AREA 291

Published by Prague Crown Publishing, Inc.

ISBN Paperback: 979-8-999339386
ISBN Hardcover: 979-8-999339393

AREA 291

BY

JENNY AHMED

CONTENTS

Other Books by Jenny Ahmed

Utopia
The Burning Sky
Seismic Eruptions
All the Kings Men
Spirals
Awake
By Dawn's Early Light
All the King's Men

I dedicate this to my assistant, Joyce. She is the biggest cheerleader of my books. If a book gets published, it's only because of her hard work.

For my part, I know nothing with any certainty,
but the sight of the stars makes me dream!

~Vincent Van Gogh

WHISPERS FROM THE DEEP

The Pacific, a vast and ancient entity, held its secrets close. Off the sun-drenched coast of Malibu, a stretch of ocean, not more than a few nautical miles across, had become a phantom limb of the charts, an area marked not by hazard buoys but by an unsettling silence that permeated everything from weather patterns to sonar readings. Malibu residents talk about the mysterious lights they see going into the ocean at night. It has become such a common occurrence; the residents are no longer surprised. It has blended into typical nightly sightings. They designated it Area 291, a sterile alphanumeric code for a place that defied explanation.

For decades, whispers had circulated throughout the maritime community—tales of ships vanishing without a trace, of fishing vessels experiencing catastrophic mechanical failures that defied diagnosis, of lone sailors driven mad by an oppressive, unnatural stillness These were not the common dangers of the sea, the rogue waves or sudden squalls. These were events that left no debris, no distress calls, only a void where a vessel and its crew once were. When they existed, the official reports used bureaucratic obfuscation, stating "unforeseen circumstances," "navigational error," and "unknown cause." But for those who looked closer, who listened to the fragmented whispers, a more chilling narrative emerged—one of many anomalies in a pocket of the world where the rules of nature seemed to bend, or perhaps, to break entirely.

Area 291 is well-known to the Ancient Alien community and also to the military, who have often supposedly conducted military drills at this site. Various military outfits have released photos of orbs and tic-tac shaped "UFOs" that would travel at enormous speeds and just plunge into the sea, then disappear.

One could logically conclude someone had already explored the area. Rob Lowe started exploring sites that had an alien component. He attempted to explore the area, but the authorities turned him around and gave a warning.

The initial reports were too fragmented, too anecdotal. A fisherman's tall tale of a silent fog bank that swallowed his boat for hours, only to release him miles off course with all his instruments dead. Surfers hallucinated an eerie, geometric light pulsing beneath the waves, followed by a bout of inexplicable amnesia. Pilots from practically every airline reported sightings of a perfectly circular atmospheric anomaly, a void in the sky that seemed to absorb all ambient sound. His aircraft experienced severe control surface issues shortly after. The lights and reports of submersible aircraft going into the sea were so common that people living in Malibu used to sit outside to watch the lights.

Also known as Sycamore Knoll, it really grew in urban myth when the public found out that Google blurred the image of the underwater knoll on Google Maps. Now why would Amazon have to blur out something that starts out 2000 feet deep and runs to extremely deep depths miles from off the shore? The public had this very question, and Google has not answered it.

Published research led to a series of highly classified naval reports from the late 1970s, detailing experimental sonar exercises near Area 291 that were abruptly terminated due to "unforeseen environmental conditions" and "equipment malfunctions." The officials heavily redacted the reports and expunged the crucial details, but the timing and location aligned perfectly with some of the earliest civilian disappearances. This confirmed the suspicion that government agencies had been aware of, and likely investigating, the anomaly for decades, adding another layer to the conspiracy that felt increasingly palpable. The sheer lack of any conventional explanation—no seismic activity, no known marine life capable of such disruption, no atmospheric phenomena that matched the descriptions. A gnawing sense of the unknown. It was a humbling and, frankly, terrifying realization. The universe was far stranger than imagined.

The investigators at MUFON still document the information people report to them. It seems ironic that with all this history, no exploration has been attempted. But is that really the truth? As of 2025, the age of disclosure is becoming a louder movement. It is unbelievable that no branch of the armed forces ever explored Area 291, or Sycamore Knoll, as it is sometimes called. Perhaps it was explored and not disclosed. Many feel there is a cabal at work suppressing information.

One thing each person in the United States needs to think about…How does this affect national security? Actually, not national security, but rather planetary security. What in the world could be under all that water, and why? Now you are asking the right questions. Is it possible this would be the underwater base? If one does even the most basic research, it will show that these anomalies appear in many places and in many countries.

The U.S. Government, to be more transparent, released what is now known as the "Tic-Tac" video. The event itself happened very close to Area 291. It is a very real occurrence; this craft was going into Area 291. One thing I find kind of credulous is a craft not of this world, threatens a military warship and poses a risk to national security is just filed away and military staff as witnesses. Anyone with common sense would have this person on the unemployment line for gambling with human lives.

There is another very common occurrence that should also be transparent: alien abductions. There are some abductions that are well-documented. While psychological evaluations are important, I'm just focusing on eyewitness testimony and artifacts that have been extracted from abductees. But those are for a different story…

While this is all true, the rest is a good story mixed in with accurate facts. I hope you sleep well tonight!

CHAPTER 1

THE SALTY SIREN

r. Rachel Katz is a physician, but often dabbles in the sciences, such as working with electronic manipulation, magnetics, physics, and astrobiology. Rachel was as sharp and precisely honed as the scientific instruments she meticulously calibrated. Her affiliation with MUFON, the Mutual UFO Network, often led her down rabbit holes conventional investigators dismissed as fanciful. Yet, Rachel possessed a rare blend of rigorous scientific discipline and an open mind that allowed her to see patterns where others saw only noise. The reports from Area 291 were a tapestry woven with disparate threads: a yacht that simply ceased to exist during a calm afternoon sail, leaving behind only a perfectly circular calm patch on the water; a freighter whose advanced navigation systems went dark simultaneously, its crew reporting a deafening silence that preceded their rescue by a passing vessel, the men visibly shaken, speaking of an "emptiness" that pressed in on them; a news story of news within the Vatican; a Coast Guard patrol that experienced a localized atmospheric phenomenon—a pocket of air so devoid of sound and movement that it felt like stepping into a vacuum. The commonality was unnerving: the abrupt cessation of all sensory input, a complete and utter blackout of the normal world, followed by mechanical failures or complete disappearance.

Rachel's study was of a life devoted to the unexplained. Throughout her entire life, Rachel lived in different time periods in history. Her father was the famous Malcomb Katz, the greatest Florida treasure hunter. Malcomb discovered so many shipwrecks there is a strait off the east coast called Malcomb's Alley. He's on the same level as Mel Fisher. Malcomb discovered one galleon after another. This is how Rachel learned the talent of map reading and all the surveillance that came with it. She pinned maps of the Pacific to the walls, crisscrossing them with colored markers denoting incident locations. Stacks of maritime manifests, cross-referenced with missing persons reports and naval logs, teetered on every available surface. The air was thick with the scent of old paper, ozone from her equipment, and the faint, metallic tang of coffee that had long gone cold. She spent her days poring over spectral analyzes of atmospheric data, searching for anomalies in magnetic fields, and scrutinizing sonar logs that offered frustratingly blank canvases where activity should have been. The oceanography reports were perplexing. Area 291, according to established charts, was a relatively featureless abyssal plain. Yet, a handful of older, more obscure charts, salvaged from forgotten maritime archives, hinted at a deeper trench, a geological anomaly that modern surveys had never fully explored or corroborated. Rachel's conviction was strengthened by these conflicting records, which suggested something significant was hidden beneath the placid surface. Area 291's lens changed the view of Malibu's picturesque coastline, just a mere six and a half miles off the coast. The cerulean waves, the golden beaches, the sprawling mansions perched on the cliffs—they all seemed to exist on the surface of a vast, indifferent entity that held a dark, silent secret. The isolation of the coastline, the sheer immensity of the Pacific stretching to the horizon, amplified the sense of unease. It was a place where the familiar world seemed to fray at the edges, where the known universe brushed against something profoundly alien and unknowable.

It was during one of her frequent visits to a discreet, low-profile maritime research facility near the coast, ostensibly to analyze oceanic data, that she first encountered Dr. Benjamin Fine. His demeanor was a blend of confident tech-suaveness and a pragmatic skepticism that initially grated on Rachel. Benjamin was a recruit to MUFON, specializing in the application of advanced surveillance technology to unexplained aerial and maritime phenomena. He had a keen eye for data that others overlooked and a knack for coaxing usable information from the most degraded signals. Rachel found herself impressed by his ability to process and analyze information at a speed she could only envy. He had been independently tracking similar anomalies, albeit with a focus on aerial signatures that sometimes dipped towards the ocean's surface near the Malibu coast. What started off as a genuine fascination with each other's work blossomed into late dinners, going to movies, and then finally admitting they had feelings for each other. They have been dating for over a year. Each date always ended in theorizing about Area 291.

Rachel, not one for sappy romances, had to admit they made a striking couple and really made an impact when they told people they were partners. Apparently, each of their mothers knew more than they did about what was going on. The important thing was that they worked well together and their personalities complemented each other.

A mutual, albeit anonymous, contact within MUFON's investigative wing orchestrated their initial meeting. They chose a quiet and unassuming seaside cafe; its weathered tables and salt-tinged air were a stark contrast to the clandestine nature of their rendezvous. The Salty Siren was her dad's restaurant and bar. A lot of the treasures he found were on display. The real Salty Siren was the big, red-headed mermaid that greeted guests as soon as they entered the restaurant. Rachel loved using the restaurant as her office. The Siren was a popular beachside hangout in Sebastian Inlet. All the tourists loved the Siren with its icy draft beer and the best wings. Rachel's father did some tense negotiating in getting her wing recipe.

Benjamin arrived with a tablet displaying intricate waveform data, while Rachel brought a worn leather satchel overflowing with printouts of her own meticulous, but less technologically advanced, research. The air between them was thick with unspoken questions. Rachel laid out her findings: the fragmented reports, the historical inconsistencies, the baffling silence. Benjamin listened intently, his initial professional curiosity gradually morphing into something akin to unease. He presented his own data: unexplained energy signatures detected by aerial drones operating near Area 291, intermittent radar blackouts that defied explanation, and a series of high-resolution satellite images showing unusual thermal patterns on the ocean's surface, localized within the very region Rachel had identified.

"It's… more than just a cluster of odd incidents, isn't it?" Benjamin finally ventured, his gaze fixed on the swirling patterns on his tablet. "The energy readings, they're unlike anything I've ever cataloged. They don't fit any known natural or man-made source. And the silence… it's like a sonic dead zone. As if something is actively *absorbing* all sound."

Rachel nodded slowly, her eyes reflecting the distant, opalescent shimmer of the setting sun on the water. "Exactly. It's the absence of data that's most interesting. Sonar logs that should show the seabed but show nothing. Audio feeds that go dead. Ships that vanish, not in storms, but on clear, calm days. It's as if the ocean itself is holding its breath in that spot." She gestured with a hand, tracing an invisible circle in the air. "And the few who have reported anything coherent… their accounts are remarkably similar, even across decades and different witnesses. Mechanical failures, systems going offline, disorienting atmospheric shifts, and always, that profound, unnatural silence."

Benjamin had been trying to capture objective data from these fleeting phenomena. He had deployed sensor buoys, operated high-altitude drones equipped with specialized audio and visual equipment, and even used modified deep-sea cameras attached to remotely operated vehicles (ROVs) in shallower waters bordering Area 291. He was hoping to find subtle infrasonic frequencies, unusual electromagnetic fluctuations, or visual distortions that could explain the anecdotal reports and provide concrete evidence of something far more than mere coincidence. The data he had gathered so far was tantalizingly suggestive: brief spikes in gamma radiation, sudden drops in ambient temperature, and audio recordings that, when processed, revealed a near-perfect absence of expected oceanic noise, punctuated by brief, unidentifiable sonic artifacts that defied classification. These patterns, when laid against Rachel's historical data, painted a picture of a recurring phenomenon.

The weight of the evidence was becoming undeniable. The sheer number of incidents eroded any remaining doubt. Rachel felt a surge of urgency.

They made the decision to pursue a more direct investigation not over a dramatic pronouncement, but in a shared, quiet understanding as they reviewed yet another chilling report of a missing fishing trawler. The phenomena of Area 291 were anything but. They were diffuse, unpredictable, and deeply unsettling. To truly understand what was happening, they needed to go beyond correlating fragmented data. They needed to witness it, to measure it, to experience it firsthand.

Skepticism still surrounded their work. Many within MUFON, and certainly within the broader scientific and governmental communities, viewed Area 291 as a statistical blip, a collection of unrelated maritime accidents. But Rachel and Benjamin knew better. They knew that the whispers from the deep were growing louder, and that the vast, indifferent ocean was hiding a truth that was about to surface. The investigation was no longer a passive observation; it was a descent, a deliberate plunge into the heart of a mystery that had claimed lives and defied understanding for far too long.

A flickering neon sign of the "Salty Siren" diner cast long, distorted shadows across Rachel's cluttered home office. The air was thick with the scent of stale coffee, old paper, and the faint metallic tang of her diagnostic equipment. To give the diner a true rustic feeling, there were crab traps, an old trawler in the middle of the restaurants. On a busy weekend, they fill the deck with ice and place shucked oysters on the ice. It's quite a tourist trap. Once it was dark outside, the red neon "Salty Siren" sign would blink, making her desk glow in the transient red neon.

Maps of the Pacific, riddled with an intricate web of pushpins and colored yarn, adorned every available wall space. Each pin represented a phantom ship, a lost crew, a vanishing act that defied rational explanation. Tonight, the focus was squarely on Area 291, the tantalizingly empty quadrant off the Malibu coast that had become an obsession.

Rachel's desk was a controlled chaos of maritime manifests, cross-referenced with missing persons reports, sticky notes and naval logs. Each sheaf of papers represented a life, a vessel, a story abruptly cut short. She traced the ghostly outline of a freighter, the *Sea Serpent*, which had reportedly encountered an inexplicable system failure near the infamous zone. Its captain, a man with decades of unblemished service, had radioed a garbled message about a "silence that eats sound" before all communication ceased. Rachel had spent weeks chasing down every lead, every obscure clue, every fragmented eyewitness account. The official report cited "catastrophic electrical surge," a phrase that sat like a stone in her gut. It was a convenient, sterile explanation for something that felt anything but.

Her fingers, stained with ink and calloused from years of handling aged documents, hovered over a faded newspaper clipping. It detailed the disappearance of a small fishing trawler, the *Lucky Star*, over thirty years prior. The report mentioned a sudden, localized fog that rolled in under clear skies. The sea swallowed their vessel without a trace, and the two-man crew was never found. Rachel had painstakingly compared the date and approximate location of the *Lucky Star*'s vanishing with the more recent disappearances. A pattern emerged. It wasn't just random chance; there was a geographical nexus, a gravitational pull towards the anomaly that was Area 291.

She leaned back in her chair and rubbed her tired eyes. The sheer volume of data was overwhelming. The recurring elements were the silence, the abrupt cessation of all sensory input, and the subsequent inexplicable malfunction or disappearance of vessels and their crews. It was a signature, albeit an elusive one. She had meticulously analyzed meteorological data for the period of these incidents. There were no recorded storms, no unusual atmospheric pressure systems, no significant seismic activity that could account for the chaos. The oceanography reports for Area 291 were equally unhelpful. Modern surveys depicted a relatively unremarkable abyssal plain. However, Rachel had unearthed older, more obscure charts from a forgotten maritime archive, charts that hinted at a far deeper, unexplored trench within the area. These discrepancies fueled her intuition, suggesting that the official records were incomplete or deliberately misleading.

Her gaze drifted to a spectral analysis chart pinned to the wall, displaying a bizarrely flat line where a typical oceanic soundscape should have been. She got anonymized sonar logs from a commercial research vessel that had inadvertently crossed the periphery of Area 291. The data were unnerving. Instead of the expected cacophony of marine life, geological echoes, and the distant rumble of shipping traffic, there was an almost perfect void. As if someone had activated a massive sound-dampening field. She had run the data through multiple analytical programs, searching for any explanation—faulty equipment, transmission interference, signal degradation. Nothing explained the complete and utter absence of expected sound.

She had interviewed dozens of witnesses, individuals who had brushed against the edge of Area 291 and emerged shaken, disoriented, and often disbelieved. There was the surfer who spoke of a "pressure" that seemed to squeeze the air from his lungs, followed by a momentary loss of consciousness and a jarring spatial displacement, finding himself miles from where he'd been paddling just moments before. There was the pilot of a small charter plane who reported a perfectly circular patch of sky, a void that seemed to absorb all light and sound, causing his aircraft to experience severe control surface issues. Their testimonies shared a common thread of profound disorientation, sensory deprivation, and an unsettling sense of being outside of normal reality.

Her colleagues in mainstream academia, when she dared to broach the subject of Area 291, would offer sympathetic smiles and veiled suggestions of overwork or an overactive imagination. The very nature of affiliation with MUFON, while allowing her access to a wealth of unexplained phenomena, also positioned her at the fringes of the scientific community. Rachel compiled a timeline, charting the disappearances chronologically. The earliest confirmed incidents dated back to the mid-20th century, with increasing frequency in the latter half. It was as if the phenomenon was growing, intensifying, or perhaps, becoming more accessible. She had never dared to imagine a more complex and mysterious universe.

"What do you think it is Sweetie?" he said while flipping the pen cap off and on.

"Daddy, I have no idea what to think!" Rachel said, wringing her hands.

"You know what is said, after all possibilities are eliminated, the one remaining is the true one." He took a sip of his coffee.

"I've discounted sea monsters, rouge waves, whales, solar output, and even things I can't even conjure up."

"What does Benjamin think?" he said, looking Rachel in the eye.

"Dad, he's just as confused as I am. An underwater base checks all of the boxes. As wild as it sounds, that is the most realistic answer, except we are talking about UFOs and aliens."

CHAPTER 2

SEASIDE SERENITY

Their partnership sprouted up a year before. Rachel sat at a secluded booth in the "Seaside Serenity," a cafe whose name was a cruel irony given the turbulent waters of her current investigation. The salt-laced breeze, a familiar comfort, did little to soothe the persistent thrum of anxiety in her chest. She'd chosen this place for its anonymity, a neutral ground far from the sterile confines of her office, where she could meet her new associate without drawing undue attention.

A young man approached her. He wasn't what she'd expected. The dossier had painted a picture of a driven, almost fanatical researcher, but this was Dr. Benjamin Fine—lean, dressed in casual but practical outdoor wear, and with a keen intelligence glinting in his eyes. He offered a polite, almost apologetic smile as he slid into the seat opposite her.

"Dr. Rachel? I'm Benjamin Fine. Sorry if I'm a few minutes late. The traffic near the coast can be a nightmare, even this early." He set a worn messenger bag on the table. Its contents suggested more than just a casual coffee break.

"The cones here are surprisingly good." Rachel announced with a hidden smile.

Benjamin scanned the menu briefly before closing it. "Just a black coffee, thank you, Rachel. And please, Benjamin is fine." He paused, his gaze flicking over the maps and printouts Rachel had carefully laid out on the table. "I've been going through the preliminary files you sent over. The sheer volume of… anomalies… is quite something."

"Anomalies" was a generous term, Rachel thought, for the spectral silence and vanished vessels. "It's the pattern that's interesting, Benjamin," she began, her voice lowering slightly, the professional detachment she usually employed struggling to surface. "Or rather, the lack of a pattern in the conventional sense. There's a geographic nexus, a specific area off the Malibu coast that seems to be a… drain. A place where ships and aircraft simply cease to be."

Benjamin leaned forward, his initial politeness giving way to a focused curiosity. "Area 291. Yes. I've cross-referenced the incident reports with historical maritime traffic data. The statistical improbability of so many disappearances in such a concentrated zone is… striking. Frankly, it's the data that makes a skeptic like me sit up and take notice." He tapped a finger on the sonar printout Rachel had displayed. "This spectral analysis really caught my eye. The complete absence of sound. It's not just low noise; it's a void. I've run simulations of equipment malfunction, deep-sea interference, even unusual geological formations that might absorb acoustic signals. Nothing fits. Nothing on this scale."

"My background is primarily in data acquisition and analysis," Benjamin explained, his eyes alight with the challenge. "I've spent years developing custom sensor arrays and analytical software for everything from tracking migratory birds with unprecedented accuracy to detecting subtle seismic shifts. The idea of a localized zone that negates all sensory input… it's a fascinating problem." He reached into his messenger bag and produced a sleek, tablet-like device, its screen displaying a complex three-dimensional topographical map. "I've been working on a concept for a deep-sea drone system. It's designed for extreme environments, equipped with multi-spectral imaging, passive acoustic sensors capable of detecting the faintest of signals, and… well, a few experimental detection arrays that might be relevant."

Rachel examined the device, impressed by its sophisticated interface. "Experimental detection arrays?"

"Think of it as a way to measure the 'quality' of space-time," Benjamin said cooly as he was typing on his pad. "It's theoretical, based on some fringe quantum field theory research. Certain phenomena might interact with the vacuum energy of space, so we can measure them and the localized distortions they create. It's a long shot, but if there's something in Area 291 that's causing a sensory void, it might also cause these subtle, energetic ripples."

"You're proposing to send your drone into this… void?" Rachel asked with a touch of trepidation in her voice. The thought of sending advanced technology into the unknown was one thing; the thought of losing it, along with any potential data, was another.

"Not immediately," Benjamin clarified. "My initial proposal is for a layered approach. We start with remote sensing. I have access to a high-altitude, long-endurance drone capable of atmospheric and surface scanning. We can deploy it for extended periods, focusing on Area 291 and its periphery. It's equipped with advanced radar, lidar, and passive infrared sensors. We can map any energy signatures, atmospheric anomalies, or unusual thermal patterns that standard satellite imagery might miss. We'll also be deploying a network of discreet buoys with hydrophones and magnetometers around the perimeter. My tech can integrate and analyze the data from all these sources in real-time, looking for correlations and deviations."

Rachel felt a surge of professional excitement, a feeling she hadn't experienced in years. This was not just about chasing ghosts in dusty archives anymore. This was about the newest technology that could finally break the secrecy about Area 291. "That sounds… incredibly thorough. Your approach is exactly what's needed. My research has been observational, piecing together fragments. Your methods promise a proactive, systematic investigation."

"The key is to gather as much objective data as possible before we even consider putting anything valuable at risk," Benjamin agreed. "We need to understand the boundaries of this phenomenon, its characteristics, and any predictable triggers. The more we know, the safer and more effective any subsequent deployment of your deep-sea drone can be." He picked up a faded newspaper clipping detailing the disappearance of the *Lucky Star*. "Thirty years ago, it was a fog. More recently, it's system failures and outright vanishing. These aren't random accidents. There's a signature, however subtle, and we need to find it."

Rachel nodded, tracing the outline of the newspaper's headline with her finger. "The maritime community whispers about it. A cursed patch of ocean. But the official narratives are always so mundane, so dismissive. 'Navigational error,' 'unexpected weather.' It's a deliberate obfuscation, I'm sure of it. The declassified documents I've found hint at naval involvement, experimental sonar exercises gone wrong. Something is being actively suppressed."

"And that's where MUFON's role becomes critical," Benjamin stated. "We operate outside the usual bureaucratic channels. We can investigate without the same level of oversight, allowing us to pursue leads official inquiries might shut down. My connections within certain tech development firms also give us an edge in acquiring and deploying specialized equipment that wouldn't normally be available to civilian researchers."

The coffee arrived — a dark, steaming comfort. As Benjamin took a sip, his expression turned more serious. "I'll be honest, Rachel, I've seen a lot of strange data in my career. Unexplained signals, anomalous sensor readings. But nothing that has this consistent, widespread, and frankly, disturbing footprint. The sheer number of these incidents, the lack of any conventional explanation, it's... unsettling. What are your theories? Beyond the obvious 'unknown phenomenon'?"

Rachel hesitated, choosing her words carefully. "I've considered everything from highly advanced, clandestine military technology to... something far less terrestrial. The silence is the most confounding element. It suggests an active suppression of energy, a distortion of physical laws. And the disappearances... it's not just destruction. It's a complete erasure. If it's an unknown technology, it's unlike anything humanity has ever conceived. If it's something else... then we're dealing with forces beyond our current understanding of physics."

Benjamin met her gaze. "Area 291 isn't just a maritime anomaly. It's potentially a window into something entirely new. Something that rewrites the rules." He tapped his tablet again. "My drone is still in its prototype phase, but the core systems are sound. I believe we can have it ready for initial atmospheric and surface reconnaissance within three weeks. Once we complete their locations, we will deploy the buoys."

"Three weeks," Rachel echoed, the timeframe feeling both exhilaratingly short and dauntingly long. The thought of finally confronting the mystery of Area 291 with such powerful tools at her disposal was almost overwhelming. "I'll have more historical data compiled by then, focusing on the oldest reports. We need to go back as far as possible."

"Excellent," Benjamin replies. "And we'll need to establish secure communication channels. We need to encrypt and compartmentalize everything related to this investigation. We don't know who else might be interested in Area 291, or what their intentions are. Given the potential naval involvement you mentioned, caution is paramount."

Rachel felt a renewed sense of purpose. The solitary pursuit had been a burden, but with Benjamin Fine, a sharp, technologically adept investigator who shared her drive for empirical truth, the path forward, though fraught with peril, suddenly felt illuminated. The whispers from the deep were about to be amplified, scrutinized, and perhaps, finally understood. Their unlikely partnership, forged in a quiet cafe overlooking the turbulent Pacific, marked the true beginning of their descent into the enigma of Area 291.

The hushed whispers of survivors, fragmented and often dismissed as the ravings of traumatized minds, held a peculiar resonance for Rachel. She craved the raw, unfiltered echoes of encounters with the inexplicable. They were the human element, the soft, breakable edges of a mystery that resisted all attempts at conventional dissection. She had spent countless hours sifting through dusty archives, poring over declassified naval reports and cryptic log entries, but it was these personal narratives, these fleeting glimpses into the abyss, that truly gnawed at her.

"With his methodical approach and his suite of advanced technological tools, Benjamin was the perfect counterpoint to her archival deep dives. Their meeting in the secluded booth of "Seaside Serenity" had been the catalyst, the moment where the solitary pursuit of understanding Area 291 coalesced into a collaborative endeavor. Now, the real work, the painstaking collection and analysis of data from the periphery of the enigma, was about to begin. Before long, the Seaside Serenity had become their office.

"The common thread is the silence," Rachel mused, her gaze fixed on a faded newspaper clipping detailing the loss of the fishing trawler *Sea Serpent* in the late 1980s. "It's not just a lack of noise; it's an active nullification. Witnesses, those who recall anything coherent at all, speak of an all-encompassing quiet that descends upon them, a silence so profound it feels like a physical presence. The engines cut out, the radio goes dead, even the wind seems to cease its howl. This reminds me of the Zone of Silence."

Benjamin was excited to told Rachel what he had uncovered about the oppressive silence that was reported. "I've been running simulations based on the acoustic void data from the few salvaged logbooks of Area 291 incidents. It's unlike anything known in acoustic physics. Standard sonar cancellation principles, even advanced noise-reduction algorithms, operate on specific frequency ranges and require a measurable input to counteract. What we're seeing here is a complete absence, a black hole of sound."

Benjamin gestured to a complex waveform displayed on his computer screen. "This represents the acoustic signature of a typical deep-sea environment, even in the quietest abyssal plains. Notice the subtle hum of the water, the faint clicks of marine life, the distant rumble of seismic activity. It's never truly silent. But in the reports from Area 291, there's a point where all of this simply... disappears. It's as if the very fabric of the medium has been altered, rendering it incapable of transmitting sound."

Rachel leaned closer, her historian's instinct for pattern recognition kicking into high gear. "And the fog. It's another recurring element. Not just any fog, but a dense, unnaturally localized bank. Some describe it as being 'thick as milk,' appearing and dissipating with impossible speed. One survivor from the *Challenger* incident, a deckhand named Miguel Rodriguez, spoke of a fog that 'swallowed the sun' and felt 'cold, yet dry.' He claimed it clung to the ship, muffling every sound, and that when it lifted, they were miles off course, their navigation systems fried."

Benjamin tapped a sequence on his tablet, bringing up a series of satellite imagery overlays. "I'm cross-referencing meteorological data with the reported incident timelines. Standard atmospheric models can't account for the sudden genesis and dissipation of such dense fog banks in that specific area, especially without significant prevailing weather systems. It suggests an external influence, something that can rapidly alter atmospheric conditions on a localized scale." He zoomed in on a particular date and time, highlighting a small, circular area off the coast. "Here, on the date of the *Challenger*'s distress call, there was a brief, anomalous spike in atmospheric moisture readings, precisely where Rodriguez described the fog appearing. The resolution isn't high enough to see the fog itself, but the data point is there, a statistical anomaly that aligns with his account."

The sheer number of such seemingly unrelated phenomena coalescing around a specific geographic point made Area 291 so compellingly sinister. It wasn't a single isolated mystery, but a nexus of bewildering events. Rachel pulled out a thick binder, its pages filled with photocopied accounts and her own annotations. "I've compiled a list of recurring elements from the survivor testimonies and distress call transcripts. Beyond the silence and the fog, there's the sudden and catastrophic failure of electronic systems. Navigation equipment, radar, radio communication—all rendered useless simultaneously. And they aren't just simple malfunctions.

"That's where my custom sensor arrays come into play," Benjamin explained, his eyes gleaming with intellectual fervor. "I've designed a suite of instruments that don't rely solely on electromagnetic principles. We're talking about passive acoustic sensors with extreme sensitivity, broadband electromagnetic field detectors that can pick up even the subtlest energetic fluctuations, and what I call a 'gravimetric resonance scanner.' It's theoretical, based on some very fringe interpretations of general relativity, but the idea is to detect localized distortions in the gravitational field. If something in Area 291 is manipulating space-time, even on a minute scale, this scanner might pick up the ripples."

He projected a schematic onto the table, a complex diagram of interconnected sensors and data-processing units. "The plan is to deploy a series of unmanned sensor pods in a grid pattern around the periphery of Area 291. These pods will be tethered to a central buoy equipped with satellite uplink capabilities. They'll be submerged to varying depths, allowing us to create a multi-dimensional profile of any anomalies. We'll be recording continuously: audio, electromagnetic spectra, atmospheric conditions, and, crucially, any gravimetric fluctuations."

Rachel traced the projected lines of the sensor array with her finger. "It's a brilliant strategy, Benjamin. By creating a perimeter, we might observe the phenomenon as it occurs, or at least detect its effects before it fully envelops a vessel. The survivor accounts often speak of a sudden onset, a feeling of being 'caught' without warning. This layered approach could provide us with crucial lead-up data."

She recalled a chilling account from a commercial diver, a man named Thomas Ashton, who had been working on a deep-sea pipeline installation near the edge of Area 291 in the late 1990s. He spoke of a profound disorientation, a feeling that his own senses were betraying him. "Ashton described it as a 'pressure on the mind,' a cognitive fog that accompanied the external silence. He said his depth gauge started fluctuating wildly, showing him plummeting to impossible depths, then soaring to the surface, all within seconds. His submersible's internal chronometer also malfunctioned, jumping hours ahead. He attributed it to extreme nitrogen narcosis, but the official inquiry found no such readings in his bloodwork."

"Cognitive disorientation and temporal distortion," Benjamin murmurs, scribbling notes on his tablet. "These are classic hallmarks of advanced theoretical physics, specifically related to spacetime manipulation. If we can correlate Ashton's reported gravimetric anomalies with his subjective experience of sensory and temporal distortion, it would be a significant breakthrough. It would suggest that whatever is happening in Area 291 isn't just affecting the physical environment, but also our perception of it."

He tapped the screen, bringing up a detailed list of the sensor pod's capabilities. "Each pod has an independent power source for extended deployment, robust data storage, and an encrypted burst transmission system. The hydrophones can capture frequencies far below human hearing, and the EM detectors can sweep across an unprecedented range. The gravimetric scanner, while experimental, has shown promising results in controlled laboratory environments simulating localized gravitational shifts."

Rachel remembered another fragmented testimony, this one from a lighthouse keeper on a remote island near the presumed epicenter of Area 291. He had reported seeing "flashes of light in the water, like underwater lightning, but with no sound." He had dismissed it as a trick of the light, perhaps bioluminescence, but the timing, coinciding with a reported surge in electrical failures at the lighthouse, had always struck Rachel as significant.

"So, the sensor array will provide us with a comprehensive environmental scan," Rachel summarized. "Audio, electromagnetic, gravimetric, and visual data, all collected simultaneously. This is far better than anything they have tried before. Previous investigations, if you can even call them that, relied on sporadic sonar pings, eyewitness reports filtered through layers of bureaucracy, and the occasional salvaged, often damaged, logbook."

Benjamin Fine reviewed the latest schematics on his tablet, echoing her sentiment. "The data points are too consistent, Rachel. Too many vessels, too many crew members reported the same sequence of events, spanning over fifty years. It defies statistical probability for it to be mere coincidence or a standard maritime hazard. We're looking at a pattern, and the pattern suggests an active, recurring phenomenon." He looked up, his gaze meeting hers, a shared understanding passing between them. "We have to do more than just analyze historical data. We need to go there."

"Funding will be the immediate hurdle," Rachel mused, pulling a worn leather-bound notebook from her satchel. The navy reports are sparse though declassified, and the historical accounts are scattered across private archives and, frankly, some less-than-reputable sources. We need to equip ourselves to deploy Benjamin's sensor arrays meaningfully." She tapped her pen against the notebook. "Official channels will probably be… uncooperative. Whenever people raised these incidents, they consistently obfuscated and denied them.

Benjamin offered a wry smile. "That's where MUFON comes in. The Mutual UFO Network. They might not have the resources of a major research institution, but they're certainly more open to investigating the unexplained. They may have limited funding, but they are independent. It means we have autonomy they can't easily revoke." He tapped his tablet, bringing up a contact list. "I've already made some preliminary inquiries. There's a regional director, a man named Arthur Finch, who's shown a keen interest in maritime anomalies. He's cautiously optimistic about allocating a small grant for 'unusual environmental sensor deployment'."

Rachel raised an eyebrow. "Cautiously optimistic. That's code for 'begrudgingly willing to throw a few thousand dollars at something he can't easily explain'." She chuckled softly. "But it's a start. We'll have to be judicious with every dollar. Your sensor pods, the data transmission hardware, the offshore support vessel… it all adds up."

He paused, with a thoughtful expression on his face. "There's also the human element. We'll need a small, trusted crew for the catamaran. Experienced sailors, discreet individuals who understand the need for confidentiality. I have a few contacts who owe me favors, people who value their privacy and are adept at keeping their mouths shut. They won't ask too many questions as long as the pay is good and the mission parameters are clear."

Rachel understood the implications. This was not just about scientific inquiry; it was about operating in a gray area, potentially brushing against forces that might prefer the anomalies of Area 291 to remain hidden. The possibility of interference, of deliberate obstruction, loomed large.

"The MUFON grant should cover the initial charter and the basic sensor array," Rachel calculated, scribbling furiously in her notebook. "We'll need to supplement that with our own funds for the advanced components, particularly the gravimetric scanner calibrations and the enhanced data processing software. I can liquidate some of my personal assets. It's a risk, but the potential reward… the potential to finally understand what's happening out there…" Her voice trailed off, filled with a potent mix of scientific curiosity and a deep-seated sense of responsibility.

He gestured expansively with his hands, his eyes alight with the vision. "We're not just charting unknown waters; we're charting unknown science. The data we collect could be the key to unlocking mysteries that have baffled humanity for centuries. It's a chance to push the boundaries of what we believe is possible."

Rachel found herself caught up in his infectious enthusiasm. The weight of the potential risks seemed to recede, replaced by the thrill of the unknown, the unadulterated pursuit of knowledge. She envisioned the moment their data streams coalesced, the hidden patterns emerging from the noise, the pieces of the puzzle clicking into place. It would be the culmination of years of solitary research, of fragmented whispers and tantalizing clues, finally rendered into coherent, undeniable evidence.

"Alright, Benjamin," she said, closing her notebook with a decisive snap. ."Let's do it. We'll pool our resources, leverage the MUFON grant, and prepare for deployment. I'll begin liquidating my assets immediately. You complete the sensor configurations and secure the catamaran charter. We'll need to establish a secure communication protocol between us, independent of any public networks. And we need to be meticulous. We must document every piece of data, every calibration, and every operational step with absolute precision.

Benjamin smiled, a genuine, broad grin that conveyed his shared determination. "Consider it done, Rachel. The deep has secrets, and we're about to ask it directly. The *Serenity* awaits." He tapped his tablet, a small, almost imperceptible hum emanating from the device. On the table, the holographic projection of Area 291 seemed to shimmer. The preparation had begun. The vast, indifferent ocean, a symbol of everything unknown and immeasurable, was about to be probed by their audacious quest for answers.

Their relationship has been going on for a year. While it had become serious, they are still taking their time. Both of them experienced pain in the past. Rachel's work has been most important to her. Benjamin went through a divorce a few years ago. His wife had an affair with his friend. He tried to make it work, but it wasn't happening. The success of their relationship is that they can both laugh at themselves. Being together was a natural feeling, like they've been together for a lot longer than they had.

And as it's said, the rest is history.

CHAPTER 3

THE NAUTILUS

The humming of the server room faded as Rachel and Benjamin turned their attention from the digital realm to the daunting, tangible reality of their impending expedition. In their quest, the MUFON grant, while a lifeline, was insufficient. The ambition to deploy Benjamin's sensor arrays into the abyssal depths of Area 291 demanded more than just off-the-shelf technology and borrowed time on a research catamaran. It required specialized knowledge, equipment far beyond their current reach, and, crucially, a vessel capable of withstanding the crushing pressures of the deep.

"We've bootstrapped as much as we can," Benjamin stated, his gaze fixed on the satellite image of Area 291 still projected on the table. "But to map the anomaly zone, at the depths where some of the more extreme readings originate, we'll need something more robust than a surface vessel with towed arrays. We need a submersible. A deep-diving, autonomous or remotely operated vehicle that can carry a substantial payload of sensors and operate independently for extended periods."

They were looking for someone with the capability, and more importantly, the willingness to take on a project with... unconventional parameters." Their search quickly narrowed to a single, legendary, and notoriously elusive figure: Dr. Winston Jasper.

Jasper was a name whispered in awe and a touch of apprehension within the tight-knit circles of deep-sea exploration and marine biology. He was also an anomaly: a prodigy who earned his doctorate at a young age, a pioneer in submersible design, and a recluse who had vanished from public life a decade before, focusing on rumored highly specialized, private deep-sea ventures. Rumors of a custom-built, state-of-the-art deep-sea vessel and a laboratory on a remote coastline, reachable only by sea or a treacherous coastal track, fueled the mystery surrounding his current operation. His unruly curly hair can easily spot him in a crowd.

Jasper was a force to be reckoned with. Nobody seems to know his age, but he earned his first doctorate at the ripe age of 14. One of his passions is designing underwater craft because it's an interesting hobby. As the late in life baby, he's an only child. People consider Jasper an odd duck. He doesn't have friends to speak of, but he has a deep relationship with his parents. Xavier and Wilfred Jasper have many patents between them, mainly in chemistry and industrial processes. It is these patents that leave the Jaspers with hundreds of millions of dollars in the bank. If not billions. Basically, Jasper can fund any mission. Even the ones that go up into space.

"Jasper," Rachel murmured, the name carrying a weight of both immense possibility and significant challenge. "He's built his own deep-sea craft, hasn't he? 'The Nautilus,' I believe the rumors call it. Something very advanced that can do much more than what's for sale. And his reputation… eccentric, to put it mildly. He's known for his disdain for conventional scientific protocols, preferring his own unique brand of empirical investigation."

"Eccentricity is a small price to pay for access to 'The Nautilus'," Benjamin counters, a glint of determination in his eyes. Jasper developed the Nautilus metal panel, by metal panel. As far as Benjamin was concerned, Jasper's sub was the only one in the world with a working bidet. "And his reputation for results is undeniable. If anyone can get us down there, into the heart of Area 291, and back with the data we need, it's Jasper. The question is, how do we even reach him? He doesn't exactly have a publicist or a readily available contact number."

Their inquiries led them to a grizzled, retired lighthouse keeper, a man named Silas Croft, who'd spent forty years tending a lonely beacon on a rocky outcrop a mile from the nearest settlement. "The scientist," Silas rasped, his voice like the grinding of pebbles on the shore. "He comes and goes. Always by sea. His vessel... a marvel. Lights that cut the dark, silent as a ghost. He likes his solitude. He doesn't take kindly to visitors. Unless they bring something, he wants nothing.

Following Silas's cryptic directions, which involved navigating a maze of unmarked sea channels and a final approach to a hidden cove, Rachel and Benjamin motored their chartered RIB towards a formidable, almost fortress-like structure clinging to the rugged cliffs. The air grew thick with the metallic tang of salt and something else... ozone, perhaps. As they drew closer, the sheer scale of Jasper's operation became apparent. Anchored in the sheltered waters of the cove was 'The Nautilus'—a vessel that defied conventional categorization. It was less a ship and more a leviathan, a sleek, dark hull of advanced composite materials, its lines suggesting immense power and an unparalleled ability to slice through the ocean's resistance. Dominating the stern was a massive, recessed bay, clearly designed to launch and recover a submersible. The size of the Nautilus was unbelievable! That was just what was visible above the water! The largest submarine in the world is 603 feet and is Russian-made; it is the Belgorod. If the Nautilus is not bigger than that, it comes a close second.

The laboratory itself was Jasper's singular vision. Built into the cliff face, it was a sprawling complex of gleaming metal and reinforced glass, punctuated by what appeared to be several smaller submersibles, each a unique design, hinting at years of iterative experimentation. Strange bioluminescent specimens pulsed in enormous tanks visible through the darkened windows. Twisted pieces of wreckage, their origins unknown and their forms alien. The entire place hummed with a low, resonant energy, a palpable sense of advanced technology intertwined with a wild, untamed connection to the ocean's deepest secrets. The Area 291 mystery is perfect for Jasper, his sub, and his lab. He gives a new meaning to the term 'mad scientist.'

As they disembarked onto a small, sturdy jetty, the heavy thrum of 'The Nautilus's' internal systems vibrated through the soles of their boots. The air here felt different, charged. A figure emerged from a side entrance of the laboratory, silhouetted against the strange internal lights. Jasper was very tall and lanky, with a weathered and, tanned face. His eyes behind thick, multi-lensed spectacles, seemed to bore right through them, assessing their every detail with an unnerving intensity. He wore a practical dark jumpsuit, stained with what could have been grease, or perhaps something more… biological.

"Benjamin," the man stated, his voice a deep baritone. It wasn't a question. "Rachel. I was expecting you. Silas is surprisingly observant for a man who talks to seagulls."

He extended a long, slender hand. "Dr. Winston Jasper. And you've come about the deep." It wasn't a greeting, but a statement of fact.

Rachel extended her hand. "Dr. Jasper. Thank you for agreeing to see us. Your reputation precedes you, of course."

Before Rachel stood a large man-child, barely of drinking age.

Jasper's grip was firm, almost unnervingly so. "Whispered rumors and misconstrued truths often build reputations. I deal in demonstrable facts, observable phenomena. And you, Dr. Rachel, have brought me some rather interesting 'observable phenomena' to consider." He gestured for them to go towards the lab entrance. "Come. My time is not inexhaustible as the ocean, but for those who offer genuine scientific merit, it can be stretched."

Inside, the laboratory was a symphony of controlled chaos. The air was cooler, filled with the distinct scent of ionized water and various chemical compounds. Glass tanks housed a mesmerizing array of marine life, some glowing with an eerie internal light, others possessing grotesque, almost alien forms. Along the walls, display screens showed complex schematics, live sensor feeds from submerged drones, and what appeared to be detailed geological surveys of the ocean floor. Scattered amongst the advanced equipment were artifacts that defied easy classification: a massive, iridescent shell of impossible size, a fragment of what looked like petrified coral in the shape of a fractal, and a series of intricately carved bone fragments that seemed too ancient to be human.

Jasper led them to a central area dominated by a holographic projector. When he flicked the switch, the three-dimensional oceanographic map bathed the room in its ethereal blue light. "Area 291," he said, his voice taking on a more animated tone. "Your area of interest. I've been observing it for some time. Sporadic energy spikes. Unexplained magnetic fluctuations. And a disturbing number of 'anomalous acoustic events' that defy any known natural or man-made source."

He manipulated the holographic display with precise hand gestures, zooming in on a particular region within the charted coordinates. "My own drones have detected... anomalies. Not biological. Not geological. Something... else. Persistent, localized energy fields. And a temporal displacement signature that's, shall we say, highly irregular?"

Benjamin cut to the chase. "Dr. Jasper, we believe there is a recurring, possibly intelligent, phenomenon occurring within Area 291! We need to deploy advanced sensor equipment directly into the anomaly zone, at significant depths. Our current resources are insufficient. We require a vessel and operational support capable of sustained deep-sea exploration. 'The Nautilus' is, as far as we know, uniquely qualified."

Jasper turned his piercing gaze onto Benjamin, then shifted to Rachel. He walked over to a large, complex console covered in a bewildering array of dials, buttons, and touchscreens. "The Nautilus," he stated, "is not a vessel for hire. She is an extension of my research, my life's work. Her purpose is to plumb the deepest mysteries, not to serve as a taxi for academic curiosities." He paused, his gaze returned to them, sharp and appraising. "However, your 'curiosities' align with certain... observations of my own. The temporal displacement signatures I've detected are particularly intriguing. If you can provide data that corroborates and expands upon my findings, if you can offer a framework for understanding what is occurring, then perhaps... a collaboration might be considered?"

Rachel seized the opening. "We have amassed decades of historical data, Dr. Jasper. Shipping logs, anecdotal accounts, declassified naval reports, even classified sonar readings that have been leaked over the years. Patterns of disappearances, equipment failures, and sensory phenomena have been identified. We currently hypothesize that a singular, powerful, and possibly deliberate force connects these events. We believe this force originates within Area 291, and its effects extend far beyond mere maritime incidents."

"Please, just call me Jasper," he laughed. "I feel like I want to call you, Mom."

"The disappearances," Jasper mused, his eyes distant as he stared at a tank filled with a swirling, phosphorescent nebula of microscopic organisms. "The 'ghost ships'. I've logged several instances. Vessels that vanished from radar, from visual range, with no distress calls, no debris. And the peculiar fog banks that seem to materialize out of nowhere, engulfing entire fleets, only to dissipate just as rapidly, leaving behind… emptiness." He tapped a finger against the glass of the tank. "The ocean guards its secrets jealously. But it also reveals them in its own peculiar language. Your data, Dr. Rachel, and Mr. Benjamin's technological acumen—these are the Rosetta stones we need."

Jasper walked over to a holographic projection of 'The Nautilus' itself, a sleek, formidable machine that dwarfed as impressive as the real thing. "The Nautilus can descend to 12,000 meters," he stated, his voice resonating with pride. "Her hull is a proprietary composite, capable of withstanding over 1,100 atmospheres of pressure. Her power core is a closed-loop thorium system, allowing for sustained operation for months at a time. She can deploy and retrieve multiple drone units, each equipped with a suite of scientific instruments. And," he added, a faint smile playing on his lips, "she is, I assure you, perfectly capable of navigating… unusual environmental conditions."

He then gestured to a series of smaller, more compact submersibles docked in a separate bay, each designed for specific tasks. "I have several specialized deep-sea drones. The 'Abyssal Eye' has advanced sonar and LIDAR, allowing it to map complex underwater topography in zero visibility. Another, the 'Chrono-Probe,' detects and analyzes temporal distortions, a project I've been working on for years, inspired by certain... persistent anomalies in the Pacific." He looked directly at Rachel and Benjamin. "You could integrate your sensor payloads into these drones, or directly onto the Nautilus." The choice depends on the precise nature of the data you wish to collect and the operational parameters we establish."

Rachel felt a surge of hope, tempered by the knowledge that Jasper's price would be steep, and likely not financial. "Dr. Jasper, we are prepared to share all our data, our methodologies, and any findings we uncover. Our aim is understanding, not profit. We believe that whatever is occurring in Area 291 has implications that extend far beyond our immediate scientific interests. It could represent a fundamental shift in our understanding of physics, of life, perhaps even of our place in the cosmos. We will grant you full co-authorship and equal scientific credit for any discoveries made."

Jasper steepled his fingers, his gaze intense. "Credit is a transient thing. Data is eternal. What I require is access. Access to your complete archives, your analytical frameworks. And I require your... participation. Not as passengers, but as integral members of the expedition. The Nautilus is a complex system, and all who command her must understand her operational parameters. I will need your expertise in calibrating your equipment, in interpreting your data streams, and in human observation. You will join me aboard the Nautilus, and we will venture into Area 291 together."

Benjamin exchanged a glance with Rachel. The implication was clear: this wasn't just about chartering a vessel; it was about becoming part of Jasper's world, a world that was clearly as deep and enigmatic as the ocean itself. The offer was extraordinary, a chance to work with technology that was light-years ahead of their own, but it also came with an implicit surrender of control.

"Dr. Jasper, we understand." Rachel replied, her voice steady. "We are prepared to commit to your terms. We will provide you with all our research, and we will join you aboard 'the Nautilus.' Our goal is the same: to uncover the truth behind Area 291."

Jasper nodded, a subtle shift in his posture showing acceptance. "Excellent. The preparations will be extensive. Your equipment will need to be integrated into the Nautilus's systems. We will conduct joint simulations. And you will need to familiarize yourselves with the vessel's protocols. The dive will begin with the next favorable lunar tide, approximately four weeks from now." He gestured to a secure data port embedded in the wall. "Upload your archives. I will begin my analysis immediately. Mr. Benjamin, I will require detailed specifications of your sensor arrays, including power requirements and data output formats. Dr. Rachel, I will expect a comprehensive overview of the historical incident timeline and any potential predictive modeling you have developed. The descent into the unknown is about to become a lot more... structured."

As Rachel and Benjamin began transferring their life's work to Jasper's secure systems, they felt a profound sense of stepping across a threshold. They had sought an expert, a tool for their mission. What they had found was something far more. They had found a potential partner, a maverick scientist whose own obsessions mirrored their own, and a vessel that promised to take them deeper into the mystery than they had ever dared to imagine. The preparations for their dive into Area 291 had truly begun, not in the quiet hum of a server room, but in the resonant hum of Dr. Jasper's extraordinary laboratory.

The submersible 'Nautilus' was not merely a vessel; it was a summation of Dr. Winston Jasper's singular vision, a fusion of groundbreaking engineering and understanding of the abyss. Its hull, a seamless shell of advanced carbon-nanotube composite layered with a proprietary ceramic matrix, exuded an aura of impenetrable strength. Unlike the bulky, utilitarian designs of most deep-sea exploration craft, the Nautilus was sleek, almost predatory in its aesthetic. The designers optimized its form for hydrodynamic efficiency. Jasper had overseen every stage of its construction. The outer plating, a matte obsidian black, absorbed sonar signals, rendering the vessel virtually invisible to conventional detection systems, and could withstand 1100 atmospheres. Beneath this formidable exterior lay a technological marvel. With capabilities tested, the 'Nautilus' was engineered for depths beyond 12,000 meters. The Nautilus was science at its best.

The descent of the Nautilus began after hours of controlled urgency. Jasper's detached demeanor, underscored by a barely perceptible tremor of anticipation, moved through the submersible's confined spaces with an almost priestly reverence. He performed the diagnostic check and each system calibration meticulously, almost like a ritual. He oversaw the loading of the scientific instruments; each piece of equipment having taken years of theoretical design and painstaking construction. Technicians secured Benjamin's custom-built gravimetric anomaly detectors in their specialized cradles, shielding their delicate sensors from the ambient electromagnetic noise of the support vessel. Rachel's advanced bio-acoustic signature analyzers, capable of distinguishing between the whisper of plankton and the potential sonic emanations of something far more profound, were also integrated, and their data streams were routed through the Nautilus's formidable processing core.

Jasper arranged the inside of the Nautilus with extreme luxury. Tufted sofas with what appeared to be Turkish fabrics and throw pillows. Thick handmade Turkish carpet runners dotted the submersible. The staterooms had beautiful dark green flowered silk wallpaper, and the bedrooms had four-poster beds in them. Feather pillows dotted the beds. The walls everywhere had artwork depicting sketched animals, shadowy boxes of butterflies, and everything else you could imagine. Someone in Jasper's family, or perhaps Jasper himself, was a fan of the Moulin Rouge, as there was memorabilia everywhere.

Unlike other runs the Nautilus had made, there was no crew for this trip. It was just the three of them. During these months they were preparing for this voyage, the three of them practiced all the roles that are needed to navigate this queen of the sea. While this was a fool's trip, they were performing willingly; they did not want to risk more lives than needed.

A canvas of deepening shadows formed outside the thick viewport. The vibrant blues of the upper ocean dissolved into an impenetrable void, a realm where light, as they understood it, ceased to exist. The only visual input was the faint, almost spectral glow of the Nautilus's exterior lights, illuminating a small bubble of visibility in the vast, crushing darkness. It was a stark reminder of their profound isolation, of the immense gulf separating them from the familiar world above.

As the Nautilus continued its silent plunge, the external lights cast an eerie, shifting illumination on the surrounding water. The initial impression was of an infinite, featureless expanse. As they descended deeper, faint, ghostly shapes materialized in the periphery of the lights—tiny sparks of light that bloomed and faded like ephemeral stars in the terrestrial night sky. They were fleeting, elusive, existing in a realm where sunlight was a distant memory and survival depended on an entirely different set of evolutionary adaptations.

The silence within the submersible was profound, broken only by the rhythmic hum of the machinery and the soft clicks of keyboards. It was a silence that amplified the awareness of the immense pressure outside, a pressure so great it could crush steel like paper. Yet, within the protective embrace of the Nautilus's reinforced hull, they were in a sanctuary, a technological marvel designed to defy the very forces that sought to annihilate them.

The sonar ping, a sharp, distinct pulse, emanated from the Nautilus, its sound waves rippling outwards into the abyssal blackness. The return echoes, interpreted by sophisticated algorithms, painted a picture of the ocean floor ahead. Initially, the topography appeared as expected for a deep-sea trench—a gradual slope descending into an increasingly rugged landscape. But as the sweeps continued and the Nautilus descended further, the readings deviated from any known geological models.

"Interesting," Benjamin murmurs, his gaze fixed on the readouts. "The gravitational fluctuations are… unusual. This type of geological formation shouldn't have higher density pockets locally. It's as if there are… irregularities in the seafloor's distribution."

Benjamin added, "Acoustically, things are also shifting. The ambient noise floor is remarkably low, almost unnervingly so, save for the predictable echoes of our own sonar. However, "I'm picking up very faint, intermittent emissions that don't correlate with any known biological or geological sources. They're too structured to be random noise, but too weak to get a clear signature yet."

Outside, the world was utter blackness, a void punctuated only by the limited reach of their lights. The sonar returns were becoming increasingly detailed, revealing a seabed that defied conventional geological understanding. Instead of the expected abyssal plains or volcanic ridges, the Nautilus was encountering formations that appeared... artificial.

"The sonar is showing a series of complex geometric structures ahead," Rachel reported, her voice a mixture of surprise and professional detachment. "They're not consistent with natural erosion patterns or known tectonic activity. They appear... segmented, almost block-like, with sharp angles and unnaturally flat surfaces."

Jasper had never been speechless before. He adjusted the course slightly, maneuvering the Nautilus to get a clearer visual of the unusual formations. The powerful external lights cut through the darkness, revealing glimpses of what the sonar had suggested. Towers, impossibly regular, rose from the seabed. Walls, perfectly planar, stretched into the gloom. It was a landscape sculpted by something other than the slow, chaotic forces of nature.

Benjamin worked feverishly at his console. "The composition appears to be primarily silicate-based, with trace metallic elements that are... highly unusual. Not impossible, but certainly not typical for this geological environment. The density is consistently higher than the surrounding rock, which explains the anomalies. As for artificial origin... the regularity of the shapes, the sharp angles, the sheer scale of these structures... it's beyond any natural geological process I'm familiar with."

The three of them stood speechless in front of the main window, observing the massive alien city. No one can move a muscle. The Nautilus drifted slowly, its lights playing across the alien landscape. What had begun as a scientific expedition into a poorly understood oceanic anomaly had transformed into something far more profound.

They had descended into a realm of darkness and pressure, only to find that the unknown was not merely a void, but a place of baffling, artificial grandeur.

Somehow there was a yellowish glow emitting from the buildings. There appeared windows everywhere and long, string-like fauna that flickered yellow and white. They were swimming around the Nautilus and would stick to the window for a minute or two. No one could say if they were studying us or we were studying them. There were thousands of these graceful creatures. An electric current shivered down the trio's spines. There was no longer any wonder if humankind was alone in this cosmic soup. Even though they were long string-like filaments, they moved with purpose and intelligence was clearly seen. This was the most beautiful grace ever seen.

Benjamin had the camera. The video was rolling as well as getting photographs. He could not wait to share this with the world.

The silence of the abyss was no longer empty; it was pregnant with questions, with the echoes of a presence that had shaped this alien world before they, the fragile explorers, had even arrived. Outside, the crushing pressure seemed to mirror the revelation's mounting pressure. They had not just entered the unknown; they had stumbled into its meticulously crafted chambers. The journey had just begun, and the depths of the mystery were already proving to be far greater than anyone had dared to imagine. Each sonar ping was a question, each faint reading a whisper from a past that defied their present. At the threshold of a forgotten world, the Nautilus, a tiny beacon of human ingenuity, was now a sentinel. crushing blackness, were no longer just explorers; they were archaeologists of the impossible. The initial descent was over, but the true dive into the enigma had only just begun. This was the moment, the culmination of dreams and calculations, that justified every risk, every sacrifice. They were witnessing the impossible made real.

The silence within the submersible was profound, broken only by the rhythmic hum of the machinery and the soft clicks of keyboards. Yet, within the protective embrace of the Nautilus's reinforced hull, they were in a sanctuary, a technological marvel designed to defy the very forces that sought to annihilate them.

The depth gauge ticked over another thousand meters. 3,000 meters. The pressure was now immense, a crushing weight that bore down on the submersible. Outside, the world was utter blackness, a void punctuated only by the limited reach of their lights. The sonar returns were becoming increasingly detailed, revealing a seabed that defied conventional geological understanding. Instead of the expected abyssal plains or volcanic ridges, the Nautilus was encountering formations that appeared… artificial.

"The radar is picking up something amazing! I don't even have to poke my head through the window to see it! It's an alien ship! There are many on the seabed!" Jasper was so excited.

"Ships!" Rachel whispered softly to herself. Now she had perfect understanding why people sitting on the beach in Malibu, they would see them diving into the water.

Benjamin leaned forward, his eyes wide. "That aligns with the gravimetric data. These structures seem to contribute significantly to the localized density anomalies. If this were a natural formation, the gradients would be much smoother, more organic. This is… different. Towers, impossibly regular, rose from the seabed. Walls, perfectly planar, stretched into the gloom. It was a landscape sculpted by something other than the slow, chaotic forces of nature."

Jasper was pulling at his hair at the temples. "I can't believe we have answers! We found man's search for meaning!"

"Depth: 4,000 meters," Jasper announced, his voice now carrying a palpable sense of awe. "Pressure approaching 400 atmospheres. We are entering uncharted territory, not just in terms of depth, but in terms of what we are seeing."

The silence in the control sphere was now electric. Each of the three members was acutely aware of the unprecedented nature of their discovery. The sonar had been accurate. The visual confirmation was undeniable. They were no longer merely descending into the abyss; they were entering a place that seemed to have been deliberately constructed, a place that existed outside the boundaries of their scientific understanding.

The Nautilus drifted slowly, its lights playing across the alien landscape. What had begun as a scientific expedition into a poorly understood oceanic anomaly had transformed into something far more profound. They had descended into a realm of darkness and pressure, only to find that the unknown was not merely a void, but a place of baffling, artificial grandeur.

The journey had just begun, and the depths of the mystery were already proving to be far greater than anyone had dared to imagine. Each sonar ping was a question; each faint reading a whisper from a past that defied their present. Now, the Nautilus stood as a sentinel, a beacon of human ingenuity, at the threshold of a forgotten world. The sheer scale of the structures, their geometric precision, spoke of an intelligence, an architect, that had operated on a timescale and with capabilities far beyond their own. The silicate composition, the metallic trace elements, the exotic isotopes—these were the breadcrumbs, the spectral fingerprints of a civilization that had perhaps once called this crushing darkness home. And the faint organic residue… it hinted at a history, a story of a life that had evolved in conditions so alien, so extreme, that it was beyond the wildest dreams of even the most speculative exobiologist.

The journey was no longer just about descending; it was about ascending in understanding, about piecing together a narrative from fragmented data, from the silent testimony of an alien landscape. Yes, the Nautilus was a probe and a Rosetta Stone, decoding a language written in the deep. The implications were staggering. If these structures were indeed artificial, then humanity was not alone in its capacity for monumental engineering, nor was it the sole inheritor of this planet's deep places. The descent into the unknown had revealed a past that was not just prehistoric, but perhaps pre-human, a chapter in Earth's history that the ocean's relentless churn had erased, only to be preserved in this isolated, impossible sanctuary.

"Jasper!" Rachel yelled, "I'm detecting a localized energy fluctuation. It's... inconsistent with any known geothermal or biological activity. It's a sharp, coherent spike, originating from the seabed directly ahead of us. And it's pulsing."

Rachel took a deep breath and continued. "It's more like a biological signal. Powerful enough to be registered on our systems. It's almost as if something is deliberately modulating its output."

Jasper slowed its descent to a crawl; the Nautilus adjusted its trajectory. The external lights, already casting their powerful beams into the abyssal gloom, now seemed to intensify, as if responding to the anomaly. The sonar, which had been painting a picture of the alien structures, now registered something more elusive.

Jasper could not contain his excitement! "Look at the sonar... It is coming from the buildings. It seems that the buildings are trying to communicate by modulating the energy they are emitting!" Everyone was amazed at the idea of using energy fluctuations to communicate.

Jasper wanted to try and experiment to communicate. He went to his room and grabbed his violin. He started playing the scales. Anyone listening could hear the heart and soul Jasper put into the violin scales. When Jasper paused, the violin music was being echoed back to the crew of the Nautilus. It was the most beautiful sounds heard and it was all recorded. Time seemed to stop once the music stopped.

The three exchanged glances, a silent acknowledgment of the profound, almost surreal, nature of their findings. The carefully constructed scientific models that had guided their expedition were fraying at the edges, unable to account for the phenomena they were now witnessing. They had prepared for the unexpected, for the unknown geological formations, for the possibility of undiscovered life forms, but the reality unfolding before them was far stranger than any theoretical prediction.

Suddenly, an unknown phenomenon materialized in the periphery of the Nautilus's forward viewport. It was not the bioluminescence of deep-sea creatures, which they had observed earlier in their descent. This was different. Faint, ethereal wisps of light coalesced, swirling and dancing in the blackness, emanating from the surface of the colossal, geometric structures. The light was not a steady glow, but a shifting, iridescent luminescence, cycling through shades of violet, emerald, and a deep, unsettling crimson.

"Visual confirmation," Rachel stated, her voice betraying none of the awe that was undoubtedly gripping each member of the crew. "Ben, can you give us light? What is it?"

Ben's fingers moved with practiced speed, his eyes wide with a mixture of scientific fascination and primal apprehension. "The light… it's not consistent with incandescence or fluorescence as we understand them. The visual lines are… bizarre. There are emission peaks at frequencies that are typically associated with high-energy particle interactions, but the intensity is far too low for that to be the primary source. It's like a controlled, low-level cascade of exotic particles. And the light itself… it's almost as if it's not interacting with the water molecules in the usual way. It's too… pure, too distinct."

The pulsating energy signatures intensified, and the strange light phenomena changed into more defined patterns. It was as if the ancient structures were awakening, responding to the Nautilus. The sonar echoes grew more complex, painting a picture of internal activity within the alien architecture. Breathless, the crew watched as the impossible unfolded

Ben focused entirely on the acoustic front, added, "The sounds I detected earlier are becoming more pronounced. They're not just random noise anymore. There are discernible modulations, almost like… data packets. But the structure is so alien, our algorithms are struggling to even categorize them, let alone decode them."

Benjamin leaned back, running a hand over his tired eyes. "The gravitational fluctuations are also increasing in amplitude. It's still subtle, but it's undeniable. It's as if these structures are not merely inert masses; they are actively manipulating forces on a fundamental level. The combination of energy emissions, unusual light, acoustic distortions, and localized gravitational anomalies… it's unlike anything ever recorded."

The implications were immense. They were no longer just observing unusual geological formations. They were witnessing the activity of something that defied their understanding of physics and biology. The initial descent had brought them to the edge of a profound mystery, and now, as they ventured deeper into Area 291, they were plunging headfirst into its heart. The sheer scale of the geometric structures was awe-inspiring, but it was the subtle, yet undeniable, signs of activity that truly sent a shiver down their spines. It suggested a purpose, an intent, behind this impossibly ancient architecture.

"Rachel's voice was hushed. "I'm detecting a molecular signature within the emitted light. It's not organic in the way we understand it, but it suggests exotic matter. This is beyond anything I've ever encountered."

The Nautilus moved slowly, its powerful lights cutting through the darkness, illuminating sections of the impossibly regular, towering structures. They looked like colossal pillars, impossibly smooth, stretching upwards into the unseen abyss. Vast flat planes, like impossible walls, connected them, forming a labyrinthine network on the trench floor. The light phenomena continued to dance and swirl, casting an eerie, pulsating glow that seemed to seep from the very material of these alien edifices. Spaceships glowed in the background, as far as it could possibly be seen.

"The energy output is increasing," Benjamin warned, his voice tight. "It's still within safe parameters for the Nautilus, but the pulses are becoming more frequent and more intense. It's as if they're… reacting to our presence. Almost like a greeting, or perhaps a warning."

"I'm getting a coherent signal!" Rachel exclaimed, her voice ringing with excitement. "It's extremely faint, but it's there. The sequence is a repeating pattern of pulses. Though it's not a language, it has structure. It's complex. It's… communication. They also keep repeating the scales."

Benjamin pointed to his display. "I'm now showing a distinct waveform. This isn't random. The acoustic pulses and energy emissions synchronize perfectly. It suggests a manipulation of spacetime on a localized but significant level. It's as if the structure itself is a colossal, complex instrument, generating a multi-layered signal."

The descent was a deep dive into the impossible. A coherent alien phenomenon had connected the incidents. The crew of the Nautilus, suspended in the crushing blackness, were no longer just scientists exploring a deep-sea anomaly; they were the first human beings to intercept a signal from a civilization that existed outside the known parameters of terrestrial existence, a civilization that communicated not through sound waves traveling through air, but through a symphony of energy, light, gravity, and acoustics, playing out in the most extreme environment on Earth. They had sought the unknown, and the unknown had answered, not with a roar, but with a whisper woven from the very essence of the universe. The implications were staggering. If this were communication, what was it saying? What ancient knowledge, what alien perspective, lay encoded in these pulses of energy and distortion? The descent into the unknown had revealed not a void, but a presence, a silent, monumental testament to intelligences that had thrived in the deep long before humanity had even contemplated the stars. The Nautilus was now a receiver, tuned to a frequency of existence that had remained hidden for eons, waiting for the right ears, the right instruments, to finally perceive it. The abyss' silence was no longer empty; the crew was on the precipice of a fundamental change.

CHAPTER 4

ECHOES FROM THE ABYSS

The descent had ceased to be a purely scientific endeavor and had transformed into an act of navigation through an alien landscape. The Nautilus now glided with a newfound fragility through a geological formation that defied all conventional understanding of oceanic trenches. This was no mere fault line or tectonic rift; it was a meticulously sculpted chasm, its walls rising in impossibly sheer, unnaturally smooth planes. The very rock seemed polished, betraying no signs of erosion or the chaotic forces typically associated with such geological features. The scale was overwhelming, dwarfing the Nautilus into an insignificant speck against the colossal architecture that loomed on either side.

Jasper maintained a precise, slow speed. "The sonar is still painting a picture of these structures, but the resolution is… peculiar. It's as if the material itself is absorbing some of the acoustic energy, or perhaps redirecting it in ways we don't understand. When we get back to the surface, the data we've collected will be unbelievable!"

Jasper's words hung in the air, echoing the unspoken astonishment of the entire crew. The external lights of the Nautilus, designed to pierce the crushing blackness of the abyss, were now reflecting off surfaces that seemed to absorb and re-emit light in an unsettling manner. There was no harsh glare, no direct reflection. Instead, the colossal structures exuded their own faint, internal luminescence. It was a ghostly illumination, a spectrum of muted blues, greens, and a subtle, pervasive violet that pulsed with the same rhythmic energy previously detected. This wasn't bioluminescence, nor was it the stark glare of volcanic activity. It was an intrinsic glow, as if the very material of the trench walls was alive with captured light, or perhaps generating it through some unknown process.

The depth gauge showed they were now well over 7,000 meters, a frontier that had previously existed only in theoretical models and the imaginations of science fiction writers. The pressure outside was a colossal, unyielding force, a constant reminder of their vulnerability. Yet within the Nautilus, the focus remained locked on the unfolding mystery. The trench itself seemed to be a vast artificial canyon, its boundaries defined by these impossibly smooth, geometrically perfect walls. They weren't the rough, fractured surfaces one would expect from tectonic activity; they were as if carved, or grown, with deliberate intent.

"Jasper, I'm detecting a significant increase in the particulate matter," reported Rachel, her voice tight with a mixture of excitement and apprehension. "It's not sediment stirred up by our passage. It's forming discrete, almost crystalline structures in the water, and they're glowing faintly, mirroring the ambient light from the trench walls. They appear to be... suspended, almost deliberately."

The implications were staggering. They were not merely observing alien geology; they were witnessing a dynamic environment that seemed to be governed by principles that defied their understanding of physics. The luminous particles, the subtle distortions, the geometrically perfect structures—pointed towards something far more profound than a unique geological phenomenon.

"Rachel, can you try to isolate the source of that acoustic resonance?" Jasper asked, his mind racing to connect the disparate data points. The structures... they seem to be subtly vibrating. It's not a constant hum, but more of a resonant frequency that shifts and changes, almost in response to our presence."

The windows and buildings were all glowing. It was beautiful. Just stunning. One mystery is where the sounds were originating.

Rachel adjusted her acoustic array settings. "I'm trying, Jasper. The soundscape down here is incredibly complex. There are faint, almost melodic undertones beneath the ambient noise, and the resonance you're describing… it's like a vast, intricate instrument is being played. There's a pattern, a distinct sequence, to these harmonic vibrations. It's almost… instructional. It seems like the sounds are coming from everywhere."

The Nautilus continued its slow, deliberate passage, its external cameras capturing the surreal panorama. The trench walls rose miles into the unseen overhead, their surfaces rippling with faint, iridescent light. They were so perfectly formed, so geometrically precise, that they resembled colossal circuit boards etched onto the planet's crust. Wide, flat planes stretched between the towering structures, creating a sense of immense, ordered spaces, like the courtyards of a city built by giants.

Ben's fingers danced across his console. "It's… astonishing, Rachel!"

The Nautilus slowly maneuvered towards a massive circular opening. As they approached, the faint luminescence within intensified, revealing a cavernous space that stretched into the unknown depths of the trench. The walls of the cavern appeared to be constructed of the same impossibly smooth, glowing material as the exterior structures. The swirling luminous particles seemed to be drawn into the aperture, disappearing into the depths.

"Jasper, the energy field is fluctuating more rapidly now," Ben reported, his voice strained. "It's becoming more complex, with multiple overlapping frequencies. And the gravitational pull is increasing, but it's… oscillating. It's not a steady draw anymore. It's like a rhythmic pulse."

"The acoustic resonance is also changing," Rachel added. "The melodic undertones are becoming more pronounced, and I'm detecting what sounds like… echoes. But they're not echoes of our own passage. They're distinct, structured sound patterns originating deep within the structure. It's like a response." Certain sound patterns have shown to have healing powers, such as the purring of a cat. This is not too different.

Jasper's analysis confirmed the increasing complexity of the energy emissions. " It's almost as if... the structure is attempting to communicate, or perhaps to calibrate its emissions based on our presence." Looking out the window, this energy looked like long strands of finely woven hair.

Rachel looked around at Ben and Jasper. "We've gathered unprecedented data. We've witnessed phenomena that rewrite our understanding of physics and biology. The echoes of the abyss are not merely geological reverberations; they are signals from a civilization that has mastered forces we can only theorize about. We will document this location, gather as much passive data as possible, and then we will ascend. We have found something extraordinary, something that will change everything. And we have visual documentation of everything."

Its cameras recorded every shift as the Nautilus held its position. Slowly, the luminous particles danced, a mystery. The descent into the trench had been a journey into the unknown, but the ascent would carry with it the weight of a discovery that would echo through the annals of human history. They had navigated the trench, and in doing so, had charted a fresh course for understanding humanity's place in a universe far stranger and more wondrous than they had ever dared to imagine. Its creators' capabilities are revealed by the audacity of the engineering in this chasm. Though only scratching the surface, the Nautilus's advanced sensors detected faint force ripples on a scale exceeding human comprehension. The pulsating energy signatures, the organized gravitational distortions, and the structured acoustic resonances were not random occurrences; they were the hallmarks of intelligent design, a symphony of physical laws manipulated with an artistry that bordered on the divine. Their mission was understood by the crew to be observation and data collection. The crew's initial theories about geothermal activity or undiscovered biological entities had been thoroughly dispelled, replaced by a far more profound and humbling realization: they had encountered evidence of intelligent design on a scale that dwarfed human ambition. The descent had been a physical journey into a progressively alien environment, but the true journey was the cognitive one, the recalibration of their understanding of life, intelligence, and the very nature of reality itself. Proving to be a repository, the abyss held unfathomable secrets. A form of first contact became the Nautilus's mission, but interacting with the alien required rethinking "contact." Now seen as potential communication, the structured acoustic modulations were no longer baffling. With staggering implications, communication could transcend physical barriers. Scientists could now interpret the glowing particles, which were once thought to be merely exotic matter, as sophisticated informational carriers, data packets suspended in a medium, or possibly even bio-luminescent technology integrated into the very fabric of the trench's environment. The Nautilus, a vessel of discovery, had become a silent witness to a lost epoch.

"Hey guys," Jasper asked comically. "Did anyone realize this is the only submersible in the world that can go this deep?"

"This was not just a geological anomaly; it was an artifact, a relic of a past or perhaps a present, that had remained hidden for millennia. The mystery of their origin gnawed at her. Rachel wondered: Were these the remnants of an ancient terrestrial civilization that had vanished without a trace? Or were they the work of an extraterrestrial presence that had established a clandestine outpost deep within Earth's oceans, using the extreme depths as an impenetrable shield?

The scans suggested a sophisticated, integrated system. If this were a city, it was a city built with a purpose that transcended mere habitation. Perhaps it was a data repository, a power nexus, a research facility, or a refuge. The possibilities were as vast as the structures themselves.

The implications of controlled gravity manipulation were immense. It suggested a level of physics mastery that was currently theoretical for human science, involving principles that might unlock faster-than-light travel or enable the manipulation of fundamental forces. The sheer age implied by these structures, existing in such a state of preservation at these crushing depths, meant that this civilization had achieved such mastery millennia, perhaps eons, ago.

"The acoustic signatures are also peculiar," Rachel added, re-adjusting her hydrophone array. "Beyond the ambient pressure noise and the faint hum of the structures, there are… patterns. Not random sounds, but structured resonances. They're incredibly low frequency, almost subliminal, but they exhibit a complexity that suggests something more than mere geological resonance. It's almost as if the structures themselves are… singing, a slow, deep thrumming that speaks of immense power and age."

Jasper presented a magnified image on the main screen. It showed a section of the wall that, under extreme magnification, revealed a surface that was not solid in the conventional sense but composed of countless, impossibly small, interconnected modules. They shifted and reformed, their movements imperceptible without specialized imaging, creating the illusion of a solid, seamless surface.

"These modules could be the key to the material's properties," Rachel theorized. "They could be collectively manipulating energy fields, modulating the pressure, and even generating the light. If this is the case, then these structures are not merely inert buildings; they are dynamic entities."

The Nautilus continued its slow, cautious traversal, its external lights sweeping across vast facades, intricate latticework that defied terrestrial architectural norms, and colossal, arched doorways that led into unimaginable darkness. The mission had begun as a geological survey, an investigation into anomalous deep-sea phenomena. It had rapidly developed into an archaeological expedition, a journey into the remnants of a lost world. Now, it felt like an encounter with something profoundly alien, a civilization whose very existence challenged humanity's understanding of life, intelligence, and the universe.

"Visual confirmation of a larger aperture ahead," Jasper announced, his voice cutting through the hushed awe within the control sphere. "It appears to be a primary ingress point, significantly larger than anything we've encountered. This is it," Jasper murmured, his gaze fixed on the immense portal. "This is the heart of it all."

Jasper reported a subtle but persistent tug on the submersible. "The gravitational field is influencing our trajectory. It's a gentle but insistent pull, guiding us... or perhaps testing us."

The rhythmic pulse of the Nautilus's floodlights, once a reassuring beacon against the crushing blackness, now seemed to cast a pale, almost timid glow against the incandescent spectacle unfolding before them. Streaks of vibrant, unearthly light, sapphire blues and emerald greens, bloomed in the inky void, originating from the colossal structures and extending outward onto the abyssal plain. These were not the ephemeral bioluminescence of deep-sea organisms, nor the diffuse glow of hydrothermal vents. These lights possessed a deliberate, almost intelligent quality, pulsing with a synchronized cadence that seemed to speak of a complex, underlying system. They flickered, intensified, and then faded, only to reignite moments later, tracing intricate patterns across the submerged metropolis.

"Jasper, are you seeing this?" Ben's voice was hushed, tinged with the same awe that had settled over Jasper and Rachel. His primary sensor array, usually a cascade of complex data streams, was now dominated by visual feeds of the cascading luminescence. "These lights... they're not natural phenomena. The spectral analysis is unlike anything we've ever recorded. They're emitting a broad spectrum, but with sharp, defined peaks that don't correspond to any known atomic or molecular emission." He tapped furiously at his console, attempting to categorize the impossible. "The intensity is variable, but consistently above background levels, even when the visible pulse subsides. It's as if there's an underlying constant energy emission, modulated into these visible bursts."

Jasper reported, "Navigation is becoming… erratic. The autopilot is struggling to maintain a stable heading. It's like there's an invisible current pulling us or pushing us. The inertial navigation system is registering anomalies, and the compass is spinning erratically." He glanced at his instruments, a flicker of concern crossing his face. "And the energy readings… they're spiking. Significantly. They're localized, concentrated around those glowing areas. It's overwhelming the sensitive magnetometers."

Rachel adjusted the gain on her analyzers. "It's a chaotic symphony, Jasper. We're detecting emissions across multiple bands—radio frequencies, microwave, even some extremely high-frequency gamma rays, but all incredibly localized and pulsed. And the power output… it's astronomical. At some of these nodes, the energy flux is orders of magnitude higher than anything we could have predicted. It's interfering with our comms, our sonar… even our structural integrity sensors are showing minor fluctuations. It's as if the entire area is a massive, fluctuating electromagnetic field."

"The energy is coalescing at specific points." Rachel announced, pointing to a cluster of readings on his display. "These aren't random bursts. They appear to be directed. It's as if they're… beaming something. Or receiving something. The interference isn't uniform; it's strongest when we approach these illuminated conduits." He brought up a 3D rendering of the energy field, a swirling, vibrant matrix that seemed to be woven into the very structure of the submerged city. "The source of these emissions isn't superficial. These structures actively generate power instead of just being inert buildings, as the source is deep within the material.

Jasper swore under his breath. "The navigational anomalies are intensifying. We're being nudged off course. It feels… deliberate. Like something is guiding us, or actively trying to prevent us from proceeding further." He fought the controls, the Nautilus groaning faintly as it resisted an unseen force. "These nudges directly correlate with the energy surges." It's like a physical manifestation of the energy field itself."

The implications were chilling. If these energy emissions were strong enough to affect a submersible as robust as the Nautilus, what were they capable of? Could they be the cause of the many unexplained disappearances of deep-sea vessels and anomalies reported in this region over the decades? Extreme geological events or equipment failure had always been blamed for the 'ghost ships,' lost sonar contacts, and sudden radio silence. Now, a terrifyingly plausible explanation was emerging.

"The energy signature is fluctuating in intensity and frequency." Rachel elaborated, her voice strained. "It's not a steady hum; it's a modulated signal. We're picking up complex waveforms, almost like… Morse code, but on an incomprehensible scale and in a spectrum we can't easily decode. It's far too complex to be natural geological processes. This is artificial. This is a deliberate transmission."

Jasper's mind raced. A transmission. What were they communicating? And to whom? Were these signals an ancient greeting, a dormant system awakening, or a warning? The presence of such advanced energy generation and transmission capabilities, coupled with the sophisticated architecture, pointed towards a civilization that had mastered forces that humanity was only beginning to theorize about. The structures did not simply cause energy readings.

Intense energy fields and gravimetric manipulation combined were terrifying The Nautilus, with its limited understanding and primitive sensors, was like a fly caught in a spiderweb of unimaginable complexity.

Jasper grunted, his jaw tight. "Barely. It feels like we're being… herded. The Nautilus can withstand extreme pressures, but this feels like wrestling with the ocean itself. The energy field is actively pushing against our thrusters. If this continues, we'll lose maneuverability entirely."

Rachel chimed in. "The energy composition is shifting as well. We're detecting a higher proportion of exotic particles, particles that we've only observed in high-energy cosmic ray interactions. And the frequency of the pulses is increasing. It's speeding up. I don't think this is just background noise anymore. I think we've triggered something. Our presence, our energy output, our very existence here is causing a reaction."

"The patterns of light are becoming more intricate," Rachel noted, zooming in on a section of the central spire. "They're forming geometric shapes, complex fractals that repeat and grow. It's almost like a visual language. And the energy readings are stabilizing around these new patterns, suggesting a feedback loop."

Ben continued scrolling through pages of data. "The crystalline structures we're encountering... their purity is astounding. We're talking about mineral formations with an almost absolute lack of lattice defects. For example, the silicate compounds forming these conduits—their molecular arrangement is perfect. Not just good, but *perfect*. In nature, even the most pristine geological formations exhibit microscopic imperfections, distortions in the crystalline lattice caused by the chaotic forces of formation. These... these are flawless. They suggest a process of creation that is beyond random accretion or slow geological crystallization. It's as if they were grown, or perhaps meticulously manufactured, atom by atom."

Rachel zoomed in on a dense reading. "And this... this is perhaps the most bewildering. We're detecting trace amounts of certain metallic alloys. Alloys that, again, under these conditions, should have long since oxidized or broken down. The molecular bonds holding them together are... anomalous. They exhibit properties that suggest an artificially induced stability. We're talking about materials that could only exist through advanced metallurgical processes, processes that involve controlled environments and precise energy inputs— techniques that are light-years beyond anything we've achieved, even in our most advanced laboratories."

The implications were staggering. The very ground beneath their theoretical feet was composed of elements that defied decay, formed into structures of impossible perfection, and imbued with an energy that seemed to interact with the fabric of reality itself. This wasn't the work of tectonic plates or volcanic activity. This was an affront to fundamental geological principles.

"The sheer scale of this is what's difficult to comprehend," Rachel continued, her voice low. "We're talking about structures that span kilometers, composed of materials that should be ephemeral. The energy required to stabilize these isotopes, to grow such perfect crystals, to forge these anomalous alloys... it's astronomical. It would require a civilization with a command over energy that makes our fusion reactors look like primitive fire-starting kits. And the processes involved... they must have manipulated fundamental forces, perhaps even the very laws of thermodynamics, to achieve this."

She brought up another projection, this one depicting a cross-section of one of the larger structures. "Look at this. The internal architecture. It's not just solid material. There are intricate networks of conduits, chambers, and what appear to be energy-distribution channels. But the design... it's not optimized for fluid dynamics or heat transfer in any way we understand. It's optimized for something else. Something that requires these specific, impossible materials, and this controlled energy flux."

The concept of terraforming, once relegated to science fiction, crept into their discussions. Could these structures result from a deliberate, colossal effort to reshape the deep-sea environment? The perfect crystalline formations might not be natural geological occurrences, but the building blocks of an artificial biosphere, designed to withstand or even thrive in pressures that would instantly crush any known Earth life.

Jasper's voice cut through the scientific fervor. "These geological anomalies are also affecting our submersible's systems in new ways. The hull integrity sensors are picking up minute, localized stresses that don't correspond to external pressure. It's as if the very material of these structures is exerting a subtle, insistent force on our hull, trying to... conform us to its own properties. It's not destructive, not yet, but it's like a constant, pervasive handshake from an alien hand."

Ben added another layer of complexity. "And the energy emissions we're detecting are not simply 'leaking' from these impossible materials; they seem to be actively *generated* by them, in a controlled manner. It's not radioactive decay as we know it. It's a sustained, modulated output. The half-lives might be short, but the processes creating and sustaining these isotopes, and extracting energy from them, are clearly incredibly advanced and long-lasting. This suggests a power source that is not only potent but also sustainable over geological timescales. This is not a dying star; this is a carefully managed, perhaps even renewable, energy system."

Rachel confirmed, her gaze intense. "It's not just a city built of strange materials. It's an entire geological stratum that defies terrestrial explanation. This implies a level of planetary engineering that is simply... mind-boggling. We're not looking at mere construction; we're looking at a transformation of the fundamental geological and energetic landscape. It's as if the builders didn't just erect buildings; they rewrote the rules of matter and energy for this entire region of the planet."

The implications for human science were profound. If such materials and processes were possible, they would revolutionize everything. But the immediate concern was understanding the *purpose* behind them. Was this merely a derelict power station, a forgotten artifact of an ancient civilization? Or was it something more active, more dangerous? The perfect symmetry of the crystals, the deliberate integration of impossible materials, the controlled energy emissions—it all pointed to an intelligence, a design, a purpose.

The sheer audacity of it was breathtaking. They had come seeking evidence of lost civilizations, and they had found something that suggested a civilization that had mastered the very building blocks of reality. A civilization that could not only create matter and energy but manipulate its fundamental properties, bending it to its will to construct an entire submerged metropolis that defied all known laws of science.

The scale of the engineering truly pressed down on them, heavier than the kilometers of water above. It wasn't just a few structures; it was an entire biome, an ecosystem of impossible materials and sustained energy. The flawless crystalline formations, perfect down to the atomic level, were not merely aesthetic choices; they were clearly functional, designed for the efficient, lossless transmission of energies that Rachel was only beginning to categorize. The anomalous isotopes, so unstable by terrestrial standards, were stabilized and harnessed, their theoretical decay rates rendered irrelevant by some unknown process. Rachel had speculated about a form of "geological engineering" on a planetary scale, a re-writing of fundamental physical laws to suit the needs of the builders. It was a concept so vast, so audacious, that it bordered on the divine.

They were now close-ranging on one of the larger edifices, a towering spire of interlocking, luminescent crystalline structures that seemed to pierce the impenetrable darkness above. The *Nautilus*'s external cameras, designed to capture every minute detail of the abyssal plains, were feeding high-definition imagery directly to the command console. As the submersible's powerful spotlights swept across the intricate facade of the spire, revealing layers of impossibly smooth, geometric planes and swirling patterns of light within the material, something flickered in the illumination's periphery. It was barely a suggestion, a whisper of motion in the oppressive stillness.

Benjamin leaned closer to his screen. "Guys," he said, his voice a low murmur, "I'm seeing something on the forward-facing cameras, quadrant three. Peripheral."

All eyes snapped to the designated monitor. The image was a dizzying kaleidoscope of the spire's glowing surface and the inky blackness surrounding it, punctuated by the *Nautilus*'s powerful, focused beams. The lights cut through the water like surgical instruments, illuminating a small section of the alien architecture. Benjamin had enhanced the relevant feed, digitally sharpened the image and adjusted contrast. For a fraction of a second, between the sweep of one light beam and the next, a series of blurs streaked across the frame. They were too fast, too indistinct, to be water currents or the natural drift of sediment. They moved with a deliberate, directional velocity that was undeniably biological, or at least, animate.

Benjamin announced, "The motion is incredibly rapid, and the ambient light conditions are making definitive identification… difficult. They're almost in sync with the light's movement, ducking into the shadows as the beams pass." He zoomed in on a dense area of the feed, where the blurs were most pronounced. What appeared was a fleeting impression of form, a suggestion of limbs, or perhaps appendages, moving with an unsettling fluidity. They were small, much smaller than the massive structures they were observing, but their presence was a stark, undeniable confirmation that they were not alone in this alien domain.

The implication sent a ripple of unease through the command center. These weren't simply passive inhabitants of the abyss. They were aware of the *Nautilus*, aware of its lights, and actively evading detection. The feeling of being watched, a vague, unsettling sensation that had lingered since they first entered this anomalous zone, now solidified into a palpable, almost suffocating presence. It was no longer a psychological projection; it was a confirmed, observed phenomenon.

The tension in the submersible was a thick, almost tangible thing. The vast, silent alien city, with its impossible materials and sustained energy, had just revealed its inhabitants. And these inhabitants were not shy. They were fast and, apparently, aware of the intruders in their midst. The scientific curiosity that had driven them thus far was now being edged out by a primal sense of caution, the innate human response to the unknown, the feeling of being observed by something that moved in the shadows.

Benjamin shook his head. "I can't get a lock on them. They're too fast, and the energy fields here are… noisy. Our sensors are struggling to differentiate their signatures from the ambient background radiation and the energy emissions from the structures themselves. It's like trying to pick out a single violin note in the middle of a symphony played by an entire orchestra with their instruments amplified."

Rachel gestured to the monitor. "Look at the way they move. There's no apparent propulsion system, no fins, no visible means of locomotion that we would recognize. They seem to glide, to flow through the water. And the speed… it suggests a mastery of fluid dynamics that is far beyond anything we have engineered." She paused, with a speculative gleam in her eyes. "It's possible they are not moving *through* the water as much as they are manipulating the surrounding water, creating localized pockets of reduced resistance or even generating micro-currents to propel themselves."

The idea of entities that could subtly manipulate their environment to move was both fascinating and terrifying. It implied a level of control over the very medium they inhabited that was profound. This wasn't just life adapting to an environment; this was a life that *shaped* its environment. Rachel remembered an old magazine that interviewed someone off the coast of Malibu and talked about how these crafts went into the water without a splash. Over the years, hundreds of people came forward telling the same story.

Jasper interjected, his voice sharp. "The hull stress sensors are showing increased activity. The localized pressure fluctuations are becoming more frequent, and slightly more intense. It's still within nominal parameters, but the pattern is changing. It's no longer random brushing; it feels more… deliberate. Like probing."

The feeling of being watched intensified. The shadows, once just the absence of light, now seemed to hold a tangible menace. Each flicker on the monitor, each fleeting blur of motion, sent a jolt through the crew. They were no longer just observers; they were participants in a silent, unseen drama unfolding in the crushing darkness of the abyss.

Rachel was already back at her console, her mind racing through the possibilities. "It's plausible. If these structures are, as we suspect, localized energy fields, they could influence a form of advanced energy conduit or generator. If these entities can generate their own modulated energy signatures, they could theoretically interact with the spire's matrix. It would explain their incredible speed and their ability to disappear into the energy flux. They might be 'surfing' the energy currents."

The image of entities "surfing" the energy currents of an alien city, a city built of impossible materials and powered by unknown forces, was a potent one. It painted a picture of a life form so perfectly adapted to its environment that it had become one with it. Fleeting blurs on the screens were no longer subtle movements.

CHAPTER 5

SHADOW'S PACT

The alien architecture now dwarfs the Nautilus. The unsettling realization that they were not alone had tempered the initial awe at the impossibly engineered structures. Jasper had sent them deeper into the labyrinthine city, towards a particular section of the colossal spire that pulsed with a more concentrated, rhythmic luminescence. It deviated from its original trajectory, a calculated risk taken in the face of growing evidence that this place was not merely a relic, but a living enigma.

Rachel guided the submersible with delicate precision. Her gloved hands, usually steady as she analyzed the data, now traced the contours of the approaching structure on his holographic display. "The energy signatures are intensifying. "There's a pattern to it, a harmonic resonance unlike anything we've encountered. It's almost as if the spire itself is… singing."

The *Nautilus* glided closer, the aperture now filling the main viewscreen. It was an entrance, a gateway into the heart of the spire. As they passed through the shimmering threshold, the environment within shifted dramatically. The oppressive darkness of the abyss gave way to a soft, pervasive twilight, a gentle luminescence that seemed to emanate from every surface. The interior was vast, a colossal chamber that defied the external dimensions of the spire. It was not a single, space, but a series of interconnected platforms and spiraling walkways, all fashioned from the same impossibly smooth, luminescent crystal. The air, or rather the fluid that filled the chamber, was perfectly clear, devoid of any sediment or particulate matter.

"Look at these! Rachel stated in absolute wonder. "They're not decorative. They appear to be… data repositories. See the intricate patterns within the crystal? They're not random. They're etched, inscribed with a precision that suggests information storage."

"That's the challenge, Jasper," Rachel replied, a hint of frustration in her voice. "The crystal lattice itself is the medium. It's not like a hard drive or a server. It's… a solidified form of data. The energy patterns we're detecting within them are incredibly complex, almost like a biological neural network. We need to translate those patterns."

For the next several hours, the *Nautilus* navigated through the colossal chamber, its external cameras meticulously scanning every detail. They observed what appeared to be holographic projectors embedded in the crystalline surfaces, dormant for millennia but hinting at the sophisticated visual displays once present. They found what looked like communal gathering spaces, vast amphitheaters of polished crystal, and smaller, more intimate chambers that might have served as living quarters or specialized laboratories. Yet, despite the evidence of a sophisticated civilization, there was no sign of the inhabitants themselves.

It was in a more secluded, recessed area of the main chamber, away from the central pulsating light source, that they found it. A series of intricately carved pedestals, each supporting a hexagonal prism of a deep, iridescent blue crystal. These prisms glowed with a soft, internal light, a stark contrast to the pervasive luminescence of the surrounding structures.

"Rebecca, I'm detecting a distinct energy signature emanating from those prisms," Ben reported, his voice sharp with focus. "It's different from the ambient energy. It's more… focused, more structured. And the complexity of the wave patterns… it's orders of magnitude beyond anything we've seen."

Rachel leaned closer to her console, her eyes wide. "These aren't just energy sources. They're emitting coherent data streams. It's a direct information transfer, Jasper. And the data… it's not just structural or scientific. It's narrative. It's history."

"Access it, Rachel? Can we tap into it?" Jasper asked.

"We can try to," Rachel explained, I'll need Ben to figure some of this out. "They designed these prisms for a direct neural or energy-based interface, not for a physical connection." We'll have to adapt our sensors, try to 'listen' to the data stream, and hope our translation algorithms can make sense of it."

It was a painstakingly slow process. The team worked in shifts, their focus unwavering, as Rachel and Ben painstakingly attempted to decode the alien data. At first, the outputs showed fragmented information, a jumble of abstract symbols and fluctuating energy patterns. But gradually, with each review of their algorithms, the pieces fell into place. The symbols gathered into coherent images; the energy patterns resolved into narrative.

The first coherent images that flickered onto the *Nautilus*'s main screen were of celestial bodies, stars and nebulae in configurations that predated human astronomical observation. Then came depictions of the planet itself, as it must have been millennia ago, teeming with life and marked by colossal geological upheavals. And then, the builders appeared.

They were not the swift entities they had glimpsed outside. These beings were tall, slender, and with limbs that moved with an effortless grace. Flowing, shimmering garments, which seemed to be made of solidified light, partially covered their forms. Their serene faces had large, intelligent eyes that seemed to hold the wisdom of the ages. They moved among structures that were remarkably similar to the spire.

The archives unfolded a story that spanned eons. They depicted the construction of the submerged metropolis not as acts of war or conquest, but as retreats, sanctuaries built to weather cataclysmic events on the surface. The energy sources, the anomalous isotopes, showed they could manipulate spacetime and stabilize matter, allowing for the creation of structures that defied conventional physics. The crystalline conduits weren't just for energy transfer; they were conduits of consciousness, facilitating collective awareness among the builders.

But the most profound revelation came when the archives depicted interactions with other species. Among them, fleetingly at first, were faint, almost spectral images of humanoids. They were primitive, their forms less refined than the builders, their technology rudimentary, but their presence in these ancient records was undeniable.

"Ben," Rachel said, her voice barely a whisper, "they knew about us. They have records of early humans."

Rachel's face was nodding grimly. "More than that, Ben, look at this! This isn't just observation! These records show them... interacting! Sharing knowledge. Not just with us, but with other species across the galaxy!"

The hexagonal prisms, the "data crystals" as Rachel had termed them, revealed a long-standing pact, a covenant of cosmic stewardship. The builders, who referred to themselves in the translated records as the "Luminaries," had not sought to conquer or dominate. Instead, they had acted as silent guardians, seeding knowledge and fostering development across the cosmos. They had established these archives—these vast repositories of their civilization's legacy.

The records detailed a specific pact, a "Pact of Shadows," as the translation rendered it. It was an agreement forged between the Luminaries and a select few species who had reached a certain threshold of technological and philosophical advancement. Humanity, it seemed, had been one of those species millennia before recorded history. The pact was not about direct intervention, but about indirect guidance, a subtle influence designed to steer developing civilizations towards enlightenment and away from self-destruction.

The Luminaries had left behind technologies, subtly integrated into the fabric of societies, that would allow for eventual breakthroughs in energy, consciousness, and interstellar travel. They had also, according to the archives, established a network of "observers," entities tasked with monitoring the progress of these chosen species. The swift, elusive beings they had encountered outside the spire? They were the current iteration of these observers, tasked with ensuring the integrity of the archives and assessing the readiness of any species that stumbled upon them.

"The pact," Rachel muses aloud, her voice echoing softly in the crystalline chamber, "it was to be revealed only when a species showed both the capacity for advanced understanding and the maturity to handle such knowledge. They didn't want to interfere directly, to foster dependence. They wanted us to find our own way, to reach this point through our own efforts."

The implications were staggering. An ancient, benevolent alien civilization had subtly influenced for millennia humanity's progress, its technological leaps. The wars, the scientific discoveries, the philosophical debates—all had occurred under the watchful, silent gaze of the Luminaries.

This cast a new light on human history, revealing a hidden layer of cosmic interaction that had shaped their destiny in ways they had never imagined. Instead of secrecy, the "Pact of Shadows" offered discreet guidance, gently shaping young civilizations' evolution. The archives held more than just a record of their past; the entities outside, the swift and silent guardians, were the living embodiment of that pact, their vigilance a constant reminder of the immense responsibility that came with accessing such ancient knowledge.

With the alien consciousness, the data crystals hummed. Unlike any human imagination, the figures flickered on the screen. Tall and impossibly slender, their bodies seemed to flow with an inherent grace, as if gravity were a suggestion they had long since learned to disregard. They moved through structures that echoed the very spire the submersible now occupied, vast, crystalline cities that pulsed with a gentle, internal light. These were not the frantic, hurried movements of explorers or conquerors, but the deliberate, measured actions of beings who had transcended the urgency of linear time. Their attire, if it could be called such, appeared to be woven from solidified starlight, shimmering and shifting with an ethereal luminescence that defied terrestrial physics.

After their faces were clearly rendered, they possessed an alien beauty that was both profound and disquieting. Their features were symmetrical, harmonious, yet devoid of the familiar expressions that defined humanity. Their eyes, large and dark, held a depth that spoke of unfathomable eons, reflecting a detached, almost clinical, curiosity. There was no malice, no aggression, but an immense, overarching intelligence that seemed to catalog and analyze everything it perceived.

The Luminaries, as the translated archives referred to them, viewed the cosmos not through the lens of emotion or conquest, but as a grand, intricate experiment. Earth, with its burgeoning life and volatile sentience, was a fascinating specimen within this boundless laboratory.

The Luminaries' interest in humanity was not an anomaly, but a part of their long-term cosmic strategy. The archives detailed their observations of early hominids, their rudimentary tool-making, their nascent social structures, and their burgeoning capacity for abstract thought. These records were not sterile, objective scientific reports; they were filled with a subtle, almost pedagogical, tone. They depicted the Luminaries, cloaked in their shimmering garments, observing nomadic human tribes from a distance, their presence so subtle that they were indistinguishable from natural phenomena. These were not direct interactions, but carefully orchestrated moments of influence. An unusually potent lightning strike that illuminated a primitive cave painting, a sudden, inexplicable surge of inspiration that led to the development of a new tool, a fleeting vision that sparked a myth or a legend—these were the subtle nudges the Luminaries employed.

One sequence showed a small group of early humans huddled around a meager fire, their faces etched with fear and uncertainty as they gazed at the stars. From the darkness, a faint, shimmering light descended, not a solid craft, but an ephemeral beacon that pulsed with a gentle rhythm. It lingered for a moment, casting an otherworldly glow upon the bewildered humans, before dissolving back into the night sky. The translated commentary from the Luminary archives described this as a deliberate act of "pattern seeding," an attempt to imbue a new consciousness with the fundamental geometry of the cosmos, to plant the seeds of curiosity and wonder that would, eons later, lead to the development of astronomy and a yearning for the stars.

Another segment depicted a scene of primitive agriculture. Early humans struggled to coax sustenance from the soil, their methods inefficient and their yields meager. Then, a Luminary, its form almost indistinguishable from the heat haze rising from the parched earth, subtly altered the electromagnetic fields around a patch of fertile land. The result was a sudden, inexplicable burst of growth, the plants thriving with a vigor that defied the harsh conditions. The archival notes explained this as an experiment in "bio-enhancement," a controlled introduction of optimized environmental stimuli to observe the resultant evolutionary adaptations in both flora and fauna, and by extension, the human societies that depended on them. They were not seeking to uplift humanity through direct intervention, but to provide subtle, almost imperceptible, catalysts for sped-up natural development.

The Luminaries' scientific curiosity was immense, bordering on the voracious. They studied the intricate dance of ecosystems, the complex interplay of genetics, and the emergent properties of consciousness. Humanity, with its chaotic blend of primal instincts and soaring intellect, its capacity for both immense cruelty and profound love, presented a rich and perplexing subject of study. The archives detailed elaborate simulations run by the Luminaries, projecting potential evolutionary pathways for humanity based on varying environmental and social inputs. They were running through countless parallel futures, attempting to understand the myriad possibilities inherent in the human experiment.

The hum of the *Nautilus* seemed to deepen, resonating with the weight of the information now spilling from the data crystals. Dr. Thorne, his face illuminated by the cool glow of the holographic display, felt a cold dread settle in his gut. The serene, almost detached curiosity of the Luminaries, as detailed in the previous archives, now took on a chilling new dimension. It wasn't just scientific observation; it was a meticulously managed experiment, and humanity, it seemed, had been a willing, if profoundly ignorant, participant in its own subjugation.

The revelation of a clandestine pact, brokered centuries ago between humanity's most powerful nations and these enigmatic alien entities, felt like a betrayal of an unimaginable scale. The data crystals showed a planned infiltration, not sudden tech. Instead of gardeners, the narrative shifted to a beneficial deal.

The Luminaries had presented their offer to a select few human leaders during periods of immense global conflict and technological stagnation. Because of the industrial age's yearnings and war threats, such a proposition flourished. The Luminaries, in their infinite patience and with their advanced understanding of causality, had foreseen these moments of desperation. They understood that a species teetering on the brink of self-annihilation might be more amenable to a partnership that promised salvation, even at a steep price.

The essence of the deal was stark and morally ambiguous. In exchange for a steady, controlled infusion of alien technology—particularly in the fields of energy generation and weaponry—humanity would grant the Luminaries unfettered access to study their developing civilization. The data crystals pulsed with images of clandestine meetings, silhouetted figures against the backdrop of moonlit deserts and ancient forests, the exchange of not just knowledge, but of something far more profound: control.

The implications for human autonomy were staggering. Every leap in technological advancement, every military breakthrough, every paradigm shift in understanding the universe, could now be re-examined. Was the atomic bomb a product of human ingenuity, or a carefully delivered package, designed to show the destructive potential of a species and the subsequent need for advanced defensive and offensive capabilities? Was the dawn of the space age driven by a natural human curiosity, or by a gentle nudge from their alien benefactors, guiding them towards a celestial stage where further observation was possible? The archives offered no simple answers, only a mosaic of evidence that painted a deeply unsettling picture.

And at the heart of this intricate deception, acting as a silent, yet crucial, intermediary, was the Vatican. The ancient institution, with its millennia-old network of influence and its unparalleled ability to maintain secrets, had become the lynchpin of the clandestine bargain. The data crystals revealed the Luminaries had recognized the Vatican's unique position, its spiritual authority, and its historical role as a repository of knowledge and a weaver of narratives. They saw in the Church a perfect tool to manage the human element of the pact, to ensure secrecy and to maintain a veneer of human control, even as the reins of power were subtly slipping away.

The archives showed the Luminaries did not engage directly with secular governments. Instead, their communications and their directives were funneled through a select, highly secretive echelon within the Vatican. This echelon, composed of individuals whose faith had been intertwined with an alien wisdom, acted as the bridge between the divine and the terrestrial, between the cosmic and the human. They were tasked with interpreting the Luminaries' subtle guidance, with translating their advanced concepts into a form that human scientists and engineers, and, most crucially, with masking the true origins of these advancements could understand and implement.

This historical role of the Vatican explained so much of the Church's enduring influence, its seemingly pronouncements on matters of science and society, and its deep involvement in global affairs. It wasn't just about faith; it was about a centuries-long stewardship of a cosmic secret. The illusion of divine power, the miracles, the prophecies—the archives hinted that many of these were not simply acts of divine intervention, but carefully orchestrated events, designed to reinforce the Church's authority and to maintain the established order, an order that was, in reality, dictated by alien architects.

The data crystals projected scenes of ornate chambers within the Vatican, hidden beneath centuries of history, where religious iconography was juxtaposed with alien schematics. It depicted hushed meetings between robed figures and beings whose forms flickered at the edge of human perception, a surreal ballet of power and faith. The archives spoke of 'sacred trusts,' of 'illuminated doctrines,' and of 'celestial mandates,' all terms used to cloak the raw pragmatism of the alien bargain. The Vatican, in this new, chilling narrative, had not been a passive observer of history, but an active participant in a grand, extraterrestrial experiment.

Holy books were crafted between the Church and the Luminaries. Over the course of time, humanity questioned parts of the bible right in the first paragraph of Genesis to the end. Were the Luminaries God? If they were, they wasn't telling anyone. The Luminaries were seeding worlds, increasing wisdom, and other factors only they knew about.

Technology exchange wasn't a benevolent gift. The Luminaries understood that a technologically advanced humanity, particularly one capable of wielding immense destructive power, was a far more interesting specimen to study. It provided them with a constant stream of data on the development of complex societies, on the ethical dilemmas posed by advanced weaponry, and on the psychological impact of rapid technological change. The arms race, the Cold War, the constant geopolitical tension—these were not simply the product of human folly, but potentially, carefully managed variables within the Luminary experiment.

The Luminaries established a complex oversight system; the archives showed. The 'swift entities,' the ethereal beings encountered by the *Nautilus*, were not merely observers; they were also the enforcers of the pact. Their speed and elusiveness were not just about stealth, but about their ability to monitor and, when necessary, to influence events to ensure that humanity remained on its predetermined course.

A chilling realization of humanity's status had replaced the initial awe and wonder inspired by the Luminaries. They were not pioneers on the cusp of an interstellar dialogue, but laboratory animals, their every move meticulously recorded, their every innovation a carefully curated response to external stimuli. The beauty of the Luminary civilization, their crystalline cities and their ethereal forms, now seemed to mask a cold, calculating intelligence that viewed humanity not as equals, but as fascinating, albeit potentially dangerous, biological constructs.

The data crystals continued to unfold, revealing the intricate mechanism of this pact. It wasn't a simple quid pro quo; it was a dynamic, evolving relationship. The Luminaries learned from humanity as much as humanity learned from them, albeit through vastly unorthodox methods.

According to the archives, the development of nuclear weapons was damning. The data depicted the Luminaries subtly guiding human scientists towards the understanding of fission and fusion, not to empower humanity, but to test its capacity for self-destruction. The subsequent proliferation of nuclear arsenals, the constant threat of global annihilation, had provided an unprecedented stream of data on societal stress, political maneuvering, and the human psyche under extreme duress.

Similarly, the rapid advancement of communication technologies, the internet, the global information network, had also been influenced. The Luminaries saw this as a way to speed up the spread of information, to create a more interconnected and thus more easily observable global society. It allowed for the rapid dissemination of ideas, the formation of global trends, and the observation of collective human behavior on an unprecedented scale. The vast amount of data generated by this interconnected world was a treasure trove for the Luminaries, providing insights into human thought processes, cultural evolution, and the dynamics of social networks.

The sheer scale of the deception was overwhelming. Centuries of human history, re-contextualized by this single, devastating revelation. The luminaries, through their intermediaries, had become the unseen puppeteers, their strings woven into the very fabric of human progress. The Vatican, once seen as a spiritual beacon holding humanity tethered to a predetermined destiny. Humanity became a fascinating experiment in stability and technology. It turned out that freedom was the price of salvation. The Pact of Shadows was more than just a historical footnote. The implications for the *Nautilus* mission, and for humanity's future, were now terrifyingly clear. They were not about to make contact; they were about to unearth a secret that could shatter the world.

A chilling weight of data crystals filled the dimly lit Nautilus. The events rewrote the narrative of human progress irrevocably. Archives painted a grim picture, not of organic evolution, but of a meticulously orchestrated dance, guided by unseen hands. The Luminaries, with their seemingly benevolent presence, had in reality become the architects of our historical trajectory, their pact of shadows a subtle but pervasive influence on the very fabric of human civilization.

The immediate aftermath of the pact was not an immediate utopia. Instead, it was a period of calculated disruption. The Luminaries, driven by an insatiable scientific curiosity, saw in humanity a chaotic variable, a species whose inherent volatility was precisely what made it such an interesting subject. This led to a disturbing pattern woven into the historical record: periods of apparent technological stagnation followed by sudden, explosive leaps, often accompanied by devastating conflicts.

The archives provided granular details of how this manipulation played out. Introducing advanced energy technologies, for instance, was not a straightforward gift designed to uplift humanity. Rather, it was a carefully controlled release, calibrated to speed up industrialization while simultaneously creating new vectors for conflict. Fossil fuel dependency, the subsequent geopolitical rivalries it engendered, and the eventual, desperate search for alternative energy sources—all of it was part of a broader experimental design. The Luminaries were not merely providing solutions; they were engineering problems, then observing how humanity grappled with them. This allowed for the study of interdependence, and of the psychological impact of scarcity.

The instigation of the conflict was perhaps the most harrowing revelation. The data crystals detailed many instances where the Luminaries, through their intermediaries, had subtly amplified existing tensions between nations. It wasn't about direct intervention, a thunderous arrival of alien fleets. Instead, it was far more insidious. The Luminaries weren't interested in world peace; they were interested in the data generated by its absence. They sought to understand the biological and sociological imperatives that drove species to conflict, and what better laboratory than a planet teetering on the edge of self-annihilation?

The archives painted a disturbing picture of the Second World War. While human historians had attributed the rapid advancements in aviation, rocketry, and radar to wartime necessity, the data suggested a more deliberate orchestration. Luminary-influenced research streams produced key theoretical breakthroughs that arrived just in time to give one side an advantage.

The Vatican did far more than simply be custodians, as shown. The data crystals, which display ancient texts previously thought to be religious allegory, now look like coded messages and technical specifications, facilitated the pact. The Church had inadvertently become the ultimate gatekeeper of an alien agenda, its sacred institutions imbued with a purpose far beyond human comprehension.

Global events subtly controlled space exploration. In the experiment, they deliberately sped up the race to the moon. The Luminaries, having guided humanity towards the development of rocketry, saw the moon as a logical next step—a stepping stone to further exploration, and more importantly, a platform from which to observe humanity's attempts at extraterrestrial endeavors. Early space missions carefully ensured that humanity's reach did not exceed its grasp, at least not to disrupt the experiment. The Luminaries were not afraid of humanity reaching the stars; they were afraid of humanity discovering them, or worse, disrupting their own clandestine operations.

Rachel, Jasper, and Ben found themselves re-examining every significant event in human history through this new, profoundly disturbing lens. The Renaissance, the Enlightenment, smallpox, the plague, the Industrial Revolution—were these organic surges of human intellect, or carefully timed injections of knowledge and stimulus? Humanity was like a child prodigy, performing marvels under the watchful eye of a demanding, inscrutable tutor, never truly free to explore its own innate talents or to make its own mistakes.

The implications for the *Nautilus* mission were now starkly clear. They hadn't stumbled upon a benevolent alien race eager to share cosmic secrets. They had discovered the keepers of humanity's cage. The knowledge they possessed was not a key to unlocking the universe, but a blueprint of their own prison. A pact of shadows was not a historical footnote but a living influence, even as humanity believed itself to be charting its own course. The data crystals continued to shimmer, each byte a history rewritten, a future mortgaged, and a present built on a foundation of deliberate deception.

The deepest and most disturbing layers of the Luminary archives finally unfolded but through a chillingly direct document titled, "Protocol: Harmonic Convergence and Subsequent Yield." Benjamin felt a cold dread snake up his spine as the holographic projections resolved into what appeared to be a multi-phase operational plan. This was not about observation and subtle manipulation anymore. This was about the endgame. The 'Harvest' Protocol.

The document laid bare the Luminaries' ultimate aim, an almost clinical description of what they intended to do with their centuries-long experiment. It wasn't about fostering humanity or guiding it towards some predetermined cosmic destiny. It was about assessment, cataloging, and then, depending on the outcome, assimilation or elimination. The word 'yield' sent a shiver through Benjamin. It spoke of a resource being gathered, a crop being reaped. Humanity, it seemed, was merely a long-term agricultural project for these alien entities.

The protocol meticulously detailed its distinct phases. Phase One, already extensively documented in the previous archives Benjamin had deciphered, was the 'Incubation and Stimulus' phase—the subtle guidance, the engineered conflicts, the sped up technological leaps, all designed to foster complexity and volatility. Phase Two, the 'Stress Assessment,' was currently underway, and Ben finally understood the true purpose of the escalating global instability. The economic collapses, the rising geopolitical tensions, the erosion of societal trust—these weren't unintended consequences of Luminary interference, nor were they simply data points in a study of conflict. They were deliberate, escalating pressures designed to push humanity to its breaking point. The Luminaries were creating the ultimate stress test, observing how a species reacted when its carefully constructed systems crumbled.

The document elaborated on the metrics they were evaluating during this phase. It wasn't just about technological capacity or military might. The protocol detailed specific parameters for assessing "societal resilience," "resource adaptability," "ideological cohesion," and, most disturbingly, "inherent existential threat potential." They were looking for emergent behaviors that showed an uncontrollable drive towards self-destruction or, conversely, the capacity to overcome insurmountable odds and achieve a harmonious equilibrium. The current global chaos was, in their alien calculus, the perfect crucible for forging such data. Each news report of famine, each flicker of escalating conflict, each economic downturn was not a tragedy for the Luminaries, but a precisely measured input into their grand, terrifying experiment.

Their plans seemed like reading the Book of Revelations. The 'Harvest' Protocol then detailed Phase Three: 'Catalytic Disruption.' This was where things escalated significantly. The document outlined a series of carefully orchestrated events designed to push humanity over the precipice, ensuring that either its potential for self-annihilation or its capacity for profound adaptation would become undeniably clear. This could involve engineered environmental catastrophes, introducing novel technologies that would shatter existing economic paradigms, or even the manipulation of biological agents to observe societal responses to widespread crisis. The goal was to create a situation where humanity could not possibly ignore the precipice they stood upon, forcing a definitive choice between extinction or radical transformation.

Luminaries weren't interested in *preventing* these crises; they were interested in the *data* generated by humanity's response to them. They wanted to see how the species navigated genuine desperation. Would they turn on each other with unprecedented savagery, or would they find common ground, demonstrating a capacity for unified action that had, until now?

The subsequent phase, Phase Four: 'Cognitive and Resource Assimilation,' was where the chilling reality of the 'Harvest' truly manifested. Depending on the data gleaned from Phase Three, humanity would either be deemed a viable resource for assimilation or a contained threat to be neutralized. Assimilation, the document vaguely suggested, involved integrating select human cognitive patterns, technological advancements, and perhaps even biological traits into the Luminary collective. This wasn't about co-existence; it was about absorption. The Luminary collective would dissect humanity's unique evolutionary path, catalog its most valuable aspects, and repurpose them, discarding or rewriting its less desirable traits. It was the ultimate form of intellectual and cultural appropriation, performed on a species-wide scale.

Conversely, if humanity proved too volatile, too inherently destructive, or simply too unmanageable, Phase Four shifted to 'Containment and Sterilization.' This was the elimination protocol. The Luminaries, with their advanced understanding of galactic ecosystems, would not permit a species that posed a significant existential threat to continue unchecked. The method of sterilization was not explicitly detailed, but the sterile, clinical language suggested something far more efficient and terrifying than a conventional war. It spoke of 'resource reclamation' and 'ecological reset,' terms that painted a picture of a planet being scrubbed clean, its dominant species eradicated with the same dispassion one might use to clear an infestation.

The document also touched upon the criteria for this grim assessment. Humanity's progress towards sustainable coexistence with its environment was a key factor. Its capacity for empathy and inter-species cooperation, beyond the confines of its own kind, was another. The Luminaries were looking for a species that could prove itself worthy of continued existence, not through displays of power or technological prowess, but through a profound ethical and evolutionary maturity. And from their perspective, humanity had consistently failed to show this maturity.

Benjamin's mind raced, piecing together the fragments of information. The ancient texts he had studied, the whispers of prophecy, the recurring themes of judgment and reckoning—they weren't religious doctrines; they were echoes of this Luminary protocol, passed down through generations, distorted and reinterpreted through the lens of human myth. The concept of a final judgment, of a cosmic weighing of souls, was a deeply ingrained human archetype, perhaps a subconscious recognition of the external forces that had been shaping their destiny for millennia. The Luminaries weren't gods; they were cosmic assessors, and humanity was on trial.

Contingency plans were also detailed in the 'Harvest' Protocol. If humanity, in its desperate struggle during Phase Two, achieved a remarkable level of unity and innovation that posed an unforeseen threat to the Luminary's long-term objectives, a preemptive 'Disruption Event' could be triggered. This would essentially reset the experiment, plunging humanity back into a period of relative stagnation or chaos, preventing it from reaching a stage where it might discover or challenge its overseers. It was a fail-safe, ensuring that the experiment could always be controlled, its outcomes always dictated.

The sheer audacity of the plan was overwhelming. For millennia, humanity had believed itself to be the sole author of its history, the architect of its own destiny. Now, Benjamin understood the truth: they had been subjects in a vast, alien laboratory, their triumphs and their failures meticulously documented, all leading to this final, terrifying assessment.

The document concluded with a series of projections and probability analysis, showing the Luminaries' current assessment of humanity's likelihood to pass the 'Harvest' criteria. The outlook was bleak. Projections heavily favored the 'Containment and Sterilization' outcome, with assimilation deemed a statistically improbable, albeit not impossible, result. The Luminaries seemed to view humanity's inherent nature as a fundamental flaw, a bug in the system that was unlikely to be patched.

Benjamin looked at the shimmering data crystals, no longer seeing them as repositories of lost knowledge, but as blueprints for humanity's potential extinction. The Luminaries were not benevolent guardians; they were cosmic farmers, tending their crop with cold, scientific detachment, ready to harvest what they deemed valuable and to cull the rest. The Pact of Shadows had indeed set the stage, and now, the ultimate act of the 'Harvest' Protocol was about to begin. The question that gnawed at Benjamin was not *whether* it would happen, but *when*, and whether humanity, even now, had any chance of altering its grim prognosis. Contrary to expectations, the data revealed a dire fate for the species.

When the revelations ended, Jasper, Rachel, and Benjamin sit in their chairs, speechless with their eyes and mouth wide open. It was a coin toss who would speak first.

CHAPTER 6

MARKED FOR SILENCE

The descent into the Luminary archives had been a descent into a terrifyingly clinical abyss. Now, the ascent of 'The Nautilus' felt less like an escape and more like a desperate flight, burdened by the crushing weight of what they had unearthed. Rachel, Benjamin, and Jasper started the complex series of maneuvers required to bring their submersible back to the surface. The familiar hum of the machinery seemed to underscore their profound isolation. They had glimpsed the true nature of their cosmic custodians, and the revelation was not one of benevolent guidance but of cold, calculated stewardship. Humanity, it appeared, was a specimen under observation, its fate subject to the whims of alien agriculturalists.

The crushing pressure of the deep, a constant antagonist during their descent, now served as a tangible manifestation of the invisible forces they had inadvertently provoked. The data they carried was not merely information; it was a declaration of war, an exposé that threatened to shatter the meticulously constructed facade of ignorance that had protected humanity for millennia. Every meter gained towards the surface was a meter closer to a world that remained blissfully unaware, a world that would soon have to confront the horrifying truth of its own precarious existence. The silence of the abyssal plains, which had once felt like a natural hush, now echoed with the unspoken threats of the 'Harvest' Protocol. It was a silence pregnant with impending judgment, a vast, indifferent expanse that seemed to mock their newfound, terrifying enlightenment. Somewhere in Jasper's mind, he wishes he could unsee these events.

Everything he learned on this trip, all Jasper could think about was all of those Bible verses. From the "us" in Genesis 1:26 all the way to the scriptures about Judgement Day. For over 2000 years, humankind got the biggest screwing ever.

Rachel felt a prickle of unease that had nothing to do with the integrity of the hull. She was acutely aware of the power structures they had challenged, not just the shadowy terrestrial organizations that served the Luminaries, but the very cosmic hierarchy that had been established. They had trespassed in the deepest sanctum of their overseers, ripped away a veil that was never meant to be lifted. The silence of the deep ocean now felt like a cloak of secrecy, a deliberate partitioning designed to keep species like humanity ignorant and contained. The dark, viscous water outside the viewport, teeming with unseen life, suddenly seemed to mirror the unseen machinations that had been playing out on a global scale for centuries. Now it made perfect sense why the U.S. government made this a no-go zone. However, that would imply they knew about this cover-up and must be in on it. Rachel kept thinking.

Benjamin found his thoughts returned to the chillingly dispassionate language of the 'Harvest' Protocol. "Yield," "assimilation," "sterilization." These were not the terms of a protector, but of a proprietor. The centuries of human striving, of art and science, of love and conflict, had all been reduced to quantifiable data points in an alien assessment. The stress tests, the engineered crises, the subtle nudges towards progress and chaos—all of it was part of a systematic evaluation, a cosmic performance review with humanity as the unwilling participant.

Jasper kept replaying the holographic projections in his mind — the statistical probabilities of humanity's demise. That their own inherent nature was the very reason for their potential extinction was a bitter pill to swallow. He had always believed in humanity's resilience, its capacity to overcome adversity. But the Luminaries saw that same resilience as a potential threat, a sign of untamed volatility. The deep sea, with its brutal competition for survival, its ancient and unyielding laws, now seemed like a pale imitation of the cosmic ecosystem the Luminaries were so adept at managing.

Now that the Luminaries made contact, the brotherhood in the Vatican was made aware. They now have a mark on them.

"There's a service road that leads out to the main highway," Rachel said, her eyes still scanning the perimeter. "It's less visible from here. We'll take 'The Nautilus' on tow, make it look like a routine maintenance operation." She knew it was a thin ruse, but it was the best they had. The goal was not to disappear completely, not yet. It was to create enough distance, enough confusion, to allow them to regroup and assess their next move. The intel they carried was too vital to be lost in a premature confrontation. They had to reach their contacts, to deliver the data, and to alert the world. But first, they had to outmaneuver those who were clearly intent on stopping them.

As they began the laborious process of preparing 'The Nautilus' for transport, Benjamin worked feverishly, his analyzer a constant hum of activity. He felt the weight of their predicament pressing down on her, a mirror of the ocean's pressure, but far more insidious. The Luminary data was a double-edged sword: a key to humanity's survival, and potentially, a catalyst for its destruction. And now, it seemed, there were factions on Earth who were just as dangerous as the cosmic custodians they had discovered. The silence of the deep had been a temporary shield, but the surface was a battlefield, and they had just been identified as the primary targets. From mere indicators of observation, the subtle signs of surveillance escalated, becoming active attempts.

The world they had returned to was not the world they had left; it was a world now aware of their presence, and actively seeking to contain the truth they carried. A black sedan and the dark van, the spectral jamming signals, the microscopic tracking tags—these were the first tangible manifestations of a force determined to silence them, a force that operated in the shadows of human infrastructure, a force that understood the profound implications of the Luminary's presence and humanity's potential response. The genuine challenge, Rachel realized, wasn't just against an alien intelligence, but against the human elements complicit in its machinations, elements that had already manifested their intent to suppress the truth. The journey back to the surface was over, but the perilous escape had just begun.

Jasper paused as he exited the submersible. He caught sight of another vehicle, a dark van this time, parked further down the road, its side door slightly ajar. A fleeting glimpse of what looked like electronic equipment, antennae, and a darkened interior, confirmed Benjamin's assessment. It was an observation post. The feeling of being watched was no longer a vague suspicion; it was a tangible, suffocating certainty. He could almost feel the unseen eyes on them, cataloging their every move, their every breath. The immensity of the Luminary revelations had been overwhelming, but this immediate, terrestrial response was chillingly concrete. It suggested that their terrestrial contacts, the shadowy entities who had facilitated their mission, were compromised or actively working against them now. The pact of shadows, it seemed, was fraying, its threads unraveling into something far more dangerous.

"The sedan, the van… they've been here since we surfaced," Rachel stated, her voice low and steady, a testament to years of ingrained professional discipline. She had a knack for observing the periphery, for noticing the details others missed. The vehicles weren't just parked; they were positioned with a tactical advantage, their placement designed to offer a clear, unobstructed view of the pier and 'The Nautilus'. "They're not coincidental. This is surveillance." She felt a cold dread seep into his bones. They had returned from the cosmic unknown, only to find themselves immediately ensnared by terrestrial intelligences, intelligences that clearly knew they were coming back, and knew they were carrying something of immense significance. The question was, who were they? And more importantly, what was their agenda? Were they acting on behalf of the Luminaries, enforcing their silence? Or were they independent actors seeking to exploit the knowledge they possessed? Paranoia thrived in the dangerous unknown of ambiguity.

The jarring transition from the crushing embrace of the deep ocean to the mundane reality of the surface had been unsettling.

'The Nautilus' breached the waves with a groan of stressed metal, the sudden influx of natural light a harsh assault on eyes accustomed to the controlled luminescence of the archives. They had returned, carrying a truth so monumental it felt like a physical weight in the cramped confines of the submersible. The dockside, usually a scene of bustling activity, appeared unnervingly quiet as they secured the vessel. The familiar scent of salt and diesel fuel was a welcome, yet somehow suspect, comfort.

Rachel was the first to disembark, her movements deliberate, a practiced vigilance overlaying her exhaustion. She scanned the immediate surroundings, her gaze lingering on a nondescript black sedan parked a little too casually at the edge of the pier. It was a vehicle that blended into urban anonymity, yet its stillness, its patient, almost predatory posture, felt out of place. She saw no one inside, the tinted windows a dark, impenetrable barrier. A prickle of unease crawled up her spine. This was a distinct threat, more insidious, more human in its execution, yet undeniably connected to the cosmic horror they had just escaped.

Benjamin followed, his senses already on high alert. He instinctively reached for his comms unit, intending to start their pre-arranged debriefing protocol with a trusted contact. The device sputtered, emitting a burst of sharp, unintelligible static. He tried again, cycling through frequencies, but the result was the same—a telltale cacophony of digital noise that felt deliberate, invasive. "Comms are down," he announced, his voice tight. "Something's jamming us. It's not typical interference. This is… targeted." He pulled out a handheld spectrum analyzer, its small screen already displaying erratic spikes, patterns that spoke of sophisticated signal manipulation, far beyond anything a casual observer could achieve. The signals weren't just disrupting their communication; they were attempting to pinpoint their location, to map their presence with unsettling precision.

Jasper paused as he exited the submersible. He caught sight of another vehicle, a dark van this time, parked further down the road, its side door slightly ajar. A fleeting glimpse of what looked like electronic equipment, antennae, and a darkened interior, confirmed

Benjamin's assessment. It was an observation post. The feeling of being watched was no longer a vague suspicion; it was a tangible, suffocating certainty. He could almost feel the unseen eyes on them, cataloging their every move, their every breath. The immensity of the Luminary revelations had been overwhelming, but this immediate, terrestrial response was chillingly concrete. It suggested that their terrestrial contacts, the shadowy entities who had facilitated their mission, were compromised or actively working against them now. The pact of shadows, it seemed, was fraying, its threads unraveling into something far more dangerous.

The encrypted message arrived not through the usual secure channels, which Benjamin had already confirmed were still compromised, but via an antiquated, almost anachronistic method: a printed note slipped beneath the windshield wiper of Rachel's repurposed support vehicle, a nondescript van that had been meticulously prepared for their exfiltration. It was a slight gesture, almost theatrical in its deliberate anachronism, designed to stand out amidst the digital chaos. The paper was thick, of a quality rarely found in everyday use, and bore the faint, elegant scent of old parchment and something else, something subtly floral and monastic.

Rachel spotted it before they even began the final loading of their equipment. Her gloved hand retrieved it, unfolding it with deliberate care. The typeface was antique, a serif font that spoke of tradition and an era when information moved at a more considered pace. The message itself was brief, almost maddeningly so, yet its implications rippled outwards, touching upon the very foundations of their predicament.

"Your discovery is known," it read, the words stark and precise against the creamy paper. "The pact endures. Silence is paramount. Those who seek to disrupt the ordained order face consequences beyond your current comprehension. Seek guidance from the whispers, not the storms. The old ways hold."

Benjamin, peering over Rachel's shoulder, noted the subtle watermark on the paper, a stylized cross intertwined with a key—an insignia he recognized with a jolt of profound unease. It was the symbol of a particular, deeply embedded faction within the Vatican. Not the public face of the Church, not the benevolent pronouncements of its leaders, but something far older, far more clandestine. The Holy See, it seemed, was not merely aware of the Luminary revelation; it was actively involved in managing it.

"The Vatican?" Benjamin breathed, the words barely audible. "This… this is from them?"

Jasper nodded slowly. "It fits. The lore we uncovered, the references to ancient guardians and celestial alignments… the Church has always been a repository of such knowledge, often deliberately obscured. They have a vested interest in maintaining a certain narrative, especially one that places humanity, and by extension, their divine authority, at the center of creation."

Rachel's jaw tightened. "A 'pact'? 'Ordained order'? This isn't just about covering up an alien discovery; it's about maintaining a carefully constructed edifice. They don't want humanity to know it's not alone. They don't want us to know that our history, our very understanding of faith, might be a carefully managed fiction." He looked at the printed note again, his eyes tracing the edges of the watermark. "They're warning us. Not just warning us to be silent, but threatening us. 'Consequences of your current comprehension' sounds like more than just a reprimand."

"The 'whispers' and the 'storms'," Benjamin muses, his mind racing through possibilities. "The storm is what we've encountered so far—the surveillance, the jamming, the immediate attempt to contain us. The whispers… that must be this message. A communication from within, from someone who opposes the current agenda, or at least understands the danger of the heavy-handed approach."

Jasper elaborated, his tone grave. "The Church has a long history of compartmentalizing knowledge. Certain orders, certain cardinals, have access to archives and traditions that are centuries, even millennia, old. They would have been privy to the Luminary signals, perhaps even expecting them, long before we did. This pact they mention… it could be a centuries-old agreement, a covenant struck with whatever entities the Luminaries represent, or with other powers who have guarded this knowledge."

"And their motive?" Rachel pressed on, the weight of their new pursuers settling heavily upon him. "Why would they want to keep this secret? It's the most significant discovery in human history. It changes everything."

"Precisely," Jasper replies. "It changes *everything*. The Church built its authority on a specific cosmology, a narrative of God's creation and humanity's unique place within it. The Luminaries, if they represent an older, more pervasive cosmic intelligence, could shatter that narrative. It could lead to a crisis of faith on an unprecedented scale. For an institution built on faith, that's an existential threat. There's power in keeping the masses contrite. "

Benjamin tapped his analyzer. Its screen now displayed a distinct set of anomalies. "I'm detecting a new intermittent signal. It's incredibly faint, encrypted, and appears to be originating from multiple, shifting points. It's not a tracking signal, not like the one on the Nautilus. This is more like a beacon, a locator for… something else." He looked up, his eyes wide. "It's broadcasting a specific frequency pattern. I've cross-referenced it with known Vatican communication protocols, older ones, almost forgotten ones. It matches the signature of certain archaic cipher transmissions used by… high-ranking ecclesiastical officials. It's a signal that's undetectable by standard military or intelligence sweeps. Only someone with very specific knowledge, very specific equipment could even register it."

Rachel felt a familiar resolve hardening within her. The layers of the conspiracy were deeper and more intricate than she had imagined. This was no longer just a scientific expedition gone awry; it was a geopolitical and theological chess match played on a cosmic scale. "We need to get to neutral ground," she declared, his voice firm. "Somewhere we can analyze this message, decode any further communications, and try to understand the 'whispers' without being swept away by the 'storms'. This Vatican connection… it's a significant development. It means our path to disseminating this information is far more complex and dangerous than we ever expected." She looked at Benjamin and Jasper, his gaze steady. "We are marked for silence, not just by shadowy surveillance teams, but by an ancient institution with an unimaginable reach. But we will not be silenced." The note, a simple piece of paper, represented a profound shift in their understanding of the forces arrayed against them. The abyss had revealed its secrets, it seemed, held its own, equally formidable, guardians of those secrets."

"Anything?" Rachel finally broke the silence.

Benjamin shook his head, his eyes never leaving the screen. "Still nothing coherent. The jamming that targeted 'The Nautilus' seems to have dissipated, or at least it's masked by background noise now. But the data logs… they're a mess. It's like someone went in with a precision scalpel and just… erased key sections. Not random corruption; it's surgical deletion." He sighed, running a hand through her already disheveled hair. The Luminary's archive timestamps are missing, the decryption keys for some core files are scrambled, and the archive's energy readings are distorted. It's as if the very signatures of the Luminary technology have been overwritten with something else. Something… artificial."

"Artificial, but not human?" Jasper's voice was quiet, but it carried the weight of his observation. He had spent the last hour scanning the skies and the water with a handheld sensor array, a tool Benjamin had salvaged from the van's diagnostic equipment.

"That's the terrifying part," Benjamin admitted, his voice barely a whisper. "The distortions… they don't match any known terrestrial electromagnetic signatures. There are transient spikes too brief, too precise to be natural phenomena. And the power signatures… they're incredibly efficient, almost elegant in their application. It's advanced, certainly beyond our current capabilities, but the *pattern* of interference feels… familiar, though I can't quite articulate why. It's as if someone is deliberately mimicking certain aspects of advanced, but ultimately mundane, technological disruption, while simultaneously introducing something far more alien."

Rachel glanced in the rearview mirror; his eyes meeting Jasper's in the dim light. "Familiar how?"

"It's the *intent*," Jasper said, his voice gaining a little more strength. "The meticulousness. It's not random chaos; it's controlled damage. Like a gardener pruning away unwanted growth. Our data logs, the Luminary archive signatures—they're the unwanted growth.

Someone, or something, is meticulously curating what we can and cannot know, and more importantly, what we can and cannot prove." He paused, tapping the console. "And there's something else. A faint residual energy signature near where 'The Nautilus' surfaced. The origin is too diffuse to pinpoint, but it's unlike anything I've seen. It flickered and then vanished, but the signature is still there, imprinted on the local atmospheric conditions like a ghost in the machine. It's… not terrestrial."

Benjamin's eyes widened as he heard Jasper's description. "That's… that's what I'm seeing too, in the energy readings. Small pockets of interference that don't conform to typical atmospheric anomalies. They're localized, transient, and they appear to be… interacting with the data corruption. It's not just human agents wiping our logs. This is something else. Something that can manipulate energy fields, influence technology, and is likely to remain unseen."

"Unseen, but not unheard," Rachel mutters, the Vatican's cryptic note echoing in her mind. "The 'whispers' and the 'storms.' We've experienced the storms: the jamming, the surveillance, the surgical deletion of data. But this… this interference feels like something far more advanced than conventional human countermeasures. This feels like the alien partners, or perhaps entities allied with them, are actively involved in ensuring our silence."

Rachel continued, "The concept of alien intervention, once the subject of their primary mission, now felt like a tangible, immediate threat. They had gone searching for proof of extraterrestrial intelligence, and they had found it, along with a chilling confirmation that this intelligence was not necessarily benevolent, or even neutral, for humanity's grasp of its existence."

"The energy signature," Benjamin said. "It's not aggressive. It's more like… a deterrent. A subtle nudge, a way of saying 'you're on the wrong track,' or 'this information is not for you.' It's the digital equivalent of a closed-door, but with the added implication that the door itself can shift and reconfigure at will." He gestured at her consoling. "I've salvaged fragments of the energy readings from the Luminary archive. There are faint traces of what appears to be… a deliberate damping field. It wasn't there when we started the download, or at least, we didn't register it. It seems that something triggered it after we began extracting the data, as if our discovery activated it. A localized nullification field, designed to obscure the true nature of the Luminary technology, or its origins, from any subsequent analysis. And the energy required to generate such a field, even for a brief period, is immense. Far beyond anything our submersible could generate, and certainly beyond any conventional human technology we possess."

Rachel's grip tightened on the wheel. "So, it wasn't just the Luminaries hiding their secrets from us; it was also their... allies? Or perhaps their overseers? Using their own advanced technology to obscure the evidence *for* us, and for anyone else who might stumble upon it."

"It's a shared agenda," Jasper stated, his voice grim. "The human element, with the Vatican involved, focuses on controlling the narrative, preventing panic, and maintaining a divinely ordained order." But this... this alien interference is about controlling the *evidence*. It's about ensuring that the true nature of the Luminaries, their technology, their capabilities, and their ultimate intentions, remains shrouded in mystery. They want us to have *some* information — enough to confirm their existence, perhaps, but not enough to understand them, not enough to truly leverage their knowledge, and certainly not enough to challenge their established dominance."

Benjamin pointed at a fluctuating graph on his screen. "Look at this. It's a secondary signal, much weaker than the primary jamming, but far more sophisticated. Disruption isn't its purpose. This is a subtle form of informational warfare. It's weaving itself into the corrupted data streams, introducing subtle inaccuracies, shifting probabilities, subtly altering the context of the remaining Luminary information. It does not delete altogether.

"What kind of influence?" Rachel asked, her mind racing to connect these technological intrusions with the cryptic message they had received.

"It's subtle," Benjamin explained. "It's like a magician's misdirection. For example, in one of the partially salvaged logs, there was a reference to Luminary propulsion systems. The original data suggested exotic matter manipulation, theoretically capable of interstellar travel. But the imprinted signal has subtly altered the energy signatures, nudging them towards a more conventional, albeit highly advanced, interpretation. But it's still extraordinary without the 'impossible' part. Instead of being alien, it's just humanly possible. It's a way to make the discovery palatable, to make it seem like a stepping stone, rather than a fundamental reframing of reality. It encourages us to look for human analogues, human solutions, when the truth is something entirely different."

"They want us to misunderstand," Jasper concluded, his eyes distant, as if seeing beyond the confines of the van. "They want us to interpret Luminary technology through our own limited lens. It's a way of containment, not through force, but through intellectual misdirection. If we believe we can eventually replicate or understand their technology through our current scientific paradigms, then we remain on a path they can expect and control. They let us have a crumb, but they ensure it's a crumb that leads us away from the feast."

Rachel brought the van to a stop in a deserted industrial lot, the skeletal remains of warehouses looming around them like forgotten giants. He turned off the engine, plunging them into a sudden, profound silence broken only by the distant rumble of the city. The sense of being watched, of being subtly yet relentlessly manipulated, was almost palpable.

"So, we have the terrestrial guardians of the narrative," Rachel said, her voice low and steady, "and we have... what? The extraterrestrial custodians of their own secrets? Both working to ensure that humanity remains ignorant, or at least, docile."

"It's more than just ignorance," Benjamin argued, tapping another section of his display. "This secondary signal... it's not just altering existing data; it's also seeding new, false data. Tiny, almost imperceptible fragments that appear to be independent observations, or even corrupted sensor readings from other missions. They're designed to corroborate the subtly altered Luminary data, creating a false consensus, a manufactured history of near-misses and misinterpreted phenomena. It's a sophisticated disinformation campaign, woven into the very fabric of our recovered information."

"They are actively trying to bury the truth," Jasper stated, his gaze sweeping the empty expanse of the lot. "Not just by silencing us, but by subtly discrediting any evidence we might recover or reconstruct. They could easily dismiss our findings as misinterpreted data, flawed readings, or even deliberate fabrications, supporting these with the phantom evidence they planted."

Rachel ran a hand over her face, the exhaustion seeping into her bones. "This is more complex than I ever expected. We thought the greatest challenge would be convincing humanity of the Luminary's existence. Now, it seems, the greatest challenge will prove that what we discovered is even real, and not some elaborate, technologically advanced deception." She looked at Benjamin. "Can you isolate any of this seeded disinformation? Can you trace its origin point, even if it's just a pattern?"

Benjamin sighed, a weary sound. "I'm trying. The sophistication is staggering. It's not a single source; it's a distributed network, mimicking random electronic noise, atmospheric anomalies, even residual cosmic background radiation. It blends in, to be the white noise that drowns out the signal. But there are... rhythmic pulses within the noise. Extremely faint, but undeniably artificial. They're like tiny digital heartbeats, hidden within the static. If I can find a consistent pattern, a repeating sequence, then perhaps..." His voice trailed off.

Jasper then spoke, his voice cutting through the tense quiet. "I've been reviewing the satellite imagery we pulled before our primary comms went dark. There was a series of... unusual atmospheric phenomena detected over the ocean several hours before we surfaced. Brief, localized distortions, almost like thermal inversions, but they were too geometrically precise. And they were moving in concert with a specific, previously uncatalogued maritime vessel. It wasn't a military ship, nor a commercial one. Its design was... unconventional. Sleek, almost organic, it emitted a faint but distinct energy signature that matched the residual readings from the Luminary archive."

Benjamin's head snaps up. "A vessel? You're saying the source of the energy damping and the data manipulation wasn't a satellite, or a land-based operation, but an actual ship?"

"It's the most likely candidate," Jasper confirmed. The speed was improbable, outside shipping lanes, with emissions matching surges. It wasn't actively broadcasting, but its systems were active, sophisticated, and clearly designed with the environment, and possibly, with any technology operating within it."

Rachel leaned back, her gaze fixed on the grimy windows in the van. "So, not only are they tampering with our data remotely, but they have physical assets in play. Advanced craft, capable of operating undetected, and possessing the technology to interfere with both our submersible and our data." She closed her eyes for a moment, the sheer scale of the conspiracy pressing down on her. "This isn't just about suppressing knowledge; it's about active technological engagement. They're not just hiding; they're *managing* the situation. They're intervening subtly but decisively to shape our understanding and ensure their secrets remain safe. The Luminary archives were not just a discovery; they were a breach, and we are now under direct, albeit covert, alien intervention. And they're working in concert with terrestrial powers to ensure that silence reigns. With chilling certainty, she realized the road ahead was perilous. The deep ocean had held its mysteries, but the surface was proving to be a far more dangerous and deceptive frontier.

Across the wet street, shadows stretched from the diner's neon, a fitting scene to their dread. The repurposed van now felt like a trap. Rachel wrestled with a growing realization: their mission had altered. The primal instinct had brutally eclipsed the thrill of discovery for self-preservation. They were no longer explorers; they were prey. The data they had painstakingly retrieved from the depths of the ocean, the irrefutable evidence of an intelligence far beyond human comprehension, had not only put them on the radar of terrestrial powers, but had also apparently alerted their extraterrestrial counterparts.

"They know we have it," Rachel continued, her voice hung heavy in the air. The Vatican's cryptic warning, "the whispers and the storms," suddenly resonated with a terrifying clarity. The storms were the overt acts of suppression, the jamming, the surveillance, the surgical obliteration of their digital trail. But the whispers, the subtle manipulation of data, the seeding of misinformation—that was the true insidious threat, designed to undermine not just their findings, but their credibility.

"Ben gestured to a complex waveform on his screen. "This new pattern… it's not human. The modulation is too complex; the energy requirements too immense. It's like a digital fingerprint, but one crafted from forces we don't fully understand. It's the signature of something that can manipulate reality on a fundamental level, not just through brute force, but through elegant, almost invisible, technological finesse."

Jasper chimed in, his voice calm but laced with a deep concern. "The vessel I identified, it's not just a passive observer or a data broadcaster. Its energy signature suggests it possesses capabilities far beyond simple transmission. The localized distortions it generates are consistent with localized spacetime manipulation, albeit on a minuscule scale. This isn't just about hiding their technology; it's about actively preventing us from understanding its true nature. They can warp the very fabric of reality around their activities, making detection and analysis incredibly difficult. It's a way of saying, 'We can be here, we can do this, but you will never truly comprehend *how* or *why*.'

Ben ran a hand over his stubbled chin, the rough texture a stark contrast to the smooth, almost ethereal nature of the forces they were up against. "So, the Luminaries themselves are not just an alien race, but an entity or entities with the power to bend the rules of physics. And they have terrestrial allies who are adept at controlling information and narrative. We've stumbled into a war, not of weapons and bloodshed, but of knowledge and perception. They possessed knowledge that could shatter the foundations of human society, and two immensely powerful, albeit disparate, forces were determined to ensure it remained buried forever.

EARTHLY PURSUITS

The realization that they were not merely being hunted, but actively managed, sent a fresh wave of dread through the occupants of the van. It was a chilling thought: their pursuit of truth had inadvertently placed them at the nexus of a clandestine struggle, a shadow war waged by forces both terrestrial and extraterrestrial. The overt surveillance and attempts to corner them were merely the blunt instruments; the real danger lay in the subtle, pervasive manipulation of information, a digital poison designed to discredit them and bury their monumental discovery. This was no longer a scientific expedition; it was a desperate fight for survival, not just of their lives, but of their sanity and their very credibility.

The magnificent three were stuck in this van with no clue where to go and what to do. The science they were learning was mind-bending, and flying by the seat of their pants.

Rachel gripped the steering wheel, her knuckles white. "So, these aren't just agencies. They're instruments. Instruments of a pact, perhaps. A global agreement to manage this… this Luminary presence. And their mandate is clear: containment. Not just of the technology, but of the knowledge. They're not trying to understand it, or even weaponized it for themselves. They're acting as gatekeepers, ensuring that humanity remains blissfully, or perhaps, willfully, ignorant."

She recalled the Vatican's veiled warnings. The "whispers and storms" weren't just abstract threats; they were the operational methods of these shadowy entities. The storms were the overt tactics—the jamming, the pursuit, the attempts to corner them. But the whispers, the subtle, almost imperceptible alterations to the Luminary data, the seeding of plausible deniability into their scientific records—that was the true insidious work, designed to make their discoveries sound like fabrications or misinterpretations.

"They operate under the guise of national security," Benjamin continued, his voice tight with a mixture of frustration and awe. "But this goes beyond any single nation's interest. The scope of their coordination, the seamless integration of disparate tracking and disruption protocols, suggests a global consortium. A covert global security council, perhaps, tasked with policing not just human activity, but potential extraterrestrial influence. And they're using technology that seems to be... borrowed. Or perhaps, reverse-engineered from the very entities they're supposed to be monitoring." He pointed to a complex energy signature on his screen. "This waveform, it's been appearing intermittently whenever we encounter a sophisticated form of interference. A faint harmonic resonance, yet distinctly non-terrestrial. It's as if they're tapping into an external power source, or using a technology that produces energy signatures remarkably similar to the Luminaries themselves. It implies a deep, perhaps even symbiotic, relationship with the very unknown they claim to be protecting us from."

Jasper nodded, his gaze distant, as if seeing beyond the mundane reality of their current hiding place. "Think about the implications, Rachel. If these agencies have access to this level of technology, technology that can manipulate energy fields, cloak entire vehicles, and subtly alter data streams on a global scale, then the power they wield is almost absolute. They can effectively control which information reaches the public, which scientific theories are validated, and which historical narratives they preserve. Without a shot fired, they can erase individuals, evidence, and entire fields. They designed their operations for zero traceability and absolute deniability. It's the ultimate form of covert action, operating in the perpetual twilight of classified operations, their existence and their actions known only to a select, self-appointed few."

They parked the van in a maze of darkened industrial alleys, where the air was thick with the scent of damp concrete and decay. The drumming of a passing rain shower had intensified, a percussive soundtrack to their escalating anxiety. Rachel chose this location deliberately because the sheer density of urban clutter and potential blind spots might hamper conventional surveillance. But he knew, with a chilling certainty, that mere physical obstacles wouldn't deter these 'shadowy agencies'. Their methods transcended the ordinary.

"They have to be ruthless," Rachel stated, her voice low. "If they must maintain the status quo and preserve humanity's current understanding of its place in the universe, then they must eradicate anything that threatens that," she said. And what we have, what we've seen, it's the ultimate threat. It's not just about a few rogue scientists uncovering a secret; it's about shattering the very foundations of human civilization, of religion, of science, of our collective identity. The Luminaries, if they are indeed as advanced and as influential as the evidence suggests, represent a fundamental change so profound that acknowledging their existence, let alone their potential capabilities, could trigger global panic, societal collapse, or worse, an existential crisis that could fracture humanity beyond repair."

"And these agencies," Benjamin interjected, his eyes still scanning the spectral analysis, "they believe they are acting in humanity's best interest. They see themselves as the guardians, the shield against a truth that would be too much for us to bear. It's a paternalistic yet terrifying rationale. They're not driven by malice necessarily, but by a cold, calculated logic that prioritizes stability over truth. They have likely developed or been given access to technologies that allow them to influence global events, suppress inconvenient discoveries, and orchestrate narratives. The coordinated chase we've been experiencing, it's not just about stopping us from reaching a certain point, or seizing our data. It's about shaping our perception of the chase itself, about making us look like fugitives, like unreliable narrators, even if we escape."

Jasper's handheld sensor, which he had been discreetly sweeping around their immediate vicinity, emitted a low, almost inaudible hum. He frowned. "There's a localized dampening field emanating from a few blocks away. It's subtle, but it's there, and it's not strong enough to disrupt our internal comms, but it's designed to blind external sensors. It's a deliberate act of concealment, a bubble of invisibility. They're anticipating that we might try to use public communication channels, or that other, less sophisticated surveillance systems might pick up on their presence. It's a layered defense. And the energy signature of this dampening field... it's similar to the residual traces left by the Luminary vessel, but it's significantly attenuated. It suggests they're either using a scaled-down version of Luminary technology, or they've replicated its effects using terrestrial, albeit highly advanced, means."

Rachel felt a prickle of unease crawl up her spine. The thought that these terrestrial agencies might possess or have access to Luminary-derived technology was both terrifying and oddly... fitting. It explained the sheer leap in their capabilities. They weren't just operating with advanced terrestrial tech; they were dabbling in forces they likely didn't fully comprehend themselves, risks they would take under the guise of protecting humanity from a greater unknown. "They've mobilized," she said, her voice firming with a renewed sense of purpose, despite the danger. "These aren't just patrols; these are specialized units, deployed with a specific aim: to neutralize us, not just physically, but informationally. They want to ensure that no traces of our findings survives. And their methods, as you've both observed, are untraceable. No fingerprints, no shell casings, no dropped equipment. Just... silence."

Benjamin was working feverishly, his eyes wide. "I'm picking up an anomalous pattern in the global financial markets. Not a crash, or a surge, but a series of meticulously placed, high-volume trades that are designed to subtly mask other, more significant transactions. It's like a financial smokescreen. The origins of these trades also route through shell corporations and offshore accounts, making them notoriously difficult to unravel, often linking back to entities with a history in discreet government operations. It's not just about suppressing scientific data; they're actively manipulating the global economic landscape to facilitate their clandestine activities, to fund their black projects, and to ensure the infrastructure remains operational without raising suspicion. It's a silent, invisible war being waged on every front, and we've somehow stumbled into the crosshairs."

The metallic tang of stale air in the van did little to mask the coppery scent of fear that had become their constant companion. They had been chasing shadows, ghosts in the machine of global surveillance, but the realization that these weren't just advanced national security agencies, but something far more deeply entrenched, far more insidious, had shifted the ground beneath their feet. Rachel's intuition had always whispered of an unseen hand guiding the more overtly aggressive terrestrial pursuers. Now, the whispers were coalescing into a discernible, terrifying voice, a voice that echoed from the hallowed halls of the Vatican. Yet, it was entirely possible to see the patterns.

The Vatican. It seemed an anachronism, a medieval relic thrust into the 21st century's high-tech theater of the absurd. Yet, the veiled warnings, the subtle pressure exerted through papal pronouncements on 'preserving societal harmony' and 'guarding against existential threats to faith,' now took on a chillingly literal meaning. It wasn't just a spiritual custodian; it was an active participant, a silent partner in a pact that predated even modern nation-states. Their faith, once a beacon of hope and knowledge, had, in this instance, become a weapon, forged in the crucible of ancient secrets and amplified by borrowed, or perhaps stolen, extraterrestrial technology.

Patterns. It's been there the entire time, but people never connected the dots. In all fairness, anyone who connected them would have been called a nut. But there is a pattern. The Catholic Church owns one of the largest and most powerful telescopes in Arizona. Now why would a church need such an observatory? The simplest questions can come up. For example, why was the third secret at Fatima not made public? They published the first two, but the third is very vague, unlike the first two.

Benjamin was talking and rapidly typing, "Rachel, I'm picking up an unusual energy signature. Almost like a religious artifact, it's radiating a subtle frequency. It is not terrestrial as we understand it. This is… different. It's intertwined with the jamming signals, acting as a kind of meta-control, a harmonizer for the disruptions. It's like the technology is being 'blessed' or 'sanctified' before deployment." He zoomed in on a complex waveform, intricate and alien, yet imbued with a strange, almost resonant beauty. "And the source of this modulation… it's localized, but the spread pattern is unusual. It's not adhering to typical signal propagation models. It's as if it's being directed through Ley lines, or some sort of esoteric network. The closer we get to Rome, the stronger it becomes."

Jasper interjected, "I've been cross-referencing those anomalous atmospheric shifts Benjamin detected earlier with historical seismic and geomagnetic data. There are patterns, subtle but undeniable, that correlate with periods of significant religious or political upheaval in certain areas. Not just earthquakes or magnetic storms, but moments where the 'veil' between the mundane and the… extraordinary, seemed to thin. And the energy signature Benjamin's describing? I'm seeing faint echoes of it in archived data from the early 20th century, linked to certain clandestine Vatican expeditions that were officially debunked as hoaxes or misinterpretations."

Rachel gripped the steering wheel, his knuckles white. The 'whispers and storms' weren't just metaphors for psychological warfare and technological disruption. They were literal. The storms were the jamming, the cloaking, the relentless pursuit. The whispers… they were the subtle manipulations, the seeding of doubt, the almost spiritual aura that these enforcers projected. They weren't just operatives; they were zealots. And their zeal was amplified by technologies that defied human comprehension.

"The Holy See has always been a master of information control," Rachel murmured, her voice gravelly. "But this… this is on another level. They're not just trying to discredit us; they're trying to *exorcise* us. We're not just fugitives; we're heretics. Heretics who have seen too much, who threaten a narrative that has been meticulously constructed over millennia. The Luminaries are not just an alien species; they are a disruption to a divine order, an order that the Vatican has, for centuries, sworn to uphold. And their pact… it's not with a benevolent creator, but with entities that demand absolute secrecy, absolute control."

Benjamin's voice was a tight wire of apprehension. "I've decrypted a fragment of a transmission that was intercepted during the last jamming attempt. It wasn't standard military jargon. It was laced with archaic Latin phrases, interspersed with what appear to be… liturgical instructions. There were references to 'purification,' 'sanctification,' and 'the banishment of impurity.' It's as if they're performing a religious rite while disabling our systems. The energy signature of the jamming, the 'blessing' I detected, it's all part of their ritual. They believe they are cleansing the electromagnetic spectrum, ridding it of the 'unclean' influence of our discovery."

Jasper's eyes scanned the data streams, his face a mask of grim understanding. "The gravitational anomalies I've been tracking, the ones that coincide with Luminary presence… they're also present, albeit on a much smaller scale, around the Vatican's extraterritorial properties. It's like they've replicated or harnessed a fraction of that Luminary influence. They're not just using terrestrial technology; they've integrated elements that are alien. This explains their ability to influence their surroundings, to create localized pockets of distorted reality. They're not just observers; they're active participants, shaping the very fabric of existence around them to serve their purpose."

Rachel felt a chill that had nothing to do with the rain pelting the van. She remembered the hushed conversations she'd had with a former contact within the Vatican, a disgraced cardinal who had spoken of a secret order, the *Custodes Veritatis*—the Guardians of Truth. They were the true enforcers, operating beneath the veneer of religious authority, their mandate to protect humanity from truths that would shatter its faith. And now, it seemed, these Custodes had discovered the Luminaries, and in their zealous pursuit of protecting humanity from the unknown, they had forged an unholy alliance.

"They see us as a threat to the faith itself," Rachel stated, her voice heavy with the weight of this revelation. "Our discovery, the existence of the Luminaries, invalidates so much of what they hold sacred. That humanity is not the sole creation of God, or that we are not at the center of the divine plan… it's anathema to them. And they've found a way to weaponize that fear. They're using advanced technology, technology that is clearly of Luminary origin, to enforce their dogma. It's a perversion of everything faith should represent."

Jasper's voice was grim. "The 'Aethelred's Hand'… the historical figure of Aethelred the Unready was known for his indecisiveness, his reliance on often brutal and misguided advisors. Perhaps this is a nod to that—a group that operates with a warped sense of readiness, a brutal conviction that overrides rational thought. And 'Inquisitores Astrae'… it's chilling. They are literally seeking the stars, but intending to purge them, or at least, control humanity's understanding of them. They believe they are acting in God's name, but their methods are clearly anything but divine."

Rachel's mind raced. This was far more complex than a simple cover-up. It was a spiritual war, waged on a technological battlefield. The Vatican, or at least a powerful faction within it, wasn't just trying to hide the Luminaries; they were actively trying to control them, or perhaps even to combat them, using their own alien technology against them. And Rachel and his team, in stumbling upon the truth, had become the ultimate heresy.

"If they are truly operating with Luminary technology," Rachel continued, the words feeling heavy on her tongue, "then they possess capabilities far beyond our current understanding. The energy manipulation, the cloaking, the data distortion… it all points to direct access to Luminary capabilities. It's not just about defending humanity from a truth that might destabilize it; it's about maintaining a position of power, a divine mandate, that is threatened by this new cosmic reality. They cannot allow the Luminaries to be revealed, because their existence, their nature, would challenge the very foundations of the Catholic Church, and by extension, much of Western civilization."

Benjamin's voice expressed a growing dread. "I'm detecting a surge in the 'blessed' energy signature, and it's focused. This is a general jamming field. It's a targeted pulse, and it's locking onto our vehicle's unique electromagnetic signature. It's like they're 'unholy'ing' us, marking us for… something. And the Latin phrases within the transmission? They're not just instructions; they're imprecations, condemnations. They're actively trying to sever our connection to… whatever they believe is our 'divine' protection."

Jasper's handheld scanner was emitting a high-pitched whine. "There's a localized distortion field being generated directly ahead. It's not just visual cloaking; it's affecting the local gravity. Objects are becoming… heavier, sluggish. It's designed to slow us down, to immobilize us. And the energy signature is identical to the 'blessed' frequency Benjamin is tracking. They're using Luminary-derived gravitational manipulation to physically impede us, to make escape impossible. It's like they're building a spiritual prison, using alien physics."

Rachel slammed on the brakes, the van skidding to a halt just meters from what appeared to be a solid wall of shimmering, distorted air. The rain seemed to fall in slow motion around it, each droplet defying gravity. "They've found us," she breathed, her heart pounding a frantic rhythm against her ribs. "The Custodes Veritatis. They're not just pursuing us; they're hunting us with the fervor of crusaders, armed with the very power they fear."

The air crackled with unseen energy. The rhythmic chanting, faint at first, grew louder, a dissonant choir singing in a language that scraped at their sanity. It was the sound of ancient dogma amplified by alien science, a symphony of faith and fear orchestrated by forces that saw Rachel and his team not as seekers of truth, but as agents of cosmic heresy, destined for purification. The pursuit had taken a terrifying turn, from a game of cat and mouse to a spiritual exorcism, waged with tools that belonged to the stars. "They believe they are doing God's work," Benjamin whispered.

Jasper pointed to a series of readings on his console. "The gravitational distortion isn't uniform. It's emanating from specific points, forming a pattern that's remarkably similar to the layout of certain ancient cathedrals. They're using Luminary-derived gravitic emitters to create a localized field that mimics the oppressive, awe-inspiring atmosphere of sacred spaces, designed to instill fear and submission. It's a psychological weapon as much as a physical one. They want us to feel utterly insignificant, crushed by a force that is both divine and technological."

"They interpret our discovery as blasphemy," Rachel stated, hervoice low and steady, a stark contrast to the rising panic within the van. "The existence of an advanced alien civilization that predates or perhaps even influenced humanity's development would alter the narrative of creation, the divine plan. For them, it's not just about covering up a scientific fact; it's about preserving the very essence of faith. They are the custodians of a divinely ordained order, and we, by seeking and revealing this truth, have become the agents of chaos, the heretics that must be purged. Their zeal is amplified by their access to Luminary technology. They have the power to enforce their beliefs, to shape reality itself to fit their dogma."

Jasper nodded, his eyes unfocused as he processed the complex data. "The patterns I'm observing in the atmospheric distortions now align with specific historical sites of supposed divine intervention. Places where miracles were reported, where apparitions were seen. They're not just trying to mimic the effects of sacred spaces; they're actively trying to *recreate* those phenomena using Luminary technology. They're not just preserving faith; they're trying to manufacture it, to prove their divine mandate through pseudoscientific displays that mirror historical religious claims. It's a terrifying manipulation of both science and spirituality."

Rachel understood then that this wasn't just about controlling information; it was about controlling belief. The Vatican enforcers, the 'Inquisitores Astrae,' weren't merely interested in suppressing the Luminaries; they were attempting to co-opt their power, to integrate their advanced understanding of the universe into their own theological framework, or failing that, to demonize them and portray humanity's discovery as a dangerous heresy. Their mandate was clear: to maintain the status quo of human belief, no matter the cost of truth or human lives.

"They believe they are acting as the ultimate arbiters of truth," Rachel said, her voice resonating with a newfound clarity. "They have seen a glimpse of the cosmic order, and it does not fit their preconceived notions of a God-centric universe. Instead of embracing the expanded reality, they have suppressed it, demonized it, and sought to weaponize the very forces that could liberate humanity. Their 'faith' has become a shield against understanding, and their 'divine mandate' a license to commit any atrocity in the name of preserving their perceived cosmic hierarchy. And they are using Luminary technology as their instrument of divine judgment."

The humming of the van's engine was a frail counterpoint to the relentless symphony of pursuit that now echoed around them. It wasn't the guttural roar of conventional engines or the whine of sirens that punctuated their flight; it was something far more unnerving. High above, almost invisible against the bruised twilight sky, a new class of aerial pursuer had joined the fray. These weren't the lumbering helicopters or the familiar shapes of military drones they had occasionally glimpsed. These were sleek, impossibly fast craft that moved with an unnerving silence, their passage marked only by a faint distortion of the air, a shimmering heat-haze that seemed to bend light and sound itself. Their designs defied aerodynamic principles as they understood them, capable of instantaneous directional changes that would tear conventional aircraft apart. Rachel had seen them described in hushed whispers in intelligence briefings as "wraiths"— drones so advanced they seemed to materialize from nowhere and disappear just as readily, leaving no thermal or acoustic signature. Their speed was phenomenal, closing the distance at a terrifying, inexorable pace.

"They're strengthening the chase," Jasper mutters, his eyes glued to the real-time tactical display projected onto the van's dashboard. The holographic map, usually a clear representation of their surroundings and pursuers, was flickering erratically. "These new units… they're not broadcasting any standard transponder signals.

They're operating on a completely different spectrum, or perhaps, no spectrum at all in the way we understand it. The jamming is still active, but these things are slipping through it like water through a sieve. Benjamin, are you getting anything on them?"

Benjamin's face illuminated by the flickering readouts. "It's like trying to catch smoke, Jasper. Their propulsion systems are… unusual. There are intermittent bursts of exotic particles, but they're so brief and so diffuse it's hard to get a lock. It's not plasma, it's not ion drives… it's something that seems to manipulate localized spacetime to achieve thrust. And the cloaking isn't just visual; it's interfering with every sensor I have. They're not just hiding; they're actively trying to erase their presence from existence." He paused. "I'm detecting a subtle gravitational lensing effect around them, though. Very minor, but it confirms the spacetime manipulation theory. They're bending space around themselves to achieve speed and stealth. It's Luminary tech, no question about it, but refined, weaponized by terrestrial hands."

Rachel was still behind the wheel and decided it was time to take some actions. Technology also escalated beyond the sky. As they navigated a desolate stretch of highway, the van's internal systems began to glitch erratically. Lights flickered, the navigation system became momentarily unresponsive, and a low, insistent hum vibrated through the chassis. Rachel felt a prickling sensation on her skin, a disquieting awareness that they were being… observed, not just visually, but in a far more invasive manner.

"They're not just jamming our communications anymore," Benjamin announced, his voice tight with a mixture of frustration and dawning horror. "They're actively probing our systems. I'm picking up a directed energy field, incredibly focused, sweeping over the van. It's designed to bypass our firewalls and penetrate our encryption. It's like they're using a hyper-penetrative sonar, but for data. They're not trying to break our encryption with brute force; they're trying to find an exploit, a quantum entanglement key, something that allows them to slip through our defenses unseen." He tapped furiously on his keyboard. "It's remarkably sophisticated. It's not just accessing our hard drives; it's trying to read the electrical impulses within our neural interfaces, the very thoughts we're having as we interface with the systems. They want to know what we know, not just what we've stored."

Jasper's gaze, usually steady, was now darting between his readouts and the surrounding darkness. "I'm seeing anomalous readings in the atmospheric composition. Tiny, almost imperceptible shifts in pressure and temperature, localized directly around our vehicle. It's like they're deploying micro-drones, too small to be detected by Benjamin's primary sensors, that are mapping our immediate environment. They're not just tracking our vehicle; they're mapping the surrounding terrain in real-time, anticipating our movements, looking for escape routes or potential ambush points." He pointed to a series of faint, shifting patterns on his display. "These are not random atmospheric disturbances. They're precise, controlled micro-environmental manipulations. They're using them to create subtle diversions, to make the road ahead seem less stable, or to obscure obstacles we might otherwise see."

Rachel gripped the steering wheel, her knuckles white. The silent, airborne wraiths were a chilling testament to their aerial superiority. The data-probing technology was an invasion of privacy on a level they hadn't even conceived. And these subtle environmental manipulations... they sowed confusion, to create the illusion of unpredictable danger, to wear down their focus. This wasn't just about catching them; it was about psychological attrition, about making them so overwhelmed and disoriented that they would eventually make a mistake, or surrender.

"They're not just relying on Luminary tech anymore, are they?" Rachel muses aloud, the gears of her strategic mind grinding against this new reality. "They're integrating it with their own advanced terrestrial capabilities. The drones are likely a combination of our best aerospace engineering and Luminary stealth and propulsion. The data intrusion... that's a terrestrial cyber warfare division working with Luminary insights into information physics. And these environmental manipulators... that sounds like experimental atmospheric control, powered by Luminary energy sources. They're not just borrowing; they're actively innovating, merging two incredibly advanced technological paradigms."

"We need to get out of this van," Rachel announced. The van was going to the Salty Siren. Rachel couldn't wait to get to her booth and sling back a few drinks to let all this information process in her head. Just a couple of hours is all she asked.

And the van headed to the Salty Siren. Rachel briefly wondered if this new ground-breaking technology predicted this?

"I could only imagine what we could do with this technology." Jasper pondered. "I hope we can reverse engineer at least 1% of what we are working with, " Jasper concluded.

Benjamin let out a frustrated sigh. "I've isolated the primary source of the data intrusion. It's not originating from a single ground station. It's being relayed through a network of micro-satellites, so small they're almost undetectable. They're acting like a distributed swarm, creating a pervasive field of surveillance that blankets an area. And the energy signature associated with them… it's not purely electrical. There's a component of what looks like modulated quantum entanglement, allowing them to establish instantaneous, ghost-like connections to our systems. It's like they're weaving a net of pure information, catching every stray bit of data before it can even be transmitted."

Jasper nodded, his gaze still fixed on his console. "And those atmospheric anomalies? They're not just about deception. I'm detecting localized fluctuations in the magnetic field precisely timed with the micro-satellite sweeps. It's as if they're using these magnetic pulses to 'reset' or 'flush' any residual data that might have been stored temporarily in our onboard systems, or even in our personal devices. They're not just trying to read our current data; they're trying to scrub our recent past clean, to eliminate any trace of our movements or communications that might have escaped their primary scans." He looked up, his face etched with concern. "It's a comprehensive technological offensive. Every angle is covered: aerial pursuit, digital infiltration, environmental manipulation, and data sanitization. They're building a bubble of technological isolation around us."

The van suddenly lurched violently, throwing them against their restraints. An alarm blared from Jasper's console. "Gravitational anomaly detected!" he shouted. "Not atmospheric. It's localized. Something's directly ahead, creating a… a spatial distortion. It's like hitting a patch of invisible molasses!"

Rachel fought the steering wheel, the van resisting his every input as if it were trying to drive through thick, invisible tar. The speed dropped precipitously, the engine straining against an unseen force. The world outside the windshield seemed to warp and blur, the familiar landscape contorting into grotesque shapes. This was a new level of engagement. Not just stealth and speed, but a direct, physical impediment.

"It's a gravity weapon," Benjamin confirmed, her voice strained. "Localized, focused gravity manipulation. They're not just slowing us down; they're actively increasing the gravitational pull in our immediate path, making it exponentially harder to move. The Luminary tech is being used to create a localized singularity, or something akin to it, just strong enough to immobilize us." He winced as a powerful surge hit them. "And they're pulsing it, just like the magnetic field resets. They're hitting us with a one-two punch: immobilize, then scan and sanitize. They want to hold us stationary while they conduct a full forensic sweep of the van and ourselves."

Rachel forced herself to think, her mind racing against the crushing weight. They were being systematically dismantled, their technological edge eroded by an opponent who was not only employing alien ingenuity but also combining it with their own formidable terrestrial capabilities. The 'Inquisitores Astrae' were not merely fanatics; they were brilliant, ruthless engineers of suppression, leveraging every available tool, terrestrial and extraterrestrial, to achieve their goal.

"They're expecting our every move because they're not just tracking us; they're predicting us," Rachel said, her voice raspy as she wrestled with the controls. "Their surveillance is so pervasive, their understanding of physics so advanced, they can model our escape vectors with terrifying accuracy. They're not reacting to us; they're pre-empting us. The wraith drones are for pursuit and engagement. Data probes and micro-satellites extract information. The environmental manipulators are for misdirection and disorientation. And now, the gravity weapon… it's the ultimate trap, designed to hold us in place for the final 'purification'."

Benjamin's eyes widened as he analyzed the energy signatures of the gravity pulses. "The pattern of the pulses isn't random. It's following a sequence… it's almost like a code. And the modulation of the gravity field… it's not uniform. There are subtle variations. I think they're trying to imprint something on us, or onto the van itself, as it's held captive by the field. A unique identifier, a bio-signature lock, or maybe even a 'tag' for future tracking. They want to ensure that even if we escape this immediate trap, they'll never lose us again."

Jasper was frantically recalibrating his sensors. "The gravity weapon is being amplified by an external source. I'm detecting a high-energy beam being directed at the focal point of the distortion. It's not just generating the field; it's powering it, strengthening it and more sustained. The source appears to be a mobile emitter, likely one of their specialized ground vehicles, disguised or camouflaged. It's moving into position to maintain the gravitic lock."

Rachel saw the grim reality: they were being cornered, not just by speed and stealth, but by an orchestrated technological assault that was both alien and unnervingly familiar in its application. The fusion of extraterrestrial power with terrestrial military and scientific might had created a pursuer unlike any they had ever encountered. The 'Aethelred's Hand' and the 'Inquisitores Astrae' were not just shadowy operatives; they were architects of a new warfare, one that blended ancient dogma with the most advanced technology imaginable. Their goal was absolute control, and their methods were developing with terrifying speed, pushing Rachel and his team to the absolute limits of their ingenuity and endurance. The chase had entered its most perilous phase, a desperate flight from an enemy that seemed to command the very forces of nature and information. The van bucked again, the engine groaning, as the invisible hand of alien physics tightened its grip. They were ensnared, and their pursuers' silence terrified them far more than any roar. There was no escaping this invisible enemy.

The shimmering distortion ahead resolved itself not into a physical barrier, but into a dizzying, disorienting mosaic of light and shadow. The gravitic weapon had ceased its oppressive hold, releasing them from its invisible vise, but the reprieve was momentary. Instead, the cityscape that had been steadily approaching them, a sprawling metropolis glittering with a million artificial stars, now seemed to pulse and warp. Streetlights flickered in unison, the neon signs of businesses bled into one another, and the distant glow of the city's core fractured into a kaleidoscope of impossible colors. It was a visual assault, designed to overload their senses and sow confusion, a tactic as insidious as the physical restraints they had just escaped.

"What in God's name is that?" Jasper breathed, his voice tight with alarm. The tactical display, which had briefly stabilized, now swam with aberrant data. Ghostly shapes flickered in and out of existence on the holographic map, too transient to be tracked, too many to be dismissed. "It's not just a visual hallucination, is it? Benjamin, are you seeing this?"

Benjamin's face pale was hunched over his console. "It's… it's a multi-spectrum optical distortion field. They're projecting it across a significant portion of the urban grid. It's layering multiple visual frequencies, overriding our natural perception, and likely affecting the city's own infrastructure sensors too. They're not just trying to blind us; they're trying to make the entire city appear unstable, chaotic. And those ghost signatures on the map…" He paused; her brow furrowed in concentration. "They're not vehicles. They're localized atmospheric and energy fluctuations, too small and too fast to be anything but coordinated micro-deployments. Like a swarm of nanobots, they're released into the air. They're probably mapping every surface, every shadow, every potential hiding place in real-time."

Rachel forced her eyes to remain fixed on the road, her grip on the steering wheel tightening until his knuckles were bone white. The chaos outside was palpable, a symphony of visual discord that threatened to unravel his focus. Yet, he could sense the underlying order of their pursuers' plan. This wasn't brute force; it was a sophisticated, multi-pronged attack, designed to overwhelm and subdue. "They want us disoriented, vulnerable. They're using the city itself as a weapon, or at least, as a canvas for their deceptions. And those micro-deployments... they're not just passive sensors. I can feel it. A subtle shift in the air pressure, a faint whisper against the chassis. They're not just mapping; they're preparing for ground engagement."

As if on cue, the van suddenly swerved, not from any input on Rachel's part, but as if a phantom hand had yanked the steering wheel. Alarms shrieked from Jasper's console. "Collision warning! Multiple ground contacts! They're converging on us from all sides!"

The van was suddenly rocked by a violent impact, not a collision with another vehicle, but a percussive force that seemed to come from below. The chassis groaned in protest. "EMP burst!" Jasper yells. "Localized, targeted! It's taking out our primary power conduit!"

Suddenly, the engine died, causing an unnerving silence, amplifying the lack of alarms. The holographic display flickered and died, leaving them in relative darkness, illuminated only by the still-warped glow of the city lights filtering through the windshield. The pursuing vehicles, which had been closing in, slowed, their menacing forms now stark and imposing.

The city, a dizzying blur moments before, now sharpened into a terrifying tableau. Sleek, matte-black vehicles, their designs menacingly utilitarian and utterly unfamiliar, emerged from alleyways and side streets, cutting off their escape routes with unnerving precision. These weren't standard police cruisers or civilian vehicles. They were low-slung, heavily armored machines that moved with an almost predatory grace. Some were clearly armed, their weapon mounts swiveling with silent menace.

"These are not standard military units," Jasper stated, his voice grim. "The chassis design, the propulsion signature... it's too advanced, too silent. And their coordination... it's like they're all part of a single, distributed intelligence. They're not communicating with radios; they're connected by something far more direct, far more instantaneous."

Benjamin pointed a trembling finger at his display. "The swarm is activating ground-level elements. I'm detecting directed energy pulses, low-frequency, designed to overload our vehicle's internal systems again, but this time, specifically targeting the steering and braking mechanisms. They're not just chasing us; they're trying to disable us in place."

Rachel gritted her teeth, fighting the phantom tugs on the wheel, the jarring, unpredictable lurches that threatened to send them careening into buildings or other vehicles. The cityscape was no longer just a backdrop; it was a labyrinth of potential traps, a deadly obstacle course. Her glimpsed figures on rooftops, silhouetted against the distorted sky, armed and observing. Ground operatives too were emerging, their dark uniforms blending seamlessly with the shadows, their movements precise and economical. They were not chaotic attackers; they were a highly trained, coordinated force, employing every facet of their advanced technology.

"We can't outrun them in the city," Rachel stated, his mind already racing through escape vectors. "They've boxed us in. The drones in the sky, the ground units, the jamming... it's a pincer movement. We need to disappear. We need to shed this vehicle, shed our current identities."

"We're dead in the water," Benjamin whispers, his voice laced with despair.

Rachel's gaze swept across the street. Across from them, a darkened, nondescript warehouse stood silently, its entrance shrouded in shadow. It wasn't on any of the schematics they had access to, but an instinct, honed by years of operating in the shadows, screamed at him. "Jasper, Benjamin, grab what you can. We're going dark. Now."

She killed the remaining lights; the van becoming a hulking, inert silhouette in the distorted urban twilight. The pursuing vehicles surrounded them, their headlights cutting through the disorienting haze. Rachel could hear the faint, rhythmic thud of their engines, the barely audible whir of their advanced propulsion systems. They were closing in, their prey immobilized.

"The warehouse," Rachel murmured, pointing with his chin. "It's our only chance."

With a surge of adrenaline, they unbuckled their restraints. Jasper grabbed a satchel containing their most critical data drives, while Benjamin secured a small, hardened case holding their emergency communication and evasion equipment. Rachel took a deep breath, the scent of ozone and something metallic—the residual energy of their pursuers' technology—filling his lungs.

"On my count," he whispered. "Three… two… one… GO!"

They burst out of the van, not towards the warehouse directly, but sprinting into a narrow, garbage-strewn alleyway next to it. The pursuing vehicles, momentarily confused by the sudden egress, lost precious seconds. Rachel could hear shouts, the clang of metal as the ground operatives disembarked.

As they ran, Rachel risked a glance back. One of the matte-black vehicles had stopped directly in front of their abandoned van. A ramp extended, and a team of operatives, clad in advanced tactical suits that seemed to absorb light, emerged with their weapons raised. The aerial drones, previously a distant threat, were now descending, their silent forms growing larger, more menacing, against the warped urban sky.

They reached the rear entrance of the warehouse, a heavy steel door that looked impossibly fortified. Jasper produced a compact device, a whisper-thin piece of technology that hummed with barely contained energy. It emitted a low-frequency pulse, and with a soft hiss, the locking mechanism disengaged. They slipped inside, plunging into an oppressive darkness that was a welcome relief from the city's disorienting light show.

Inside, the air was thick with dust and the scent of forgotten industrial processes. The space was vast, filled with the hulking shadows of dormant machinery. Rachel could hear the sounds of their pursuers in the distance, the metallic footsteps, the muffled commands. They had found them. But they had also bought themselves a sliver of time.

"They know we're here," Benjamin stated, his breath coming in ragged gasps. "Their surveillance network is too comprehensive. They'll have mapped the building's internal structure by now, if not already projected it onto their tactical displays."

Jasper was already at a small, grimy window, peering out into the alley. "They're securing the perimeter. We're trapped in here. And that EMP burst wasn't random. They knew van was a liability, a beacon. They disabled it to force us into a more contained environment, where they could… manage us."

Rachel felt a familiar prickling sensation, the sense of being observed, amplified by the close confines. "They want us alive. They want information. The EMP was to ensure we couldn't escape with the van, to minimize collateral damage. But they're not taking chances. This is a containment operation. They'll flood the building. We need to find a way out, a way to disappear from their grasp entirely."

Jasper spotted a rusted ladder leading to a catwalk high above. "Up there," he said, gesturing. "We need to move vertically. Try to break their line of sight, disrupt their sensor sweeps. This isn't just about evasion anymore; it's about going completely off-grid. We need to shed every trace of our former lives, every piece of technology that can be tracked. From here on out, we're ghosts. Their pursuers' sounds grew louder, echoing through the cavern. The close call in the city had ended, but the true pursuit, the one that would force them into the deepest shadows, was just beginning.

The suffocating darkness of the warehouse, once a sanctuary, now felt like a tomb. Each creak of metal, each distant echo from the city's distorted pulse filtering through the walls, was a potential harbinger of discovery. They had shed the van, a beacon of their previous existence, but the act of shedding had also severed their lifelines. The hum of advanced technology, once their shield, was now their enemy, capable of betraying their presence with every stray emission. Rachel's assessment had been chillingly accurate: this was no longer about outrunning their pursuers; it was about erasing themselves from the global map, about becoming phantoms in a world that was meticulously designed to track and apprehend.

Benjamin, hunched over a makeshift workbench cobbled from discarded crates and salvaged metal, worked with a feverish intensity. His fingers, usually so precise on holographic interfaces, now fumbled slightly with the delicate circuitry of a disassembled communication scrambler. The surrounding air crackled with a nervous energy, a stark contrast to the oppressive stillness of the warehouse. "I'm trying to neutralize any outgoing signals from the equipment we brought with us," he explained, his voice a low murmur, barely audible above the persistent hum of the city outside. "Even passive sensors can pick up residual energy. We need to go dark, truly dark. No transmissions, no pings, nothing that can be triangulated. If they have any kind of spectral analysis running on urban grids, even a faint whisper from our gear could lead them back here."

Jasper, meanwhile, was meticulously cataloging their remaining assets, his movements economical and deliberate. He laid out a small collection of items on a dusty tarp: a handful of untraceable currency, a set of blank identity cards, a compact multi-tool, and a single, encrypted data chip that represented their last tangible link to any semblance of their former lives. "Everything we had is compromised," he stated, his voice devoid of emotion. "Our secure channels, our established safe houses, even our digital footprints. They're not just looking for *us*. They're looking for *evidence* of our existence, evidence of what we know. This chip... it's the only thing that might still be clean, but even then, I wouldn't bet my life on it." He ran a gloved thumb over its smooth surface. "Every piece of technology we've relied on, every network we've accessed, is now a potential trap. They've showed an extraordinary ability to infiltrate and manipulate not just our systems, but the very fabric of the city itself."

"They won't stop," Rachel said, the hushed atmosphere. It's likely that they'll think we're close by. They'll be sweeping the area, not just with overt patrols, but with covert surveillance. Thermal imaging, acoustic sensors, even biological markers if they have the capability. The EMP that disabled the van was a precision strike. They knew our vulnerabilities. They're learning our patterns, our reactions. And the longer we stay here, the more they can refine their approach."

Benjamin looked up, his eyes hollowed with fatigue. "I've disabled the active transmissions from our gear, but it's a temporary measure. These systems are resilient, to be hard to shut down completely. And even if I can scrub every signal, they know we're here. They saw us enter. Their drones will have mapped this building by now. They'll have eyes on every entrance, every exit. We're in a locked box, and they're holding the key."

Jasper sighs, the sound heavy with resignation. "Which means the next step isn't about hiding *in* here. It's about disappearing *from* here. We need to move, and we need to move unseen. But how? Every route out is likely being monitored."

Jasper pointed towards a large, defunct industrial furnace, its metallic maw gaping open. "That thing looks like it hasn't been operational for fifty years. But it's connected to something. There's a good chance there's an old flue, a disused access point that might lead down, or even laterally, away from the main structure." He knew it was a long shot, a gamble based on sheer desperation, but it was a gamble that bypassed their pursuers' most immediate surveillance.

Benjamin frowned, already accessing his limited offline mapping software, cross-referencing it with the rudimentary blueprints he'd downloaded before their digital lives were shattered. "The schematics for this era of industrial buildings are notoriously incomplete. But there are notations for older subterranean infrastructure. If there's a flue, it's likely connected to a lower-level network. It's a risk, though. Those spaces could be collapsed, flooded, or filled with toxic gases."

"We've faced worse," Jasper said, his voice regaining a sliver of its former resolve. He picked up the small satchel containing the data chip. "And we're running out of time. The longer we delay, the more they'll solidify their cordon. They'll have time to bring in specialized units, to deploy more sophisticated containment technologies. We need to move before they decide containment isn't enough, before they start a 'sterilization' protocol." The unspoken threat hung in the air, a chilling reminder of the stakes.

Rachel nodded. "Benjamin, can you rig a temporary bypass on our comms gear? Something that can emit a localized decoy signal? Enough to draw their attention for a few minutes while we make our move?"

Benjamin's eyes lit up with a spark of inspiration. "Yes. I can create a phantom signature; make it look like a system reboot or an unauthorized data transfer. It will buy us a window. But it will drain our remaining power reserves on the portable units."

"It's a trade-off we have to make," Rachel replies. "Jasper, you're with me. Benjamin, you set the decoy, then follow us. Keep that data chip secure. It's our only bargaining chip, our only leverage, if it comes to that."

The descent into the forgotten depths of the warehouse was a descent into an even more profound darkness. The air grew heavy, damp, and carried the metallic tang of stagnant water and decay. Rachel, using a salvaged industrial flashlight that cast a weak beam, led the way. Jasper followed closely behind, his senses on high alert, his hand never far from the compact energy pistol concealed within his jacket. The flue was indeed old, a gaping maw of corroded metal that led them down a treacherous, winding path. The sounds of their pursuers, though muffled, seemed to grow more distant with each downward step, to the effectiveness of their chosen route.

They emerged into a vast, echoing space—an old, forgotten subway tunnel, its tracks long since rusted and reclaimed by the earth. The air here was slightly fresher, but carried a distinct chill, the chill of immensity and of a world that had long since moved on. The city above, with its distorted lights and its relentless pursuit, felt a thousand miles away. But the knowledge that they were still being hunted, that the price of their secrets was a constant, gnawing pressure, remained.

"This is where we shed the last vestiges of our former lives," Rachel stated, his voice resonating in the vast emptiness. "No more relying on traceable currency, no more using fabricated identities that might be flagged. From this point on, we live by our wits, our skills, and our ability to become completely invisible.

We become ghosts in the machine."

Benjamin nodded grimly. "The decoy signal was successful. I got a flurry of automated reports from the drone net showing a significant energy spike within the warehouse. They're almost certainly converging at that location. They'll be expecting us to escape through the main exits, or perhaps even try to salvage something from the van. They won't expect us to vanish into the earth."

Jasper looked down the dark, imposing tunnel. "But where do we go? This tunnel could stretch for miles, leading us anywhere, or nowhere. We're cut off from everything. No communication, no support. It's just us."

Rachel turned towards the darkness of the tunnel, the weak beam of flashlight cutting a narrow swathe through the oppressive black. "We move south. Towards the old industrial district. There are more forgotten spaces there, more places to melt away. We travel by night, we avoid populated areas, and we trust no one. We are no longer operatives, no longer agents. Our escape has begun. And our only mission now is survival until we can expose what they are hiding."

The weight of their situation pressed down on them, a palpable force. They were adrift in a sea of shadows, their former lives erased, their future uncertain. The pursuit had shifted from a high-speed chase to a silent, insidious hunt. The earthly pursuers, armed with advanced technology and an unwavering mandate, were relentless. But the true battle, the one for the soul of humanity, had just begun, and it would be fought in the deepest recesses of secrecy, where the cost of discovery was absolute. They had to learn to live without being seen, without being heard, without leaving a trace. They had to become the ultimate phantoms for the sake of a truth that was too dangerous to be known. The price of that secrecy was their very existence, reduced to a whisper in the dark, a flicker in the periphery, a ghost in the machine of a world that desperately wanted to believe it was safe, even if that safety was built on a foundation of lies. And they were the only ones left to remind it of the truth.

CHAPTER 8

ALIEN COUNTERMEASURES

The suffocating darkness of the warehouse, once a sanctuary, now felt like a tomb. Each creak of metal, each distant echo from the city's distorted pulse filtering through the walls, was a potential harbinger of discovery. They had shed the van, a beacon of their previous existence, but the act of shedding had also severed their lifelines. The hum of advanced technology, once their shield, was now their enemy, capable of betraying their presence with every stray emission. Rachel's assessment had been chillingly accurate: this was no longer about outrunning their pursuers; it was about erasing themselves from the global map, about becoming phantoms in a world that was meticulously designed to track and apprehend.

"They won't stop," Rachel said, breaking the hushed atmosphere with her voice. It'll be assumed that we're still close by. They'll be sweeping the area, not just with overt patrols, but with covert surveillance. Thermal imaging, acoustic sensors, even biological markers if they have the capability. The EMP that disabled the van was a precision strike. They knew our vulnerabilities. They're learning our patterns, our reactions. And the longer we stay here, the more they can refine their approach."

Benjamin looked up, her eyes hollowed with fatigue. "I've disabled the active transmissions from our gear, but it's a temporary measure. These systems are resilient, to be hard to shut down completely. And even if I can scrub every signal, they know we're here. They saw us enter. Their drones will have mapped this building by now. They'll have eyes on every entrance, every exit. We're in a locked box, and they're holding the key."

Jasper sighs, the sound heavy with resignation. "Which means the next step isn't about hiding *in* here. It's about disappearing *from* here. We need to move, and we need to move unseen. But how? Every route out is likely being monitored."

He pointed towards a large, defunct industrial furnace, its metallic maw gaping open. "That thing looks like it hasn't been operational for fifty years. But it's connected to something. There's a good chance there's an old flue, a disused access point that might lead down, or even laterally, away from the main structure." He knew it was a long shot, a gamble based on sheer desperation, but it was a gamble that bypassed their pursuers' most immediate surveillance.

The descent into the forgotten depths of the warehouse was a descent into an even more profound darkness. The air grew heavy, damp, and carried a metallic tang. Rachel, using a salvaged industrial flashlight that cast a weak beam, led the way. Jasper followed closely behind, his senses on high alert, his hand never far from the compact energy pistol concealed within his jacket. The flue was indeed old, a gaping maw of corroded metal that led them down a treacherous, winding path. The sounds of their pursuers, though muffled, seemed to grow more distant with each downward step.

They emerged into a vast, echoing space—an old, forgotten subway tunnel, its tracks long since rusted and reclaimed by the earth. The air here was slightly fresher, but carried a distinct chill, the chill of immensity and of a world that had long since moved on. The city above, with its distorted lights and its relentless pursuit, felt a thousand miles away. But the knowledge that they were still being hunted, that the price of their secrets was a constant, gnawing pressure, remained.

The weight of their situation pressed down on them, a palpable force. They were adrift in a sea of shadows, their former lives erased, their future uncertain. The pursuit had shifted from a high-speed chase to a silent, insidious hunt. The earthly pursuers, armed with advanced technology and an unwavering mandate, were relentless.

But the true battle, the one for the soul of humanity, had just begun, and it would be fought in the deepest recesses of secrecy, where the price of discovery was absolute. They had to learn to live without being seen, without being heard, without leaving a trace. They had to become the ultimate phantoms for the sake of a truth that was too dangerous to be known. The price of that secrecy was their very existence, reduced to a whisper in the dark, a flicker in the periphery, a ghost in the machine of a world that desperately wanted to believe it was safe, even if that safety was built on a foundation of lies. And they were the only ones left to remind it of the truth.

Rachel noticed it first in Benjamin. His movements were fractionally less precise than usual. She kept glancing at his wrist-mounted chronometer, though it was functioning perfectly. "Just… a feeling," she'd murmured when Rachel had enquired. "Like I'm forgetting something important. A step missed, a detail overlooked." It was self-doubt that could cascade, undermining confidence and fostering paranoia.

Jasper was exhibiting a different symptom. His reflexes, usually razor-sharp, seemed to be slightly dulled. He'd stumbled once, a minor misstep on the uneven ballast, but the recovery was slower than Rachel would have expected. He'd also complained of an unusual fatigue, a weariness that no amount of rest seemed to ease. "It's like my energy reserves are being leached away," he'd confessed, his voice rough with exhaustion. "Like I'm running on fumes, even after a full night's sleep."

Rachel understood. This wasn't about brute force; it was about attrition. The alien presence, or those acting on its behalf, wasn't just interested in apprehension. They were interested in neutralization, and that meant dismantling their targets from the inside out. The psychological realm was the prime battlefield. They were being subjected to a form of environmental conditioning, subtle but pervasive. The constant low-frequency hum that seemed to emanate from the very earth beneath their feet. The strange atmospheric shifts, imperceptible but potent, induced a mild but persistent sense of unease.

During the few precious hours of uneasy slumber, they managed in abandoned service shafts or derelict maintenance tunnels, they'd all reported unsettling dreams. Benjamin dreamed of falling, of being trapped in an inescapable maze. Jasper dreamed of being watched, of unseen eyes scrutinizing his every move, his every thought. Rachel herself dreamed of her lost colleagues, their faces distorted, their voices whispering accusations. These nightmares were not random.

The technological disruptions, while less overtly psychological, served the same purpose: to isolate and disorient. A flickering streetlamp that cast the wrong shadow, a public transport announcement that seemed to loop endlessly on a single, nonsensical phrase, a malfunctioning traffic light that caused minor but frustrating gridlock—these were not accidents. Someone carefully orchestrated these disruptions to sow chaos and make their environment feel unreliable. They were messages, delivered not through words, but through the subtle degradation of the familiar, the erosion of order.

As they navigated a desolate stretch of disused industrial infrastructure, Benjamin's portable scanner, a device designed to detect residual energy signatures, emitted a series of discordant chirps. It was picking up something, or rather, the absence of something. "It's like a localized distortion in the ambient energy field," he explained, her voice tight with concern. "Not a signal, but a… gap. Something is actively dampening the background radiation in this area."

"They're not just trying to find us anymore," Rachel stated, her voice low and grim. "They're trying to break us. Our own senses and perceptions are being used against us. They want us to doubt what we see, what we hear, what we feel. They want us to become unreliable witnesses of our own reality."

Jasper nodded, his eyes scanning the shadows with renewed intensity. "The goal is to make us doubt ourselves. If we can't trust our own judgment, we can't possibly outmaneuver them. Every decision will be second-guessed. Every path taken will be fraught with indecision."

"And that's when they'll strike," Benjamin added, his voice barely a whisper. "When we're most vulnerable, most fractured. When we're arguing about whether that shadow is real, or whether that sound is just the wind, or whether we're both hallucinating."

"They're trying to isolate us not just physically, but mentally," Rachel reiterated, the words tasting like ash in her mouth. "They want us to feel utterly alone, even when we're surrounded by people. To doubt our own minds and perceptions is their goal. This is their primary weapon: to make us our own worst enemy."

Benjamin had been meticulously documenting these anomalies, creating a separate, offline log on a heavily shielded, analogue device. "The patterns are too consistent to be random," he stated, tapping the screen of her notepad. Areas we've recently occupied show concentrated environmental disturbances. The glitches in our equipment seem to correlate with periods of heightened stress or critical decision-making. It's a deliberate, intelligent campaign."

Jasper leaned against a damp, grimy wall in what they hoped was a forgotten ventilation shaft, sighed. "So, they don't need to corner us physically to win. They just need to make us surrender to our own minds. Make us believe we're trapped, even when there's a path forward. Make us doubt the truth we're trying to protect."

"Exactly," Rachel confirmed. "This is the countermeasure. Not a missile, not a capture net, but the slow, insidious erosion of our will to fight. They are the ultimate manipulators, using the very fabric of reality as their tool. They've seen our resilience, our ability to adapt and survive. So, they're changing the game, forcing us to fight ourselves. She looked at her companions, "We have to be vigilant, not just for their physical presence, but for the subtle whispers of doubt they are implanting in our minds. We have to hold on to the truth, to our mission, even when our senses try to tell us otherwise."

"We can't stay here indefinitely," Jasper stated one cycle, his voice raspy from the damp air. He was meticulously cleaning their few remaining tools, a ritual that seemed to anchor him in the face of the pervasive disorientation. "The environmental conditioning is becoming unbearable. Benjamin's sleep has been almost nonexistent, and even I'm questioning if that shadow in the corner is just a shadow."

Benjamin nodded in agreement. He had been pouring over a salvaged, offline hydrological map of the city's subterranean network. "The air quality is degrading. These drains aren't designed for long-term habitation. And the further we penetrate this network, the more isolated we become. If we need to move, we need a better option than simply deeper darkness."

"We need to consider the possibility," Rachel conceded. "If they can deploy sophisticated surveillance and psychological warfare on land, it's logical they would extend that to their aquatic domain. But what form would these underwater sentinels take?"

Benjamin tapped a section of the map that showed a deepwater channel leading out to sea. "My analysis of the aberrant acoustic data suggests formations that contradict natural phenomena or known submersible technology. There are… patterns. Rhythmic pulses, complex sonar pings that don't align with any known marine life. And the energy readings are off the charts, localized and highly focused."

"Drones?" Jasper ventured. "Automated patrol units designed to detect and neutralize any intrusions."

"Possible," Rachel mused. "But the sheer scale of the energy readings, and the complexity of the acoustic signatures, suggest something more. Something biological, perhaps. Bio-engineered creatures, designed for deep-sea reconnaissance and defense. Or perhaps something even more advanced. Energy-based entities, as some of the more speculative theories suggest. Beings that exist as pure energy, capable of manipulating the water itself, or of projecting their consciousness across vast distances."

"If these entities are indeed patrolling the waters, any attempt to exit via the bay would be… problematic," Jasper stated, the understatement hanging heavy in the humid air. "We'd be swimming directly into their hunting grounds."

"But if their focus is solely on preventing interference with Area 291 and the submerged structures," Rachel countered, "then perhaps there's a way to use that to our advantage. If we can identify their patrol patterns, their operational parameters, we might slip through. Or, failing that, to create a diversion that draws their attention away from a potential extraction point."

"The drones are minimal in capability," Jasper pointed out. "Their range is limited, and they lack stealth." And even if we could deploy one, getting it past whatever patrols the surface and the immediate shoreline would be a challenge in itself."

"Possible," Rachel mused. "But the sheer scale of the energy readings, and the complexity of the acoustic signatures, suggest something more. Something biological, perhaps. Bio-engineered creatures, designed for deep-sea reconnaissance and defense. Or perhaps something even more advanced. Energy-based entities, as some of the more speculative theories suggest. Beings that exist as pure energy, capable of manipulating the water itself, or of projecting their consciousness across vast distances."

The thought of confronting an entity composed of pure energy, or a bio-engineered leviathan, was almost as daunting as the psychological torment they were already experiencing. Their current arsenal was woefully inadequate for such a scenario. Their salvaged energy pistol was effective against conventional technology, but against something that defied physical form or possessed an alien biology, it would be useless.

"If these entities are indeed patrolling the waters, any attempt to exit via the bay would be… problematic," Jasper stated, the understatement hanging heavy in the humid air. "We'd be swimming directly into their hunting grounds."

A 'heat' elsewhere, a simulated breach perhaps, it might draw their focus. But it would require precise timing and an understanding of their sensory capabilities."

"And a means of delivering that simulated threat," Rachel added. "We'd need to get close enough to the bay to deploy something. Perhaps one of our remaining reconnaissance drones, changed to emit a high-energy signature, something that would scream 'intruder' to their systems."

"The drones are minimal in capability," Jasper pointed out. "They have a limited range and are not stealthy," he said. And even if we could deploy one, getting it past whatever patrols the surface and the immediate shoreline would be a challenge in itself."

Suddenly, the sonar emitted a sharp, piercing whine. The readings spiked erratically, displaying a complex, overlapping array of signatures. "Multiple contacts!" Benjamin exclaimed, his voice rising in alarm. "And they're closing in. Fast. They're not just one sentinel, Rachel. There are several. And they're not moving parallel anymore. They're converging on our position."

Jasper voiced a thought. "I think it's the Guardians who want to take us out. The Luminaries have no reason. The Guardians lose their control, their technology, and all the benefits."

The surrounding water seemed to shimmer, a distortion that was not a product of their failing senses, but of something far more tangible. The faint glow from the phosphorescent growths intensified, then flickered out, plunging them into absolute darkness save for the weak beam of Rachel's flashlight, which now seemed woefully inadequate. A low, guttural hum filled the tunnel, a sound that vibrated not just in their ears, but deep within their bones. It was a sound that spoke of immense power, of alien purpose, of a primal, ancient hunt.

The water churned violently, as if a colossal force was stirring beneath the surface. Shadows detached themselves from the deeper darkness, impossibly vast and fluid, coalescing into vaguely defined forms that seemed to pulse with an internal, otherworldly light. They were not sleek mechanical constructs, but organic, almost amorphous entities, their shapes shifting and reforming like sentient currents.

"They're bio-engineered," Benjamin gasps, his eyes wide with a horrified understanding. "Look at the way they move. The bioluminescence… it's not just for display. It's a weapon. It's disrupting the energy fields around us, interfering with our equipment, probably our own neural pathways too."

One entity, a colossal, serpentine shape of shimmering, iridescent light, drifted closer, its form defying conventional biology. It seemed to possess no discernible features, yet Rachel felt an undeniable sense of being observed, of being analyzed with intelligence that was both alien and terrifyingly precise. The hum intensified, a dissonant chord that seemed to resonate with the very fear that was gripping them.

"We need to retreat," Jasper urged, his voice a desperate plea. "Back into the tunnels. We can't fight these things."

Rachel nodded, his mind racing. Direct confrontation was suicide. The psychological warfare they had endured on land had prepared them for this subtle form of attack. These were not mere guards; they extended the alien presence, designed to deter, to disorient, and ultimately, to destroy anything that threatened their submerged dominion.

"Benjamin, can you reverse the sonar? Make it produce a wide burst? Something chaotic, to overload their sensors for a moment?" Rachel commands.

"I can try!" Benjamin fumbled with the controls; his hands slick with nervous sweat. "It'll drain the remaining power, but it might buy us a few seconds."

As Benjamin started the sonar, a wave of disorienting energy washed over them. The alien entities recoiled, their bioluminescence flaring erratically, the hum momentarily breaking into a discordant shriek. It was a fleeting moment of reprieve, a crack in their otherwise perfect defense.

"Now!" Rachel yelled. "Back the way we came! Don't look back!"

The oppressive weight of their subterranean existence had worn on them. Days bled into nights, marked only by the changing cycles of their meager rations and the dwindling power of their portable lights. The city above, a sprawling entity of light and noise, felt like a forgotten dream, a memory of a world they could no longer inhabit. Rachel, Benjamin, and Jasper had established a temporary base in a network of disused storm drains beneath the industrial district, a labyrinth of concrete and flowing water that offered a semblance of concealment. But the psychological warfare they were enduring, the subtle erosion of their senses and sanity, had not ceased. It had in fact intensified.

The thought of confronting an entity composed of pure energy, or a bio-engineered leviathan, was almost as daunting as the psychological torment they were already experiencing. Their current arsenal was woefully inadequate for such a scenario. Their salvaged energy pistol was effective against conventional technology, but against something that defied physical form or possessed an alien biology, it would be useless.

They were deep within the outer shell, a forgotten chamber choked with dust and the skeletal remains of outdated server racks, when the anomaly occurred. Benjamin had bypassed a significant portion of the alien encryption, his fingers dancing across the salvaged console, coaxing fragments of information from the digital ether. The air crackled, not with the familiar static of interference, but with a sudden, profound silence. The ambient hum of the city's dormant systems, the faint trickle of water, even the ragged rhythm of their own breathing seemed to cease, as if the universe itself had held its breath. Then, the light changed.

It wasn't a flicker or a sudden blackout. It was a *deepening* of the darkness, a saturation of shadow that seemed to absorb all illumination. The emergency lights on their suits, designed to cut through the gloom of subterranean environments, flickered and died, not from malfunction, but as if their photons were being actively leached from existence. A cold seeped into the chamber, far more profound than the ambient chill of the underground. It was an ancient cold, a cold that felt as though it had existed before the stars. Rachel felt a primal fear coil in her gut, a terror that transcended logic, a recognition of something immeasurably vast and utterly indifferent.

Then, they saw them.

They weren't entities that occupied space in the way humans understood it. They were more like… absences given form, voids that pulsed with an internal, alien luminescence. At first, they appeared as shifting. They were tall, impossibly so, their forms elongated and fluid, lacking the rigid structure of organic life as they knew it. Their limbs, if they could be called limbs, moved with a languid grace that defied physics, seeming to flow rather than stride. There was no discernible head, no face, no sensory organs that they could identify. Yet, Rachel had the undeniable sensation of being observed, of being scrutinized by an intellect that spanned millennia, an awareness that perceived them not as individuals but as insignificant blips in a cosmic tapestry.

One figure drifted closer, its form resolving into a more coherent, yet still terrifying one. It comprised what appeared to be interwoven strands of pure energy, shimmering with a spectrum of colors that had no name in human language. These strands pulsed and reconfigured themselves with a mesmerizing, almost hypnotic rhythm. Within this dynamic structure, Rachel thought he could perceive patterns, intricate geometric designs that shifted.

Benjamin gasped, a choked sound that was instantly swallowed by the suffocating silence. His eyes were wide, fixed on the entity before him, his scientific curiosity warring with an overwhelming sense of existential dread. "Jasper … look at the energy readings," he whispered, his voice strained. "They're… they're not registering. It's like they're not there, but… but they're distorting the very space around them. There are anomalies, localized warps… it's impossible."

Jasper slowly raised his weapon, the targeting laser a thin, defiant red line against the encroaching void. But even as he did, he seemed to hesitate. There was no heat signature, no discernible mass to target, no conventional vulnerability. The entities were not solid objects to be shot; they were manifestations of a power that seemed to operate on principles far beyond their comprehension.

The closest entity tilted, or perhaps simply reoriented itself, and Rachel felt an alien presence brush against her consciousness. It wasn't a thought, not a word, but a pure *knowing*. It was a sensation of immense age, of witnessing the rise and fall of civilizations, of understanding the fundamental forces of the universe in a way that made human knowledge seem like the ramblings of a child. She felt a wave of profound insignificance wash over her, the weight of eons pressing down, threatening to crush her very being. It was a glimpse into a consciousness that had no beginning and no end, a vast, ancient intelligence that viewed humanity as fleeting and ultimately irrelevant.

Each of them saw flickers of their own history flash before his eyes, not as memories, but as objective observations. The birth of stars, the formation of galaxies, the slow, agonizing march of evolution on countless worlds. And then, a brief, almost dismissive focus on Earth. He saw the primitive stirrings of life, the slow ascent of humanity, the frantic scramble for knowledge and power, all presented with a detached, clinical air. It was as if they were viewing a laboratory experiment that had run its course, a fleeting phenomenon of biological and technological complexity.

Then, the perception shifted. The ancient gaze seemed to focus on their immediate situation, on their purpose within this forgotten data nexus. It wasn't a threat, not in the way they understood it. It was more like a simple, irrefutable assessment. *You are attempting to interfere with that which you do not comprehend. Your actions are... inconvenient.*

The implications were chilling. These were not conquerors seeking to enslave or exterminate. They were something far more ancient, something that operated on a scale of cosmic stewardship, perhaps. And humanity, in its desperate attempt to understand and potentially defend itself, was merely an annoyance, a minor disruption to their grand, unfathomable designs.

Benjamin, in his own moment of terror, experienced a similar psychic intrusion. Images flooded his mind—not of nightmares or personal fears, but of vast, incomprehensible cosmic structures, of forces that shaped galaxies like clay. He saw the underlying mathematics of reality, the elegant, terrifying equations that governed existence, rendered not in symbols, but as tangible, flowing constructs of light and energy. It was overwhelming, a torrent of data that threatened to overload her senses, to shatter the very framework of his understanding. He felt the intricate, interconnected web of the universe and humanity's place within it as a fragile, almost accidental, occurrence.

Jasper fought against the profound sense of existential dread. He focused on the physical, on the tangible aspects of their situation, even as the intangible pressed in on him. He felt the alien entities' immense power not as a directed force, but as a passive, inherent property, like the gravity of a black hole. They weren't *trying* to intimidate them; their mere presence was an overwhelming force. He recognized a profound, almost unbearable sadness within their alien perception, a sense of witnessing the cyclical nature of existence, the inevitable rise and fall, and the often-futile struggles of emergent lifeforms. It was a sorrow born not of empathy, but of an ancient, detached understanding of cosmic impermanence.

An eternity of heartbeats filled the silence. The pulsing energy forms remained, their alien luminescence painting the dust-choked chamber in hues that defied earthly description. The sense of observation was relentless, a silent, unwavering scrutiny that stripped away all pretense. Rachel felt his own thoughts laid bare, his motivations analyzed, his fears cataloged, all without a flicker of judgment, simply as data points in a cosmic ledger.

Then, as abruptly as it began, it ended. The oppressive silence fractured. Once again, the faint hum of dormant machinery returned, and the distant trickle of water was audible. Their suits' emergency lights flickered, creating a weak, familiar glow. The encroaching darkness receded, not as if pushed back, but as if the entities had simply ceased to occupy that sliver of reality. The ancient cold dissipated, replaced by the damp, earthy chill of the underground. It was as if they had blinked, and an epoch had passed, leaving only the ghost of an encounter.

Benjamin slumped against a defunct server rack, his breath coming in ragged gasps. "They... they were not hostile," he stammered, her voice trembling. "Not in the way we think. It was... a classification. We were... assessed. And found wanting." She looked at her datapad, its screen now displaying a jumble of corrupted code; the precious data they had almost secured was now lost. "They didn't destroy it. They just... shifted the parameters. Made it irrelevant."

Jasper lowered his weapon, his knuckles white. "They are... ancient," he stated, his voice rough with an emotion Rachel couldn't quite place—awe, perhaps, or a profound, unsettling realization of their own insignificance. "Older than anything we can comprehend. Their power isn't in weapons; it's in their very existence. They are... the universe, in a way we are not."

Rachel felt a profound exhaustion settle over her, a weariness that seeped into her bones. The psychological countermeasures they had been experiencing—the paranoia, the doubt, the manufactured fear—now seemed like a mere prelude, a childish game compared to the true, immeasurable power they had just witnessed. These entities were not aliens in the typical sense. They were something far older, far more advanced, beings who perceived reality on a fundamental level that humanity could barely grasp. They were not engaged in a war of conquest, but perhaps in a cosmic balancing act, and humanity's technological ambition had placed them on the wrong side of a geological, or perhaps even a galactic, fault line.

"They showed us," Rachel said, her voice quiet, resonating with the gravity of what they had seen. We were shown the scale of what we're up against. And they showed us that our focus on technology, on physical confrontation, is... misguided. They are not just an enemy to be defeated; they are a force of nature to be understood, or perhaps, to be avoided." She looked at Benjamin, then at Jasper, their faces etched with the shock of the encounter. "Our mission parameters have changed. We are not here to fight them. We are here to survive. And to learn."

Losing the data thwarted their immediate aim. However, they found the glimpse revealed a terrifying paradigm shift. They had sought schematics and data streams, but they had found a glimpse of the Masters, the ancient architects of the cosmos, and in doing so, had discovered a truth far more profound and far more humbling than they had ever imagined. The aliens' true countermeasures were not technological jamming or psychological warfare. They were the overwhelming, existential truth of their own vastness, their own antiquity, a silent testament to humanity's fleeting existence in the grand, indifferent theater of the universe. The true battle was not for control of Earth, but for humanity's very perception of its place within the cosmic order.

CHAPTER 9

RACE AGAINST TIME

Before a pronouncement, the silence in the conduit exhaled cosmically. The encounter with the entities, the Masters as Rachel had called them. The alien threat wasn't a tangible enemy with observable motives; it was a force of nature, indifferent and ancient, a testament to humanity's infinitesimal place in the grand, unforgiving tapestry of existence. Their mission, once a desperate scramble for technological advantage, had morphed into a grim race against a much larger, far more abstract clock. The datapad Benjamin had painstakingly worked on was a mosaic of corrupted data, not so much erased as obsolete, its carefully gathered fragments of alien schematics now as relevant as hieroglyphs in a quantum physics lecture. The schematics were useless because the Masters' true operational logic wasn't something that could be reverse-engineered from broken circuits or scrambled code. It was woven into the very fabric of reality, a manifestation of principles that defied their most advanced scientific understanding.

"They're accelerating," Benjamin stated, his voice a low, urgent hum that cut through the still, damp air. He was poring over a secondary terminal, salvaged and jury-rigged, its screen flickering with a chaotic cascade of data streams they had intercepted from less sophisticated alien probes and heavily encrypted human transmissions. The sheer volume of information was staggering, a digital ocean of fragmented reports, panicked dispatches, and eerie, statistically anomalous data points that spoke of a coordinated, systematic approach to global destabilization. "The energy signatures, the atmospheric shifts, the anomalies in global financial markets… it's all converging. The chaos isn't a side effect. It's the engine."

Rachel leaned closer, her gaze fixed on the pulsing graphs and cryptic alphanumeric sequences. "You mean they're actively engineering the collapse?"

Benjamin nodded, his eyes glinting with a mixture of fear and fierce determination. "The patterns are undeniable. Economic downturns that defy all logical modeling, mass migrations triggered by fabricated environmental crises, societal unrest that seems to be… amplified, curated. It's like they're preparing a petri dish. We're being cultured for something."

Jasper ran a diagnostic on his sidearm, the metallic click echoing in the confined space. "Cultured for what? To be nutrients?"

"Worse," Benjamin replied, his voice barely above a whisper. "For assessment. For harvest."

Rachel hugged herself as an icy chill passed through her. "I'm afraid, terrified to tell you what I'm thinking."

Jasper, who must have been feeling the same chill, said, "I think we are thinking the same thing. I have been for some time. Scared shitless. I'll just come out and say it…what we learned in Sunday school."

"Shit!" Benjamin added. He got serious quickly.

"Ben and I are Jews," Rachel added. "But Jasper, you're Catholic, right?"

"Yes, I grew up Catholic." Jasper stated. "But they weren't religious fanatics. We went to Easter Mass and Midnight Mass on Christmas Eve."

"I only say that because our theology says the same thing many times. Non-Jews think of the Old Testament as a historical book with no meaning"

"I always thought it grounded the faith in the New Testament." Jasper added.

"Ah ha! That's what I wanted to hear! Revelations came from many parts of the Old Testament." Benjamin felt like he was finally figuring things out. "Both faiths spoke about the harvest…" He left that last statement hanging in the air."

The words hung in the air, heavy and suffocating. Harvest. One did not associate the term with advanced extraterrestrial intelligence. It implied reaping, collecting, and using. It spoke of a purpose, a function that humanity was being groomed to fulfill. Rachel remembered the overwhelming sense of insignificance she had felt in the presence of the Masters, their detached, ancient gaze that had cataloged their history with the clinical detachment of a biologist examining a microbial colony. "The 'harvest' protocol… we intercepted fragments of that term before," Rachel mused, recalling their initial, desperate attempts to decipher the alien agenda. "We assumed it was about resource acquisition, or perhaps biological samples. But this… this is something else entirely. Everything is about a farmer."

"It's about integration," Benjamin explained, gesturing to a disturbing cluster of data that showed correlated spikes in societal breakdown and localized anomalies in biological and neurological readings. "They're not just watching us fall apart; they're facilitating it. Complexity and noise are being stripped away. They're simplifying us. Think of it like pruning a garden. They're removing the weeds, the overgrowth, the diseased branches, so that the essential elements, the parts that serve their purpose, can thrive."

Rachel's mind raced. The chaos wasn't an accidental byproduct of an alien presence; it was the deliberate, meticulously orchestrated prelude to something far more sinister. Their advanced tech, which disrupted systems, didn't cause the economic collapse. The societal unrest, the riots, the fractured governments—these weren't just signs of human frailty; they were the intended outcome of alien manipulation, designed to break down the established order and leave humanity vulnerable.

"They want us manageable," Jasper stated, his voice grim. "Easier to process."

"Precisely," Benjamin affirmed. "The more fractured and desperate humanity becomes, the less resistance there is to whatever their goal is. They're creating a state of global triage. The strongest, the most adaptable, the ones who can survive the stripped-down conditions—they will be the ones left. And those who are left will be deemed… suitable."

The implication was horrifying. Humanity wasn't facing an invasion of conquerors seeking to subjugate or destroy. They were facing a cosmic gardener, a shepherd tending to its flock, preparing for a selective culling. The Masters, with their unfathomable antiquity and their perspective that spanned epochs, viewed humanity not as equals, but as a species to be managed, its future dictated by their inscrutable needs. The current global pandemonium, the economic freefall, the escalating violence—it was all part of a meticulously planned phase, a systematic reduction of humanity to a more manageable, more exploitable form.

"How much time do we have?" Rachel asked, the question a heavy weight in her chest. The encounter in the data nexus had provided a terrifying glimpse of the scale of their adversaries, but it had also imparted a sense of urgency. The window for intervention, for disrupting this inexorable process, was shrinking with every passing hour.

Benjamin's fingers flew across the interface; he was in deep concentration. He overlaid satellite imagery with atmospheric composition data, cross-referenced it with seismic activity logs and encrypted military intelligence that their network had scraped together. A stark, terrifying graph displayed a steep, almost vertical acceleration. "The models predict critical mass within… weeks, maybe a month at most," she reported, his voice tight. "The 'harvest' protocol is no longer a theoretical future event. It's actively underway. The current global chaos isn't just a consequence of their presence; it's the final phase of their preparation. They're not waiting for us to break; they're ensuring we do, on their terms."

A chilling realization settled over Rachel. Their previous efforts, their focus on acquiring alien technology and understanding their weapons systems, had been misguided. The Masters didn't operate on the same plane of existence. Their power wasn't in ships that could vaporize cities or energy weapons that could pierce armor. Their power was in their understanding of fundamental cosmic principles, their ability to subtly manipulate the very fabric of reality, to guide the course of civilizations with an unseen hand. They were like gods, not of creation, but of cosmic husbandry, and humanity was a crop ripe for the reaping.

"We need to disrupt their assessment phase," Rachel stated, her mind already shifting gears. "If chaos is the mechanism of their evaluation, then we need to introduce a variable they haven't accounted for. Something that throws off their readings, something that makes us appear... unsuitable for harvest."

Jasper slammed his hand against a metal bulkhead; the sound was sharp and resonant. "How do you disrupt chaos? They created it. They control the levers."

"We don't disrupt the chaos," Benjamin counters, his eyes alight with a new idea, a dangerous spark of defiance. "We introduce something that invalidates the *purpose* of the chaos. If they're stripping us down, simplifying us, to identify the most manageable elements, then we need to become... unmanageable. We need to become something they can't categorize, something that doesn't fit their parameters for 'harvest'." He pointed to a section of the data showing a sudden, inexplicable surge in localized neurological activity across several major urban centers, correlating with spikes in what we're being labeled as 'mass hysteria events'. "They're looking for patterns of submission, of breakdown. We need to show them``9+ patterns of... redirection. Of adaptation that defies their logic."

The pressure was immense. Every fragment of intelligence they gathered pointed to a rapidly closing window. The global stage was being set; the actors—a demoralized, fractured humanity— were being primed for their last role. They were the only ones who understood the true nature of the threat, the cosmic scale of the operation. The rest of the world was unaware of the unseen hand guiding their descent through the currents of the manufactured crisis.

Rachel felt a surge of adrenaline, a desperate energy that pushed back against the crushing weight of despair. The Masters operated on an immense scale; their plans unfolded over eons. Humanity's struggle, its very existence, was a fleeting blip in their consciousness. But even a blip could be unpredictable. Even a microbe could resist sterilization if it mutated in the right way. "Benjamin, focus on identifying the core metrics they're using for their assessment. What are they measuring? Compliance? Resource depletion? Population density? Jasper, we need to assess our remaining assets. What can we leverage they wouldn't expect? What unconventional capabilities do we have that they cannot easily quantify or dismiss?

Benjamin's fingers danced, his mind already in overdrive, sifting through the torrent of data, searching for the alien algorithm that dictated survival. Jasper began a silent inventory of their dwindling resources, his gaze sharp and assessing, his military mind already calculating probabilities and potential avenues of unconventional resistance. Never had the race against time felt so real, so critical. The 'harvest' was impending, a cosmic scythe poised to sweep across humanity, and they were the last, desperate hope to make themselves invisible, or perhaps, unpalatable, to the celestial reapers. The chaos they were witnessing wasn't just a prelude to destruction; it was a carefully curated environment, and their only chance was to introduce an element that would make the curated product unsuitable for the intended purpose. They had to become anomalies within the anomaly.

The raw data painted a terrifying picture, but data, even the most damning, could be spun, buried, or outright denied. Rachel knew this intimately, having spent years navigating the murky waters of intelligence and disinformation. The fractured narratives the Masters were weaving across the globe, manifesting as economic collapses, fabricated environmental crises, and amplified societal unrest, were a testament to their mastery of manipulation. Governments, already teetering on the brink of collapse, were complicit or too overwhelmed to discern the true orchestrator behind the curtain. The Vatican, a bastion of ancient knowledge and influence, had its own agenda, a historical predisposition to control narratives and maintain its spiritual authority, which likely meant suppressing any evidence that contradicted their carefully constructed worldview, or worse, aligning with it for perceived future benefits. Possessing the intercepted transmissions or the analysis of anomalous patterns wouldn't be enough. It would be dismissed as fringe conspiracy, state-sponsored propaganda, or the ramblings of a desperate few.

"We're drowning in information, but we're starving for validation," Benjamin stated, his voice raspy with fatigue. He had been working tirelessly, his eyes red-rimmed, the glow of the holographic displays reflecting in their depths. The sheer volume of disparate data points—the statistical anomalies in weather patterns, the synchronized plunges in global stock markets, the eerily coordinated waves of civil unrest that seemed to erupt simultaneously in strategically chosen flashpoints—all pointed to a singular, intelligent design. But how to present this deluge of digital evidence to cut through the manufactured fog? How to create a Rosetta Stone for a reality-altering revelation?

Jasper, meticulously cleaning and reassembling a piece of salvaged alien hardware, grunted in agreement. "Think about it. Even if we broadcast everything we have—the energy signatures, the spectral analysis of those probes, Benjamin's breakdown of the 'harvest' protocol—it would be dismissed. They'll say it's a hack, a deepfake, a psy-op by a rogue nation. They've already laid the groundwork for denial by creating the very chaos that makes coherent thought impossible for the majority." He tapped the metallic component against his palm. "We need something tangible. Something that screams 'alien' without a translator or a degree in astrophysics."

Rachel paced the confined space of their makeshift sanctuary, the recycled air thick with the scent of ozone and desperation. The encounter in the data nexus had been their first, terrifying, irrefutable brush with the Masters. But the 'proof' of that encounter was locked within their own consciousness, an experience too profound and alien to be captured by any conventional recording device. Even if they had secured a recording, its transmission would be fraught with peril, its authenticity questioned by a world deeply invested in maintaining its illusion of control. They needed more than just data; they needed an artifact, a broadcast, a phenomenon that bypassed all human and Vatican-controlled filters and directly impinged upon the collective consciousness.

"The data," Rachel said, her words echoing with a newfound conviction. "The vision they showed us. It was a simulation, an interpretation. But it was based on something. A historical record.

They have access to information, to the past, that we can only dream of. What if we could access a fragment of that raw, unadulterated data? Not their curated version, but the unfiltered stream of events as they unfolded. Something so monumental, so incontrovertible, that even the Masters couldn't spin it."

Benjamin's eyes widened, a flicker of understanding crossing his face. "You're talking about finding a temporal echo. A residual imprint of an event so significant that it left a mark not just on our planet, but on the fabric of spacetime itself. Something they *observed* firsthand, or perhaps even influenced, that predates their current 'harvest' protocol. Something that proves their awareness and manipulation of our history."

"Exactly," Rachel affirmed. "If we can find a verifiable, objectively recorded event that shows their direct or indirect involvement in shaping human civilization in a way that contradicts our accepted historical narrative, that would be proof. Not just of their existence, but of their ancient, ongoing interference. It would shatter the illusion of self-determination that governments and the Vatican rely on. It would be a beacon in the fog."

The challenge, however, remained immense. The data nexus had been a fleeting, almost hallucinatory experience. Recreating the conditions, or finding another access point, seemed an almost impossible task. What would such a 'temporal echo' even look like? How could they distinguish a genuine cosmic imprint from natural phenomena or historical misinterpretations?

Rachel pulled up at the Salty Siren. She whispered a small prayer. "Thank you, Dad, for not putting the internet in the Siren. No fancy restaurant equipment. They took orders in the old-fashioned way. There is not a single computer at the Siren. Now they had a quiet place to work, and that would leave no digital footprint.

Jasper leaned forward, his gaze sharpening. "If they're observers and manipulators, they'd be interested in key junctures. Moments of great societal shift, technological leaps, perhaps even the genesis of major belief systems. If we can pinpoint a period where our history diverged sharply from expected evolutionary paths, or where an unexplained leap in knowledge occurred, and if that divergence coincides with their observed presence, that could be our anchor."

"But how do we find that anchor?" Benjamin counters while pulling up databases of historical anomalies, unexplained archaeological finds, and contested scientific theories. "They have a subtle influence; they don't leave footprints; they guide the tides."

"Perhaps they leave something else," Rachel said, a new line of inquiry forming. She remembered the feeling of immense age, the overwhelming sense of cosmic perspective he'd experienced in the nexus. These were not beings who operated on human timescales. Their actions would be deliberate, patient, and likely to leave signatures that were subtle and overlooked by those focused on the immediate present. "Think about their technological signatures. The energy fluctuations, the gravitational distortions they might have caused when they first arrived, or at pivotal moments in our past. If we can correlate those with major historical shifts, with events that defy conventional explanation, we might find our proof."

Benjamin began cross-referencing seismic data with historical records of unexplained phenomena. He overlaid astronomical observations with archaeological timelines, looking for any anomalies that couldn't be explained by terrestrial or celestial mechanics alone. The process was painstaking, a needle-in-a-haystack search across millennia of human history and geological epochs. They were looking for a ghost in the machine of time, a whisper from the void that confirmed humanity was not, and had never been, alone, and that an unseen hand had guided their trajectory.

"The Sumerian civilization," Benjamin suddenly murmured, her eyes fixed on a complex graph. "There are theories, fringe theories, of course, about their rapid advancement. The sophisticated astronomical knowledge, the early development of writing, the complex societal structures that seemed to appear almost fully formed. Conventional explanations cite isolated genius or fortunate circumstances, but the jump is... statistically improbable, even for a cultural renaissance."

Rachel felt a prickle of anticipation. "And the energy signatures? The atmospheric anomalies? Is there anything correlated with that period?"

Benjamin pulled up spectral analysis logs from deep-earth probes, cross-referenced them with satellite imagery from decades ago, and even scoured declassified meteorological archives. "There are... faint, residual energy traces," he reported, her voice tinged with excitement. "Extremely faint, almost undetectable. Consistent with certain exotic particle decay patterns. And some highly anomalous, localized atmospheric sensing events were recorded in the region during that approximate period, events that were dismissed as optical illusions or rare weather phenomena."

"Or actively guiding it," Rachel said, the implication sending a shiver down her spine. "If they were seeding knowledge, accelerating development, that would explain the Sumerians' rapid rise. It would be an obvious demonstration of their long-term manipulation. The proof isn't just that they exist; it's that they've been meddling for millennia, shaping us into... whatever it is they intend to harvest."

The challenge now was to present this fragmented evidence to resonate. A few faint energy traces and some anomalous atmospheric distortions wouldn't be enough to convince a skeptical world, let alone the entrenched powers. They needed something more definitive, something that couldn't be explained away.

"We need to go deeper," Rachel declared, his gaze hardening with resolve. "The Sumerian period is a starting point. But if they've been influencing us for millennia, there must be other moments. Other divergences. We need to trace their footprints through history, find undeniable proof of their intervention at key junctures. Think of major technological leaps that seem to have appeared out of nowhere. The construction of ancient megaliths. The sudden emergence of complex philosophies or religions. These are the moments when the veil thins, where their influence might leave a more substantial mark."

He looked at Benjamin, his voice low and urgent. "Benjamin, focus your efforts on identifying these historical inflection points. Look for patterns, for correlations between unexplained advancements and the subtle energy signatures we've detected. Cross-reference with any anomalous astronomical events or geological activities that might have coincided. Jasper, I need you to assess our remaining secure communication channels. We need to broadcast this information once we have it to a network of trusted, independent journalists and scientists, bypassing traditional media and governmental gatekeepers. We're not just looking for proof anymore; we're preparing for a global unveiling. We need to shatter the narrative once and for all."

The urgency was palpable. The 'harvest' was no longer a distant threat; it was a meticulously orchestrated plan unfolding in real-time, disguised as global chaos. Their window to find irrefutable evidence, to compile a case that would resonate beyond the controlled narratives, was rapidly closing. They were no longer just trying to survive; they were fighting for humanity's right to self-determination, a fight that required not just courage, but undeniable, irrefutable truth. The Masters sought to cultivate a compliant crop, but Rachel was determined to show them that humanity, even in its current fractured state, possessed a spirit of defiance, a capacity for truth-seeking, that could not be so easily pruned or harvested. They had to find the cosmic smoking gun, a piece of evidence so profound that it would force the world to confront its true place in the universe, and the ancient, insidious hand that had been guiding its every step.

The raw data painted a terrifying picture, but data, even the most damning, could be spun, buried, or outright denied. Rachel knew this intimately, having spent years navigating the murky waters of intelligence and disinformation. The fractured narratives the Masters were weaving across the globe, manifesting as economic collapses, fabricated environmental crises, and amplified societal unrest, were evidence of their mastery of manipulation. Governments, already teetering on the brink of collapse, were complicit or too overwhelmed to discern the true orchestrator behind the curtain. The Vatican had a historical predisposition to control narratives and maintain its spiritual authority, which likely meant suppressing any evidence that contradicted their carefully constructed worldview, or worse, aligning with it for perceived future benefits. Possessing the intercepted transmissions or the analysis of anomalous patterns wouldn't be enough. It would be dismissed as a fringe conspiracy, state-sponsored propaganda, or the ramblings of a desperate few.

Rachel paced the confined space of their makeshift sanctuary, the recycled air thick with the scent of ozone and desperation. The encounter in the data nexus had been their first, terrifying, irrefutable brush with the Masters. But the 'proof' of that encounter was locked within their own consciousness, an experience too profound and alien to be captured by any conventional recording device. Even if they had secured a recording, its transmission would be fraught with peril, its authenticity questioned by a world deeply invested in maintaining its illusion of control. They needed more than just data; they needed an artifact, a broadcast, a phenomenon that bypassed all human and Vatican-controlled filters and directly impinged upon the collective consciousness.

"An artifact," Benjamin muses, his fingers hovering over a projection of the atmospheric anomalies. "What kind of artifact could withstand their influence, their ability to control information? And more importantly, what artifact could we even hope to get?"

"Not necessarily something they brought with them," Rachel countered, her mind racing through possibilities. "Think about their modus operandi. They're not a conquering force in the traditional sense. They're gardeners, cultivators. It's their job to manipulate the environment, the species. What if the proof isn't an alien weapon, or a crashed ship, but something *they've* been manipulated *by*? Or something they've inadvertently left behind that serves as a marker of their presence, a scar on reality that even they can't erase?"

She stopped pacing, a sudden thought igniting a spark of fierce hope. The 'Masters' had shown them a vision, a projection of humanity's history, vast and complex, yet presented with a dispassionate, almost clinical overview. It was as if they were reviewing a historical record, cataloging events with an objective detachment that transcended human emotion. But what if that record wasn't entirely accurate? What if their interpretation of history, their curated narrative of human evolution and societal development, was flawed?

"The data nexus," Rachel said, the words echoing with a newfound conviction. "The vision they showed us. It was a simulation, an interpretation. But it was based on something. A historical record. They have access to information, to the past, that we can only dream of. What if we could access a fragment of that raw, unadulterated data? Not their curated version, but the unfiltered stream of events as they unfolded. Something so monumental, so incontrovertible, that even the Masters couldn't spin it."

Benjamin's eyes widened, a flicker of understanding crossing his face. "You're talking about finding an echo. A residual imprint of an event so significant that it left a mark not just on our planet, but on the fabric of spacetime itself. Something they *observed* firsthand, or perhaps even influenced, that predates their current 'harvest' protocol. Something that proves their awareness and manipulation of our history."

"Exactly," Rachel affirmed. "If we can find a verifiable, objectively recorded event that shows their direct or indirect involvement in shaping human civilization in a way that contradicts our accepted historical narrative, that would be proof. Not just of their existence, but of their ancient, ongoing interference. It would shatter the illusion of self-determination that governments and the Vatican rely on. It would be a beacon in the fog."

The challenge, however, remained immense. The data nexus had been a fleeting, almost hallucinatory experience. Recreating the conditions, or finding another access point, seemed an almost impossible task. What would such a 'temporal echo' even look like? How could they distinguish a genuine cosmic imprint from natural phenomena or historical misinterpretations?

"Perhaps they leave something else," Rachel said, a new line of inquiry forming. She remembered the feeling of immense age, the overwhelming sense of cosmic perspective she'd experienced in the nexus. These were not beings who operated on human timescales. Their actions would be deliberate, patient, and likely to leave signatures that were subtle and overlooked by those focused on the immediate present. "Think about their technological signatures. The energy fluctuations, the gravitational distortions they might have caused when they first arrived, or at pivotal moments in our past. If we can correlate those with major historical shifts, with events that defy conventional explanation, we might find our proof."

Benjamin began cross-referencing seismic data with historical records of unexplained phenomena. He overlaid astronomical observations with archaeological timelines, looking for any anomalies that couldn't be explained by terrestrial or celestial mechanics alone. The process was painstaking, a needle-in-a-haystack search across millennia of human history and geological epochs. They were looking for a ghost in the machine of time, a whisper from the void that confirmed humanity was not, and had never been, alone, and that an unseen hand had guided their trajectory.

"The Sumerian civilization," Benjamin suddenly murmured, his eyes fixed on a complex graph. "There are theories, fringe theories, of course, about their rapid advancement. The sophisticated astronomical knowledge, the early development of writing, the complex societal structures that seemed to appear almost fully formed. Conventional explanations cite isolated genius or fortunate circumstances, but the jump is... statistically improbable, even for a cultural renaissance."

Rachel felt a prickle of anticipation. "And the energy signatures? The atmospheric anomalies? Is there anything correlated with that period?"

Benjamin pulled up spectral analysis logs from deep-earth probes, cross-referenced them with satellite imagery from decades ago, and even scoured declassified meteorological archives. "There are... faint, residual energy traces," he reported, his voice tinged with excitement. "Extremely faint, almost undetectable. Consistent with certain exotic particle decay patterns. And some highly anomalous, localized atmospheric sensing events were recorded in the region during that approximate period, events that were dismissed as optical illusions or rare weather phenomena at the time."

Jasper whistled softly. "So, they were there back then? Watching the beginning stages of civilization?"

"Or actively guiding it," Rachel said, the implication sending a shiver down her spine. "If they were seeding knowledge, accelerating development, that would explain the Sumerians' rapid rise. It would be a simple demonstration of their long-term manipulation. The proof isn't just that they exist; it's that they've been meddling for millennia, shaping us into… whatever it is they intend to harvest."

The challenge now was to present this fragmented evidence to resonate. A few faint energy traces and some anomalous atmospheric distortions wouldn't be enough to convince a skeptical world, let alone the entrenched powers. They needed something more definitive, something that couldn't be explained away.

"We need to go deeper," Rachel declared, her gaze hardening with resolve. "The Sumerian period is a starting point. But if they've been influencing us for millennia, there must be other moments. Other divergences. We need to trace their footprints through history, find undeniable proof of their intervention at key junctures. Think of major technological leaps that seem to have appeared out of nowhere. The construction of ancient megaliths. The sudden emergence of complex philosophies or religions. These are the moments when the veil thins, where their influence might leave a more substantial mark."

He looked at Benjamin, his voice low and urgent. "Benjamin, focus your efforts on identifying these historical inflection points. Look for patterns, for correlations between unexplained advancements and the subtle energy signatures we've detected. Cross-reference with any anomalous astronomical events or geological activities that might have coincided. Jasper, I need you to assess our remaining secure communication channels. We need to broadcast this information once we have it to a network of trusted, independent journalists and scientists, bypassing traditional media and governmental gatekeepers. We're not just looking for proof anymore; we're preparing for a global unveiling. We need to shatter the narrative once and for all."

The urgency was palpable. The 'harvest' was no longer a distant threat; it was a meticulously orchestrated plan unfolding in real-time, disguised as global chaos. Their window to find irrefutable evidence, to compile a case that would resonate beyond the controlled narratives, was rapidly closing. They were no longer just trying to survive; they were fighting for humanity's right to self-determination, a fight that required not just courage, but undeniable, irrefutable truth. The Masters sought to cultivate a compliant crop, but Rachel was determined to show them that humanity, even in its current fractured state, possessed a spirit of defiance, a capacity for truth-seeking, that could not be so easily pruned or harvested. They had to find the cosmic smoking gun, a piece of evidence so profound that it would force the world to confront its true place in the universe and the ancient, insidious hand that had been guiding its every step.

The analysis of the Sumerian period, though tantalizing, was merely a whisper in the cacophony of the Masters' grand deception. Rachel knew they needed more than faint energy traces and dismissed atmospheric anomalies. They needed the roar of undeniable proof, a deafening testament to humanity's manipulated past. The holographic display, still shimmering with data points from ancient Mesopotamia, seemed to mock their efforts. It was a breadcrumb, not the feast of evidence they required.

"The Sumerian connection is promising, but it's ancient history," Benjamin stated, her voice tight with the ever-present strain. "The Masters are still active. Their current harvesting operation… it's happening *now*. If we can find evidence of their past interventions, imagine what we might uncover by observing their present activities. Where are they *now*? What are they *doing*?"

Jasper looked up, his brow sweating. "We've been chasing ghosts across millennia. Ghosts that might be echoes of their presence but not the living, breathing threat they represent today. The data from the initial probe of Area 291… it was incomplete. Fragmentary. We barely scratched the surface of those submerged structures. What if the primary archive, the unedited, uncorrupted record, is still down there?"

"The archive," Rachel echoed, the word a low rumble in the confined space. "If the Masters are meticulous record-keepers, as their historical interventions suggested, then the heart of their operation, the central hub for their current global 'harvest,' must be at. The epicenter of their most significant Earth-based operations. Area 291 is the logical nexus."

Benjamin was already pulling up the schematics of the submerged structures. "The initial scans were inconclusive. Significant interference, powerful localized energy fields that jammed the sensors. We got a snapshot of the external architecture, the unusual metallic alloys, and the non-terrestrial geometry. But the internal layout... it remained largely a mystery. We detected a massive energy signature emanating from its core, far exceeding anything we'd encountered before."

"And if they are actively managing the harvest," Jasper mused, "then this nexus is likely a live data stream. We might not just find historical records; we might witness their current manipulation in real-time. Imagine capturing raw footage of the harvest protocol, the energy siphoning, the psychological conditioning—all of it, unfiltered."

The thought sent an icy dread through Rachel, but also a surge of adrenaline. To witness it, to record it, to broadcast it—that was their goal. Not just to prove the Masters' existence, but to expose the brutal reality of their dominion.

"We need to be prepared for anything," Rachel stated, his voice hardening. "The drone is our primary tool for data acquisition, but we also need a plan for direct engagement, however unlikely that may be. The deeper we go, the more dangerous it becomes. They've been here for a very long time. They know this territory better than we ever will."

"Our submersible's weapons systems are limited," Benjamin pointed out. "They're designed for defense, not offense. Especially not against technology as advanced as what we encountered last time. The energy pulses we detected... they could disable our primary propulsion system in seconds."

Rachel looked at Benjamin, then at Jasper. "This is the most critical mission we've undertaken. Failure has catastrophic implications. The Masters are merging their control. The global chaos is escalating. If we don't expose them now, if we don't find the definitive proof within that submerged archive, humanity will be nothing more than a farmed commodity. We have to succeed."

"Benjamin, Jasper," Rachel's voice, tensed, held a new urgency, "we can't go back to Area 291 as we are. The drone is our best bet for data retrieval, but its range is limited, and interference is a significant threat. And our submersible, while reinforced, is still vulnerable to active countermeasures. We need to expand our toolkit and perhaps our personnel."

Benjamin nodded without looking up. "The energy-dampening fields were the primary obstacle. However, they designed Jasper's upgrades for passive interference, which is promising. If the Masters employ active jamming or directed energy weapons, the drone's current shielding will be insufficient. And the submersible's cloaking is only effective against passive detection; it won't mask us from a deliberate scan or an energy sweep."

Jasper chimed in, "We've also been experiencing persistent network intrusions. Sophisticated, designed to look like standard traffic. They're probing, testing our digital defenses. If they can breach our systems, they can expect our moves, and more importantly, they can locate Area 291 with pinpoint accuracy. We need a more robust firewall and a way to disrupt their reconnaissance.

Rachel leaned back, her eyes scanning the holographic display that depicted the intricate, alien geometry of the submerged structures. "This isn't a battle we can win alone. The Masters have been operating with impunity for millennia. They have embedded themselves so deeply into our world that they are practically invisible. We're like fleas on a whale, trying to understand the ocean. We need to find others who understand the whale, or at least, know how to spot it."

The word "allies" hung in the air, a tantalizing yet dangerous prospect. In their line of work, trust was a commodity rarer than unobtanium. The Masters' influence was so pervasive that even those who might suspect the truth were silenced, manipulated, or simply too afraid to speak out. But desperation was a powerful catalyst.

"Reactivating 'The Nautilus'," Rachel mused, the name a phantom from their past, a whispered legend among a select few. "That was always the contingency, wasn't it? A deep-sea exploration vessel with capabilities far beyond anything we currently possess. But it's been offline for years, its location a closely guarded secret, and its reactivation would be an enormous undertaking. The risks involved…"

"Are considerable," Benjamin finished for her. "The energy signature required to power it, the retrieval of its specialized crew, if any are still alive and willing… it would draw attention. This is the kind of attention we cannot afford right now. We're trying to be discreet, Rachel."

A plan was coalescing, a dangerous but plausible strategy emerging from the chaos. But it relied on a cascade of successful operations, each step a potential point of failure. The digital reconnaissance, the drone modifications, the submersible's enhanced sensors, the delicate dance of bypassing alien defenses, and finally, the daring cyber-intrusion. Area 291 conceals the truth about the Masters and their pact with humanity. And we cannot let it remain buried forever." Rachel was determined.

The weight of their undertaking settled upon them again, heavier this time, imbued with the added burden of building an arsenal, both digital and physical, and seeking the elusive echoes of potential allies. They were not just a team anymore; they were the resistance, arming themselves against an ancient, unseen enemy.

The race against time had just entered a new, more perilous phase. They had to gather their tools, their resources, and perhaps their allies before the Masters completed their next devastating harvest. The silence of the depths was still their target, but now, the strategy to breach it was far more complex, far more dangerous, and far more dependent on the hidden strengths they could unearth, both within their own capabilities and from the world at large. The fight for humanity's narrative was about to escalate, and they were desperately trying to ensure they had the weapons to win it.

CHAPTER 10

THE MASTERS

The decision was made to go back undersea. There was a lot of work to do. They could not pick-up the phone and explain what is happening off the cost of California. The Luminaries and the Guardians knew their activities and there was no doubt the Guardians would take them out using the Luminaries technology.

A shift occurred in the mobile command center's hum. The frantic external anxieties were still there, a low thrum beneath the surface, but the immediate focus had coalesced into something sharper, more dangerous. The pronouncements of global collapse were still blaring from the screens, but they were now merely the cacophony against which a singular, desperate plan was being forged. Rachel's quiet resolve, Benjamin's calculated efficiency, and Jasper's grim determination had converted into a singular, perilous imperative: they had to go back. Back to the crushing, unfathomable darkness beneath the waves. Back to Area 291.

Benjamin nodded, his eyes already scanning schematics that materialized on his personal display. "The original plan was to conduct limited incursions, gather intelligence, and retreat. However, the incursions assumed we had more time and could afford a more cautious approach. The escalating global crises they've engineered have stripped us of that luxury. They've created a smokescreen so dense, so all-encompassing, that direct action is now the only viable path."

Jasper chimed in. "The energy signatures around Area 291 are indeed intensifying, as Benjamin noted. It suggests a greater power draw, an increased operational tempo. It's their systems preparing for a final deployment, or… the archive itself is becoming more accessible, perhaps even actively responding to their imminent timetable. Either way, it's a signal that the window is closing, and rapidly."

"And our current assets," Rachel continued, her gaze sweeping over the room as if assessing every piece of equipment, every member of their small, beleaguered team, "are insufficient for a mission of this magnitude and urgency. Our reconnaissance drones, while advanced, are too easily detected, too limited in capacity for the data we need. Our analysis of the Masters' communications, while ongoing, remains a monumental task given their quantum encryption. We need a direct conduit, a deep-sea platform capable of sustained operations within their zone of influence."

Her gaze settled on Jasper. "The submersible. Jasper, your craft. It's our best, perhaps our only, option."

Jasper met Rachel's gaze, a flicker of something unreadable in his eyes—a mixture of apprehension, pride, and a deep-seated concern for his creation. "The Nautilus. Jasper designed it for extreme depths, and for extended autonomous missions. Its stealth capabilities are unparalleled; its sensor suite is among the most advanced ever developed. But… it's been compromised."

Benjamin's head snaps up. "Compromised? How? We thought someone simply disabled and hid it.

"Disabled, yes. Hidden, perhaps. But 'compromised' suggests more than just a temporary malfunction or a strategic concealment," Jasper explained, his voice taking on a more analytical, though no less urgent, tone. "When I attempted to access its diagnostic logs remotely prior to its disappearance, I found… irregularities." Falsified data streams, encrypted sub-routines that were not part of its original programming, and evidence of attempted system overrides that went far beyond simple sabotage. It was as if someone had been trying both to disable it and then… reassert control. Or perhaps, to erase specific elements of its mission profile."

Rachel leaned forward, his gaze intensifying. "The Masters. They knew you were developing it, its potential. They would have seen it as a threat, an anomaly they needed to neutralize. If they attempted to control it, to weaponize it, or even just to access its capabilities for their own purposes…"

"Precisely," Jasper confirmed. "They didn't just want it out of commission; they wanted to understand it, or worse, to repurpose it. The systems I designed for its deep-sea resilience, its unique propulsion signature, its ability to navigate the extreme pressures of the abyssal plains—these are all things that would significantly interest them. They could have been trying to extract its technological secrets, or to integrate its capabilities into their own clandestine operations."

Jasper tapped a few commands into his console. A holographic map of the Pacific formed, overlaid with cryptic markers. "Its last known transmission pinged from a deep-sea trench, approximately 800 kilometers off the coast of an uninhabited archipelago. It was a 'dead man's switch' protocol I embedded, designed to activate only in the event of total system failure or prolonged external interference. It transmitted a low-power distress signal and then entered a dormant state, masking its signature. They clearly intercepted that signal, or its proximity, because they responded with the EMP. But they didn't find it. Or perhaps they found it, couldn't fully disable it, and left it as a decoy or a trap."

Rachel considered the implications. This was not a simple recovery; it was a deep-sea salvage operation, a clandestine reactivation, and a race against time, all conducted under the shadow of an omnipresent, technologically superior enemy. Jasper, this goes beyond equipment repair. This is about reactivating our most powerful tool. It's about reclaiming a strategic advantage. We need to be prepared for the possibility that the Masters may have left something behind within The Nautilus itself—a beacon, a tracking device, a listening post."

Jasper paled slightly. "I've considered that. The EMP burst that disabled the navigation array was also designed to disrupt sensitive electronics. If they planted a tracker, it's likely they would have attempted to mask it within that surge. But I have developed a series of resonance scanners designed to detect anomalous energy signatures at specific frequencies. These scanners will find anything hidden within the Nautilus. It will be part of the initial diagnostic sweep. We will strip it down, piece by piece, until we are absolutely certain it is clean."

Benjamin brought up a new set of projections—submersibles, deep-sea drones, and the limited range of their current fleet. "Our current submersible cannot reach that depth. Its operational ceiling is significantly lower than the Nautilus's design. We need a vessel that can support a mission of this magnitude, a vessel that can transport the equipment, personnel, and sustained power for the reactivation process."

Rachel's gaze swept over their limited resources. The mobile command center, while advanced, was not a deep-sea exploration craft. They were a team of analysts, strategists, and a brilliant, if somewhat unorthodox, scientist. "We need a mother-ship," he stated, his voice firm. "A larger, more capable vessel that can serve as our primary platform. It needs to deploy the repair and diagnostic equipment, and to provide a secure environment for Jasper to work. And it needs to operate within hostile waters without detection."

Benjamin was trying to solve this puzzle. "There's the 'Triton.' It's an old research vessel, decommissioned but still theoretically operational. They designed it for extended oceanographic surveys in extreme environments. It's slow, but it's stealthy, and it has the cargo capacity and power generation capabilities. We could outfit it with the repair bay, the fabrication unit, and the resonance scanners."

"And its operational history?" Rachel inquired.

"Its last known deployment was several years ago, conducting research in the Arctic. The Navy officially retired it because of budget cuts, but reported its hull integrity as excellent. We could gain it through… less conventional channels," Benjamin said, a hint of a smirk playing on his lips. "It would require careful planning and a significant amount of diversionary activity, but it's workable."

Jasper nodded, the pieces beginning to fall into place. "If we can get The Nautilus to a secure location where we can perform the repairs and data extraction, the 'Triton' would be ideal. It could act as a mobile workshop, allowing me to rebuild the comms system and bypass the Masters' modifications without the constant threat of immediate discovery."

"The risk, however, remains considerable," Rachel interjected, her tone sober. "The Masters are aware of our existence. They are aware of our aim. If they believe we are actively pursuing the archive, they will escalate their countermeasures. They will increase their surveillance, deploy their own deep-sea assets, and potentially start direct engagement."

"Which is why stealth is paramount," Benjamin emphasized. "The 'Triton,' despite its size, has a surprisingly low thermal and acoustic signature. We can change its propulsion systems to minimize detection. And its operational range, while not as extensive as a military vessel, would allow us to approach the target area without raising immediate alarms. Once we locate the Nautilus, we can deploy the Nautilus itself, a true stealth operative, to retrieve its own systems and bring them aboard the Triton for repairs."

Jasper, however, still had reservations. "Retrieving The Nautilus... it's a delicate operation. Towing or lifting it by a larger vessel poses a significant risk of further damage to its hull, especially given its existing vulnerabilities, as its hull is not designed for such stresses. It would be far more efficient, and safer, if I could perform the initial reactivation and data extraction while it remains in its current location."

"And risk immediate detection by any Masters' assets in the vicinity?" Rachel counters. "If they discover us attempting to reactivate it in situ, they will converge. We need to extract it, bring it to a secure environment where we can work undisturbed. The Triton provides that environment. We will devise a method for secure transfer, Jasper. Perhaps a specialized cradle or containment unit, designed to minimize stress on the hull."

"The fabrication unit on the Triton," Benjamin muses, his mind already working on solutions. "We can design and build a cradle capable of housing and transporting the Nautilus safely. It will need to handle the immense pressures of the deep, even if we only need to bring it to a certain depth for the transfer. It's an engineering challenge, but one that our resources can meet."

"Every crisis they engineer, every moment of fear they amplify, is a step towards their goal," Rachel added. "They are not merely waiting for us to falter; they are actively pushing us towards collapse. They are creating the conditions for their own dominance, a world so fractured and desperate that it will readily accept their sterile, ordered control. We are not just fighting their technology; we are fighting their narrative."

Rachel nodded, the logistical complexities of the mission weighing on her. "Which is precisely why the 'Triton' is essential. It will provide a controlled environment. Once we have 'The Nautilus' aboard, you'll have the resources you need to restore its functionality. But we must proceed with the utmost caution. The Masters are not passive observers. If they detect our movements, they will respond. And their response will not be subtle."

The decision to proceed with the reactivation of 'The Nautilus' was a calculated gamble, a bold stroke born of desperation and a profound understanding of the stakes involved. It was a commitment to venturing into the heart of the enemy's operational territory, armed with a compromised, but potentially invaluable, asset. The abyss, once a symbol of mystery and scientific exploration, had become a battleground, and 'The Nautilus,' once a vessel of discovery, was now their only hope of unraveling the labyrinthine plot that threatened to consume humanity. Soon, the journey back into the crushing darkness would begin.

'Triton's' hull groaned, an indistinct sound that revealed years of silence and an unscheduled awakening. It was less a ship and more a leviathan stirred from a deep-sea slumber, its massive frame now housing a hive of activity. The transformation of a decommissioned research vessel into a covert deep-sea command center was a testament to Benjamin's almost supernatural ability to bend bureaucratic systems and technical limitations to his will. Scaffolding snaked across its cavernous hangar bay, illuminating the skeletal remains of 'The Nautilus' with diagnostic lamps, meticulously positioning them. The air thrummed with the upgraded hum of auxiliary power cores, their output carefully managed by Jasper's intricate bypass systems, each capacitor bank a testament to his genius and their desperate need.

The preliminary scans are... less than encouraging," Jasper announced, his voice a low murmur that barely cut through the cacophony of the repair bay. He gestured to a holographic display showing a series of complex schematics overlaid with a disturbing array of red indicators. "The Masters didn't just disable 'The Nautilus'; they started a cascade of micro-fractures within its primary propulsion manifold. They're minuscule, almost imperceptible to standard diagnostics, but under extreme pressure, they could lead to catastrophic failure. It's like they were trying to cripple it slowly, ensuring it would implode rather than simply cease to function." He ran a hand through his already disheveled hair; his gaze fixed on the intricate patterns of stress fractures. "Replicating the original manifold's molecular structure with the fabrication unit will be a significant challenge. The alloys needed are incredibly specialized, designed for deep-sea resilience. Standard synthesized materials won't withstand the pressures."

Benjamin brought up a distinct set of data. "I've been cross-referencing the materials science databases. There are some theoretical alloys that, while not explicitly designed for submersibles, exhibit similar tensile strength and resistance to hydrostatic pressure. They're experimental, primarily used in deep-crust geological sampling probes. It'll require a higher energy input for the fabrication process, and the resulting material might have... subtle variations in its electromagnetic signature. But it's our best chance."

"Subtle variations can be our undoing," Jasper counters, the inherent caution of a creator reasserting itself. "If their surveillance detects even the faintest anomaly, they'll expose us before we reach Area 291." We're not just navigating a physical labyrinth; we're navigating a minefield of its detection grids. Every system, every component, must be indistinguishable from its original design, or it must be completely undetectable."

The journey back to Area 291 was not a direct transit; it was a serpentine ballet of evasion. The 'Triton,' despite its enhanced stealth capabilities, was still a vessel of considerable size. Navigating the ocean's surface, even under the cloak of perpetual twilight and the cover of increasingly frequent, and ostensibly natural, storm systems, was a precarious act. Benjamin had orchestrated a symphony of misdirection, fabricating distress signals from other, far-off vessels, spoofing transponder signals, and even generating phantom sonar contacts to draw potential patrols away from their path.

"We're approaching the outer perimeter of their known surveillance network," Benjamin announced, his voice tight with concentration. The bridge of the 'Triton' was a stark contrast to the utilitarian chaos of the hangar bay, a command center humming with sophisticated displays and the quiet efficiency of its crew of three. "A series of deep-sea sensor arrays is triangulating our projected trajectory. They're designed to detect anomalies in water temperature, pressure, and acoustic signatures. Standard deep-sea vessels have a significant thermal and acoustic footprint, but... the 'Triton's' changed propulsion system is minimizing that. Still, we can't afford to linger."

Jasper pointed to a series of swirling patterns. "They're using bio-luminescent organisms, genetically engineered or perhaps even naturally occurring, to create a living sonar net. The patterns are complex, designed to mimic natural plankton blooms, but there are subtle, almost imperceptible, harmonic resonances that betray their artificial nature. My acoustic sensors are picking them up, but they're incredibly difficult to differentiate from the background noise of the deep."

"How do we thread that needle, Jasper?" Rachel asked, her gaze fixed on the illuminated map, his mind already picturing the crushing depths.

"Unconventional methods," Jasper replied, a glint in his eye. He tapped a sequence of commands, and an extra layer of data appeared on the screen. "The Masters' technology detects predictable patterns, deviations from the norm. They expect ships to move in straight lines, to follow charted courses. We need to behave like the ocean itself. I've been studying the migration patterns of deep-sea cephalopods and certain species of whales. Their routes are not linear; currents dictated them, by prey availability, by complex biological imperatives. We need to mimic that erratic, instinctual movement."

He piloted the 'Triton' not on a direct course, but through a series of calculated, almost organic, maneuvers. The massive vessel would drift, seemingly aimlessly, only to surge forward in a sudden burst of controlled thrust, weaving through perceived gaps in the sensor net. It was a dance of desperation, each maneuver requiring precise calculations of current flow, pressure differentials, and the predicted response times of the Masters' surveillance systems.

"Their drones are becoming more prevalent," Benjamin reported, his voice strained. "We're detecting multiple signatures, small, agile craft designed for deep-sea reconnaissance. They're not directly observing us, not yet, but they're mapping the area, probing for any deviation from the expected environmental parameters. They're like a swarm of metallic gnats, and they're getting closer."

Jasper adjusted his approach, guiding the 'Triton' into a deep thermal vent field. The extreme temperature gradients and volatile chemical signatures of the vents masked their own thermal and acoustic output, creating a temporary blind spot. "These vents are a double-edged sword," he explained. "They provide excellent cover, but they're also incredibly unpredictable. A sudden eruption could rupture the 'Triton's' hull, or worse, create a massive energy surge that would betray our presence to their most sensitive instruments."

The tension in the bridge was palpable. Each kilometer gained was hard won, a victory against an unseen enemy that seemed to expect their every move. The Masters were not just a technological force; they were a force that understood the ocean's complexities, its hidden currents, its crushing pressures, and they had weaponized that knowledge.

Jasper grimace. "Those aren't standard sonic pulses. They're using modulated frequencies that resonate with the specific alloys of the 'Triton's' hull. It's a sophisticated form of acoustic echolocation, designed to pinpoint any structural irregularities. This is where the experimental alloys Benjamin sourced become a liability. While they offer strength, their unique resonance might be exactly what the Masters are looking for."

"The technical maneuvers of getting the Nautilus and the Triton down to Area 291 required enough science to make the head spin." Rachel pondered.

"Not directly," Jasper admitted. "We can't alter the fundamental resonance of the hull. But we can try to overwhelm their system. I've been jury-rigging a series of broadband sonic emitters designed to flood their sensors with so much conflicting data that their triangulation becomes impossible. It's a brute-force approach, and it will draw attention, but it might buy us the time we need to slip through their net."

The 'Triton' emitted a series of low-frequency thrums, a sound that vibrated through the deck plates and into the very bones of the crew. On the displays, the intricate patterns of the Masters' sonic probes distorted, breaking apart into a chaotic jumble of readings.

"It's working," Benjamin breathed, a flicker of relief in his eyes. "Their targeting is destabilizing. They're not receiving clear readings anymore."

But their temporary respite was short-lived. The disruption of the sonic net had not gone unnoticed. "Increased drone activity," Benjamin reported, his voice tight again. "Multiple contact signatures converging on our position. They've triangulated our general location based on the sonic anomaly. They know we're here."

Jasper's jaw tightened. "They're likely deploying their own submersibles now, faster and more agile than our drones. Area 291 is a critical nexus for their operations; they won't let us approach it unopposed." He pointed to a section of the map, a deep canyon that plunged into impenetrable darkness. "We need to go deeper. The pressure down there is immense, far beyond the operational limits of most conventional submersibles. But it was designed for 'The Nautilus'. If we can reach that trench, we might use its abyssal depths as cover."

"The 'Triton' can escort us to the edge of the trench," Rachel stated, her voice resolute. "But it cannot descend into it. The pressure will be too great. That's where 'The Nautilus' must take over. Jasper, are you confident we can pilot it through that descent, even in its compromised state?" Rachel was wrapping her arms around herself to block out the deep-water chill. The heat doesn't work very well at these depths, Rachel thought.

Jasper looked at the holographic representation of 'The Nautilus,' now a fragile, intricate web of newly fabricated components and salvaged systems. He pictured the unknown dangers lurking in the crushing darkness, the possibility of their own creation being the instrument of their demise. "Confidence is a luxury we cannot afford," he said, his voice steady despite the immense weight of the question. "But I have designed that vessel to withstand the impossible. We will descend. And we will reach Area 291. We are about to walk into the labyrinth's heart. The 'Triton' slowed and dimmed its lights as they readied 'The Nautilus' for its solitary descent into the abyss' crushing maw. The gauntlet had truly begun.

The abyss's crushing embrace prevailed. Each meter 'The Nautilus' descended was a testament to its reinforced hull and Jasper's meticulous engineering, yet it was also a constant reminder of the unforgiving environment they were now venturing into. The 'Triton,' a behemoth of human ingenuity, had deposited them at the precipice of the trench, its own operational limits reached by the sheer, overwhelming pressure. Now, only 'The Nautilus,' a ghost of alien design retrofitted with desperate human ambition, could navigate the true depths.

"The water pressure is exceeding initial projections," Jasper's voice crackled through the comms, strained but steady. His fingers danced across the controls; his gaze locked on the multitude of readouts that painted a grim picture of their descent. "We're at Mach 1.7 on the pressure gauge, and it's still climbing. The hull integrity is holding, but there's a… subtle harmonic distortion emanating from the starboard quadrant. It's within tolerance, but it's definitely there."

Benjamin's voice, usually calm and commanding, held an unfamiliar edge of tension. "Subtle is relative down here, Jasper. Can you identify the source?"

"I'm trying," Jasper replied, his brow furrowed in concentration. "It's not a structural anomaly from the fabrication. It's… external. Almost as if something is applying localized pressure to the hull. But there's nothing on the external sensors."

Rachel, positioned at the tactical display, scanned the dark, featureless expanse outside their viewport, a void that swallowed the feeble glow of their external lights. "At these depths, the external sensors are notoriously limited." The pressure itself can distort readings, let alone any actual interference. "She tapped a symbol on her screen. "We're picking up faint energy signatures. Irregular pulses, not consistent with any known geological or biological activity. They're… deliberate."

"Deliberate is the operative word," Benjamin stated, his eyes fixed on a different array of readings. "They know we're coming. Or at least, they know *something* is descending into their domain. These aren't just passive sensors; they're active probes. They're trying to get a lock on us."

Jasper adjusted the 'Nautilus's' trajectory, weaving the submersible through an unseen current. "I'm attempting to mask our thermal signature by mimicking the ambient temperature of the surrounding water. It's a delicate balance; too much deviation and we become a beacon, too little and we risk being crushed by unseen thermal gradients." He paused, his voice dropping slightly. "There's a new signature appearing, Benjamin. It's coalescing. And it's moving towards us."

On Rachel's display, a faint, swirling pattern resolved itself, emanating from the darkness ahead. It wasn't a distinct shape, but a disturbance in the abyss's fabric, like a ripple in a cosmic ocean. "It's a localized gravitational anomaly," Rachel reported, his voice hushed. "Highly focused. They're manipulating spacetime, Benjamin. Not just using the ocean as a barrier, but as a weapon."

"Gravitational lensing?" Benjamin muses, his mind racing. "If they can bend spacetime, they might distort our perception, disorient us, or even pull us off course. Jasper, can you compensate?"

"I'm trying to counteract the gravitational pull by adjusting our thrust vectors and ballast, but it's like trying to swim against a tsunami," Jasper replied, his knuckles white on the controls. "The anomaly is localized, but it spreads its influence," he said. It's affecting the 'Nautilus's' internal systems. Power fluctuations are becoming more frequent. The life support is drawing more energy than it should."

Suddenly, a deep, resonant hum vibrated through the hull of 'The Nautilus,' a sound that seemed to bypass their auditory sensors and resonate directly within their bones. It was not the groan of stressed metal, but a coherent, almost melodic frequency.

"What was that?" Rachel demands, her hand instinctively reaching for her sidearm, a futile gesture in the face of such alien power.

"It's… a sonic weapon," Jasper stammers, his eyes wide with a mixture of terror and awe. "But not like anything we've ever encountered. It's not a concussive blast; it's a resonant frequency. It's designed to disrupt molecular bonds. They're not trying to break our hull; they're trying to unravel us, atom by atom."

Benjamin's mind worked at lightning speed. "Jasper, can you identify the frequency?"

"I'm getting multiple harmonic overlaps," Jasper replied, his fingers flying across his console. "It's a complex waveform. But there are… sub-harmonics. If I can isolate them, I might generate a counter-frequency. It's a long shot, and it will require a significant energy expenditure. We'll have to reroute auxiliary power from non-essential systems. That includes the primary navigation suite."

"Meaning we'll be blind if your counter-frequency fails," Rachel stated, her gaze unwavering.

"Precisely," Jasper confirmed, his face grim. "But the alternative is disintegration. We have to try."

He started the process, a low whine building within the submersible as power conduits surged with a redirected, desperate energy. As the external hum intensified, the vibration within the hull became almost unbearable. On the tactical display, the swirling gravitational anomaly flickered, as if struggling against an unseen force.

"It's working!" Jasper exclaimed, a surge of adrenaline momentarily overcoming his fear. "The counter-frequency is disrupting their sonic attack. They're pulling back."

The oppressive hum receded, leaving behind an unsettling silence. The gravitational anomaly on Rachel's display dissipated, shrinking back into the darkness from which it had emerged. But the reprieve was short-lived.

"Another anomaly detected," Rachel announced, her voice flat. "This one is different. It's mobile. And it's fast."

A series of sharp, metallic clicks echoed through the submersible, far too rapid and precise to be natural. Then, the viewport was momentarily illuminated by a blinding flash of cerulean light, followed by a violent lurch that threw them against their restraints.

"Impact!" Jasper yelled, wrestling with the controls. "Multiple impacts! They're not drones, Benjamin. They're… something else. Swarming. And they're armed."

On the external cameras, now flickering and distorted, they could glimpse them: swift, darting shapes, no larger than a human fist, their metallic bodies glinting in the intermittent flashes of their own weaponry. They moved with unnerving insectoid precision, their attacks coordinated and relentless.

"Automated attack craft," Benjamin deduced, his voice tight. "Designed for deep-sea saturation. They're using a directed energy weapon, narrow-beam, high-frequency. It's designed to penetrate our hull plating without causing immediate catastrophic failure, but to cause internal damage. It's a surgical approach to destruction."

"They're overwhelming our shielding," Jasper reported, his breath coming in ragged gasps. "The energy output is too high. We can't sustain this for long."

"We need to find cover," Rachel urged, scanning the sonar for any geological features. "A cave, a fissure… anything that can block their line of sight."

Jasper pointed to a section of the trench wall on his display. "There! A thermal vent field deeper down. The heat and chemical signatures should mask us. But the currents are highly volatile. It's incredibly dangerous."

"It's our only chance," Benjamin decided. "Jasper, take us in. Full evasive maneuver. Rachel, monitor those swarmers. See if you can predict their attack vectors."

The 'Nautilus' plunged deeper, the swarmers relentlessly pursuing. The submersible weaved and dodged, Jasper's piloting a desperate ballet against overwhelming odds. Each near miss sent shudders through the hull. The cerulean flashes of the swarmer weapons illuminated their path, painting fleeting, terrifying patterns on the abyssal darkness.

"They're adapting," Rachel reported grimly. "They're predicting our evasive maneuvers. We are being flanked by them."

"I'm losing power to the starboard thrusters!" Jasper cries out. "Direct hit! They've compromised a crucial system."

The submersible listed, its descent becoming uncontrolled. The heat and chemical signatures of the vent field grew stronger on their sensors, a desperate beacon in the encroaching darkness.

"We're going in too fast!" Jasper shouted, fighting the controls. "We won't survive the impact with the vent structures!"

Benjamin's eyes narrowed, a fierce determination burning within them. "Jasper, focus on maintaining hull integrity. Rachel, scan for any immediate structural weaknesses in the vent field we can exploit. We need to force an entry, not crash."

Rachel's fingers flew across his console. "There! A large fissure, partially obscured by a plume of super-heated water. It might offer some protection, but the current within it is extreme."

"It's our only option," Jasper agreed, his voice strained. With a burst of controlled desperation, he angled the 'Nautilus' towards the fissure. The submersible plunged into the torrent, the crushing force of the vent's current threatening to tear them apart. Boiling water and mineral-encrusted rock swirled in the external cameras. The current tossed and buffeted them, and the hull groaned under the immense strain.

Then, a jarring impact. The submersible shuddered violently, and for a terrifying moment, silence fell, broken only by the hiss of escaping steam from a minor hull breach. They rested, wedged precariously within the maw of the fissure.

"Status report!" Benjamin demands, his voice hoarse.

"Hull integrity at seventy-two percent," Jasper reported, his voice shaky but clear. "Major breach in the aft ballast system, but we're contained. Life support is stable, though power reserves are critically low. The swarmers… they're not following us in. The heat and chemical composition of the vent field are deterring them."

Rachel peered at his display. "They're hovering outside the main plume, Benjamin. They are waiting. One thing about them is they are aware of the damage, but they will wait patiently."

"Patience is their strength, and our current weakness," Benjamin acknowledged, taking a deep, steadying breath. "We're trapped, but we're alive. Jasper, can you access the fabrication unit? We need to repair that ballast system. And we need to reroute all available power to the forward sensor array. We need to know what's happening out there."

Jasper nodded, his weary eyes meeting hers. "I can attempt the repairs. It will be slow, and we'll have to cannibalize secondary systems. But we can do it. We have to."

Jasper began the painstaking process of repairing the 'Nautilus' with the limited tools and resources available. With the faint glow of their internal lights reflected off the mineral-laden walls of their temporary sanctuary, the crew of the submersible knew they had only bought themselves a fleeting moment of respite. The labyrinth beneath the waves was alive, and its guardians were far more cunning and dangerous than they had ever imagined. The true test of their resolve, and of the Nautilus, had only just begun. They were deep within alien territory, and the silence outside their hull was a deceptive mask for the constant, predatory vigilance of their unseen enemy. The journey to Area 291 was not merely a descent into the crushing depths; it was a gauntlet, a series of trials designed to break them, to dismantle them, and to ensure that no unauthorized entity ever breached the sanctity of their abyssal domain.

"We don't need to last long," Benjamin stated, his voice regaining a measure of its usual command. "We need to find the critical data. Rachel, focus on those energy nodes. Can you identify which ones are likely to contain significant data archives based on their energy output and spectral analysis?"

Rachel manipulated the sensor feeds, cross-referencing the energy signatures with theoretical models of alien data storage. "The largest node within the central spire of the primary structure… its energy signature is immense. It's unlike anything I've ever seen. It's radiating complex, patterned data packets, even though the ambient distortion. If there's a repository of their knowledge, it's likely there."

"The central spire," Benjamin repeated. It was a monument of an unknown civilization. Now, it was also a direct threat, the center of an actively hostile defense system. "That's where we need to go."

"Are you serious, Benjamin?" Jasper exclaimed. "That's essentially walking into the heart of the beast! The energy output alone could fry our systems before we even get close. I don't want to know what else they have guarded that place."

"We don't have a choice, Jasper," Benjamin reported. "We came here for a reason. If we retreat now, if I let them simply push us back into the darkness, then everything we've endured to get this far will be for nothing. Besides," he added, a grim smile touching his lips, "we've already proven we can survive their initial welcome. We can adapt. We have to."

Rachel pointed to a secondary structure, smaller and less prominent than the central spire, but still emitting a significant energy signature. "There's another cluster of nodes here on the western flank of the main edifice. The energy output is lower, more controlled. It might be a secondary archive, or perhaps a communication hub. Less risk, potentially less reward. But it could be a viable alternative if the spire proves too dangerous."

"A secondary target," Benjamin considered, his mind already calculating probabilities and risks. "It's a compromise. We might not get the primary objective, but it's a chance to salvage something. And if that node is less guarded, it might allow us to test their defensive protocols more cautiously. Jasper, can you get us to that secondary structure? Can you navigate the currents around the primary spire without drawing its full attention?"

Jasper sighed, the sound a weary exhalation that seemed to carry the weight of the abyss. "I can try. The currents are still treacherous, and the structures themselves are emitting some kind of localized gravitational field that's making maneuvering difficult. But if we move slowly, and try to use the shadows cast by the larger formations, we might approach it without triggering a full-scale alarm."

"Do you want to ring the bell or should I?" Jasper had a good laugh. This entire mission has been insane from the beginning, but he loved it!

"Then that's what we'll do," Benjamin declared, his resolve hardening. "Rachel, keep feeding me data on the energy fluctuations around that secondary structure. I want to know every shift, every ripple. Jasper, prepare for a slow, stealthy approach. We're going in. We're going to find out what they're hiding."

The battered hull of the *Nautilus* shuddered as it settled into a more stable position, the groaning of stressed metal now a more settled ache than an immediate threat. They had navigated the treacherous currents, using the colossal forms of the alien structures as both shield and guide, a risky maneuver that had brought them perilously close to the pulsating heart of the western flank edifice. Benjamin's voice, though weary, resonated with a newfound urgency. "Rachel, we're in position. What's the energy signature look like from here?"

"It's… stable, Benjamin. The localized fields seem to dampen the emissions from the primary spire. The nodes on this structure are still active, but the intensity is… manageable.

It's like a quiet annex to the main library." She pointed to a section of the display, highlighting a series of pulsating points of light that mirrored the geometric patterns on the exterior of the structure they now nestled against. "These are the nodes. They're dense, concentrated energy sources. Benjamin, the spectral analysis… it's consistent with advanced data storage matrices. This is it. This is where the core data is." Rachel summed up.

Jasper's hands were slick with sweat and muck, yet he had managed to jury-rig a temporary patch for the most critical hull breach. He leaned back, his chest heaving, his gaze sweeping over the alien architecture that loomed around them. "Manageable is relative, Rachel. I can still feel the hum of this place. It's like a giant sleeping beast. What if our presence wakes it up?"

The next few minutes were a blur of intense activity within the confines of the *Nautilus*. Benjamin's fingers blurred across his console, his system weaving a complex web of digital tendrils into the alien network. Rachel fed him a constant stream of data, identifying and isolating the secondary nodes, their pulsed emissions like distant beacons in the alien edifice. Jasper worked miracles with their dwindling power reserves, rerouting everything he could to Benjamin's interface, the hum of their life support systems dropping to an almost imperceptible whisper. The lights of the *Nautilus* flickered precariously, casting long, dancing shadows that seemed to mimic the shifting patterns on the alien structures outside.

"Accessing primary conduit," Benjamin announced, his voice tight with concentration. "Beginning core data extraction. My God! It's… immense! The data isn't just narrative; it captured consciousness itself." He winced as another energy surge coursed through the *Nautilus*. "The defenses are adapting."

"I'm getting a breach warning!" Jasper shouted, his eyes wide as he stared at his external sensors. "A significant energy spike from the main spire. It's… a focused beam. Directed this way!"

Benjamin didn't hesitate. "Rachel, how far along is the download?"

"Fifty percent on the primary conduit!" Rachel yelled back, her voice strained. "The secondary nodes are buffering, trying to catch up. We need more time, Benjamin!"

"We don't have it," Benjamin replied grimly. "Jasper, evasive maneuvers! Get us out of the direct line of fire!"

Jasper fought alien currents as the Nautilus lurched violently. The sub's hull groaned under the strain, the temporary patches groaning in protest.

"The download is fluctuating," Rachel reported, her voice laced with panic. "The energy surge is disrupting the connection. We're losing data!"

"No, we're not," Benjamin said, his voice surprisingly calm amidst the chaos. He made a rapid series of keystrokes, rerouting the interface through a series of unstable, secondary nodes that Rachel had identified as potential gateways, bypassing the main conduit's now-compromised connection. "I'm starting a localized data capture. It's not a complete archive, but it's enough. It's focusing on the parameters we need: the pact, the harvest schedule, and the purpose of this facility."

The external monitors flashed red as the alien energy beam swept across their previous position. Jasper weaved the *Nautilus* through a narrow gap between two colossal, obsidian-like structures, the sub scraping against their alien surfaces.

"Twenty seconds," Rachel said, her voice barely audible over the cacophony. "That's all the stable connection I can maintain. We have to pull out now, Benjamin."

Benjamin watched as the data stream on her console coalesced into a manageable file, a compressed kernel of the vast archive. Humanity revealed the pact, a chilling agreement forged in the depths of prehistory with an ancient, inscrutable alien race. The 'harvest' was not a literal taking of life, but a subtle, generational manipulation of human evolution, a slow, insidious seeding of traits and behaviors designed to ultimately serve the aliens' unknown agenda. These structures, the labyrinth beneath the waves, were not merely archives; they were vast, planetary-scale gene banks and evolutionary control centers, meticulously maintained over millennia.

"Got it," Benjamin breathed, a mixture of triumph and dread washing over him. He started the disconnection, severing their link to the alien network just as another energy beam sliced through the water, wider and more powerful than the last.

"Get us out of here, Jasper!" Benjamin commanded, his voice raw.

Jasper didn't need to be told twice. With a surge of its remaining thrusters, the *Nautilus* broke free from the suffocating embrace of the alien structures, its scarred hull groaning in protest. The lights of the western flank edifice seemed to pulse with a malevolent intensity, a silent promise of pursuit. But for now, they had retrieved the core data, a terrifying glimpse into the true nature of humanity's origins and the alien architects who had shaped their destiny. The labyrinth had yielded its secrets, but the escape from its depths had only just begun.

CHAPTER 11

CONFRONTATION
& REVELATION

A deafening klaxon that ripped through the submersible's interior, a jarring intrusion into the tense silence, instantly shattered the delicate dance of data extraction. Red emergency lights pulsed erratically, bathing the steampunk cabin in a hellish glow. Benjamin's fingers, moments before gliding with surgical precision across his console, froze mid-keystroke.

"What in God's name was that?" Jasper's voice, already strained from the constant pressure, now carried a distinct edge of panic. He spun in his seat, his eyes darting between the various readouts that now flashed with urgent, insistent warnings.

Rachel's face was a mask of alarm. "It's an internal alert," she stammered, her usual composure dissolving. "An intrusion detection system. It's… it's flagging *us*. They know we're here. The download… it must have tripped a silent alarm we couldn't detect until it reached a critical threshold."

Benjamin's mind was already racing, analyzing the cascade of data flooding him consoled. "Not just detection," he said, his voice tight, his eyes narrowing as he interpreted the alien glyphs that now scrolled at an alarming rate. "It's escalating. Defensive protocols are activating. Power surges are being rerouted, and… oh God, Jasper, get us moving! Now!"

The *Nautilus* lurched violently, not from an external force, but from an internal tremor that shook its very foundations. A series of sharp, metallic clangs echoed from the hull, followed by the chilling sound of something heavy scraping against its metallic skin.

"External sensors are going wild!" Jasper shouted, wrestling with the submersible's controls, his knuckles white. "There are... apertures opening up on the structure. Like gun ports. And they're tracking us!"

A searing white light, impossibly bright, lanced through the murky depths, striking the *Nautilus* with concussive force. The submersible bucked, throwing them against their restraints. Sparks showered from an overhead panel, and the acrid smell of ozone filled the air.

"Hull breach on section gamma!" Jasper roared, his voice strained against the physical onslaught. "We're losing pressure! Rachel, status on the download?"

Rachel's fingers moved quickly over her console. "It's... it's holding, but barely! The energy surges are disrupting the data flow. We're losing packets, Benjamin! Significant loss. It's like trying to catch smoke in a hurricane." She grimaced, sweat beading on his forehead. "And the defensive systems... they're not just passive. They're adapting. They're learning our vulnerabilities in real-time. This isn't a pre-programmed response; its reactive intelligence!"

Benjamin's own console was a chaotic symphony of alien code and rapidly fluctuating energy readings. "I can't maintain the direct interface!" he yelled over the din. "The defenses of the primary conduit are too strong." It's like trying to hack into the central nervous system of a god. I need to reroute. Rachel, those secondary nodes you identified... are they still accessible?"

"Some are," Rachel replied, her voice tight with desperation. "But they're being targeted too. I can see their energy signatures dimming as the structure focuses its defenses. It's like a swarm of digital antibodies hunting down our intrusion points." He slammed his fist against the console in frustration. "We're being overwhelmed, Benjamin!"

Another violent tremor rocked the submersible. The exterior cameras, flickering intermittently, showed glimpses of sleek, metallic projectiles, impossibly fast and silent, launching from the newly opened apertures. The appearance was sleek, aerodynamic, and alien.

"They're not just energy beams," Jasper gasps, narrowly avoiding a direct hit that sent a shockwave through the water. "They're physical projectiles! Guided. These aren't automatic defenses;

"Benjamin, the pact data... it's critical!" Rachel pleaded, her eyes wide. "The schedule, the purpose... if we don't get that, this entire mission is for nothing!"

Benjamin's gaze was fixed on his console, his mind a whirlwind of calculations. The direct download was becoming impossible. The sheer defensive might of the alien structure was like a tidal wave, overwhelming their every attempt to breach its core. She saw the energy signatures of the secondary nodes sputtering, one by one, like candles in a gale.

"We have to change tactics," Benjamin stated, his voice a low, urgent growl. "Jasper, can you isolate us from the main network? Force a disconnection? I need to go dark for a moment, try a different approach."

"Isolate from what?" Jasper asked, his hands still fighting the controls. "The entire structure is our adversary now!"

"The primary data conduit," Benjamin clarified. "It's a sinkhole for our resources. If we can't get the full archive, we need a targeted extraction. Rachel, focus all available processing power on analyzing the fragments we've already received. Look for patterns, keywords, anything that shows the location of the pact and harvest information. I'm going to try to brute-force a connection to a compromised node, a backdoor."

"Brute-force?" Rachel echoed, her voice trembling. "The energy signature that would generate... it would be like a flare in the dark! They'll pinpoint us instantly!"

"They already have," Benjamin counters, his jaw set. "And they're already firing. This is our only chance. Jasper, prepare for a rapid power surge, then a blackout. I need a few seconds of absolute focus."

Jasper nodded, his face a mask of grim determination. He rerouted power, bypassing non-essential systems, dimming the cabin lights further until only the glow of their consoles illuminated their faces. The hum of their life support systems dropped to an almost imperceptible whisper.

Benjamin started the process. A wave of raw energy coursed through his interface, a focused blast designed to overwhelm the decaying defenses of a specific, identified secondary node. The *Nautilus* shuddered again, this time with a different stress, as it diverted nearly all its remaining power into Benjamin's aggressive digital assault. The klaxons blared louder, the red lights strobed with greater intensity, and the alien structure responded with a furious surge of retaliatory fire.

"They're hammering us!" Jasper yelled as another projectile slammed into their port side, the impact jarring their teeth. "We can't take much more of this!"

"Almost... there..." Benjamin grunted, his brow furrowed in concentration. The alien glyphs on his screen flickered, twisting and reforming as his system fought against the structure's countermeasures. Despite the heavy damage to the targeted node, its disorganized defenses still fought. It was a desperate gamble, like trying to pick a lock during an earthquake.

"Data fragments are coalescing!" Rachel shouted, her voice a mixture of hope and terror. "I'm seeing recurring temporal markers... references to 'cyclical replenishment'... and 'gestation phases'! Benjamin, I believe the harvest depends on astronomical cycles!

"Keep analyzing!" Benjamin commands. The alien structure seemed to sense the imminent breach, its defenses converging with renewed ferocity. A massive energy beam, far larger than anything they had seen before, coalesced directly above them, a silent, ominous threat.

"Benjamin, that beam... it's building!" Jasper warned, his voice cracking. "It's targeting our current position!"

"I've got it!" Benjamin cries, a sudden surge of triumph in his voice. "A partial download! It's not the entire archive, but it's a significant chunk. The system secured the core parameters of the pact and the harvest cycle. The purpose of these structures... it's to act as nurseries, incubators for something… something they're cultivating over millennia!"

"We have to go!" Jasper yelled, instinctively throwing the submersible into a violent evasive maneuver as the massive energy beam unleashed its destructive power. The beam came close, and the heat warped the water, as if the Nautilus was in molten glass.

The klaxons finally died down, replaced by the groaning protest of their damaged hull and the ragged breaths of the crew. Long, weary shadows were cast as the red emergency lights stabilized.

"Status?" Benjamin asked, his voice hoarse, his eyes still glued to the data on his console.

"Hull integrity at forty percent," Jasper reported, his hands still slick with sweat. "Multiple micro-fractures, but holding for now. Power reserves are critical, but we have enough for a shallow ascent."

Rachel slumped back in her seat, a weak smile spreading across her face. "I've got it, Benjamin. The data. It's… it's more disturbing than we could have imagined. The 'harvest' isn't about what they take from us, but what they *make* of us. They've been subtly guiding our evolution for millennia, shaping our societies, our conflicts, even our very biology, all to prepare us for… for whatever their ultimate purpose is."

Benjamin looked at the data, a chilling tableau of ancient manipulation unfolding before her eyes. They had pushed the *Nautilus* to its absolute limits, and beyond. They had survived the initial assault, but the true confrontation, the one with the implications of the data they had retrieved, was only just beginning. The deep, dark heart of the alien structure had fought back with unimaginable ferocity, but in its desperate defense, it had inadvertently yielded the very secrets they had risked everything to uncover. The silence that followed the klaxons was heavy, pregnant with the weight of their discovery and the dawning realization of the monumental task that lay ahead. They had downloaded the truth, but the cost had been immense, leaving the *Nautilus* battered and bleeding in the alien depths.

The silence that descended upon the battered *Nautilus* was a fragile thing; a temporary reprieve earned at a harrowing cost. The alien structure, still pulsing with a residual defensive energy, had unleashed its fury, a brutal, sophisticated system designed to protect its ancient purpose. But in its desperation, it revealed fragments of truth, enough to confirm Rachel's chilling pronouncements: unseen hands meticulously cultivated humanity's evolution, and humanity had not forged its own destiny for an unknown end. Benjamin, Jasper, and Rachel were no longer just explorers; they were accidental custodians of a secret that could shatter the foundations of human society.

It was during this tense, exhausted aftermath, as Jasper painstakingly maneuvered the damaged submersible towards the surface, that the next wave of their ordeal began. The sonar, which had been a near-useless cacophony of alien interference, suddenly cleared, resolving into a pattern that sent a fresh wave of unease through the cabin.

"Company," Jasper grunted, his voice raspy. He tapped a control, bringing up a new display. "Multiple contacts. Approaching fast. They're… not alien. These are human signatures. And a lot of them."

Benjamin's eyes started scanning the fragmented data from the alien archive. He looked up puzzled. "Human? Out here?" The trench was a realm of crushing pressure and profound darkness, not a venue for naval exercises. "What are they doing?"

Rachel was in shock too. In her mind, she was already cross-referencing the sonar pings with known vessel profiles. "Military. And not just any military. That's… that's a pattern I recognize from classified intelligence briefings. Advanced sonar jamming, state-of-the-art hull plating, coordinated formations… This isn't a search and rescue, Benjamin. This is an interception."

The implications settled upon them like the crushing weight of the ocean itself. They had stolen something precious, something guarded by an unfathomable alien intelligence, and now, it seemed, their own species was poised to reclaim it, or more likely, to bury it—and them—forever. The data they held, the truth about humanity's engineered past, was not a discovery to be celebrated, but a contagion to be eradicated.

"The Vatican," Benjamin whispers, the words tasting like ash. "It has to be. Who else has the resources, the reach, and the motive to deploy such a force this deep, this quickly?" For centuries, the Holy See had been a shadowy player in the hidden corners of global politics, its influence extending far beyond the spiritual. Whispers of its clandestine activities, its vast archives of forbidden knowledge, and its network of agents woven into the fabric of world governments were legion. If any entity on Earth had known about the alien presence, about the structures and their purpose, it would have been them. And if they knew, they would act to protect their millennia-old secret.

Jasper slammed a fist against his console. "They knew we were coming, didn't they? This wasn't just about us stumbling upon something. They were *waiting* for us. And they've brought their whole damn navy."

The sonar display resolved further, painting a chilling picture of their predicament. A formidable array of submersibles, some sleek and predatory like their own *Nautilus* but clearly more advanced, and larger, more heavily armed vessels capable of operating at extreme depths, were converging on their position. These were not exploratory craft; they were instruments of war, designed for a singular, ruthless purpose. Their presence confirmed the chilling truth: the alien secret was not just a matter of extraterrestrial origin, but a cornerstone of human history, a truth so profound, so dangerous, that certain factions within humanity would commit mass murder to keep it buried.

"They're not just intercepting us," Rachel said, her voice unnervingly calm, a sign of her deep focus. "They're attempting to box us in. Look at the vectors. They're trying to herd us, to prevent us from reaching the surface, or any neutral territory."

Benjamin snapped into analytical mode. "They want the data. And they don't care how they get it, or who they have to kill to get it. The alien defenses fought us, but these humans... they'll try to capture us, to interrogate us, to take the drive. And if that fails, they'll eliminate the evidence." The alien guardians of the deep had proven to be terrifyingly effective protectors of their charge. Now, it seemed, humanity had its own guardians, equally ruthless, equally dedicated to maintaining the grand illusion.

Jasper's jaw tightened. "We can't outrun them. Not in this condition. And fighting them… that's suicide."

The *Nautilus* responded sluggishly, its damaged systems groaning under the strain. Jasper engaged the interference burst, and for a fleeting moment, the sonar display flickered, the precise lines of the approaching vessels blurring into a chaotic haze. It was a fragile shield, a momentary deception, but it was all they had. Jasper then engaged the main thrusters, pushing the *Nautilus* upwards with a desperation born of sheer survival.

"We're going for the surface," Jasper announced, his voice strained. "It's a one-way ticket. We're burning all available power for ascent."

"Emergency buoy deployment," Benjamin orders, his voice regaining a measure of its earlier steel. "The auxiliary transmitter. It's slower, less secure, but it might be our last hope." She knew the risks. The buoy's signal would be far easier to track, but it was a desperate gamble to get any part of the data out.

Jasper, with a grim nod, started the sequence. A small orange beacon detached from the *Nautilus* hull, ascending rapidly towards the surface, a tiny defiant spark against the crushing darkness and the encroaching threat.

"Brace for impact!" Jasper roared, throwing the *Nautilus* into a wild, evasive dive, a desperate attempt to outmaneuver the inevitable.

The world dissolved into a maelstrom of noise and violent concussion. The *Nautilus* groaned and shrieked, its hull protesting against the savage assault. Red emergency lights pulsed erratically once more, painting the cabin in a hellish, flickering crimson. Benjamin slammed into his console, and the world spun. Amidst the chaos, he caught a last glimpse of Rachel's screen. The auxiliary buoy's signal was weakening, being actively suppressed, but a single, tenacious packet of data, a small but vital fragment of the alien pact, had registered as successfully transmitted. It was a victory, albeit a hollow one, amidst the overwhelming defeat. The Vatican armada, a force born of human fear and the desperate need to control an uncomfortable truth, had silenced the investigators. But the seed of revelation, however small, had been sown. The arm of the Holy See, it seemed, was long, and its reach extended to the very depths of the ocean, a chilling testament to the lengths to which humanity would go to preserve its comfortable, engineered reality.

Violent redirection, not the end, was the explosive impact of the torpedoes. The *Nautilus*, crippled and listing, found itself enveloped not in the cold, inert embrace of the abyss, but by a different disruption. A high-pitched, resonant hum, a sound that seemed to bypass the hull and vibrate directly within their very bones, suddenly overlaid the deafening roar of impact. It wasn't the chaotic, destructive energy of the alien defenses or the brutal, kinetic force of human weaponry. This was something else entirely.

Jasper, despite the alarms screaming throughout the submersible, his face a mask of disbelief, stammered, "What the hell is that? My instruments... they're going haywire. All of them. Power readings fluctuating wildly, navigation systems offline, even the hull integrity sensors are showing impossible anomalies."

A pervasive, almost soothing pressure that somehow counteracted the violent shuddering of the *Nautilus*. It was as if the ocean itself had become sentient, not in a hostile way, but with a profound, dispassionate curiosity. The alien data drive, which had survived the initial torpedo blast, pulsed with a faint, internal light, as if resonating with this unknown phenomenon.

Rachel pointed a trembling finger at his primary sensor display. "Look! The human fleet... its signature is vanishing. Not breaking off, not retreating, but... dissolving. Their weapons systems are going dark. Even the Vatican subs are... they're just... gone from the scopes."

A wave of silent, alien energy seemed to wash over them, a tangible presence that felt both ancient and impossibly advanced. It wasn't an attack; it was an erasure. As if a divine hand had intervened, the human armada's pursuit stopped. The hum intensified, not unpleasantly, but with a purposeful frequency that seemed to reorder the very fabric of their surroundings. The chaotic readings on Jasper's console stabilized, not back to normal, but to a new, unified state.

"It's… it's them," Rachel breathed, his voice a mixture of awe and terror. Their goal was to prevent our fighting. They didn't want *us* to have the data. They've stepped in, not to help, not to harm, but to… contain."

The implications were staggering. The aliens, the architects of humanity's curated past, were not merely passive observers. They possessed the means to intervene, not with the brute force of lasers or plasma, but with a subtle, absolute control over technology itself. They could silence weapons, scramble sensors, and perhaps even manipulate the very physics that governed their submersible. The Vatican's formidable fleet, so intent on eradicating them and their discovery, had been rendered utterly inert, their sophisticated machinery rendered meaningless by intelligence that operated on a level far beyond human comprehension.

Benjamin felt a profound sense of unease. This was not the intervention they had feared from the alien structure itself. This was an intervention on a planetary scale, a demonstration of power so immense and so subtle that it left no trace of destruction, only of absolute control. They had been so focused on the immediate threat of the Vatican, on the desperate race to get the data to the surface, that they had failed to fully appreciate the active role the alien presence might play. They had assumed the aliens' role was primarily defensive, a reaction to intrusion. But this intervention suggested a far more proactive, and perhaps more chilling, agenda.

"They're not trying to help us," Benjamin said, his voice barely a whisper. "They're trying to stop the conflict. They've disabled the human fleet, yes, but what about us? What about the data?" He looked at the data drive. It was still glowing, its internal luminescence now a steady, soft blue, mirroring the strange, almost ethereal glow that now permeated the ocean outside their viewport. The hum, instead of being a threat, felt almost like a lullaby, a force that was gently nudging everything into a state of perfect, enforced stillness.

Outside the viewport, the ethereal glow dimmed, receding. The silence that returned was even more profound than the one that had followed the alien structure's attack. It was a silence pregnant with unspoken implications. The human fleet was gone, not destroyed, but rendered immobile, their crews trapped in a sudden, inexplicable technological paralysis. The *Nautilus* was still damaged, but its systems were no longer erratic; they were simply... inoperable by their command.

"They've contained the immediate threat," Rachel observed, her mind already racing through the possibilities. "By neutralizing both sides, they've prevented a potential escalation. If the Vatican had captured us, or destroyed us, and then tried to reverse-engineer our findings, or worse, engaged in open conflict with whatever alien presence was guarding this place... that would have been catastrophic. Not just for them, but for the entire planet, perhaps."

"They've put the genie back in the bottle," Benjamin said, the words tasting like ash. "They've stopped the fight, but they've also ensured that no one gets the information. Our data is probably inaccessible now, locked down by the same energy that disabled the Vatican's fleet." She looked at the data drive. Its glow had faded, its pulse extinguished. Transmitting a fragment of data was a brief, triumphant moment, a small victory snatched from overwhelming cosmic indifference.

Jasper tried to engage the thrusters, but they remained stubbornly inert. "Nothing," he reported, his voice flat. "Everything seems locked down. We're adrift, but not because we're damaged anymore. We're adrift because someone else has taken the helm."

"So, what now?" Jasper asked, his gaze sweeping across the inert control panels. "Are they going to… take us? Study us? Or just leave us here, stuck in the dark, a monument to our own hubris?"

Rachel shook her head slowly. "I don't think they 'take' in the way we understand it. Their intervention was about control, about preventing a larger disruption. They've neutralized the immediate conflict. The Vatican will probably find its subs mysteriously functional again once they're further away, with no memory of what happened, or perhaps with their memories subtly altered. As for us…" She paused, considering. "They might deem us too much of a risk to leave operating independently. Or, they might simply wait. Wait for us to exhaust our resources, to become a problem for gravity and pressure to solve. Or, they might decide that our knowledge, however incomplete, is a contagion they need to contain more directly."

Benjamin's mind, however, was already working on a different angle. If the aliens could disable technology with such precision, what else could they do? Could they influence thought? Could they manipulate consciousness? It was deeply unsettling that they had orchestrated their very pursuit of knowledge, and that their "discovery" was merely a part of a larger, pre-determined narrative. The aliens were not gods, nor demons, but something far more alien: meticulous scientists, conducting an experiment on a global scale, with humanity as their unwitting, and now carefully managed, subject.

"They stopped the fight," Benjamin reiterated, a flicker of defiance returning. "But they didn't erase the knowledge from our minds. They can disable our technology, but they can't disable us. Not yet." He looked at Rachel, at Jasper. They had survived the alien defenses and the human assault. They had glimpsed a truth that few had ever even suspected. Even if they locked away the data and their journey ended silently, they still remembered what they had learned and understood humanity's manufactured origins.

"They may have intervened to prevent a war between species," Rachel mused, "or even a war for knowledge. But they have also revealed a far more profound truth. The aliens are here. They have been here. And they are actively managing our development. This wasn't just a confrontation; it was a declaration. A declaration that we are not alone, and we are not free. We are... a project."

In the dark, the Nautilus remained silent, a tomb of technology. The human fleet was a phantom, their aggressive pursuit a forgotten nightmare. The alien intervention, so absolute and so dispassionate, had achieved its aim: containment. But for Benjamin, Jasper, and Rachel, trapped in their metallic shell, the revelation was far from over. It had merely shifted from a physical confrontation to an existential one. The aliens had intervened, not to help them discover the truth, but to ensure that the truth remained precisely where they wanted it: under their watchful, scientific gaze. And in doing so, they had delivered a chilling insight, not into alien hostility, but into a far more unnerving form of cosmic control. Humanity's struggle for self-determination had not even begun; it had merely been cataloged.

"Jasper, can you access the emergency logs?" Benjamin's voice, though quiet, cut through the suffocating silence. "The tertiary data buffer. It's shielded, designed for catastrophic events."

Jasper's face showed a weariness that went beyond mere exhaustion, and he nodded slowly. He now moved with a deliberate, almost mournful precision. The instruments remained unresponsive to standard commands, but the emergency log was a separate, more resilient beast. It recorded system failures to capture the moments leading up to a vessel's demise, a grim chronicle for posthumous analysis. They hoped they would never need it for such a purpose.

"It's... it's got power," Jasper reported, a hint of surprise coloring his tone. "Barely. But it's active. And it's... it's logged something. A compressed data packet. It wrote just as everything went dark."

Rachel's eyes fixed on Jasper's screen. "Can you isolate it? Can you decrypt it?"

"The encryption is alien, of course," Jasper said, a grim smile touching his lips. "But the alien drive… it seems to have left a key. A residual echo of its own code. It's attempting a partial decryption. It's… it's working."

The next few minutes stretched into an eternity. The only sounds were the faint whir of the life support systems, a constant reminder of their precarious existence. Benjamin watched, his heart a tight knot of anticipation and dread. Had the aliens expected this? Had this emergency data been a deliberate trap, or a final, desperate offering from the drive itself, a last act of defiance against its own creators' will?

Then, a series of text files populated the screen. Not schematics, not alien hieroglyphs, but plain, albeit ancient, English. Dates, names, locations, and a chilling narrative that unfolded with an almost clinical detachment. This was not a history; it was a ledger. A ledger of betrayal, of manipulation, of a pact forged in the shadows of human history, a pact that dictated the very trajectory of their civilization.

"The Pact of Lumina," Rachel read aloud, his voice barely a whisper, as a damning document unfurled on the screen. "Signed. Dated. 1477. And the signatories…" He trailed off, his face draining of color. "These are names… titans of their eras. Scientists, philosophers, powerful figures who shaped the Enlightenment, the Renaissance… figures we revere. They weren't just thinkers; they were collaborators."

Jasper scrolled further, his fingers trembling. "And this… this is a record of transmissions. Encrypted communications between Earth and… well, they're referred to here as the 'Overseers.' Dates spanning centuries. Responses to human societal development. Directives on technological advancement, on religious dogma, on suppressing certain lines of inquiry." He pointed to a passage. "Here, they discuss the 'Great Filter'—not as a theoretical concept, but as a deliberate policy. A series of engineered setbacks to prevent humanity from reaching a certain level of technological or philosophical maturity too quickly."

Benjamin felt a wave of nausea. The "Great Filter." The paradox that suggests intelligent life should be common, yet we see no evidence of it. It had always been a philosophical puzzle, a theoretical hurdle. Now, the paradox proved to be a meticulously constructed cage.

"Look at this," Rachel interjected, her voice strained. "This describes the 'mechanism of control.' It's not just about suppressing knowledge. It's about subtle psychological manipulation, about fostering division, about ensuring that humanity remains perpetually on the brink of self-destruction, but never quite crosses it. They've been playing us like instruments for millennia. Every war, every plague, every major societal upheaval... were they all orchestrated? Were they simply... adjustments to the experiment?"

The files continued to pour in. Names of individuals, some long dead, others disturbingly present in modern-day power structures, all linked to a clandestine network dedicated to upholding the Pact. They deliberately withheld the precise details of certain technologies. It was a tapestry of deceit woven over generations; a narrative of humanity's perceived immaturity being managed by an unseen, unfeeling intelligence.

"The alien drive," Jasper murmured, "it contained the evidence. It was the key to proving everything. And they—the Overseers, the collaborators, the humans who served them—they knew it. That's why they were so desperate to stop us, to retrieve it."

Benjamin's mind raced, connecting the dots. The Vatican's relentless pursuit, with its agents using exceptional intelligence and resources that surpassed public knowledge, suddenly made horrifying sense. They weren't just a religious organization; they were the terrestrial enforcers of the Pact, the guardians of the Overseers' carefully constructed illusion. Their fanaticism wasn't about faith; it was about maintaining the status quo, about preventing the truth from destabilizing the system they had protected.

"The torpedoes... that was their attempt to destroy the drive," Rachel said, her voice gaining strength. "When that failed, they ordered the Vatican fleet to intercept." They knew the drive contained the proof. They couldn't risk it reaching the surface.

"But then… the aliens intervened," Rachel said, her gaze drifting towards the viewport, now just an opaque blackness. "They didn't intervene to save us. They intervened to preserve the pact. To prevent humanity from destroying itself, or from discovering the truth that would shatter their carefully managed narrative. They disabled both sides—us, and the Vatican—because the conflict itself was a threat to their experiment."

Jasper continued to focus on the data. "There's more. Details about how they monitor our progress, how they introduce subtle 'nudges' to steer our development. And the consequences for breaking the Pact… it's not just about suppression. There are records of 'containment protocols' that are… deeply unsettling." He wouldn't elaborate, but the grim expression on his face was enough.

"Containment protocols," Benjamin repeated, the words chilling him to the bone. The aliens' intervention, which had seemed so benevolent in its immediate effect of de-escalating the conflict, now felt like a prelude to a far more sinister form of control. They hadn't just stopped a war; they had reinforced the walls of the cage.

"So, the data is secure," Rachel stated, her tone a mixture of triumph and despair. "We have it. The proof that our history is a lie, that our progress has been carefully curated, that we are not masters of our own destiny."

"But what can we do with it?" Jasper asked, her voice hollow. "We're adrift. Our systems are locked down. We can't transmit. We can't even move. And even if we could, who would believe us? The very people who have been perpetuating this lie are in positions of power, controlling the narrative."

Benjamin looked at the data drive, now just a dull piece of inert metal. The breakthrough was monumental, a truth that could redefine humanity. However, the architects of their confinement now controlled them, trapping them as microscopic cogs in a cosmic machine. The confrontation had yielded its prize, but the revelation was a heavy burden, a truth too dangerous to share, and too profound to ignore. Forces beyond comprehension slammed shut the door to the future after they saw the key to the past.

"They disabled our technology," Benjamin said, his voice hardening with a resolve that seemed to push back against the crushing despair. "They neutralized the Vatican's fleet. For now, they have kept their secret hidden. But they haven't erased our memories. They haven't taken the knowledge out of our minds. The pact is broken, not by us, but by its own internal contradictions, by the desperate need for truth that drives us."

Jasper finally looked up from the screen, his gaze meeting Benjamin's. "You're saying… even without the data, we carry it?"

"Exactly," Benjamin affirmed. "This information, these names, these dates… they're not just abstract records anymore. They represent individuals, networks, and a systemic corruption that has shaped our world. Even if we can't broadcast it, we can understand it. We can see the patterns. We can identify the threads of control that still bind us."

Rachel nodded, a new spark in her weary eyes. "The Overseers and their human collaborators have contained the immediate threat. They've silenced our ship, and they've neutralized the Vatican's aggressive response. But they haven't accounted for human resilience, for the innate drive to question, to uncover. They've locked down our technology, but they can't lock down our minds. This is not the end; it's a forced pause."

The implications of the downloaded files were staggering. Far from being a relic of the past, the Pact of Lumina was a living entity. Those listed names connected to current power structures, global organizations, and institutions that ostensibly governed the world. It was a revelation of a shadow government, a clandestine authority that had, for centuries, manipulated human progress for its own inscrutable ends.

"Think about it," Rachel continued, his voice gaining momentum. "The reason they went to such lengths to suppress the alien drive was that it contained concrete evidence of their pact. Not just vague rumors or esoteric theories, but factual documentation: signed agreements, direct communications, a detailed operational history. This is a smoking gun. This is the truth that undermines their entire millennia-long deception."

"Because those milestones were deliberately obstructed," Benjamin counters, her voice firm. "The Overseers have kept us in a state of arrested development. They feared our potential, our capacity for self-discovery and genuine innovation. They wanted us to remain predictable, manageable, dependent."

The weight of the information was immense. It painted a picture of humanity not as an evolving species, but as a captive one, its history a carefully constructed narrative, its present a managed reality. The alien intervention, in this light, was not a display of power meant to inspire awe or fear, but a practical application of control, a recalibration of their experiment to ensure it remained on track.

"They silenced us," Jasper said, with a note of grim determination in his voice. "They took away our tools, our ability to communicate. But they can't take away the fact that we've seen it. We have read it and now know all the details and know the entire Pact of Lumina."

"And they know we know," Benjamin added, his gaze steady. "That's why we're still here, adrift, our systems locked. They can't afford to let us surface with this information, nor can they simply eliminate us without creating martyrs or attracting unwanted attention. We are a problem they need to manage."

Rachel looked around the silent, still interior of the *Nautilus*. "So, what is our next move, then? Assuming of course we can ever get these systems back online."

"We learn," Benjamin stated, his voice resonating with a quiet intensity. "We absorb every detail of this data. We commit it to memory. We understand the enemy, their methods, their network. They may have contained our technology, but they have inadvertently armed us with knowledge. And knowledge, even when buried, has a way of eventually surfacing."

The retrieved data was a double-edged sword. It provided irrefutable proof of humanity's manipulated past and its covert controllers, yet it also highlighted the overwhelming power of those controllers, including the seemingly benevolent aliens who had ultimately reinforced the system of control. The pact was no longer a historical curiosity; it was a present, active threat. But for Benjamin, Jasper, and Rachel, trapped in their silent vessel, the revelation was not a cause for despair, but a call to arms. They had a glimpse of the truth, a truth that was both damning and liberating. The challenge now was to share it, to ignite the spark of awareness in a world deliberately kept in darkness, and perhaps, finally, to break the chains of the Pact of Lumina. Their journey into the depths had ended not with a definitive answer, but with a far more profound and dangerous question: how does one fight an enemy that has shaped history itself?

The silence that had descended upon the *Nautilus* was not a lull, but a breath held in anticipation of further chaos. The data was secured, a digital ghost of humanity's longest-held secret, now living within their crippled vessel. But securing it had been a prelude to a new, and perhaps more lethal, act. The alien intervention had been a stark demonstration of power, a brutal clarification of their role not as saviors, but as custodians of a cosmic experiment. And now, the experiment was threatening to boil over, with the *Nautilus* caught precariously at its volatile epicenter.

Benjamin's eyes, now blazing with a ferocity that belied his exhaustion, met Rachel's. "They disabled us, but they didn't destroy us," she stated, the words a low, steady current beneath the hum of the life support. "They want to control the narrative, and that means controlling this data. They can't let us surface with this truth."

"And the Vatican?" Rachel murmured, his gaze flickering to the inactive console that had once displayed their enemy's positions. "Their response was immediate, aggressive. They know what we have. They're not going to just let us drift into oblivion."

A tremor ran through the hull, a deep, guttural groan that spoke of stressed metal and immense pressure. The screens flickered momentarily, regaining a semblance of life, displaying a chaotic jumble of sensor data. "What was that?" Rachel demands, gripping the edge of his console.

"The submerged structures," Jasper replied, his voice tight. "They're... reorienting. Weapons systems coming back online. It's not a coordinated attack, not like before. It's more like... a territorial defense. And we're an intrusion." He pointed to a rapidly forming a cluster of blips on the tactical display. "Multiple signatures. And they're not just targeting us anymore. They're... firing at each other."

The reality of their situation slammed into Benjamin with the force of a rogue wave. They weren't just trapped; they were pawns in a war that had just fractured into a thousand skirmishes. The aliens had imposed their order, but in doing so, they had unleashed a primal, untamed force within the deep.

"We can't stay here," Benjamin declared, his voice ringing with urgency. "If those structures are firing indiscriminately, if the Vatican is still hunting us, we're sitting ducks. We need to move. We need to use this chaos."

"There are... unusual geological formations. Seismic activity is high. There are areas of intense geothermal output. The alien structures themselves seem to be anchored at these points. They're harnessing that energy. It's... volatile. But if we can navigate the... fewer volatile zones, there might be an escape route." Rachel was happy to have made this discovery and to have a plan at last.

"No gamble is too great," Rachel replied, her gaze unwavering. "We have the data. We have the truth. The question now is how to survive long enough to reveal it."

Jasper weaved the *Nautilus* through the treacherous seascape, a ballet of calculated desperation. The immense submerged structures loomed on either side, their alien architecture an unsettling blend of organic curves and sharp, functional angles. Occasionally, a blinding flash of energy would erupt from one of them, a silent, cataclysmic explosion that sent shockwaves rippling through the water, momentarily blinding their sensors. The Vatican's remaining vessels, now acting on instinct rather than orders, darted through the debris field, their sonar pulses a nervous tic in the otherwise deafening silence.

"There!" Rachel exclaimed, pointing to a patch of the display where the energy readings spiked erratically. "A series of... vents. They're unstable, but they follow a path. It seems to lead away from the main cluster of structures, towards a deeper trench."

"A trench?" Jasper echoed, his voice laced with concern. "That's going to put us under immense pressure. We're not designed for those depths, not without full power."

"The data drive is in its shielded housing," Benjamin reminded him, his gaze fixed on the glowing indicator that represented their precious cargo. "And we have enough power for emergency life support. We can weather the pressure for a time. It's better than being caught in a crossfire."

Jasper nodded, his jaw set. He started a sequence, and the *Nautilus* drifted, propelled by the subtle manipulation of its ballast tanks and the almost imperceptible nudges of its maneuvering thrusters. They were no longer fighting the ocean; they were becoming a part of its currents, a ghost within the maelstrom.

The journey was agonizingly slow. Each shift in the water, each distant detonation, sent a jolt of adrenaline through the crew. The submerged structures receded behind them, becoming darker, more indistinct shapes against the crushing blackness. But the threat remained. They could still detect the faint, persistent signatures of Vatican vessels, and the erratic energy pulses of the alien constructs continued to paint the tactical display with flashes of imminent danger.

Rachel was meticulously charting their course. "The trench is deep. Very deep. We'll need to conserve every watt of power. And there's something else... an anomaly. Something that doesn't correspond to any known geological or artificial signature."

She zoomed in on a section of the display, a small, pulsating circle of... something. It wasn't emitting heat, nor was it registering on the sonar conventionally. It was a void, a ripple in the fabric of their sensor readings.

"What is it?" Benjamin asked, his voice barely above a whisper. "I don't know," Rachel admitted. "It's... elusive. Almost as if it's deliberately trying to avoid detection. It's deep within the trench. But... it's also a potential blind spot. A place where we might pause, to assess, to... breathe."

Jasper decided. "We head for it. If it's a blind spot, it's our best chance. We'll use the last of the thruster power to get us there, and then we go dark. Completely dark.

"The *Nautilus* descended, the pressure gauges climbing steadily. Outside the viewport, the world became a blackness that was suffocating. The hum of the life support systems, once a comforting constant, now seemed like a deafening roar in the profound silence. The immense forces pressing in on them amplified each creak and groan of the hull.

They reached the anomaly. It was an impossible pocket of… stillness. The usual ambient currents seemed to dissipate around it, leaving a pocket of tranquil water. Their sensors, which had been struggling to penetrate the dense oceanic environment, suddenly found a clarity they hadn't experienced since before the alien pulse.

"We're in it," Jasper announced, his voice hushed. "It's… calm. And our signatures are almost undetectable here. It's like a pocket of silence in a storm."

Benjamin looked at the data drive, its faint, internal glow now more pronounced in the absence of external interference. "We've escaped the immediate danger," he said, his voice filled with a weary relief. "But we're far from safe. They know we have this. They know we survived. And they will haunt us."

Rachel was already working on the diagnostics, her fingers moving with a renewed purpose. "The power conduits fried, but the core systems remain surprisingly intact." The alien pulse seems to have incapacitated, not destroyed. They wanted to prevent us from transmitting, from reaching the surface. They didn't want to kill us… yet."

"Which means they have plans for us," Jasper added, his gaze distant. "Plans that involve this data."

"Then we need to make sure those plans go awry," Benjamin declared, her resolve hardening. "We are adrift, yes. Our technology is crippled. But our minds are not. We have the knowledge. We have the proof. And we have a chance, however slim, to survive and share it."

The escape from the depths was not an end, but a desperate, precarious beginning. They had navigated the maelstrom of conflict, dodged the ghosts of their pursuers, and found refuge in an anomaly that defied understanding. The *Nautilus*, a wounded beast of metal and ingenuity, rested in the silent pocket, its crew now faced with the daunting task of survival, and the even more profound challenge of revealing a truth that had been buried for millennia, a truth that the architects of their reality would undoubtedly fight to keep hidden. The confrontation had been brutal, the revelation shattering, and now, in the suffocating silence of the abyss, their escape was an act of defiance, a desperate bid for a future where humanity could finally chart its own course, free from the invisible strings of the Pact of Lumina. They had slipped through the fingers of their captors, but the eyes of the Overseers, and their alien custodians, were still upon them, waiting for their next move in the grand, terrible experiment. The chase had just begun.

CHAPTER 12

THE BROADCAST IMPERATIVE

For a short while, the trench's crushing blackness was a safe haven. The anomaly, a pocket of improbable stillness in the deep, had offered a reprieve from the immediate threats that had hounded the *Nautilus* since the alien pulse ripped through the ocean's equilibrium. Benjamin stared at the data drive, its faint internal glow a beacon in the oppressive dark. It was the prize, the burden, the reason for their near-annihilation.

"It's intact," Rachel stated, her voice carried a smile because of this good news that barely disturbed the unnatural quiet of their refuge. He had coaxed a flicker of life back into a localized diagnostic display, projecting a stream of code that confirmed the integrity of the downloaded information. "Every bit. The encryption held. They couldn't corrupt it, not remotely."

Jasper leaned over his console. "That pulse was designed to disrupt, to disable our external comms and targeting. But it seems to have been too broad-spectrum for specifically targeting the data drive's internal architecture. Or perhaps," he added, a grim note entering his voice, "they wanted to ensure we *couldn't* transmit it. They want to control the narrative, not just prevent it from being released."

Benjamin nodded, his gaze sweeping over the confines of the *Nautilus,* a vessel now more akin to a wounded whale than a cutting-edge submarine. "Which means they know we have it, and they know we survived. This silence won't last. They'll be searching. The Vatican will coordinate with whatever alien intelligence is pulling the strings."

The concept of "safe harbor" felt like a cruel joke in their current circumstances. They were adrift in the deepest known abyss, their systems crippled, their pursuers formidable and relentless. The alien constructs, even in their apparent disarray, remained a potent threat, their territorial skirmishes a chaotic ballet of destruction. The Vatican was now a terrifyingly efficient hunting party, its advanced sonar and weaponry likely already re-calibrating to pierce the veil of the deep.

"We need to get out of this trench," Jasper stated, his fingers already tracing potential escape routes on a rudimentary map generated from their limited sensor data. "This anomaly is a null zone, a blind spot, but it's also a trap. We're exposed if they decide to bombard the area, and we have nowhere to go if we're discovered."

"Where can we go?" Rachel countered, his tone devoid of hope. "Our primary propulsion is slag. Navigation is unreliable. We're essentially a glorified submersible, reliant on currents and auxiliary thrusters that are running on fumes."

"We go for the remnants of humanity," Benjamin said, her voice gaining strength. "The forgotten outposts, the clandestine facilities. There has to be someone, somewhere, who can help us. We need someone who isn't compromised, someone who believes us.

"How can we find absolute certainty in a world where an alien species rewrote the rules?" Benjamin retorts, his frustration beginning to fray the edges of her composure. "We have to take a calculated risk. We need a place to go dark, a secure location where we can understand the scope of what we've found and plan our next move. Somewhere we can analyze the data, not just guard it."

Jasper chimed in. Governments and corporations are rumored to have abandoned deep-sea research stations when the depths became too hazardous or too expensive. Some of them were built to withstand extreme pressures, designed for long-term, independent operation. If any of them are still functional, or even partially so…"

"They'd be off the grid," Rachel mused, his mind already sifting through encrypted databases and clandestine intelligence fragments. "Unmarked on any official charts. Hard to find, even harder to access without a specific key or knowledge of their location. Perfect for hiding, but also perfect for being forgotten entirely."

Benjamin stated firmly, "Choice is not a luxury we have." "We need to prioritize survival and protecting this data. We can't afford to be hunted in the open; rather, disappear, and we need to do it fast."

Their limited sensors, miraculously, could still detect faint energy signatures, anomalies that hinted at the possibility of derelict or forgotten structures. Jasper, with painstaking precision, overlaid these faint whispers of artificiality onto their navigational charts. The process was agonizingly slow, each potential location requiring cross-referencing with fragmented historical records and speculative intelligence reports.

"There's a cluster of anomalies west-southwest of our current position," Jasper reported after what felt like an eternity of silent concentration. "They're deep, very deep. The energy signatures are faint, consistent with dormant life support or residual power sources. One in particular... it's labeled vaguely as 'Project Nightingale' in some of the older, less classified archives. It was supposedly an independent deep-sea biological research facility, abandoned in the late 2010s after a... funding dispute. No official confirmation of its existence, of course."

"Nightingale," Rachel repeated, the name itself carrying a hint of obsolescence, of a time before the profound cosmic shift they had just experienced. "If it's truly abandoned, truly off the grid, it might be our best bet. It would be a ghost, a shadow on the ocean floor. And if its original purpose was biological research, it might have the independent power and life support to sustain us for a while."

"It's a gamble," Jasper cautions. "We don't know its condition. It could be flooded, crushed, or worse, repurposed. But it's the most promising lead we have."

Benjamin looked at her crew. The exhaustion was palpable, the fear a constant companion, but beneath it all, a flicker of resilience. They had faced the incomprehensible, stared into the abyss, and emerged with a truth that could shatter the world. They were damaged, vulnerable, but not broken.

"Then we make for Project Nightingale," she declared, her voice resonating with a newfound resolve. "Jasper, plot the most direct course. Rachel, keep scanning for any sign of pursuit. We use the terrain, the currents, whatever we can to mask our approach. We go dark, and we pray this forgotten haven is still standing."

The journey to "Project Nightingale" was a grueling test of their dwindling resources and fragile hope. The *Nautilus* was a wounded beast, limping through the crushing blackness. Its maneuvering thrusters groaned with each subtle change. They navigated a landscape of jagged underwater canyons and volcanic vents, the very forces that had once threatened to destroy them now serving as their reluctant shields. The alien constructs, though receding, still flickered on their passive sensors, ephemeral ghosts in the periphery of their awareness. The scattered Vatican vessels, their pursuit now more desperate and less coordinated, occasionally pinged their vicinity, their sonar waves a chilling reminder of the ever-present danger.

Each moment of relative calm was fraught with tension. The silence of the deep was a deceptive blanket, easily torn by the sudden roar of a distant detonation or the telltale ripple of displaced water. They spoke in hushed tones, conserving their limited battery power for essential functions, their world reduced to the confines of the submersible's hull and the dim glow of their essential readouts.

"Energy fluctuations," Rachel reported, her voice tight. "Localized, high-intensity. It matches the signature of the alien weaponry, but… the patterns are erratic. Almost as if fighting," Jasper confirmed, his knuckles white as he gripped the auxiliary helm. "Or they're firing on themselves, or on residual targets from the initial engagement."

"They're still perhaps the alien custodians conducting a systematic sweep, eliminating any remaining threats. Either way, it's more noise to hide us. But we can't rely on it indefinitely."

Benjamin watched the tactical display, a chaotic tapestry of blips and energy signatures. The sheer scale of the conflict unfolding around them was a testament to the stakes involved. They were not just fleeing; they were running from a war that had been brewing in the depths for millennia, a war now brought to a violent, chaotic surface by their alien overseers.

"The data," Rachel murmured, her gaze fixed on the secure housing of the drive. "It's proof of their manipulation, their control. It's the key to understanding why they've kept this from us, and what their ultimate objective is."

"And the 'Pact of Lumina' seems to be the mechanism for their control," Rachel attempted to cross-reference fragments of intercepted communications with the newly gained data. "It's not a treaty, not an alliance. It's a system of imposed order, enforced through technological and biological means. They've been grooming us, shaping our evolution, all while maintaining the illusion of our free will."

"It's a parasitic relationship," Jasper said, his voice grim. "They feed on our progress, our discoveries, directing them for their own ends. And the Vatican… they've been willing participants, guardians of the lie. Remember, they put this into place in the 1400s. The Vatican was a powerful government. The Overseers would naturally go to the Vatican because that's where all the power rested. Popes came and went, so a deep secretive agency would rest in the Vatican, who were part of the Pact of Lumina."

The concept was staggering; the implications profound. Humanity, believed to be at the forefront of its own destiny, had been a carefully cultivated garden, its growth meticulously managed. The revelation was not just about alien contact; it was about a cosmic deception of unimaginable scale.

"Approaching the last known coordinates for Nightingale," Jasper announced, his voice hoarse. "Sensors are picking up… a faint, artificial signature. It's weak, intermittent, but it's there. Not dormant, not entirely dead."

Everyone held their breath. The promise of sanctuary, of a respite from the relentless pursuit, hung heavy in the air. As they drew closer, the signature solidified. A colossal dark mass resolved out of the inky blackness, an architectural anomaly against the natural contours of the seabed. It was immense, its surface a mosaic of corroded metal and what appeared to be bio-luminescent panels, many of them dark, but some still faintly glowing.

"It's… still here," Rachel breathed, a flicker of awe in his voice. "Remarkable. After all this time, against these pressures…"

The facility was a relic, a testament to a bygone era of ambitious, perhaps reckless, scientific endeavor. A seabed landslide partially obscured its primary docking bay, a cavernous maw in its side, but a secondary access port, smaller and more weathered, remained visible.

"It's operational," Jasper confirmed, his eyes wide with a mixture of relief and trepidation. "Emergency power is still online. Life support is functional, albeit at minimal capacity. The docking port… it's damaged, but I think I can guide us in. It will be a tight fit."

Benjamin's gaze was fixed on the looming structure. It represented their last hope, a fragile sanctuary in a hostile universe. "Let's hope it's not occupied," he said, the words carrying the weight of their desperate gamble. "And let's hope whoever built it was discreet enough to leave us some privacy."

With painstaking care, Jasper maneuvered the *Nautilus* towards the secondary access port. The thrusters fired in short bursts, the vessel groaning as it scraped against the corroded metal of the aperture. The air within the control room crackled with anticipation and the acrid scent of ozone. Then, with a final, jarring shudder, they were in.

The interior of Project Nightingale was a stark contrast to the crushing darkness outside. Emergency lights flickered, casting long, dancing shadows across cavernous chambers and decaying laboratories. The air, though stale, was breathable, a welcome change from the recycled atmosphere of the *Nautilus*. The facility was a ghost town, a monument to forgotten ambitions, but it was also, crucially, a haven.

"We're in," Jasper announced, his voice filled with a weary triumph. "The docking bay is secure. Systems are responding. Minimal power, but enough to keep us alive and… relatively hidden."

Rachel was already working on the facility's internal network, her fingers dancing across a salvaged console. "This place is a time capsule. The data logs are ancient, pre-Singularity event. But the infrastructure… it's surprisingly robust. And completely isolated. No external network connections, no active broadcasts. They wanted to keep their research private, and they succeeded. Perhaps too well."

Benjamin surveyed their surroundings. The lab equipment was archaic, the research notes indecipherable without context, but the sheer magnitude of the facility suggested a significant undertaking. "We need to secure the *Nautilus* and then assess what resources this place offers. We need to analyze the data, understand the Pact, and figure out how to disseminate this information without becoming immediate targets."

The silence that descended upon them now differed from the suffocating quiet of the trench. This was the silence of a tomb, of a place long abandoned by its creators, but it was also a silence that offered the promise of peace, of a moment to regroup. They had reached a temporary safe harbor, a forgotten outpost on the fringe of a world irrevocably changed. The fight was far from over, but for the first time since the alien pulse had shattered their reality, they planned their next move, to craft a strategy for survival and, perhaps, for revelation. The ghost of Project Nightingale had become their sanctuary, a silent witness to the dawn of a new, terrifying truth. They had escaped the immediate clutches of their pursuers, but the information they carried was a beacon that would continue to draw unwanted attention, forcing them to remain in the shadows, to become ghosts themselves. The derelict facility, with its dormant machinery and faded research papers, held the potential for answers, for a deeper understanding of the forces that now governed their existence. The analysis of the data drive, combined with whatever secrets Nightingale held. They were safe for now, but the imperative to broadcast remained, a silent, burning imperative driving them forward into the unknown.

The hum of the *Nautilus*'s auxiliary power was a meager comfort in the vast, silent expanse of Project Nightingale. It was a sound that promised life, but also a constant reminder of their precarious situation. Outside the salvaged docking bay, the deep sea pressed in, an indifferent, crushing weight. Inside, however, a distinct pressure was mounting, a pressure born not of water, but of knowledge. The data drive, still cradled securely within its reinforced housing, was no longer just a prize; it was a Pandora's Box, its contents both terrifying and essential.

Rachel hunched over a jury-rigged console connected to the data drive. The alien architecture of the files was a labyrinth, designed for obfuscation as much as for storage. Yet, with each passing hour, she chipped away at its defenses, revealing the skeletal structure of a conspiracy that dwarfed anything they had previously imagined. "It's all here," she murmured, her voice raspy from disuse and strain. "The treaties. Not just vague agreements, but specific, ratified documents. Dates, signatory nations, explicit concessions. They didn't just stumble into this; humanity *invited* them in, or at least, segments of it did."

Benjamin stood behind her, her gaze fixed on the flickering holographic projections that Rachel was coaxing into existence. The images were stark and clinical. Abstract representations of interstellar entities, their forms both elegant and unsettling, intersected with the stylized insignia of various Earth governments, some recognizable, others belonging to clandestine agencies Benjamin had only heard whispered about in hushed tones. "Who signed them?" he asked, betraying none of the chill that snaked down his spine. Benjamin put his arms around Rachel, his jaw resting on the top of her head.

"I can't even imagine a world where this could happen. Benjamin whispered into her hair ,"I grew up loving God, and now I feel like something kicked me in the gut."

"I really believe in God, just not organized religion. Consider this: God created even the Watchers. There is still a creator. Don't let this attack your faith," Rachel hugged him back.

Rachel continued to share the information she got hold of. "A shadow council, it seems," Rachel replied, zooming in on a complex web of interdependencies. "The 'Pact of Lumina,' they called it. A unified global authority ostensibly formed to manage extraterrestrial contact and resource sharing. But the reality, as these logs show, was far more insidious. It was a mechanism for control, disguised as cooperation." She tapped a series of cascading data points. "Communication logs between the Lumina Council and... them. The 'Overseers,' as they refer to themselves. It's all here: directives, resource allocation requests, timelines for 'planetary integration.'"

Jasper, who had been painstakingly working to re-establish a semblance of functional environmental controls within Nightingale, joined them, his brow furrowed with concern. He had seen the preliminary data Rachel had extracted, the terrifying implications of a species willingly subjugating itself. "Integration? What kind of integration?"

"The kind where we become a farm," Rachel stated flatly, her gaze hardening as she navigated to another section of the archive. "These are the 'Harvest Protocols.' Detailed operational plans, phased and segmented. They outline the systematic extraction of... biological and geological resources. And the 'biological resources' aren't just flora and fauna. They're us, Jasper. Humanity itself. They've been preparing for this 'harvest' for centuries, perhaps millennia."

The word hung in the stale air of the research facility, heavy with dread. Harvest. It conjured images of slaughter, of a farm animal brought to slaughter, its life purpose reduced to its utility. Benjamin felt a wave of nausea, but forced it down. They couldn't afford to succumb to despair. "The pulse," he said, hismind racing. "That was the precursor, wasn't it? A final system check, a demonstration of their power, a way to sow chaos and make us more receptive to... whatever comes next."

"Precisely," Rachel confirmed. "This data explicitly details the 'Veil Initiative'—the systematic suppression of advanced human technology and societal development that could pose a threat to the established order. They didn't want us to achieve warp drive, to colonize the stars independently. They wanted us contained, predictable, and ripe for the taking. Our space programs, our breakthroughs in energy and AI—all subtly redirected or stifled. The 'Pact of Lumina' wasn't just a political entity; it was an extraterrestrial stranglehold."

She brought up a schematic, a three-dimensional rendering of a vast, complex network of orbital platforms and subterranean installations. "This is their global infrastructure. The orbital stations are monitoring and control hubs. The subterranean facilities... they're the processing centers. And this," he highlighted a series of pulsing nodes across the Earth's surface, "these are the primary collection points for the harvest. Entire cities, regions... designated for resource extraction. The Vatican's deep-sea operations? Not just about studying marine life. They were clearing the decks, preparing access points for sub-aquatic extraction, likely from underwater resource deposits and... other things."

Jasper whistled, a low, disbelieving sound. "They were terraforming Earth, not for us, but for themselves. And the Vatican... they're not just complicit; they're the primary agents of this terrestrial control, the enforcers of the 'Pact.'"

"A tiny secret society in the Church is running this bullshit. If we brought this to the Pope, he would be just as shocked as we were," Benjamin added.

"They even have contingency plans for 'unforeseen resistance,'" Rachel added, scrolling through another document. "And they're detailed. Military assets, population centers, genetic markers for specific vulnerabilities. They've mapped us, studied us, cataloged our every strength and weakness for centuries. The alien pulse wasn't just an attack on our sub; it was a surgical strike to disable any opposition and to flush out any remaining pockets of untainted humanity, like us. They knew we had something they didn't want revealed."

Benjamin felt a profound sense of despair wash over him. The weight of this information was crushing. Humanity had to swallow a bitter pill when it realized its hubris and internal divisions had allowed others to deceive and systematically enslave it so thoroughly. "They've been playing us for fools," he said, his voice barely a whisper. "Every war, every ideological conflict, every technological race... all orchestrated to keep us fighting amongst ourselves, to prevent us from ever uniting against a common enemy. And the 'Pact of Lumina' is the ultimate manifestation of that divide-and-conquer strategy."

"It's worse than that," Rachel said, her voice grim. "This data suggests a symbiotic, or rather, parasitic relationship. They provide us with certain technologies, advancements that we attribute to our own genius, but which are in fact carefully curated gifts designed to keep us dependent and steer our development in specific directions. Think about the energy breakthroughs that seemed to stall, the propulsion systems that never quite made it to market. They were deliberately throttled. They meant for us to remain earthbound, vulnerable, and technologically inferior.

She brought up a series of historical logs dating back centuries. They wrote them in a complex, evolving dialect of human languages, interspersed with alien glyphs, instead of encrypting them. They detailed the initial "contact"—not a joyous revelation, but a calculated negotiation. The aliens, posing as benevolent guides, had offered solutions to humanity's most pressing problems: famine, disease, and environmental collapse. In exchange, they subtly extracted concessions, demanding oversight of global governance and access to certain planetary resources. The "Pact of Lumina" was the formalization of this insidious exchange, a legal framework for humanity's eventual subjugation.

"The 'harvest' isn't just about raw materials," Rachel explained, her voice tight with suppressed anger. "It's about genetic diversity, about unique biological processes that have developed on Earth, processes that are valuable to them. They see us as a biological repository, a living library from which they can draw at will. Our art, our music, our very consciousness—it's all data to them, something to be cataloged, analyzed, and potentially used."

Benjamin clenched his fists, the metal of the salvaged console digging into his palms. The sheer audacity of it, the cold, calculated cruelty, was almost beyond comprehension. To view an entire species not as sentient beings, but as a resource to be exploited, a crop to be harvested. "And the Vatican," he stated, his voice gaining an edge of steel. "They were the stewards of this deception on Earth. Their religious dogma, their historical pronouncements—all designed to subtly steer our collective consciousness, to prepare us for a divinely ordained order that was in fact dictated by alien overlords.

"They even have specific directives for religious institutions," Rachel confirmed, revealing a section detailing the 'Spiritual Alignment Protocols.' "How to interpret scripture, how to frame the concept of benevolent higher powers, how to quell dissent by framing it as heresy or a rejection of divine will. They've weaponized faith itself."

Jasper looked at the holographic projections, his face pale. "The implications are staggering. Everything we thought we knew about our history, our place in the universe… it's all a lie. A carefully constructed narrative designed to keep us docile and compliant."

"And now," Rachel said, her gaze meeting Benjamin's, "they know we have this data. They know we've seen the blueprints for their harvest. This isn't just about survival anymore. This is about the future of our species. They will haunt us relentlessly. We are now the single greatest threat to their millennia-long plan."

The silence that followed was heavy with the unspoken realization of their predicament. They had escaped the immediate danger, found refuge in a forgotten scientific outpost, but they were now fugitives in a cosmic game of chess, holding the king's downfall in their hands. Their weapon and mark was the data drive. Broadcasting was no longer a choice; it was an absolute necessity. Despite how devastating, the truth had to be revealed. The question remained: how could they possibly broadcast such a truth to a world so thoroughly deceived, and against an enemy so powerful and entrenched? There were detailed reports on agricultural output, projections for human population growth and decline, even analyzes of artistic trends, all framed within the context of their eventual "harvest." It was as if an accountant were meticulously documenting the inventory before a massive sale.

Rachel pointed to a series of spreadsheets meticulously detailing resource extraction schedules. "Look at this. It's not just about raw minerals. They've been cataloging unique biological compounds, rare earth elements, and even specific atmospheric gases. These are not the actions of explorers or even colonizers; these are the actions of resource managers liquidating assets. And Earth is their prime asset." He then shifted the display to a series of interlinked communication logs. "And this is where it gets truly chilling. These are logs between various heads of state and their appointed liaisons to the 'Pact of Lumina.' The level of complicity is astounding. They're discussing population control measures disguised as public health initiatives, economic policies designed to create dependence, and even the subtle redirection of scientific research away from potentially threatening fields."

Benjamin leaned closer, his eyes scanning the translated text. A senior official from a major global power was discussing the "managed decline" of certain industrial sectors, framing it as environmental responsibility, but the underlying directive was clear: stifle technological advancement that could lead to independence. Another log detailed how they carefully manipulated media narratives, ensuring that any talk of extraterrestrial life remained in fringe conspiracy theories or sensationalized fiction, which made any genuine revelation unbelievable.

"They've been creating a narrative of human exceptionalism," Jasper observed, his voice hushed. "That we are the sole architects of our destiny, that our advancements are entirely our own. It's a masterful illusion. By controlling the flow of information and subtly guiding our technological trajectory, they've ensured we never even considered the possibility of an external, guiding hand."

Rachel brought up a projection of Earth, overlaid with glowing red zones. "They designated these as 'Harvest Zones,' and they intend to extract from most of the planet." And the protocols for these zones are grim. They detail phased depopulation, often framed as natural disasters or localized conflicts. The Vatican's role in managing those narratives, in spiritualizing the suffering and loss, is also documented here. They've been the ultimate arbiters of truth, twisting reality to fit the alien agenda."

He then focused on a series of encrypted files, a new hurdle. "This is the core operational data for the 'Veil Initiative' itself. The specific technologies and methods used to suppress our progress. It seems they've deployed a form of localized temporal distortion and subtle psychic dampening on a global scale to slow our understanding of fundamental physics and to discourage any unified, 'dangerous' thought patterns."

"Temporal distortion?" Benjamin echoed, a shiver running through him. "That explains why certain breakthroughs felt so close, yet so out of reach. It's like running on a treadmill that subtly shifts its speed."

Rachel worked with renewed urgency, her algorithms battling the alien encryption. Finally, a cascade of data flowed, revealing the mechanics of the 'Veil Initiative.' It was a sophisticated system, using orbital satellites, buried terrestrial nodes, and even subtle manipulation of the Earth's magnetosphere. The goal was not to halt progress entirely, but to guide it, to ensure it never veered into territory that could challenge the Overseers.

"They've even developed countermeasures against potential discovery," Rachel revealed, pointing to a section titled 'Containment of Anomalous Data.' "This includes the development of sophisticated disinformation campaigns, the infiltration of scientific and governmental bodies, and, as we experienced, direct kinetic intervention when necessary. The pulse that crippled the *Nautilus* was a prime example of their 'containment' protocols in action."

Benjamin looked at the overwhelming evidence, the sheer scope of the conspiracy laid bare. It was not a matter of belief anymore; it was an undeniable fact. The treaties, communication logs, and operational plans for the 'harvest' revealed a humanity systematically groomed for exploitation. The alien pulse had been the final nail in the coffin of their autonomy, a brutal reminder of their true status as subjects, not partners.

"This data confirms it," Benjamin stated, his voice firm despite the tremor of fear and anger within him. "The 'Pact of Lumina' is the mechanism, the treaties are the legal framework, and the 'harvest' is the ultimate objective. We are not alone, but our cosmic neighbors are not benevolent guides. They are farmers, and we are their crop."

The weight of that statement settled upon them, a tangible presence in the dimly lit control room. The silence of Project Nightingale, once a symbol of refuge, now felt like a shared burden, the silence of a tomb that held the secrets of a dying species. They had stumbled upon the evidence of humanity's greatest betrayal, a betrayal orchestrated from the stars and perpetuated by some of Earth's own leaders. A desperate race against time, a race to expose a truth so profound, so shattering, that its revelation could either save humanity or shatter it completely, had just begun in the fight for survival. The broadcast imperative was no longer an option; it was the only path forward, a path fraught with unimaginable peril.

A terrifyingly clear picture emerged from the raw data. Humanity, unknowingly, was on the precipice of systematic extinction, not through natural disaster or self-inflicted wound, but as a managed resource. The 'Pact of Lumina,' the 'Veil Initiative,' the 'Harvest Protocols'—these weren't abstract concepts or theoretical machinations. They were blueprints, meticulously detailed plans for the complete subjugation and eventual liquidation of the human species. Rachel's weary eyes, burning with a mixture of righteous fury and profound despair, swept across the holographic projections. "The sheer audacity of it is what gets me," he rasped, his voice hoarse. "Not just the control, but the utter lack of empathy. They view us as cattle. Or rather, like a complex crop that requires careful cultivation and eventual harvesting."

Benjamin ran a hand over the cool, metallic surface of the console, the vibration of the salvaged vessel a distant thrum against his fingertips. The weight of their discovery pressed down on him, a crushing, existential dread. How do you tell a world that believes itself the apex of creation that it is, in fact, livestock? "We have to get this out," he stated, his voice firm, a stark contrast to the turmoil churning within him. "Every minute we delay, they get closer to the harvest. We can't let them. We *won't* let them."

Jasper nodded. He had spent years working with clandestine communication systems, understanding the intricate webs of global surveillance. "The problem is," he began, his tone laced with the pragmatism born of experience, "is how. Every major broadcast network, every deep-space communication array, every terrestrial internet backbone–it's all either directly controlled by the Lumina Council's signatories or heavily influenced by them. Even if we bypassed the primary infrastructure, attempting to broadcast directly would be like shouting into a hurricane. They'd detect it, jam it, and likely triangulate our position within minutes."

Rachel leaned back, the strain clear in every line of her face. He'd been the one to decipher the deepest layers of the alien archive, to understand the true mechanics of their control. He understood the challenges better than anyone else. "They've woven themselves into the very fabric of our global communications. Not just the visible channels, but the hidden ones, the encrypted backdoors, the dormant satellites. They've had centuries to prepare this, to ensure that any truth that might disrupt their 'harvest' is suffocated before it can even draw breath." He gestured to a complex schematic of global communication nodes. "This isn't just a communication network; it's a cage. And we're trying to unlock it from the inside, with only a tiny sliver of the key."

Benjamin's gaze hardened. The thought of their painstaking efforts being rendered moot, of this vital information being silenced, was unbearable. "So, anonymous leaks? Dropping pieces of this data onto the dark web? It's too fragmented. They can dismiss it as a conspiracy theory, bury it under a mountain of misinformation. We need undeniable proof, a full account. Something they can't spin, can't deny."

"And a direct broadcast from here," Jasper added, his eyes scanning the salvaged console, "even if we could get it out, would admit our location. They'd have our coordinates, and with the 'Veil Initiative' and its containment protocols, they wouldn't hesitate to deploy whatever force is necessary to silence us permanently. Think of the pulse that disabled the *Nautilus*. That was a warning shot, a demonstration of their ability to neutralize us. A full broadcast would be an act of open defiance, and they would respond with overwhelming force."

Rachel's mind raced, sifting through the data, searching for any potential loophole, any forgotten pathway. "The 'Veil Initiative' isn't perfect," she mused, more to herself than to them. "It's designed to suppress technological advancement and critical thinking, but it relies on maintaining a certain level of predictability. Unpredictability is our only weapon. We need to do something they haven't accounted for, something that bypasses their conventional control mechanisms."

"What about the old protocols?" Benjamin suggested, recalling fragments of his training, the contingency plans for catastrophic global events. "Before the Lumina Council's dominance, there were independent broadcast networks, redundant systems designed for national security emergencies. Some might still be functional, isolated from the main grid."

Jasper's brow furrowed. "You're thinking of the Cold War era. They decommissioned and dismantled many of those systems. It's likely that the remaining systems are heavily secured, inaccessible without proper authorization, or Lumina has quietly absorbed them into its infrastructure without public knowledge. But... there were always whispers. Redundant emergency broadcast systems, rumored to be self-sufficient, powered by independent energy sources, and designed to operate completely off-grid. They were almost mythical, a fail-safe against total societal collapse."

"Mythical or not, it's a lead," Rachel said, her fingers already dancing across the console, his algorithms delving into the historical archives of communication infrastructure. "If such systems exist, they would be the most vulnerable to our current predicament, but also the most likely to remain untainted by the 'Veil Initiative.' Their isolation would be their strength, and ours." She paused, a flicker of excitement in her eyes. "There are mentions, deep within these archives, of 'Project Echo.' A series of ultra-low-frequency, long-range broadcast stations, built during the peak of Cold War paranoia, designed to penetrate deep underground and even withstand atmospheric disturbances. Officials supposedly decommissioned most of them because they were too expensive to maintain and too antiquated for modern communication.

"Supposedly," Benjamin emphasized. The word echoed the insidious nature of the alien deception. Nothing was truly as it seemed. "Can you find them, Rachel? Can you locate any of these 'Project Echo' sites?"

Rachel nodded, her focus intensifying. "The data is fragmented, encrypted within older, less accessible servers, but yes. It appears there were at least three primary sites identified, strategically located across different continents. One in the desolate regions of Siberia, another in the Australian Outback, and a third... deep within the Andes mountains. The Siberian site seems to be the most promising to remain operational, data suggesting ongoing, albeit minimal, maintenance."

"Siberia," Jasper murmured. "That's deep within former Soviet territory, now a vast, sparsely populated region. If anything survived the Lumina Council's purge of independent communication capabilities, it might be there. But accessing it? That's a whole other challenge. We'd need to travel there, physically reach the site, and then figure out how to activate it. And given their control, they likely subtly sabotaged or retrofitted any operational 'Project Echo' site with monitoring equipment.

"The data suggests otherwise," Rachel countered, his fingers flying across the holographic keyboard. "The 'Veil Initiative' focused on suppressing *advancement*. These were not advanced systems, even by their original standards. The technologies were robust and brute-force. They could have monitored it, but active sabotage probably would have required too much effort for such an obsolete system. They focused on the newest technology that might pose a future problem. An old, slow, low-frequency broadcaster wouldn't have registered as a significant risk."

Benjamin considered this. It was a gamble, a desperate one, but it was the only glimmer of hope they had. "If we can get to that Siberian site..., how do we ensure the broadcast is effective? Even if we transmit, how do we guarantee it reaches the vast majority of the population, not just a handful of isolated individuals?"

"That's where the 'echo' comes in," Rachel explained, bringing up a technical diagram of the Project Echo system. "Its design was based on broadcasting at an extremely low frequency, one that could penetrate the ionosphere and travel vast distances, even bouncing off the Earth's curvature. It's not high-definition video or rapid data transfer. It's a raw, persistent signal. Imagine it as a beacon. We transmit the core data—the treaties, the harvest protocols, the evidence of the Lumina Council's complicity. It won't be a polished documentary, but it will be undeniable. We'll focus on the most critical data points, the irrefutable evidence."

"And how do we get that data *to* the broadcast site?" Jasper asked, his mind already calculating logistics. "We have the data drive, but it's here on the *Nautilus*. We can't exactly take it on a spacewalk and hope to make it to Siberia."

Rachel replied, her eyes gleaming with renewed purpose, "We digitize it." "We compress the essential data into the smallest possible file size, encrypt it with multiple layers of robust, alien-proof encryption, and then we transmit it wirelessly. The *Nautilus* has a limited-range directional transmitter. If we can position ourselves at the optimal distance and aim for the estimated location of that Siberian site, we might send the data packet. It's a shot in the dark, but it's the only way to get the information from this secure location to a potential broadcast point."

Benjamin nodded; the plan, however audacious, formed. "So, the strategy is: locate the Siberian 'Project Echo' site. Transmit the critical data from the *Nautilus* to that site. Physically reach the site and activate the broadcast. And hope that the sheer persistence of the low-frequency signal cuts through the noise of their controlled media. It's a multi-stage operation, each step fraught with immense risk."

Jasper, with a sober voice, interjected, "The primary risk is that the site is compromised." Even if we transmit the data, it will be intercepted, and they will trace the transmission back to us. Or that the site itself is a trap, a dormant monitoring station waiting for a signal to activate it."

Rachel's expression was unreadable for a moment, then he spoke. "The data suggests that while they monitor, their protocols for handling 'obsolete' infrastructure are less aggressive. They expect us to use the established, monitored channels. A rogue, long-range, low-frequency transmission would be an anomaly, but not necessarily a direct threat that triggers immediate, overwhelming counter-measures. They might log it, analyze it, but they wouldn't assume it's a harbinger of a global broadcast *from* an obsolete site. It's our best chance to fly under their radar, at least initially."

"The data includes operational manuals," Rachel stated, a touch of weariness returned to his voice. "The authors made them incredibly detailed, as if they expected every failure." It seems the original designers of Project Echo were paranoid enough to document every eventuality. These manuals are complex, but they are in human languages, and the technical specifications are understandable. We can work with them. The challenge will be the physical environment, the isolation, and the potential for unexpected security measures that weren't accounted for in the original documentation."

Benjamin looked at the flickering holographic data, the culmination of centuries of alien deception laid bare. It was a terrifying legacy, a testament to a parasitic relationship that had enslaved humanity. But within that terror lay a seed of hope. The very thoroughness of the alien planning, their reliance on predictable systems, their underestimation of human ingenuity and desperation – these were their vulnerabilities.

"We need a plan for extraction, too," Benjamin said, his gaze sweeping across the control room. "We will be exposed once we start the broadcast. Staying there is not an option. We need to disappear."

Jasper nodded. "The *Nautilus* might be our only option for immediate exfiltration. If we can manage a rapid departure after initiating the broadcast, we might use its stealth capabilities to evade initial detection. But the range is limited, and we'll need to reach a safe-haven, a place where we can continue to evade pursuit."

Rachel brought up a detailed holographic map of Earth, highlighting the estimated location of the Siberian site. "The region is unforgiving. Extreme temperatures, vast, featureless plains, and limited infrastructure. Traveling there will be arduous. We'll need to scavenge for supplies, prepare for extreme conditions, and rely on the *Nautilus* for support during transit, if workable. It's a journey into the unknown, into the heart of a forgotten world, to ignite a spark of truth."

Benjamin took a deep breath, the cool, recycled air filling his lungs. The dilemma of dissemination was immense; the odds stacked impossibly against them. But they found it unthinkable to allow the systematic harvesting of humanity, leading it to vanish into the cosmic void with no protest. His voice resonated with resolve as she declared, "We're doing it." "We're going to Siberia. We're going to find Project Echo, and we're going to broadcast the truth. It's the only imperative that matters now. The broadcast imperative was no longer a theoretical debate.

The hum of the *Nautilus*, a constant thrum beneath their feet, had become the soundtrack to their desperate undertaking. Benjamin, Rachel, and Jasper's determined faces glowed ethereally from flickering holographic displays. The previous hours had been a blur of frantic data analysis, deciphering the alien architecture of control, and planning a plan that, by all conventional logic, should have been impossible. Now, the reality of that plan solidified, demanding meticulous preparation.

"The data packet is ready," Benjamin announced, his voice a low, steady tone that cut through the ambient noise of the ship. The holographic projection before him shimmered, displaying lines of code interspersed with what appeared to be complex wave patterns. "I've distilled the most damning evidence—the core treaties, the operational directives of the 'Harvest Protocols,' the Lumina Council's own internal communications regarding the 'Veil Initiative'—into a compressed, multi-layered encrypted file. It's small enough to be transmitted wirelessly, and the encryption… well, let's just say it incorporates elements from their own security systems, twisted and repurposed. If they can't even break their own encryption, they certainly won't break ours."

Jasper nodded approvingly. "Good. The crew calibrated the directional transmitter on the Nautilus. We're within the optimal range for a targeted transmission towards the estimated coordinates of the Siberian site. The window for this transmission is narrow, though. Atmospheric conditions are shifting, and there's a subtle increase in anomalous energy signatures nearby. It suggests they might conduct sweeps, or perhaps there's an unseen presence we're not fully aware of."

Rachel's eyes still glued to the intricate schematics of the 'Project Echo' system, chimed in, his voice a little rougher than usual, betraying the strain of prolonged concentration. "The operational manual for 'Project Echo' is extensive, but it also outlines a rudimentary diagnostic sequence for initial activation. It involves bypassing several manual overrides and starting a power-up sequence through a series of cascading commands. It's designed to be a brute-force method, less about finesse and more about a sheer force of will. We'll have to translate those commands into a format compatible with the salvaged components of the broadcast array, and then, of course, get them physically to the site."

"Physically is the key word," Benjamin counters, his gaze shifting to a holographic representation of Earth. The vastness of Siberia, a desolate white expanse on the map, seemed to mock the audacity of their plan. "The transmission is only the first step. We get the data there, assuming it arrives undetected. Then, someone has to go to that desolate wasteland, find the buried hardware, and start the broadcast. That's a journey fraught with peril. We'll be relying on limited resources, extreme environmental conditions, and the constant threat of detection."

Jasper pulled up geological surveys and atmospheric data for the region. "The terrain itself will be a significant obstacle. Deep snowdrifts, the potential for avalanches, and the sheer remoteness of the location. It's not exactly a tourist destination. Even if the site itself was isolated, people might live in the surrounding areas. There could be remote research stations, military outposts, or even indigenous communities who would be... curious, to say the least, about strangers appearing in their territory. And we can't rule out hidden Lumina Council observation posts. They've had centuries to embed themselves. This isn't just about overcoming the elements; it's about navigating a potentially hostile, occupied territory."

"Which is why," Rachel interjected, her voice regaining a measure of its earlier urgency, "we need to perfect the transmission. The more robust the data packet, the less likely it is to degrade during transit. I'm running a last series of integrity checks. We must ensure the core message remains intact even if the transmission is interrupted or partially corrupted. The 'Harvest Protocols,' the 'Veil Initiative'—these are the undeniable truths. You can add the details later, but the core indictment must be clear and present.

He gestured to another holographic display, this one showing a dense network of interconnected lines representing global communication pathways. "Their control is pervasive, but it's also layered. They've secured the primary channels, the public-facing networks. But the 'Project Echo' system operates on a different stratum. It's a relic, designed for a world that no longer exists in the way they've engineered it. Its signal is primitive, persistent, and difficult to jam or intercept by conventional means. That's our advantage. It's like trying to stop a glacier with a hairdryer."

Benjamin nodded, his mind already racing ahead, anticipating the next set of challenges. "Once we start the broadcast from Siberia, we'll be revealing our position, at least temporarily. They will triangulate. Even with the low-frequency signal, the source will eventually be detectable. We need a plan for immediate exfiltration. The *Nautilus*, with its stealth capabilities, is our best bet for a rapid departure. But we can't outrun them indefinitely. We'll need a destination, a sanctuary, a place where we can lie low and continue the dissemination effort. The dark web is an option, of course, but it's a double-edged sword. It offers anonymity, but it's also a breeding ground for misinformation, and any entity with sufficient resources can monitor it.

"The 'dark web' is more of a metaphor than a physical space," Jasper stated, his tone analytical. "It's an encrypted portion of the internet, difficult to access without specific software. While the Lumina Council might not have direct control over every node, they certainly can monitor traffic, disrupt connections, and deploy sophisticated intrusion software. If we were to attempt a broadcast through those channels, it would be a constant game of cat and mouse. Every upload, every message, would be a risk. They could trace the origin, even if it's disguised. We need a broadcast method that is both widespread and, paradoxically, untraceable in its origin."

"That's where the 'echo' becomes our greatest ally," Rachel affirmed, his gaze intent on the technical readouts. "The system's inherent design is to create a pervasive, low-frequency hum. Imagine it as a global ripple. Instead of being targeted like a satellite broadcast, the signal will persistently permeate the atmosphere. Consider it this way: when 'Project Echo' sends a message, it goes not only from point A to point B. It bounces off the ionosphere, reflects off the Earth's curvature, and penetrates deep into the planet's crust. It's designed to be heard, not just received. It's meant to be inescapable, a constant reminder. And that's exactly what we need."

He then brought up another set of data, detailing the projected reach and impact of the 'Project Echo' signal. "According to these simulations, based on the system's theoretical capabilities, a successful activation could reach about 80% of the global population within 72 hours. It would penetrate even the most isolated communities, underground bunkers, and shielded environments. It's not about instantaneous global saturation; it's about a relentless, growing awareness. Once broadcast, nobody can simply switch off or erase that signal. It will exist, a constant testament to the truth."

Benjamin considered the implications. This wasn't a single explosive announcement that someone could instantly debunk or suppress. It was a slow burn, a seed of doubt planted in the collective consciousness. "So, the strategy remains: transmit the data, reach Siberia, activate the broadcast, and then... disappear. We need to prepare for immediate evasion. The *Nautilus* can get us away from the immediate vicinity, but we'll need to find a more permanent haven. And we need to have contingency plans for continuing the dissemination. If they jam or corrupt the initial 'echo,' we need alternative methods."

"Alternative methods that are less likely to be detected," Jasper added, his gaze sharp. "Perhaps smaller, localized broadcasts? Using salvaged equipment to transmit portions of the data in encrypted bursts through less conventional channels? We could disseminate data fragments through repurposed communication networks used by... shall we say, less regulated elements of society. The groups that already operate outside the Lumina Council's purview. They might be more receptive to such information and less likely to cooperate with its suppression."

Rachel nodded slowly. "It's a valid point. The primary broadcast is our silver bullet, but we need secondary and tertiary measures. We can't afford to put all our eggs in the Siberian basket, as enticing as that basket may be. Once the main broadcast is underway, we can begin preparing smaller, more targeted transmissions. Perhaps using the *Nautilus*'s communication suite for encrypted data drops onto specific dark web forums or even public channels that have a reputation for hosting dissenting viewpoints. It would be a constant war of attrition, a continuous stream of information designed to overwhelm their censorship efforts."

She paused, a hint of weariness creeping back into her voice. "But the immediate hurdle is the physical journey. The cold, the isolation, the sheer unforgiving nature of the Siberian wilderness. We will need specialized gear, survival training, and a vehicle that can handle the terrain. The *Nautilus* might ferry us close to the site, but we'll likely need to travel the final distance on foot or with a surface-level transport if we can find or salvage one. And then there's the activation itself. The manuals are extensive, but they are also highly technical. We'll need to decipher them under duress, in an environment that will be actively trying to kill us."

Benjamin looked at the holographic map, the daunting expanse of Siberia stretching before them. The cold, calculated efficiency of the Lumina Council's control had always been their most formidable weapon. But they had underestimated something fundamental: human resilience, human desperation, and the inherent need for truth. "We prepare," Benjamin stated, his voice firm and resolute. Preparing for the fight, the cold, and the journey is what we do. We gather every piece of specialized equipment we can find on this ship. We study those manuals until we can recite them in our sleep. And we make sure that when we start that broadcast, it's not just a signal; it's an earthquake. An undeniable tremor that will shake the foundations of their carefully constructed lies."

Jasper was already cross-referencing the *Nautilus*'s inventory with the projected needs for the Siberian mission. "Thermal suits, emergency rations, navigation equipment, portable power sources for our personal devices, medical supplies – I'm compiling a comprehensive list. We'll need to prioritize. And we should consider any salvaged weaponry. While our primary objective is to broadcast, we cannot afford to be defenseless if we encounter opposition. The

Lumina Council may view 'Project Echo' as obsolete, but they won't hesitate to deploy their own security forces to prevent its activation."

Rachel was meticulously dissecting the alien encryption protocols, identifying potential vulnerabilities and backdoors that they could exploit for future transmissions. "The encryption is layered, designed to degrade over time and distance, but also has a self-correcting mechanism." It's a formidable system. However, every system has its limitations. And their overconfidence, their belief in the infallibility of their control, might be the very thing that blinds them to our more unconventional methods of information dissemination."

The weight of their impending journey settled upon them, a palpable presence in the sterile confines of the *Nautilus*. The preparation for the broadcast was not merely a technical exercise; it was a commitment to an act of profound defiance. It was the culmination of Rachel's relentless deciphering, Jasper's strategic foresight, and Benjamin's unwavering resolve. The very act of preparing for the broadcast was a testament to their refusal to be a silent harvest. They were not just preparing to send a message; they were preparing to ignite a rebellion, a whisper that would, with every passing moment, grow into a roar. The fate of humanity rested on their ability successfully to navigate the technological labyrinth, conquer the unforgiving wilderness, and unleash the unvarnished truth upon a world held captive by lies. The hum of the ship seemed to deepen, a subtle acknowledgment of the monumental task that lay ahead.

CHAPTER 13

GLOBAL AWAKENING

The ethereal hum of the *Nautilus* had faded, replaced by a deafening silence that spoke volumes. They launched the data packet, a meticulously crafted digital skeleton key to millennia of suppressed truth. Benjamin, Rachel, and Jasper watched, breath held captive, as the transmission indicator on the main console pulsed a final, resolute green. Then, nothing. The signal had been sent, a whisper into the vast, indifferent expanse of the global network. But the true test, they knew, was not in the sending but in the reception.

Hours bled into a tense, agonizing eternity. They monitored conventional channels, their alien-honed senses straining against the digital noise. The world outside the *Nautilus* was a slumbering giant, blissfully unaware of the seismic shift about to occur. Then, it began. A tremor, subtle at first, rippled through the fringes of the internet. Anonymous forums, long-dormant repositories of fringe theories and whispered dissent, flickered to life. Encrypted messages, once confined to the shadows, surfaced, their origins masked by layers of anonymizing proxies.

Rachel's eyes were glued to a cascade of incoming data streams, glowing nodes. Tiny sparks of alien data, minuscule yet potent, were igniting across the globe.

Jasper added, "The volume is still manageable. The Lumina Council's infrastructure filters out anomalies to suppress erratic data spikes. But this isn't a spike; it's a deluge. The sheer volume of interconnected fragments, all referencing similar core data points—the 'Harvest Protocols,' the 'Veil Initiative'—it's creating a pattern too complex to whistled softly. "It's... it's happening. The initial packet is breaching the firewall. They're fragmenting, dispersing, but they're getting through. The encryption we repurposed is holding, for now. They're like digital ghosts, slipping through the Lumina Council's nets." She pointed to a real-time visualization of the internet, a complex web of glowing nodes. Tiny sparks of alien data, minuscule yet potent, were igniting across the globe.

Jasper added, "The volume is still manageable. The Lumina Council's infrastructure filters out anomalies to suppress erratic data spikes. But this isn't a spike; it's a deluge. The sheer volume of interconnected fragments, all referencing similar core data points— the 'Harvest Protocols,' the 'Veil Initiative'—it's creating a pattern too complex to dismiss as mere noise. It's like a global infection, and their conventional defenses are faltering."

Benjamin watched, a grim satisfaction tightening his jaw. The initial breach was crucial. The seeds of doubt had been sown. Now, they had to wait for the first shoots of realization to break through the cultivated ignorance. He nudged a holographic projection of Earth, focusing on major population centers. "The initial ingress is primarily through the more... decentralized networks. But it won't stay there. The Lumina Council will try to contain it, to discredit it. That's where the raw, undeniable evidence comes into play. The archival data, the council's own pronouncements, the historical logs. Once they get ahold of that, the narrative shifts."

The first undeniable wave of what would become known as the "Global Awakening" didn't arrive with a bang, but with a collective, disbelieving gasp. It started with a series of leaks from independent journalism collectives, groups that had long operated on the fringes, fueled by anonymous tips and a relentless pursuit of truth. These were not the mainstream media outlets, tightly controlled by Lumina Council operatives or their human proxies, but the digital underground, the inheritors of the free press spirit in an age of pervasive censorship.

A well-known investigative blog, which is famous for its in-depth reports about government wrongdoing, shared a highly encrypted file named "The Harvest." A decentralized collective of cryptographers and data cracked within hours of the decryption keys, cleverly hidden within a series of seemingly innocuous online puzzles and disseminated through clandestine channels, analysts who had been expecting such a reveal. What they found was staggering. Detailed records of resource extraction on a planetary scale, meticulously logged and categorized by species and purpose. The "Harvest Protocols" were not abstract concepts; they were operational directives, chillingly clinical in their description of sentient life as mere biomass.

Simultaneously, another leak emerged, this one focusing on the "Veil Initiative." It was a compilation of Lumina Council internal communications, captured and decrypted through Rachel's masterful manipulation of their own surveillance technology. These documents laid bare a centuries-long strategy of deliberate misinformation, of carefully curated historical narratives designed to obscure humanity's true cosmic origins and its subjugated status. The Council's own words, devoid of the soothing rhetoric they used in public pronouncements, painted a picture of a deliberate, systematic suppression of knowledge, a millennia-long deception to maintain their control.

The internet, a vast and interconnected nervous system, convulsed. Social media platforms, designed for the dissemination of fleeting trends and personal opinions, became unwilling conduits for an inconvenient truth. Hashtags like Harvest Protocols, Veil Initiative, and Lumina Truth exploded, initially dismissed as fringe conspiracy theories. But the sheer volume of shared data, the cross-referencing of information across disparate platforms, and the unassailable authenticity of the leaked documents chipped away at the wall of denial.

Governments, especially those with close ties to the Lumina Council, were utterly surprised. Their carefully constructed narratives unraveled. The governments held an emergency session behind closed doors. Initial responses were predictable: outright denial, labeling the leaked information as sophisticated disinformation campaigns orchestrated by hostile foreign powers or rogue AI. They attempted to scrub the data from public access and silence the emerging voices of dissent. But it was like trying to hold back the tide with a sieve.

"They're in damage control mode," Jasper observed, pointing to a news feed scrolling across one of his monitors. The anchor, whose face was pale and drawn, earnestly discussed the "unverified nature" of the alleged leaks and parroted talking points that someone had clearly fed him. "They're trying to discredit the sources, to sow confusion, to reassert their control over the narrative. But the information is too pervasive. It's like a virus, replicating faster than they can quarantine it."

Benjamin nodded. "Their mistake was underestimating the interconnectedness of the modern world. They've been so focused on controlling the large, visible channels that they overlooked the myriads of smaller, independent pathways. Every decrypted message, every shared file, every whispered conversation online, is another node in a network that is rapidly coalescing around the truth."

The initial shock gave way to a potent cocktail of fear and anger. People who had lived their entire lives under the Lumina Council's benevolent facade questioned everything they had ever known. The chilling realization that they were wards of an alien power replaced the comfortable illusion of human sovereignty. This existential crisis manifested in a variety of ways. Stock markets plummeted as global economies, built on the Lumina Council's stability, teetered on the brink of collapse. Religious institutions, many of which had integrated Lumina Council doctrines into their own theological frameworks, found themselves in crisis, their sacred texts re-examined through the lens of alien manipulation.

In the more technologically advanced nations, public discourse became a battlefield. Debates raged on encrypted forums and in virtual reality spaces, with proponents of the Lumina Council's narrative clashing fiercely with the newly awakened. Differing interpretations of the unfolding reality fractured online communities and tore families apart. The sheer scale of the deception was so profound that many found it easier to retreat into denial, to cling to the familiar comfort of the lie rather than confront the terrifying truth.

But for others, the awakening was a clarion call. Dissident groups, once scattered and marginalized, found a common cause. Underground networks, accustomed to operating in secrecy, suddenly had a global audience. The data shared by the *Nautilus* wasn't just evidence; it was a blueprint, a detailed exposé of the Lumina Council's methods, their weaknesses, and the historical trajectory of their control. It gave context, allowing individuals to understand the complex manipulation they had endured for generations.

"Look at this," Rachel said, her voice hushed with awe. She projected a series of visualizations onto the main screen. They showed the projected spread of awareness. The initial wave, originating from the data leaks, was now cascading into broader societal discussions. Images of Lumina Council propaganda being defaced, of public protests erupting in major cities, of news anchors hesitantly questioning official statements, flickered across the display. "The truth isn't just going viral; it's becoming the narrative. They're losing their grip. Their attempts to control the flow of information are being overwhelmed by the sheer momentum of human curiosity and the innate desire for authenticity."

The Lumina Council's response, initially one of denial, shifted towards a more aggressive, authoritarian stance. As the truth spread, their facade of benevolent stewardship crumbled, revealing the iron fist beneath. Attempts to silence key whistleblowers and independent media outlets escalated. Reports of sudden disappearances, of individuals being forcibly apprehended by unseen forces, surfaced. The global awakening was not a peaceful transition; it was a violent convulsion, a species waking up to find itself shackled.

Benjamin watched the escalating chaos with a mixture of dread and grim satisfaction. "This is a predictable reaction. They've maintained control through manipulation and fear. Now that people have exposed the manipulation, they will use overt fear. But they are playing a dangerous game. Every suppression, every act of coercion, will only validate the information we've released. It will become further proof of their guilt, further fuel for the fire."

The alien archive wasn't just a collection of facts; it was a testament to their long history of manipulation. It detailed how they had subtly influenced human development, guiding technological advancement in directions that served their own needs, while suppressing anything that might lead to true human autonomy or cosmic awareness. It spoke of how they had orchestrated conflicts, manipulated economies, and even influenced religious and philosophical movements to maintain a balance of power that kept humanity dependent and divided. The sheer scope of the deception was mind-boggling, a masterclass in long-term strategic control that now, thanks to the *Nautilus* and its intrepid crew, was being laid bare for all to see.

Jasper tapped a stylus nervously against his data pad. "The data also shows specific vulnerabilities within their control network. They overlooked points of leverage because they were too mundane and human for an advanced alien intelligence to consider. The Lumina Council operates on a logic of absolute control. They struggle to comprehend the power of decentralized resistance, the impact of widespread public opinion, and the inherent unpredictability of human emotion. In their view, we're biological machines to manage. They don't understand that sometimes, the most powerful force is a collective, unyielding will."

The initial wave acted as a catalyst, while the ongoing sharing was a struggle. Facing an enemy, the Lumina Council found themselves unable to silence dissent with precision, as they encountered a network of awakened individuals. The encrypted data packets, once a lifeline, were now being used by the masses, re-uploaded, re-shared, and dissected across countless platforms. The very nature of the internet, its ability to facilitate rapid and widespread communication, was now a weapon turned against its former controllers.

Rachel was monitoring the Lumina Council's attempts to intercept and suppress the data. "Their firewalls are robust; and their jamming technology is sophisticated. But they're like a single monolithic entity. We are a million scattered embers, each capable of reigniting the blaze. They can shut down one server, intercept one transmission, but they can't silence the collective voice. They can't un-ring this bell."

The truth, once a tightly guarded secret, was now a wildfire, consuming the carefully constructed illusions of the Lumina

Council's dominion. It was a moment of global reckoning, a chaotic, terrifying, yet ultimately liberating dawn. Echoing the growing roar of humanity, the distant hum of the Nautilus seemed a sound that, suppressed for millennia, was now unleashed. The awakening's start meant there was no turning back. Now, the question was not whether humanity would rebuild, but how it would begin. The viral spread of truth was only the first step in a long, arduous journey towards genuine liberation.

The initial tremors of revelation had already fractured the bedrock of human society. Undeniable, albeit alien, data now proves that what people dismissed as the ramblings of the deluded and the fantastical narratives spun in the shadowed corners of the internet was true. The carefully constructed edifice of human history, built upon generations of carefully curated narratives and enforced ignorance, was showing cracks that widened with every passing hour. Everyone now recognized the Lumina Council as the architect of a cosmic deception that had spanned millennia; people had only whispered about or found the council in speculative fiction before.

The immediate aftermath was not a unified surge of outrage or a swift, decisive call for liberation. Instead, it was a cacophony of confusion, fear, and the deep, unsettling realization that the very foundations of their perceived reality were a carefully constructed illusion. Trust, once a fragile commodity even within human societies, evaporated entirely. Governments, long perceived as the legitimate stewards of human affairs, found themselves utterly discredited. Their pronouncements, once imbued with an aura of authority, were now met with derision and suspicion. How could people trust them when they fabricated the history they represented? How could they guide a future when their past was a lie? The Lumina Council's subtle influence, woven into the fabric of global governance for centuries, meant that many national leaders, whether or not aware, had been unwitting participants in the grand deception. Their attempts to manage the crisis, to control the narrative, were seen not as acts of leadership, but as further evidence of their complicity.

This erosion of institutional trust affected not only political bodies. Scientific establishments, which had meticulously cataloged the cosmos within the narrow parameters dictated by Lumina Council-approved theories, faced a crisis of identity. Scientists abruptly reevaluated astronomical observations, which they had long disregarded as anomalies or misinterpretations. The very understanding of humanity's place in the universe, the meticulous scientific reasoning that had led to the conclusion of human isolation, was now seen as a deliberate blindfolding. Religious institutions, too, found themselves in a state of profound upheaval. Many faiths had incorporated elements that, in retrospect, eerily echoed the Lumina Council's narrative—prophecies of external intervention, tales of celestial beings, and the concept of humanity as a creation or a subject of higher powers. The leaked data provided a stark, secular explanation for these echoes, stripping away the divine mystery and replacing it with the cold, calculating logic of alien manipulation. Protests interrupted sermons, people debated holy texts with renewed passion, and entire congregations split as believers struggled with the possibility that alien overseers had guided, or even created, their spiritual journeys.

The existential dread that permeated the globe was palpable. For so long, humanity had operated under the assumption of self-determination, even if that self-determination was often fraught with internal conflict and self-destructive tendencies. The revelation that they had been a cosmic experiment, a herd of livestock managed by unseen hands, was a profound blow to the species' collective ego. It raised unsettling questions about free will, about the very nature of consciousness, and about the purpose of human existence. Were their triumphs genuine achievements, or merely milestones on a path deliberately laid out for them? Were their struggles, their wars, their innovations, organic developments, or carefully orchestrated events designed to shape them into a particular form? The data revealed the Lumina Council's long-term projections, their calculated interventions, their meticulous management of human evolution, which stripped away the romantic notion of organic progress and replaced it with the chilling reality of engineered development.

This profound sense of disorientation led to a deep societal fracture. The initial unity, born from the shared shock of the revelation, splintered. Some individuals, overwhelmed by the sheer magnitude of the deception, retreated into denial. They clung to the familiar comfort of their former beliefs, dismissing the leaked data as an elaborate hoax or a sophisticated form of psychological warfare. These "Believers," as they came to be known, often formed insular communities, reinforcing each other's skepticism and viewing those who accepted the truth as gullible or misled. Their fear was understandable; accepting the truth meant dismantling their entire worldview, a process that was psychologically arduous, if not impossible for many.

On the other side were the "Awakened." These were individuals who, having processed the evidence, embraced the new reality with a mix of anger, determination, and a profound sense of urgency. The Lumina Council's deception was a call to action, not despair, for them. They organized to share information more widely, and to seek ways to actively sever the Council's control. They often moved in a decentralized manner, mirroring the network that had spread the truth, and a burning desire to reclaim human autonomy fueled their actions. These groups explored the vulnerabilities within the Lumina Council's network, seeking to understand how the Council had used the levers of power against them and how to dismantle them.

Between these two poles existed a vast middle ground of uncertainty and fear. Millions found themselves adrift, their previous anchors of belief and trust ripped away, unwilling or unable to fully commit to either the path of denial or the path of radical awakening. This group was susceptible to manipulation, their confusion exploited by various factions seeking to gain influence in the unfolding chaos. Some governments, attempting to regain a semblance of control, leaned into authoritarianism, using the widespread fear justifying increased surveillance and suppression of dissent, inadvertently playing into the Lumina Council's hands by creating the very conditions of fear they had always exploited. Others, recognizing the futility of denial, attempted to bridge the gap, advocating for a measured approach to understanding and rebuilding, but often found their voices drowned out by the more extreme sentiments.

The Lumina Council's calculated counter-measures exacerbated the deep-seated divisions. While the initial data release had caught them off guard, their sophisticated intelligence apparatus, even if temporarily disrupted, was far from inert. They exploited the societal fractures, subtly amplifying existing anxieties and distrust. They launched disinformation campaigns that were far more sophisticated than anything humanity had previously encountered. These weren't mere fabrications; they were insidious blends of truth and falsehood, designed to sow maximum discord. Rumors of impending alien retaliation, of internal human betrayal, and of the dangers of unchecked skepticism spread through the same channels that had initially spread the truth, creating a bewildering fog of conflicting narratives.

The consequences of this societal fracture were immediate and far-reaching. Global markets, already destabilized by the initial shock, experienced unprecedented volatility. The economic systems intrinsically linked to Lumina Council-approved stability metrics and resource allocation strategies, unraveled. Industries reliant on alien-derived technologies or resources faced immediate disruption, leading to widespread shortages and economic collapse in some regions. The interconnectedness that had facilitated the spread of truth now also facilitated the rapid spread of economic panic and social unrest.

In cities across the globe, protests erupted. These were not the organized, politically motivated demonstrations of the past. They were spontaneous outpourings of fear, anger, and confusion. Some protesters directed their anger at government buildings, demanding answers and accountability. Others were chaotic riots, fueled by desperation and a breakdown of law and order. However, Lumina Council agents or their proxies later subtly influenced many of these gatherings, steering them towards violence or acts that would discredit the awakened population and justify increased crackdowns. Unable to entirely suppress the truth, the Council sought to control the reaction to it, ensuring that the awakening led not to liberation, but to further subjugation through chaos.

The psychological toll was immense. Reports of widespread anxiety, depression, and even mass hysteria flooded the increasingly strained mental health services. The feeling of being insignificant, of having been a pawn in a game played by cosmic giants, was a crushing burden for many. The Lumina Council's own historical records, detailed in the leaked data, spoke of similar societal collapses on other worlds they had subjugated, a grim testament to the effectiveness of their methods. They understood that breaking the spirit of a species was as crucial as controlling its resources.

Someone had carefully hidden detailed schematics of Lumina Council technology from humanity, and the leaked data also contained this information. This offered a tangible path forward for the Awakened. Teams of human scientists and engineers, working in secret, reverse-engineer these alien systems, not for further subjugation, but for liberation. The knowledge that the Lumina Council's technology, long perceived as an insurmountable barrier, could be understood and potentially replicated, provided a powerful counter-narrative to the overwhelming sense of helplessness. This knowledge offered the potential for humanity not only to resist, but to eventually match, the technological prowess of their oppressors.

The immediate aftermath was not a unified surge of outrage or a swift, decisive call for liberation. Instead, it was a cacophony of confusion, fear, and the deep, unsettling realization that the very foundations of their perceived reality were a carefully constructed illusion. Trust, once a fragile commodity even within human societies, evaporated entirely. Governments, long perceived as the legitimate stewards of human affairs, found themselves utterly discredited. Their pronouncements, once imbued with an aura of authority, were now met with derision and suspicion. How could they be trusted when the very history they represented was a fabrication? How could they guide a future when their past was a lie? The Lumina Council's subtle influence, woven into the fabric of global governance for centuries, meant that many national leaders, whether or not aware, had been unwitting participants in the grand deception. Their attempts to manage the crisis, to control the narrative, were seen not as acts of leadership, but as further evidence of their complicity.

Within the United States, the response was a microcosm of the global chaos. The president, a figurehead increasingly disempowered by the revelations, found himself caught between entrenched factions. The Pentagon, which had long benefited from advanced alien technologies, was deeply divided internally. A vocal minority within military intelligence acknowledged the Lumina Council's true nature and began discreetly feeding information to trusted journalistic outlets, fueling the transparency movement. However, the dominant narrative within the military-industrial complex was one of damage control and continued cooperation, albeit with greater secrecy. They argued that any disruption to the established technological pipeline would be catastrophic, leaving America vulnerable. Powerful tech corporations, whose fortunes were inextricably linked to Lumina Council-derived innovations, launched massive disinformation campaigns, flooding online spaces with fabricated "counter-evidence" and discrediting independent researchers.

On Capitol Hill, the political landscape fractured. A bipartisan coalition of lawmakers, horrified by the implications of the Lumina Council's manipulation, advocated for full disclosure and immediate severance of all ties. They argued that human freedom and self-determination were non-negotiable, regardless of the perceived benefits of alien patronage. They proposed legislation to declassify all known records pertaining to alien contact and to start a global effort to develop independent, human-centric technologies. Opposing them was another coalition, composed of members who had either been knowingly complicit or who genuinely believed in the necessity of the Lumina Council's guidance. They pushed for legislation that would further regulate information flow, classify any mention of the Lumina Council as a national security threat, and reinforce existing clandestine cooperation. The debates were acrimonious, often devolving into personal attacks and accusations of treason, reflecting the profound ideological chasm that had opened within the nation.

Initially, the Vatican attempted to maintain its traditional role, issuing pronouncements that emphasized faith, resilience, and the inherent sanctity of human souls, regardless of external influences. Cardinal Valerius, a prominent figure within the Curia and a known proponent of a more open dialogue regarding extraterrestrial life, found himself at odds with the more conservative elements of the hierarchy. He argued that the Church's credibility was on the line; to ignore the overwhelming evidence of alien influence would be to alienate millions of faithful who were already grappling with doubt. He believed the Church should embrace the truth, reinterpreting scripture considering this new cosmic reality, and guide humanity through this existential awakening, asserting that God's creation was far grander and more complex than previously imagined.

The world, once numb to the insidious hum of alien influence, stirred. The leaked data from the Lumina Council, a digital Rosetta Stone to humanity's collective subjugation, had served as a harsh awakening, peeling back the layers of manufactured reality to reveal a stark, unsettling truth. Governments grappled with the ensuing chaos, their pronouncements a cacophony of denial, justification, and desperate damage control. Yet, beneath the veneer of official responses, something far more potent and organic was taking root: resistance.

Across continents and cultures, individuals who had absorbed the undeniable evidence coalesced. These were not soldiers or seasoned politicians, but the inheritors of a future stolen, the custodians of a sovereignty compromised. Scientists had dedicated their lives to the universe, and then they discovered its intricate manipulation on their doorstep. They were activists who had fought for human rights and self-determination, now confronted with an existential threat that dwarfed any previous struggle. They were ordinary citizens, the quiet majority, who, upon grasping the magnitude of the deception, felt an unshakeable resolve to reclaim their agency.

Across the Atlantic, in the bustling metropolises of Europe, a different resistance was brewing. Noor Hassan, a fiercely independent investigative journalist, whose career exposed corporate malfeasance and governmental overreach, found the Lumina Council's revelation dwarfed her life's work. She had faced the usual stonewalling and veiled threats after exposing a shadowy global financial network that had profited immensely from Lumina Council-derived innovations. But now, armed with the leaked data, she possessed irrefutable proof of the alien entities' hand in shaping global economics and political power structures. She organized a network of independent media outlets and citizen journalists, creating decentralized platforms to disseminate information that mainstream media, heavily influenced by pro-Council factions, either ignored or actively suppressed. Her approach was not one of scientific jargon, but of raw, unvarnished truth, translating the complex implications of alien pacts into a language that resonated with the common person. She focused on the erosion of human autonomy, the clandestine control over resource allocation, and the subtle manipulation of cultural narratives, all orchestrated to maintain a facade of human governance while ensuring continued alien dominance. Hassan's network became a vital counter-narrative, a bulwark against the tide of disinformation, fostering critical thinking and encouraging grassroots activism.

In the digital ether, a new form of protest emerged. Online communities, once the domain of memes and social discourse, transformed into virtual battlegrounds. Hashtags like #ReclaimOurDestiny and #EndThePact trended globally, fueled by a new generation of activists who understood the power of the internet to mobilize and inform. These digital natives, born into a world already shaped by Lumina Council technologies, felt a profound sense of betrayal. They organized virtual rallies, launched sophisticated disinformation counter-campaigns against pro-Council propaganda, and created secure channels for whistleblowers to share information without fear of reprisal. One such group, operating under the moniker "The Ghost Network," composed of anonymous hackers and cybersecurity experts, dedicated themselves to disrupting Lumina Council-controlled infrastructure and exposing their clandestine operations. They were the unseen saboteurs, the digital phantoms haunting the edges of the alien-controlled network. Their actions, though often shrouded in secrecy, were crucial in sowing discord and providing moments of vulnerability in the otherwise impenetrable facade of Lumina Council dominance. Their daring breaches into secure data vaults revealed not just financial transactions but also sensitive intelligence on the Lumina Council's long-term colonization strategies, information that was then carefully curated and disseminated by journalists like Hassan.

Amidst this burgeoning global awakening, a few individuals found themselves thrust into the unwanted spotlight. Dr. Evelyn Reed, the brilliant xenolinguistics whose initial decryption of Lumina Council communications had inadvertently triggered the leak, became an unwitting symbol of the resistance. Her nuanced understanding of the alien language and her profound ethical qualms about the implications of their presence made her a beacon for those seeking genuine answers. Though she recoiled from the attention, her public statements, carefully worded but resolute, articulated the core of the resistance's demands: transparency, accountability, and the immediate cessation of all Lumina Council interference in human affairs. She spoke not of war, but of dialogue, of establishing a true, uncoerced relationship between species, one founded on mutual respect rather than paternalistic control.

The council's patience was not solely a function of time, but also of resource allocation. Their observation and intervention protocols were energy intensive, requiring vast amounts of power and computational resources. The escalation of their activities meant a diversion of these resources from other, less critical sectors of their vast interstellar domain. This created internal pressure to resolve the Earth situation efficiently. Their analysis showed that a prolonged period of uncertainty and active resistance could cause more direct and potentially destructive interventions, a path they preferred to avoid because of the inherent risks of provoking an unmanageable conflict and damaging the very civilization they intended to absorb.

In the silent, vast expanse of space, the Lumina Council's Great Archive accumulated an unprecedented volume of data concerning Earth. Previously, records had been sparse, focusing on the planet's geological and biological evolution, its early technological aspirations. Now, the archive was being flooded with real-time sensory input, economic indicators, social media sentiment analysis, and the intricate, rapidly developing tapestry of human response to a paradigm-shattering revelation. The Council's central processing units, capable of analyzing information on a galactic scale, were working overtime, trying to find patterns in the apparent chaos, to predict the next move of a species that was, for the first time, truly aware of its cosmic isolation and the alien presence within its own sphere. Their detached study had indeed escalated into something far more active, a desperate attempt to regain control over a narrative that was rapidly slipping through their ancient, multi-jointed fingers. The era of passive observation was unequivocally over.

Since the cat was let out of the bag, the pact went viral within five minutes. Since then, the world was literally in a new place. Rachel, Jasper, and Ben were sitting at the computers on Project Nightingale watching media after media break the story. Being an armchair quarterback, the Vatican really had no believable excuse for what's been done. Perhaps the authorities initially had a good reason to sign that compact, but as centuries passed, it seemed criminal to continue it. Overnight, something changed humankind. Things that were close to the heart, such as family, became the most important things in a person's life. Things that used to be important, such as careers, disappeared in relevance overnight.

The world was in a place it's never been in before. Countries became concerned with global life and strengthening relations. There was no more talk of war or other nonsense. The stock markets in every country crashed. And the world's citizens couldn't have cared less. The days of chasing the almighty buck were over. Farmers sold their crops to families. Doctors would have gladly accepted a chicken instead of cash for payment on a bill. The world was becoming a nice place for once. People walked across their yards to meet their neighbors. The days of living next to someone for years and not even knowing their names were over. The days of sitting on the front porch and waving at passersby were back.

School-age children were back to learning the three Rs again. The internet remained, but a big pause happened to it. It no longer carried the weight and popularity it once did. Its heyday was over. It became entertainment again. Mothers and fathers became a household again.

One strange thing happened to the fabric of the world: God. The Vatican was trying to figure out how it would become part of the world again and was having its issues with the Overseers. People were living God-fearing lives. They went to churches that just worshipped God. No one knew if the Catholic Church could recover from this. In a way, Rachel felt kind of sad about their position. Overnight, Rachel, Benjammin and Jasper received Nobel Peace Prizes. The world became a peaceful place. Everyone had the belief of "#Earth first."

The world did not care about the aliens. The world spoke loudly. Get them out. The military told the Vatican to get the visitors to leave before the bombings began. The council held its ground. They just did not take the hint and were still fighting to get their standing back in the world.

CHAPTER 14

THE GLOBAL AWAKENING

The Lumina Council, observing the increasingly volatile state of humanity, recognized that their carefully calibrated approach was no longer sufficient. Instead of a controlled release, the initial revelation ignited a global firestorm. The predicted descent into manageable fragmentation had not materialized. Instead, a new sense of global unity, albeit born out of shared uncertainty and healthy defiance, had coalesced. Their long-term objective remained the orderly integration of Earth into their galactic federation, a process that demanded predictability and a certain level of manageable conformity. Humanity's current trajectory, characterized by pockets of organized resistance, rapid technological adaptation, and an increasingly vocal challenge to the established order, threatened to derail this carefully laid plan.

It was within this context of escalating unpredictability that the Council activated what they termed the 'Accelerated Harvest Protocols.' This was not a sudden shift, but an advanced phase of a pre-existing operational matrix, designed for scenarios where slower, more organic integration proved infeasible. In its purest form, the 'harvest' meant collecting a species' data. Sped-up protocols should expedite this process, turning gradual data accretion into a more concentrated acquisition. The process was expedited when the natural harvest was too slow, or when the subject showed signs of self-determination.

The initial display of these protocols subtly altered the planet. These were not direct acts of terraforming or overtly destructive meteorological events, but intricate adjustments to existing environmental patterns. The Council's advanced climate manipulation technologies, far beyond human comprehension, introduced minor, yet cumulative, anomalies. Forecasts that had been reliable for decades deviated. Unseasonal weather patterns, random and isolated, appeared with unnerving frequency. Prolonged droughts in some regions coincided with unprecedented rainfall in others, not to cause immediate mass devastation, but to create a state of constant, low-level environmental stress. The goal was not to break humanity outright, but to induce a state of perpetual anxiety, forcing societies to divert resources and attention away from resistance efforts and towards immediate survival needs.

This environmental destabilization served a dual purpose. First, it generated tangible, immediate crises that would naturally fragment global focus. Governments had to address food shortages, water scarcity, and mass displacement, which all required immediate attention and resources. Second, it served as a testing ground for humanity's resilience and adaptability in the face of prolonged, externally induced pressure. The Council meticulously analyzed how human societies responded to these cascading environmental challenges, observing their ability to innovate, their patterns of cooperation or conflict, and their reliance on existing technological infrastructure, much of which, the Council knew, still contained subtle vulnerabilities traceable to their own past influences. The chaos, therefore, became an instrument, a tool to gauge and ultimately manipulate the pace of human societal evolution.

Beyond environmental manipulation, the Council started more direct, yet still subtly veiled, forms of psychological conditioning. They understood that humanity, now aware of its cosmic context, was susceptible to narrative manipulation. Using their deep understanding of human psychology, amplified by data gathered from their advanced surveillance systems, they influenced global discourse subtly. Compromised media channels, both overt and covert, were used to propagate a carefully curated stream of information. This stream often highlighted the futility of resistance, the overwhelming power of the unknown, and the inevitable subjugation of any species that dared to defy a higher cosmic order. The Council didn't invent new fears; they amplified existing ones, weaving them into a tapestry of pervasive dread.

One significant faction emerged, characterized by a profound sense of awe and an overwhelming belief in the superiority of the Lumina Council. These were the 'Appeasers,' a diverse group encompassing disillusioned politicians, corporate leaders eager to secure new avenues of profit and influence, and a segment of the populace that found solace in the idea of benevolent overlords guiding humanity's destiny. Their argument was simple, yet chillingly persuasive to some: resistance was futile, and survival lay in subservience. They reasoned that the Lumina Council, with its seemingly omnipotent technology and advanced civilization, was not merely conquerors but potential saviors, offering humanity a place, albeit a subordinate one, within a grander cosmic order. Leave it to the politicians to make a buck.

These appeasement factions lobbied actively, both publicly and through covert channels, for a conciliatory approach. They spoke of negotiation, of seeking favorable terms for humanity's integration into the Lumina framework. This often translated into advocating for policies that prioritized cooperation with the Council's directives, even if those directives involved the gradual dismantling of human sovereignty. They pointed to the Council's initial subtle interventions as evidence of their non-hostile intentions, framing the environmental disruptions as necessary adjustments for a species deemed not yet ready for full galactic citizenship. Their rhetoric painted a picture of benevolent guidance, a firm but fair hand leading humanity out of its self-imposed darkness. This practice was causing big issues on the world stage. Most of the world wanted the aliens to leave and not to be on Earth anymore.

Within these circles, individuals and groups formed what they termed 'Liaison Committees' or 'Interstellar Integration Task Forces.'

Their members, often drawn from the ranks of former diplomats, international business executives, and technologists who had once harbored dreams of space exploration, now focused their energies on understanding and complying with the Lumina Council's unspoken demands. They scoured intercepted communications, analyzed the subtle shifts in global atmospheric patterns, and attempted to decipher the Council's overarching objectives, not to resist them, but to align with them. The hope was that by demonstrating their willingness to cooperate, they could secure preferential treatment, perhaps even immunity from the more invasive aspects of the 'harvest.' Some even posited that by actively assisting the Council, they could position themselves as intermediaries, ensuring that humanity's limited knowledge and resources were exploited in the least damaging way possible. This often involved proposing the establishment of specialized human research units dedicated to understanding Lumina technology, or suggesting the selective sharing of Earth's biological and cultural archives, presented as a gesture of goodwill. The underlying fear was that if humanity presented a unified front of defiance, the Council would resort to more direct and devastating methods of subjugation.

Conversely, the resistance, spearheaded by Jasper, Benjamin, Rachel, and others, faced a formidable challenge in uniting a world so eager to embrace division. Their message of defiance, of the inalienable right to self-determination, resonated deeply with a growing segment of the population. However, the constant barrage of Lumina-induced psychological manipulation, coupled with the environmental stressors, made sustained, cohesive action incredibly difficult. Fear, doubt, and apathy were potent weapons in the Council's arsenal, and they were being wielded with devastating effect.

Rachel navigated a treacherous path. Her initial broadcasts, which had once been met with a surge of hope and defiance, now often found themselves drowned out by a cacophony of conflicting narratives. The Lumina Council, through its sophisticated manipulation of global information networks, was adept at amplifying dissent within the resistance itself.

Within Rachel's own network, this division manifested in stark, often painful ways. Some operatives tasked with gathering intelligence questioned the efficacy of their dangerous missions, whispering about the appeasement factions and their promises of a less painful future. Others, disheartened by the lack of widespread global support, advocated for a more passive approach, focusing on preserving local communities rather than engaging in large-scale defiance. The constant pressure from the Lumina Council, both overt and covert, achieved precisely this outcome: to make the idea of organized resistance seem not only futile but also dangerous, a reckless gamble that threatened the fragile peace some were trying to secure.

One faction within the resistance, disillusioned by the lack of progress and the overwhelming power of the Lumina Council, advocated for a strategy of 'selective engagement.' They argued that instead of attempting to fight the Council on all fronts, humanity should focus its efforts on protecting specific, vital resources and knowledge bases. It seemed each person had a belief and wanted their opinion to be the new idea.

The Lumina Council, observing this fragmentation with detached precision, found it to be an ideal catalyst for their sped-up harvest protocols. The division within humanity was not merely a consequence of their actions; it was an integral part of their strategy. A united humanity, driven by a shared sense of purpose, would have been a formidable adversary. A fragmented humanity, however, was a collection of vulnerable targets, each susceptible to manipulation in its own unique way.

Conversely, the resistance, fractured and struggling for cohesion, was being subjected to a more targeted form of disruption. The empathic resonance disruptors were fine-tuned to exacerbate existing tensions within the resistance cells. In areas where Rachel's message of defiance was gaining traction, the frequencies would be adjusted to induce paranoia and infighting, making communication and trust incredibly difficult.

Even though the Nautilus mission brought the Pact to light. Unfortunately, the world did not know how to handle this and how to react. The trio was thrust into the limelight, and that benefited no one. They went off the grid and continued the fight, and pursued other interests. The trio found a large parcel of land in the mountains of Tennessee. Becoming self-sufficient in these turbulent times and be ready for any emergency was very important. They had years of food stored, generated their own electricity, and had their own fresh spring drinking water.

"We thought revealing their plan was enough," Rachel murmured, her voice barely disturbing the charged silence. "We thought showing them what the Lumina Council intends—the systematic depletion of our biosphere, the harvesting of our planet's core resources, the gradual assimilation of our collective consciousness—would ignite a global firestorm of defiance. But the Council framed it all differently."

Benjamin sighs, the sound heavy with resignation. "They've done more than frame it, Rachel. They've *reshaped* it. For a significant portion of the population, the Lumina Council isn't an invading force; it's a necessary evolutionary step. They're selling salvation through servitude, a comfortable cage for a species they deem too reckless to be trusted with its own freedom." He gestured towards the projection, where shimmering lines showed the intricate network of Lumina influence reaching into Earth's communications and energy grids. "And we're still playing defense. We're reacting, not acting. We're exposing their moves, but we're not stopping them."

Jasper looked up, his eyes sharp. "Rachel, the window is closing. The spectral analysis shows that the primary energy conduits are nearing their full operational capacity. The atmospheric manipulation is reaching its apex, creating the perfect conditions for the... extraction." He hesitated, the clinical detachment of his scientific training warring with the chilling reality of the situation. "We're talking about the final stages of the 'harvest,' as they've subtly termed it in their own communications. This isn't about preliminary data gathering anymore. This is about the core process."

Rachel met Jasper's gaze, a flicker of resolve igniting within her. "Which means our mission has to change. We can't just be whistleblowers anymore. We have to be saboteurs." The words hung in the air, heavy with implication. Their previous efforts had focused on intelligence gathering and dissemination, on arming humanity with knowledge. Now, knowledge was not enough. They needed to actively disrupt, interfere with , and directly counter the alien technology and its insidious influence.

"Sabotage requires resources we don't have, Rachel," Benjamin said, his tone pragmatic, though his eyes betrayed a hint of hope at the shift in strategy. "Their technology is light-years beyond anything we possess. We can't fight their energy weapons with our own. We can't disrupt their orbital control systems with our antiquated satellites."

"But we can exploit their systems," Jasper counters, his fingers flying across a holographic interface. "We've identified critical nodes within their planetary energy grid. Not the main conduits, which are too heavily shielded, but the tertiary distribution networks. These interface with our existing infrastructure to make the assimilation seamless. They are, by definition, the weakest points of integration."

Rachel leaned forward, her focus sharpening. "Weak points. What kind of weakness?"

"Interference patterns," Jasper explained, bringing up complex waveform visualizations. "Their technology relies on hyper-precise energy frequencies for communication, environmental control, and data assimilation. If we can introduce precisely timed resonance frequencies into these tertiary networks, we can create cascading failures. Think of it like introducing a specific harmonic into a glass structure; at the right frequency, it shatters."

"Shatter their control?" Rachel mused. "What would that look like?"

"Localized outages," Benjamin said, his mind already working through the tactical implications. "Disruptions in their atmospheric regulators, potentially causing temporary but significant environmental fluctuations. Glitches in their data assimilation streams, forcing them to re-route and re-process, buying us precious time. It's not a knockout blow, but it's a way to fight back, to disrupt the rhythm of their harvest."

"And the psychological aspect?" Rachel pressed. "We saw how effective their subtle manipulation of our emotions and perceptions had been. Can we counter that?"

"A cognitive shield," Rachel repeated, picturing a mental buffer, a personal fortress against the alien onslaught. "How would it work?"

"It's highly speculative," Jasper admitted, "but the theory involves projecting a low-level, modulated electromagnetic field around a subject, attuned to specific neural frequencies. This field would act as an agent, essentially creating a 'noise' that scrambles the targeted empathic broadcasts. It would require individual emitters small enough to be portable and a centralized system to coordinate and calibrate the fields across a network of individuals."

Benjamin leaned back, running a hand through his hair. "Rachel, this is a massive undertaking. Figure out how it all works and where to deploy. Once again, you would have minimal resources and maximum risk. Are you up to it again? Of course you can count me in."

"We are the remnants of a resistance that never truly coalesced," Rachel said, her voice gaining strength. "But we are not defeated. The appeasement narrative has taken hold, yes, but it hasn't extinguished the spark of defiance in everyone. There are still pockets of resistance, individuals and groups who understand the true stakes. We need to find them, and we need to equip them. Not with weapons, but with Thorne's cognitive shields and Jasper's disruptor devices."

Jasper projected a series of schematics. "These are the disruptor units. They are discreet, masquerading as standard atmospheric sensors or communication relays. Someone can deploy them remotely or install them manually. The energy requirements are significant but manageable for short, targeted bursts of interference. Synchronized activation is the critical factor. We need a network, a way to coordinate these devices to achieve the desired cascading effect."

"And the cognitive shields?" Rachel asked, her gaze fixed on Jasper.

"The prototypes are functional, but crude," Jasper admitted. "They are bulky, need frequent recharging, and have a limited range." Thorne's calculationssuggest we'd need a minimum of several thousand active shields within a localized area to create a noticeable ripple effect. The challenge is mass production. We lack the manufacturing capabilities, and any attempt to scale up would immediately draw Lumina's attention."

Benjamin's eyes narrowed as he studied the schematics of the disruptor units. "We can't mass-produce them openly. But what if we don't have to? What if we leverage the very infrastructure the Lumina Council is trying to integrate?"

Rachel caught his drift. "The appeasement faction. They're eager to show their loyalty, to prove their worth to the Council. They're setting up the 'Interstellar Integration Task Force' and 'Liaison Committees.' They are creating centralized hubs for research and development, ostensibly to understand and implement Lumina directives. What if we can infiltrate those hubs? What if we can use their own labs, their own resources, to build these devices?"

Jasper's eyes widened. "It's audacious, Rachel. And incredibly dangerous. If the Council detects our presence within their favored human collaborators, the retaliation would be swift and severe."

"But it's also our best chance," Benjamin counters. "They are actively seeking to integrate, to cooperate. We can use that desire against the Council. We can become the hidden hand within the appeasement movement, seeding disruption from the inside. Rachel, your ability to navigate complex social and political landscapes, to understand motivations and exploit vulnerabilities, is precisely what's needed here. You can be the face of our... internal infiltration."

Rachel felt a cold knot tighten in her stomach, but a growing sense of purpose tempered it. Her previous work had been about revealing the truth to a world that was rapidly losing the capacity to hear it. Now, her task was more clandestine, more dangerous, and arguably more vital. She would have to become a phantom, weaving through the very fabric of humanity's capitulation, planting the seeds of rebellion where hope had withered.

"The cognitive shields are the priority for deployment," Rachel declared, her voice firm. "We need to equip key individuals, those who are still capable of critical thought and who can inspire others. We can't protect everyone, but we can create focal points of resistance, individuals who can act as conduits of defiance in the Council's pervasive influence."

Jasper refined the schematics for the shields. "The current prototypes require a direct neural interface. This makes them difficult to conceal and administer. Thorne was exploring non-invasive methods, but those are still in their beginning stages. For now, we'll have to adapt. We can build smaller, more discreet emitters and integrate them into personal devices such as watches, pendants, or even rudimentary implants if needed. The energy source is still a bottleneck, though. We'll need a reliable, portable power solution."

"We'll have to scavenge," Benjamin stated. "Divert power from Lumina-controlled grids where possible; use hidden caches of pre-collapse technology. And we'll need a network of trusted technicians, individuals who understand the risks and are

committed to the cause, to build and maintain these devices. They'll need to operate in the shadows, beneath the Council's notice."

The plan coalesced, a fragile but determined framework built from desperation and ingenuity. Their mission had irrevocably shifted. It was no longer about waiting for humanity to awaken; it was about forcing its eyes open, one mind at a time, and disrupting the alien machinery that was slowly, inexorably, siphoning the life from their world.

"We need to identify potential targets for the cognitive shields," Rachel said, her gaze sweeping across the holographic displays. "Not just resistance fighters, but influential figures who are wavering, those who are still capable of independent thought but are being swayed by the appeasement narrative. We can offer them a choice: continued servitude, or the chance to fight back, to reclaim their agency."

Jasper brought up a list of individuals, cross-referenced with known communication patterns and potential ideological leanings. "This list is speculative, but it represents a range of individuals: scientists, artists, community leaders, even some disillusioned figures within the appeasement factions themselves. The key is to target those who have the potential to influence others, to create a ripple effect that spreads outwards."

"And the disruptor units?" Benjamin asked. "Where do we deploy them for maximum impact?"

"Critical infrastructure nodes," Jasper replied, highlighting specific geographical areas. "Places where Lumina control is most deeply entrenched. Power generation facilities, atmospheric processing centers, key data hubs. A synchronized disruption in these areas could create significant chaos, not just physically but psychologically. It could sow doubt, remind people that the Lumina Council's control is not absolute, that there is still resistance."

Rachel felt a surge of adrenaline, a potent cocktail of fear and determination. The path ahead was fraught with peril, a labyrinth of alien surveillance and human betrayal. But for the first time in a long time, she felt a tangible sense of purpose. They were moving beyond passive observation and into active engagement. They were no longer just fighting for humanity's future; they were actively trying to carve out a space for it.

"We need to establish secure communication channels," Rachel stated, her mind already racing through operational protocols. "Thorne's methods of encryption, combined with Jasper's understanding of Lumina signal patterns, should allow us to create a network that is largely invisible to their surveillance. We'll need mobile command units, not just this one fixed location. The appeasers are creating centralized hubs, but that makes them predictable. We need to be decentralized, fluid, and unpredictable."

Benjamin nodded, his tactical mind already mapping out deployment strategies. "We can adapt existing underground networks, abandoned pre-collapse facilities. We'll need to move frequently, to erase our digital footprints. And we'll need a constant stream of intelligence. We can't afford to be blindsided by their next move."

"That's where our existing network comes in," Rachel said, her gaze steady. "The few who still trust us, who are still willing to risk everything. They'll be our eyes and ears on the ground, feeding us information about Lumina movements, about the effectiveness of the appeasement agenda, and about potential recruits for Thorne's shields. Every bit of data, every intercepted whisper, will be crucial."

Jasper began to sketch out a preliminary timeline, his fingers dancing across the interface with renewed vigor. "The initial phase will focus on establishing these secure networks and commencing the discreet manufacturing of the disruptor units within the appeasement facilities. Simultaneously, we will begin developing and testing the refined cognitive shield emitters. This will take weeks, perhaps months."

"Months we may not have," Rachel interjected, her voice grim. "The acceleration of their harvest protocols is undeniable. We need to move faster. We need to take calculated risks. Perhaps we can't mass-produce Thorne's shields, but we can produce a limited number of highly effective units and deploy them strategically. Not to protect the masses, but to empower key individuals, to create nodes of active resistance that can inspire others and sow discord among the appeasers."

"And the disruptors?" Benjamin asked. "How do we deploy them without revealing our hand too early?"

"We use their own systems against them," Rachel said, a dangerous glint in her eyes. "We identify moments of peak Lumina activity, when their energy grids are most strained, their surveillance networks most engaged. A precisely timed disruption, a flicker of chaos in their meticulously planned operation, could be more effective than a sustained attack. It will be a war of attrition, fought in the shadows, with our minds and their own technology as our primary weapons."

The weight of their new mission settled upon them, heavy and exhilarating. They were no longer merely observers of humanity's impending doom; they were its reluctant, defiant architects of a counter-revolution. The final countdown had indeed begun, but perhaps, just perhaps, they had found a way to alter its tempo, to introduce a discordant note into the Lumina Council's symphony of conquest. The path was perilous, the odds stacked against them, but the alternative – a silent, subservient surrender – was no longer an option. They would fight. They would disrupt. Resistance would be their response.

The archived data, a vast and labyrinthine repository of Lumina Council communication intercepts, scientific observations, and fragmented historical records, lay before Rachel like an indecipherable tapestry. Weeks had blurred into a relentless cycle of analysis, each researcher poring over their specialized domain, searching for the single thread that would unravel the alien dominion. They had sifted through Lumina energy signatures, cross-referenced atmospheric anomalies with reported societal shifts, and delved into the psychological profiles of Lumina operatives—or rather, the carefully curated public personas they presented. The challenge, however, was not a lack of information, but an overwhelming surfeit of it, each piece a potential clue, each correlation a siren song leading to a dead end.

"It's like trying to find a specific grain of sand on an infinite beach," Dr. Jian Li Jasper sighed, rubbing his temples. The holographic display before him shimmered with intricate geometric patterns, representing the complex network of Lumina's psionic resonance projectors. "Their technology is so elegantly integrated, so seamless, that identifying a singular point of failure feels… impossible. They've accounted for every contingency, every potential disruption we could conceive of."

Rachel traced a line on a different holographic projection, one that detailed the Lumina Council's intricate terraforming initiatives. The projected changes to Earth's atmosphere and magnetic field were staggering, far exceeding the initial intelligence reports. "But how do we disrupt something so fundamental? We've tried jamming their frequencies, overwhelming their emitters with decoy signals. It's like shouting into a hurricane. They simply recalibrate."

It was during one of these late-night, caffeine-fueled sessions, amidst the sterile hum of the subterranean command center, that Rachel stumbled upon something incongruous. There was no present in their technology, nor any weakness in planning. It was something far more… subtle. The Lumina archives contained not only technical data but also cultural records, fragments of their own history and societal evolution. They cataloged these meticulously, almost as a form of detached anthropological study, but for Rachel, they offered a different perspective.

She had been studying their linguistic patterns, the nuances of their diplomatic protocols, and the subtle ideological undercurrents within their internal communications. The Lumina, as a species, projected an image of absolute logic, of dispassionate efficiency. Their framework for actions was always overarching, seemingly irrefutable, and rational. They presented themselves as benevolent custodians, guiding humanity towards a more stable, ordered future, devoid of the "chaotic variables" that plagued pre-Lumina civilizations.

But buried within their historical narratives, within their philosophical treatises, was a recurring theme: a deep-seated aversion to genuine, unadulterated *creativity*. Not the calculated innovation that propelled their own technological advancements, but the wild, unpredictable spark of novel thought, the act of creation that sprang from instinct, emotion, and pure, unbridled imagination. They described it as a dangerous anomaly, a source of instability, something they needed to manage carefully and, if possible, suppress.

"They fear what they cannot quantify," Rachel mused, the realization dawning with an almost palpable intensity. She projected a series of Lumina philosophical texts onto the main screen, highlighting passages that spoke of "entropic deviations" and "the necessity of predictable outcomes."

Jasper looked up from his own research, intrigued. "What are you seeing, Rachel?"

"The Lumina Council operates on a principle of absolute control, of predictable causality," Rachel explained, her voice gaining a new urgency. "They built their entire civilization on algorithms, extrapolating data to its most logical conclusion." They have perfected the art of prediction, of control, by minimizing the variables. And what is the ultimate variable? True, unscripted creativity. The thinking that leads to leaps of intuition, to the creation of something entirely new, something that defies existing paradigms."

Benjamin, ever the pragmatist, raised an eyebrow. "So, what? We paint murals and write poetry at them?"

Rachel chuckles, a rare sound in the tense atmosphere. "Not exactly. But consider this: their psionic resonance technology, their atmospheric regulators, their assimilation protocols—all of it maintains a state of controlled equilibrium. They are masters of optimization. But what happens when they encounter something that is *un-optimizable*? They cannot predict, streamline, or categorize something within their rigid logical frameworks.

She pulled up data on human cultural output prior to Lumina's arrival. Not just grand artistic movements, but individual acts of spontaneous expression: street art that appeared overnight, impromptu musical performances in public squares, underground literary zines that circulated anonymously, even complex, emergent patterns in crowd behavior that defied simple explanation.

"Their system assimilates, to integrate, to bring everything into alignment with their own ordered existence," Rachel continued. "They've successfully dampened overt resistance by manipulating emotional responses, by promoting apathy and compliance. But they've also inadvertently created a void. A space where raw, untamed creativity can flourish, especially in the hidden corners of society that still resist assimilation."

Jasper's eyes widened as he grasped Rachel's line of reasoning. "Are you suggesting they calibrate their control mechanisms to handle predictable dissent and emotional outliers?" They can process fear, anger, even overt rebellion, because these are understandable responses within a logical framework of opposition. But genuine, emergent creativity… that's a different order of anomaly."

"Precisely," Rachel affirmed. "They built their system on pattern recognition and response." They can identify a threat based on known parameters. But what if the 'threat' isn't a direct confrontation, but a disruption of the very substrate upon which their control operates? Imagine introducing a chaotic, unpredictable element into their hyper-ordered systems. Not a physical attack, but a *conceptual* one."

Benjamin remained skeptical, but he was listening intently. "How would we even go about that? We can't just unleash artists on their orbital platforms."

"We leverage what we have," Rachel said, sweeping her gaze across the research terminals. "We have Thorne's work on cognitive shields, imperfect as it is. Our company has Jasper's disruptor technology. What if we combine them in a new way? What if we don't aim to block Lumina's influence, but to *scramble* it by introducing chaotic, unpredictable mental 'noise'? Thorne believed a shield created enough static to make manipulation difficult. What if we could amplify that static to make it actively disruptive, not just passively resistant?"

Jasper sketched out new schematics, his fingers flying across the holographic interface with renewed purpose. "The current shield technology relies on synchronizing with specific neural frequencies. If we could introduce random, non-repeating waveforms into that synchronization process... it would be like trying to tune a radio to a thousand different stations at once. A cacophony of cognitive dissonance would drown the Lumina empathic resonance out."

"And we could use these units to send out these confusing messages," Rachel added, figuring it out. "Instead of targeting their energy grids, we target their resonance projectors. We will create localized zones, and in these zones, their ability to influence minds will severely degrade, allowing individuals to think freely.

"This is... unprecedented," Jasper murmured, staring at the developing designs. "The energy requirements for such a wide-spectrum, chaotic output would be immense. And the calibration would need to be incredibly precise, not to achieve a specific outcome, but to ensure a constant state of unpredictability."

"That's where the human element comes in," Rachel stated, her voice firm. "We can't automate true creativity. But we can identify individuals, pockets of humanity that still possess that spark. Artists, musicians, writers, and even scientists have been forced into sterile, Lumina-approved research. We find them, we equip them with these amplified shields, and we give them a platform. A platform to create, express, and simply be in a way that the Lumina cannot predict or control.

Benjamin leaned forward, the initial skepticism giving way to a grudging admiration for the sheer audacity of the plan. "So, we're not trying to destroy their technology. We're trying to overload it with something it cannot process: unpredictable human expression. We're turning their strength – their logic and order—into a vulnerability."

"Exactly," Rachel confirmed. "They optimized their system for control." It cannot account for genuine novelty, for the chaotic beauty of emergent consciousness. By creating these pockets of amplified cognitive freedom, we sow doubt not just in the minds of humans, but potentially within the Lumina's own understanding of our species. If they cannot predict our reactions, if our collective consciousness exhibits unpredictable, creative patterns, their entire model of assimilation breaks down."

The implications were vast. The solution didn't involve brute force or direct confrontation. It was about a subtle, pervasive subversion, an act of intellectual and artistic sabotage. It was about weaponizing humanity's most fundamental trait: its capacity for boundless, unpredictable creation.

"We'll need to identify individuals who are already exhibiting signs of creative resistance," Jasper suggested. "Those whose work, even under Lumina censorship, still carries a unique signature. We can discreetly approach them, offer them the amplified shields, and then encourage them to express themselves freely. Imagine a concert where the music itself acts as a disruptor, or a piece of art that, when viewed, generates a field of cognitive chaos. Lumina would confuse them.

"And the deployment strategy?" Benjamin asked, his mind already whirring with the logistical challenges. "Where do we create these zones of amplified creativity?"

"We start small," Rachel decided. "In areas where Lumina influence is strong, but where pockets of independent culture still linger. We establish these zones, and we observe the Lumina response. If they attempt to suppress it with brute force, they expose their own limitations. If they try to analyze and control it, they enter a realm of logic that is inherently unstable for them. It's a trap, laid with the tools of human ingenuity."

Rachel looked at the complex network of Lumina resonance projectors on the main screen. "They designed their system for harmonious integration." We're going to introduce a symphony of controlled chaos. We're going to remind them that humanity is not just a resource to be harvested, but a force of nature that cannot be tamed, only endured. This is not about fighting their technology; it's about out-thinking their logic. It's about finding the alien weakness in their utterly alien perception of what it means to be alive." The search for a conventional weakness had been a dead end. Now, they were forging a new path, one that led not to the enemy's arsenal, but to the very heart of their philosophical limitations.

The hum of the subterranean command center had become a constant companion to Rachel, a low thrum that vibrated in her bones, a testament to the tireless, often futile, efforts of the Lumina Council's opposition. The archived data, once a daunting abyss of alien information, now pulsed with a nascent understanding, a fragile hypothesis taking root in the fertile ground of desperation. Dr. Jian Li Jasper's holographic projections, once intricate maps of Lumina's psionic network, now swirled with abstract, vibrant patterns, representing the cacophony of creative thought Rachel envisioned as their weapon. Benjamin's gaze was fixed on the flickering satellite imagery, charting not troop movements, but potential points of strategic vulnerability within the Lumina's grand, chillingly logical design.

"The archival data on Lumina's own cultural evolution is our most potent weapon," Rachel reiterated, her voice resonating with a conviction that she had painstakingly forged in the crucible of weeks spent deciphering alien philosophies. "They don't just present themselves as logical beings; they *are* logic, amplified to an evolutionary peak. Predictability and the elimination of variables underpin their entire existence, technology, and societal structure. And what is the ultimate variable, the ultimate source of unpredictability they so deeply fear and try to suppress?"

Jasper, his brow furrowed in concentration, adjusted a complex waveform on his display. "Creativity. Pure emergent creativity. The kind that defies algorithms, that springs from instinct and emotion, the very elements they strive to homogenize and control."

"Precisely," Rachel confirmed, gesturing to a series of stark, geometric patterns representing Lumina's assimilation protocols. "Their system categorizes, analyzes, predicts and neutralizes threats based on established parameters. They can understand anger, fear, rebellion – these are logical responses to oppression. But they cannot comprehend genuine, spontaneous innovation. They cannot quantify inspiration. They cannot predict art."

Benjamin, who had been meticulously tracking the atmospheric recalibration sequences, looked up, a flicker of understanding in his eyes. "So, we're not trying to break their machines. We're trying to break their *minds* by introducing something they can't process."

"Exactly," Rachel affirmed. "We will not attack their energy conduits or their command structures. Instead, we will target their psionic resonance projectors, not to disable them, but to overload them with a form of cognitive dissonance they cannot interpret. We will weaponized human creativity."

Jasper nodded, his fingers dancing across the holographic interface, weaving a tapestry of projected energy fields. "The amplified cognitive shields Thorne developed, combined with our disruptor technology, can generate localized zones of extreme mental turbulence. Instead of simply blocking Lumina influence, these zones will actively broadcast a chaotic symphony of unfettered thought. Imagine it: a constant barrage of unpredictable ideas, emotions, and perceptions, a signal so complex and alien to their ordered minds that it will effectively drown out their own subtle manipulations."

"We're not just creating static," Rachel elaborated, her gaze sweeping across the schematics. "We're creating a storm of novelty. A place where human thought can manifest in ways Lumina cannot anticipate, cannot categorize, and therefore, cannot control. Their system is designed for optimization; it thrives on predictable inputs. We will provide an endless stream of unpredictable, un-optimizable output."

The implications were staggering. This wasn't a war of attrition or a conventional strike. It was an act of subtle, pervasive subversion, a philosophical counter-offensive. They would leverage humanity's most inherent, and for the Lumina, most dangerous, trait: its boundless capacity for creation.

"We'll need to identify individuals who already embody this spirit," Jasper mused, his eyes alight with the challenge. "Artists, musicians, writers, thinkers whose work, even under Lumina censorship, still carries that spark of originality. We equip them with the amplified shields, give them a platform, and encourage them to simply… create. A concert where the music itself becomes a disruptor. A public installation that, when viewed, generates a field of cognitive chaos. The Lumina would be utterly baffled."

Benjamin, ever the strategist, began to assess the deployment. "Where do we establish these zones? We need to choose locations where Lumina influence is strong, but where pockets of independent human culture still persist, however suppressed."

Rachel turned her attention to a detailed topographical map of Earth, highlighting several key geographical and urban centers. "We start small, but strategically. In areas where Lumina has established significant resonance projector networks, but where the echoes of human expression, however faint, still remain. We establish these pockets of amplified creativity, and we observe. If the Lumina attempt to suppress them with force, they reveal their limitations, their inability to grasp the nature of the 'threat'. If they try to analyze and control it, they are entering a realm of logic that is inherently unstable for them. It's a trap, baited with the very essence of human ingenuity."

She pointed to a specific region on the map, a vast, sprawling delta known for its rich artistic heritage, now heavily saturated with Lumina infrastructure. "Area 291. It's where their primary subsurface structures are located, the nexus of their control grid. It's also a place where, according to fragmented historical records, human artistic expression once flourished. If we can reawaken that spirit, even in a localized, amplified fashion, within the shadow of their greatest power… it could be the key."

Jasper's brow furrowed. "Area 291? Rachel, that's considered Ground Zero for their terraforming efforts. The atmospheric anomalies are at their most extreme there. The subsurface structures are heavily fortified, and their energy signatures are unlike anything we've encountered. It's the most dangerous place on Earth."

"And precisely why we must go there," Rachel countered, her voice unwavering. "If their primary control nexus is also the focal point of their most aggressive environmental manipulation, then disrupting their ability to influence minds at that very nexus could have cascading effects. We've spent weeks analyzing Lumina's strengths—their logic, their technology, their control. Now, we must acknowledge their greatest weakness: their inability to comprehend, let alone control, the wild, untamed, unpredictable force of human creativity. And if there is one place where that force could be most impactful, it is at the heart of their dominion, where they are most confident in their absolute power."

The decision hung in the air, heavy with the weight of its audacity and the chilling specter of the risks involved. To return to Area 291, the very epicenter of the Lumina's influence, the source of the most profound and unsettling anomalies, felt like a suicidal gamble. Yet, it was also the only logical conclusion derived from Rachel's revolutionary hypothesis. The key to dismantling the alien dominion wasn't to fight their machines, but to wage war on their philosophical foundations, to confront them with the very essence of what they sought to suppress: the chaotic, beautiful, and irrepressible spirit of human creation.

"We go back to Area 291," Rachel declared, her gaze sweeping across the faces of her team. "Not to fight their technology, but to sow the seeds of its dissolution. We go back to where it all began, to the anomaly that first revealed their presence, and we confront them with the one thing they cannot quantify, cannot control, and ultimately, cannot defeat: the unpredictable spark of human consciousness."

With grim determination, they undertook the journey to Area 291. The subterranean command center, a bastion of their resistance, was left behind, its hum fading into the silent, oppressive atmosphere that characterized the Lumina-controlled zones. Rachel, Jasper, and Benjamin, along with a select team of specialists, boarded the heavily modified stealth transport, its hull etched with experimental patterns designed to disrupt Lumina's passive scanning technologies. As they ascended, the familiar blue and green hues of Earth gave way to a sickly, unnatural ochre, a testament to the Lumina's pervasive terraforming efforts. The air outside, even within the transport's hermetically sealed environment, seemed to press in, heavy with an alien stillness.

"Atmospheric readings are… erratic," Jasper reported, his voice strained as he monitored the external sensors. "The localized energy fluctuations around Area 291 are beyond anything we've recorded. It's like the planet itself is under immense, localized stress."

Benjamin, his hand resting on the transport's control yoke, nodded grimly. "The Lumina have poured immense resources into this sector. It's not just a control hub; it's their primary laboratory for planetary transformation. They're pushing the boundaries of what's possible, experimenting with environmental manipulation on a scale that defies our understanding of planetary physics."

Rachel gazed out of the reinforced viewport, her heart a mixture of dread and a strange, exhilarating anticipation. The landscape below was a haunting tableau of alien ambition. Vast, crystalline structures, impossibly geometric and shimmering with an internal light, pierced the scarred earth. Rivers of iridescent liquid, not water, flowed through unnatural canyons, and the sky was a perpetual twilight, illuminated by the eerie glow of Lumina energy projectors that hung like malignant stars. This was the heart of their dominion, the ground zero of their grand, terrifying harvest.

"The subsurface structures are the key," Rachel stated, her voice cutting through the tension. "The data suggests they are not merely power conduits or data storage. They are the nexus of the psionic resonance projectors, the very instruments through which the Lumina influence minds and manipulate environments. If we can introduce our amplified cognitive dissonance fields directly into that nexus, the resulting feedback loop could destabilize their entire network, at least temporarily."

"But the resonance projectors are designed to operate in harmony with the Earth's natural electromagnetic fields," Jasper counters, his fingers flying across his console. "Our disruptive signals are essentially… noise. Introducing that much chaotic energy into a system built for perfect order could have unforeseen consequences. Not just for the Lumina, but for Earth itself."

"That is the calculated risk," Benjamin stated, his gaze fixed on the emerging signature of Area 291 on his tactical display. "Their control is absolute in this region. If we are to have any chance of disrupting their final phase, it must be here, at the source. We've tried to fight them on the fringes, to intercept their operations. Now, we go to their heart, armed with a weapon they cannot comprehend."

As the transport descended, the oppressive atmosphere thickened. The Lumina structures, once shimmering monuments to alien power, now felt like predatory sentinels, their cold, calculating presence palpable. The ground beneath them began to warp, the very fabric of reality seeming to bend to the Lumina's will. Rachel felt a familiar pressure behind her eyes, the subtle, insidious tendrils of Lumina influence attempting to assert their dominance, even though the transport's advanced shielding.

"They know we're here," she stated, her voice low. "The shield isn't perfect. They're probing. Trying to understand our intent, our capabilities."

"Let them probe," Benjamin said, his knuckles white on the yoke. "Our objective is singular. Reach the primary subsurface access point. Deploy the disruptor units, and initiate the cascade sequence. This is our final gamble. If it fails, the harvest will commence, and humanity as we know it will cease to exist."

The landing zone was a desolate expanse of cracked, sterile earth, punctuated by the jagged silhouettes of Lumina machinery. The air was thick with an almost tangible psionic hum, a constant, unnerving pressure that frayed the nerves. Rachel felt a profound sense of unease, the kind that settled deep in the bones, a primal awareness of being in a place utterly inimical to life as she knew it. This was the anomaly, the origin point, now the epicenter of their last stand.

"The access shaft is approximately three kilometers north-northwest," Benjamin reported, his voice amplified by the comms system. "Minimal Lumina presence detected in the immediate vicinity, but that doesn't mean it's safe. Their defenses are likely integrated into the very fabric of this place."

Rachel nodded, strapping on her suit's environmental controls. "The success of this mission hinges on surprise and speed. We deploy the disruptors, establish the cognitive dissonance zones, and hope the resulting chaos buys us the time we need to enact the next phase. It's not about defeating them here, but about creating a ripple effect that spreads through their entire network."

As they disembarked, the sheer scale of Lumina's operations became overwhelmingly apparent. Colossal crystalline towers pierced the alien sky, their surfaces rippling with contained energy. The ground itself seemed to pulse with a low-frequency vibration, a testament to the immense power being channeled through the subsurface structures. This was not merely a military installation; it was a planetary-scale organ, integrated into the very being of Earth, and now, poised for its final, terrible function.

"The data indicated a significant convergence of resonance projectors beneath this region," Jasper explained, his gloved fingers tracing the lines on his handheld scanner. "They're not just projecting influence; they're actively reshaping the planet's core energy matrix. If Rachel's theory is correct, disrupting that convergence at its source could cause a chain reaction, a feedback loop that paralyzes their control grid."

"The risks are astronomical," Benjamin cautioned, his rifle held at the ready. "We're walking into the belly of the beast. One wrong move, one miscalculation, and we'll be the first to experience the 'ultimate phase' firsthand."

Rachel met his gaze, a steely resolve in her eyes. "We've come this far, Ben. We've uncovered their greatest vulnerability, a weakness born from their very strength. To retreat now, knowing what we know, would be a far greater failure. We are the anomaly. We are the unpredictable variable. And we will deploy that variable right here, at Ground Zero."

The hum of the Lumina's control intensified as they moved deeper into the desolate landscape. The air grew colder, charged with an alien energy that seemed to prickle the skin. This was it. The final countdown had begun, and the fate of humanity rested on a desperate gamble, played out in the very heart of the alien dominion, where the ultimate harvest was about to commence.

CHAPTER 15

DAWN OR OBLIVION

Lumina's planetary assimilation projects brought with them an invaluable, albeit terrifying, knowledge of the alien infrastructure's weaknesses and, more importantly, its blind spots.

The pressure outside the submersible mounted with every meter of descent. The Lumina's psionic resonance projectors, designed to influence and terraform, were most potent in this submerged sector, their energy signatures weaving a complex tapestry of environmental manipulation that defied conventional scientific understanding. The ocean floor here was not a natural formation but a testament to alien engineering – vast, obsidian structures pulsed with an inner luminescence, interconnected by conduits that seemed to writhe like bioluminescent veins. The water itself shimmered with an unnatural iridescence; a byproduct of exotic energies being channeled through the Lumina's grand design.

"The primary nexus is directly below us," Jasper's voice, usually filled with a scientist's detached curiosity, now carried a tremor of grim urgency. His holographic display projected a three-dimensional rendering of the seabed, a complex network of alien architecture pulsating with power. "The archival data we recovered, combined with insights from our new allies, confirms it. This isn't just a processing hub; it's the central nervous system of their entire global operation."

Rachel's gaze was fixed on the main viewport, the alien landscape outside a testament to humanity's encroaching oblivion. Gigantic crystalline formations, impossibly sharp and geometric, jutted from the seabed like the teeth of some slumbering leviathan. The Lumina had chosen this locale not for its natural beauty, but for its geological stability and its strategic position, a place where they could exert unparalleled influence over both the planet's core and its emerging sentient life.

"They expected a direct assault," Benjamin stated, his voice a low growl that echoed the rumble of the submersible's engines. His tactical display showed a swirling vortex of energy signatures, representing Lumina's advanced defensive grid, interwoven with what appeared to be bio-engineered guardians patrolling the abyssal plains. "But they don't expect a psychological one. Not one that weaponized their own greatest fear."

The defectors, faces grim and etched with the weight of their betrayal and their hopes, confirmed Benjamin's assessment. "The Lumina perceive emotion as a chaotic variable," explained Elara, a former Lumina bio-engineer, her voice barely audible above the submersible's hum. "They strive for absolute order, for a predictable, homogenized existence. They cannot comprehend art, spontaneous acts of creation, or the profound irrationality of human love. These are anomalies their logic cannot process, let alone suppress. They've built their empire on predictability; we will inundate it with chaos."

The plan was audacious as it was desperate. Instead of a direct frontal assault on the Lumina's heavily fortified nexus, they intended to deploy a series of amplified psionic dissonance emitters at key points around the primary structure. These emitters, using the principles of emergent creativity Rachel and Jasper had pioneered, would not simply disrupt Lumina signals; they would flood the alien network with a torrent of pure human thought—music, poetry, abstract art, moments of profound joy and sorrow, the entire spectrum of human consciousness, amplified and weaponized. An influx of sentiment and irrationality would overwhelm the Lumina they could neither categorize nor control.

"The primary nexus is a nexus of control, but also a nexus of vulnerability," Jasper elaborated, projecting schematics of Lumina energy conduits. "Their projectors harmonize with planetary frequencies to create a stable, predictable resonance. We will introduce a discordant symphony, a cacophony of human emotion that will overload their predictive algorithms. It's like introducing a virus into a perfectly optimized operating system."

The journey to the primary nexus was fraught with peril. Lumina's automated defense systems, a terrifying blend of advanced alien technology and bio-engineered organisms, awakened. Luminescent tendrils, sharp as obsidian shards, snaked out from the abyssal structures, probing the submersible's hull. Benjamin expertly maneuvered the Nautilus, the reinforced plating groaning under the immense pressure and the glancing blows of these alien sentinels.

"They're aware of our presence," Benjamin announced, his voice tight with concentration. "Their initial response is defensive, probing. They don't seem to recognize our vessel as a direct threat yet, but that won't last."

The first true confrontation came not from alien machines, but from human collaborators. A fleet of submersible craft, sleek and armed with weaponry clearly reverse-engineered from Lumina technology, emerged from the shadows of the alien structures. These were the 'harmonizers,' humans who had willingly embraced the Lumina's promise of order and progress, sacrificing their own humanity.

"My God," Elara whispers, her face pale. "The harmonizers. They augmented them. They're... extensions of the Lumina consciousness."

The battle that ensued was unlike anything humanity had ever witnessed. It was a ballet of destruction in the crushing darkness of the deep sea. The harmonizers' offensive capabilities outgunned the Nautilus, designed for stealth and infiltration. Benjamin, however, had expected this. The submersible's hull embedded micro-disruptors designed to interfere with Lumina-derived technology.

"Deploying countermeasures!" Benjamin shouted over the din of weapon fire. "Jasper, start the harmonic resonance disruption. We need to create a window!"

Jasper's fingers flew across his console. He activated a series of sonic emitters, not to destroy, but to destabilize the harmonizers' control frequencies, introducing a controlled dissonance into their Lumina-augmented brains. The effect was immediate and horrifying. The harmonizer craft veered erratically, their synchronized formations breaking apart. Some vessels fired wildly, their targeting systems compromised, while others simply tumbled out of control, their pilots overwhelmed by the sudden influx of unfiltered human emotion.

"It's working!" Rachel cries, watching the chaos unfold on the tactical display. "They can't process the disruption. Lumina's ordered control built their minds.

Even though they temporarily neutralized the harmonizer threat, the Lumina, the true enemy, retaliated. From the depths of the primary nexus, colossal bio-luminescent entities, resembling immense, ethereal jellyfish with razor-sharp tentacles, emerged. These were the Lumina's living defenses, biological constructs infused with psionic energy, designed to crush any intrusion.

"These are the 'Guardians of the Nexus'," Elara explained, her voice strained. "They feed on psychic energy. Our weapons, our very thoughts, will only empower them if we're not careful."

The Nautilus was no longer a stealth craft; it was a cornered animal fighting for survival. Benjamin fought valiantly, dodging the crushing embrace of the Guardians' tentacles and the retaliatory fire from the remaining harmonizer craft. Meanwhile, Jasper focused on the primary aim.

"We're close to the deployment zones," Jasper reported, his voice strained. "But they heavily shielded the primary nexus." We need to get closer to deploy the emitters effectively."

Rachel knew this was their moment. The plan had always involved a high risk of sacrifice. "Ben, get us as close as you can. Elara, you know the Lumina's energy routing better than anyone. Which conduits are most susceptible to a localized overload?"

Elara pointed to a cluster of pulsating conduits on Jasper's holographic display. "Those. They feed directly into the central processing core. If we can disrupt them simultaneously with the emitter deployment, it might create a cascading feedback loop."

Benjamin, with a grim nod, pushed the Nautilus to its limits, weaving through the maelstrom of alien defenses. The submersible shuddered violently as it scraped against the obsidian structures. Alarms blared, and the lights flickered.

"Hull integrity is at thirty percent!" Benjamin yelled, his face a mask of grim determination. "We have one shot at this!"

Rachel, Jasper, and Elara worked with feverish intensity. Rachel began activating the psionic emitters, small drones that detached from the Nautilus and darted towards the designated deployment points. Jasper tuned the energy output precisely to induce maximum cognitive dissonance. Elara, meanwhile, guided them, her intimate knowledge of Lumina architecture proving invaluable.

"Now!" Elara shouted as the Nautilus stabilized near the target conduits. "Deploy the final emitter directly into the conduit cluster! And activate the primary broadcast!"

Rachel started the primary broadcast after launching the last emitter. A wave of raw, untamed human consciousness erupted from the Nautilus, not as a sound, but as a psychic wave. It was a symphony of chaos, a torrent of creativity, emotion, and sheer being. On Jasper's display, the Lumina's ordered energy signatures began to flicker and warp. An infinite spectrum of subjective experience suddenly flooded the psionic resonance projector.

Instantly, the effect was devastating. The colossal Guardians of the Nexus recoiled, their bioluminescent forms flickering violently as they struggled to process the influx of alien sentiment. The remaining harmonizer craft, their Lumina-infused minds shattering under the psychic onslaught, began to self-destruct in spectacular explosions of light and energy.

But the true impact was on the primary nexus itself. Rather than physical damage, the obsidian structures cracked from logical implosion. The Lumina's grand design, built on the suppression of all that was unpredictable and irrational, was being undone by the very forces it sought to eradicate.

"The network is becoming unstable!" Jasper exclaimed, his voice hoarse with elation and disbelief. "The feedback loop is escalating! They can't contain it!"

Battered and barely functional, the Nautilus drifted in the aftermath. The neutralization of the immediate threat occurred, but the victory was fragile. The Lumina was a vast empire, and this was but one nexus, albeit a critical one. Yet, in the crushing darkness of Area 291, humanity had struck a blow not with brute force, but with its most intrinsic, and for the Lumina, its most terrifying weapon: the boundless, chaotic, and irrepressible power of the human spirit. For now, the fragile glimmer of a new beginning, forged in the deepest trenches of the ocean, had replaced the averted Dawn of Oblivion.

The descent had been a calculated plunge into the heart of the beast, a journey into an alien abyss where Lumina's dominion was absolute. The 'Nautilus,' their submersible ark, had navigated the crushing pressures and the unnerving silence of Area 291, a sector teeming with Lumina's bio-engineered infrastructure. Rachel, the driving force behind this desperate gambit, had watched the alien landscape unfold, a stark testament to humanity's precarious existence. The defectors, individuals who had once served the Lumina and now risked everything to betray them, had provided the crucial intel – the alien consciousness, built on logic and order, recoiled from the chaos and irrationality of human emotion. Their plan was not to blast their way in, but to weaponize the very essence of humanity, to flood the Lumina's perfectly ordered network with a tidal wave of subjective experience.

The immediate threat had been the 'harmonizers,' corrupted humans augmented by Lumina technology, their forms and vessels a grotesque mockery of human design. Benjamin's tactical brilliance, coupled with Jasper's harmonic resonance disruption, had thrown them into disarray, their Lumina-controlled minds unable to cope with the sudden influx of raw human sentiment. But even as the harmonizer threat waned, the deeper, more terrifying defenses had awoken. Colossal bio-luminescent entities, the 'Guardians of the Nexus,' had emerged, their ethereal forms hinting at immense power, their tentacles poised to crush any who dared intrude. Elara, the former Lumina bio-engineer, had identified their weakness: they fed on psychic energy, meaning direct combat could be a double-edged sword.

Now, the Nautilus, battered but functional, was maneuvering through a minefield of alien technology. A colossal structure loomed, its energy signatures flaring like a dying star. The goal was not to destroy the nexus outright, but to dismantle its core functionality, to introduce a fatal flaw into its central processing unit. The defectors had been invaluable; their knowledge of Lumina's internal architecture far exceeded any theoretical calculations. They had pinpointed specific energy conduits, channels through which the Lumina directed their psionic resonance projectors and managed their vast data streams. Disrupting these conduits, Elara had insisted, would create a cascading feedback loop, a localized singularity of Lumina's own making.

"Approaching deployment zone alpha," Benjamin announced, his voice taut with concentration. The submersible's internal lights flickered erratically, a testament to the strain on its systems. Outside, the ocean floor was a chaotic tapestry of alien constructs, interconnected by conduits that pulsed with an internal, venous glow. These were not mere cables; they were living arteries of Lumina's consciousness, carrying the lifeblood of its control across the planet.

Jasper's hands moved with practiced speed across his console, calibrating the psionic dissonance emitters. These were not weapons in the conventional sense.   Each emitter, a small, crystalline drone, emitted a focused burst of amplified human consciousness. They had spent months in clandestine labs, distilling the essence of human creativity and emotion into these potent devices. They contained fragments of Bach's Brandenburg Concertos, the raw grief of a wartime elegy, the abstract brilliance of Picasso's Guernica, the unbridled joy of a child's laughter, and the profound, often illogical, devotion of human love.

"Elara, confirm the conduit integrity at alpha," Rachel requested, her gaze fixed on the main viewport. The sheer scale of the Lumina's construction was overwhelming, a testament to their alien perspective, their mastery of materials and energies beyond human comprehension. It was a world built on efficiency and control, a stark contrast to the messy, vibrant chaos of Earth.

"Conduits are stable, but heavily shielded," Elara replied, her voice barely a whisper. "Standard Lumina protocols for energy flow. They expect fluctuations, but not... this." She gestured vaguely towards the console, a subtle nod to the non-traditional nature of their assault. "The shielding absorbs and recalibrates aberrant energy signatures. We will need to tune our emitters precisely to bypass this recalibration and overload the buffer before it can compensate.

Benjamin brought the Nautilus to a halt, its hull groaning under the immense pressure, its stealth systems working overtime to mask their presence. The ambient hum of the Lumina network, a subtle, pervasive frequency that had once been imperceptible, now felt like a palpable weight, a constant reminder of the alien intelligence surrounding them.

"Deploying emitter drones," Rachel announced. Three small, dart-like craft detached from the Nautilus's underbelly, their bioluminescent trails a fleeting whisper against the dark obsidian. They moved with almost organic grace, guided by Jasper's precise commands, weaving through the intricate network of conduits.

"First emitter is in position," Jasper reported. "Starting localized dissonance pulse."

A soft, almost imperceptible ripple of energy emanated from the drone. On Jasper's primary display, a section of the Lumina's energy signature flickered. It was a tiny tremor, a barely noticeable hiccup in an otherwise flawless system.

"The buffer is attempting to compensate," Elara observed, her brow furrowed. "It's… analyzing the energy. It's trying to categorize it as a known anomaly. But it can't. The sheer diversity of emotional resonance is baffling, is not it?"

The second emitter moved into position, followed by the third. As they settled, Jasper started the synchronized pulse. This time, the effect was more pronounced. The energy signatures of the conduits at zone alpha began to warp and distort, not with explosive force, but with an internal dissonance. It was as if the very fabric of Lumina's ordered logic was fraying.

"They're detecting a significant anomaly," Benjamin stated, his hand hovering over the evasive maneuver controls. "Automated defenses are activating. I'm detecting bio-signatures. Guardians incoming."

From the shadows of the nexus, massive forms coalesced. The ethereal jellyfish-like creatures, their bioluminescence shifting from a calming blue to an agitated violet, drifted towards the Nautilus. Their psychic emanations, once a low thrumming, now felt like a sharp, piercing whine, a desperate attempt to impose order on the encroaching chaos.

"We need to move!" Rachel urged. "Zone Beta is our next target. It's a data-processing nexus. If we can disrupt their information flow, it will compound the confusion."

Jasper expertly maneuvered the Nautilus, the submersible dancing between the advancing Guardians. Laser-like energy bursts, originating from the nexus's crystalline structures, lanced through the water, narrowly missing their hull. The Guardians themselves seemed to speed up, their tentacles unfurling, razor-sharp tips glinting in the alien light.

"The harmonizers are also reacting," Jasper noted, pointing to his tactical display. "Their augmented minds cannot handle this level of cognitive overload. They're experiencing extreme psychological distress." Several Lumina-derived craft, their movements jerky and unpredictable, fired wildly, their targeting systems compromised by the escalating dissonance.

As they reached deployment zone beta, a more complex network of conduits came into view. These were thinner, more delicate, carrying vast streams of data.

"These conduits handle informational uploads and downloads," Elara explained, her voice strained. "They're the arteries of Lumina's knowledge base, the pathways through which they assimilate and distribute information. If we introduce a torrent of unclassifiable data, it could corrupt their entire archival system."

The deployment of emitters in Zone Beta was more challenging. The Guardians were closer, their psionic pressure a suffocating weight. One tentacle, impossibly long and strong, lashed out, narrowly missing the Nautilus. Benjamin's evasive maneuvers were a masterclass in controlled desperation.

"Second wave of emitters deployed," Rachel announced, her voice tight with exertion. "Jasper, start the broadcast."

The emitters in zone beta pulsed in unison. This time, the effect was immediate and dramatic. On Jasper's display, the Lumina's data streams, once represented by neat, ordered lines of code, fractured into a million shimmering, chaotic fragments. The pure, objective data was being interwoven with the subjective, emotional content of the human consciousness broadcast. It was like introducing a virus not into a computer system, but into a collective consciousness.

The Guardians recoiled visibly, their bioluminescent forms flickering wildly. They seemed to struggle to process the influx of sentiment, the illogical connections and abstract concepts that their programming could not parse. Their psychic emanations intensified, becoming a cacophony of confusion and distress.

"The Guardians are destabilizing," Elara observed, a flicker of hope in her eyes. "They're not designed to process subjective experience. Their existence depends entirely on objective reality."

Suddenly, an additional threat emerged. From the deeper recesses of the nexus, Lumina agents, their forms sleek and metallic, appeared. These were not biological constructs but sophisticated drones, programmed to hunt and neutralize any intruders. They moved with a terrifying, silent efficiency, their energy weapons spitting focused beams of destructive power.

"We're being targeted!" Benjamin yells as a beam grazed the Nautilus's aft section, sending a violent jolt through the vessel. "Hull integrity dropping! We need to reach the primary nexus, or we're trapped!"

The primary nexus was the heart of the operation, the central processing unit where all Lumina's global data converged. It was a colossal, crystalline structure, radiating an immense power, its surface shimmering with an iridescent glow. Encircling it was a formidable energy shield, a pulsating barrier of pure force.

"The shield is too strong for direct emitter deployment," Jasper stated, his face grim. "We need to find a way to breach it, or to introduce the dissonance directly into the core nexus itself."

Elara pointed to a series of massive conduits snaking away from the primary nexus, feeding into the surrounding structures. "Those are the main power conduits. They draw energy directly from the planetary core, and they also carry the core processing data. If we can disrupt those, we can create a feedback loop that will overload the primary nexus from within."

Benjamin, with a determined glint in his eye, steered the Nautilus towards the conduits. The Lumina agents were relentless, their attacks becoming more coordinated. The Guardians, though disoriented, were still a formidable threat, their tentacles flailing wildly.

"We have to get close enough to deploy the final emitter directly into the conduit cluster," Rachel said, her voice firm, her resolve unwavering. "It's our only chance. Give us everything you've got."

Benjamin pushed the Nautilus to its absolute limits. The submersible, already heavily damaged, shuddered and groaned under the strain. Alarms blared, warning of imminent system failure. The alien agents closed in, their weapons firing in a concentrated barrage.

"Hull integrity at twenty percent!" Benjamin shouted, sweat beading on his forehead. "We're running out of time!"

Jasper and Elara worked with frantic urgency, calibrating the final emitter. This was the primary key, designed to unleash the full spectrum of human consciousness onto the Lumina's core. Rachel stood ready, her hand hovering over the activation sequence.

"Almost there!" Jasper yelled as the Nautilus scraped against one of the massive conduits. Sparks flew, and the submersible lurched violently. "Deploying final emitter!"

A small, yet potent, drone detached from the Nautilus, its crystalline structure humming with contained power. It darted into the nexus of conduits, a tiny beacon of defiance against the overwhelming Lumina presence.

"Now, Rachel!" Elara cries. "Activate the primary broadcast!"

Rachel slammed her hand down on the activation sequence. A wave not of sound, but of pure human consciousness, surged from the Nautilus. It was a symphony of emotion, a torrent of creativity, a kaleidoscope of subjective experience. On Jasper's display, the Lumina's perfectly ordered energy signatures exploded into a chaotic, vibrant mess. Irrationality, love, art, poetry, and the messy, beautiful, contradictory essence of humanity suddenly bombarded the core processing data, which was designed for absolute logic.

It had a catastrophic effect. Lumina's control center, the main nexus, shuddered. Cracking the crystalline structures was logic, not force. The energy conduits overloaded, spewing uncontrolled bursts of psionic energy. The Lumina's meticulously crafted network, built on the suppression of all that was unpredictable, was being consumed by the very chaos it had sought to eradicate.

"It's working!" Jasper exclaimed, his voice raw with triumph. "The feedback loop is escalating! They can't contain it!"

Flickering erratically, the colossal nexus's iridescent glow intensified as it collapsed inwards. The Guardians, overwhelmed by the psychic deluge, dissipated into wisps of ethereal energy. The Lumina agents, their programming corrupted by the illogical influx, began to self-destruct, their metallic forms erupting in silent, blinding flashes of light.

A deafening silence replaced the oppressive hum that had permeated the depths. Shattered was the Lumina's once absolute control. Drifting in the aftermath, the battered Nautilus barely held, a testament to humanity's improbable victory.

The cascade failure rippled outward from the nexus, not with the violent cacophony of destruction, but with a chilling, profound silence. Discordant static reduced the Lumina's intricate network, a symphony of perfectly orchestrated data and psionic control. On board the battered Nautilus, the surviving crew members, Rachel, Benjamin, and Jasper, exchanged weary glances. The victory was immense, a reprieve from the imminent "harvest" that had loomed over humanity like a shroud. Yet, as the echoes of their daring exploit faded, a new, more insidious challenge presented itself. The Lumina's grip had loosened, but the seeds of their control, the subtle indoctrination that had seeped into the very fabric of global society, remained.

"The network is… fractured," Jasper murmured, his voice hoarse, his eyes glued to the dwindling energy signatures on his console. "They're not completely gone, Rachel. Although they were crippled and disoriented, their consciousness was distributed. Like a shattered mirror, the pieces still reflect."

Benjamin ran a diagnostic on the submersible's compromised systems. "We achieved our aim. We severed the primary nexus, disrupting their global operation. But the defectors warned us. They said Lumina isn't a single entity. It's a collective, a distributed intelligence. This was a blow, not an annihilation."

Rachel leaned back, her gaze fixed on the distorted holographic display of Earth's surface that flickered to life. Under the alien subjugation, the planet was a tapestry of muted lights, a testament to the Lumina's efficient, yet soulless, governance. But now, a subtle shift was occurring. Anomalies bloomed across the continents—pockets of localized chaos, flickering signals of unrest, and the nascent stirrings of independent thought. The Lumina's control had been so pervasive, so absolute, that most of humanity had simply accepted it as the natural order. Now, with the central nervous system of their captors compromised, the dormant capacity for self-determination was awakening.

"We gave them a window," Rachel said, her voice a low, resonant hum that seemed to vibrate with a newfound urgency. "A chance to choose. The broadcast… it went through, didn't it, Jasper?"

Jasper nodded, a weary smile gracing his lips. "The data streams we repurposed, Rachel. They carried not only the truth about Lumina's plans but also the raw, untamed essence of our own consciousness. The despair and resilience of those who resisted, the defiance of the defectors, the unadulterated hope we injected into those emitter drones… it was all broadcast. The Lumina couldn't censor it, couldn't categorize it. It's out there, in every network node, every communication channel they once controlled."

The implications of this broadcast were profound and terrifying. Humanity had been in a false sense of security for years because every need was met, and someone had subtly guided every decision. The Lumina had offered order, stability, and an end to the inherent messiness of human existence. In return, they demanded compliance, a passive surrender of free will that culminated in the horrific "harvest" – the psychic extraction and absorption of humanity's consciousness into the Lumina collective. Now that the Lumina's immediate threat was blunted, humanity faced a stark, unvarnished truth. The Lumina's order was a cage, their stability a prelude to oblivion.

The question was, would humanity recognize it? Had the years of enforced peace and effortless existence eroded their capacity for self-governance? Or would the broadcast, a concentrated dose of raw human experience, ignite a spark of rebellion, a yearning for the freedom to err, strive, and simply be?

"The problem," Benjamin interjected, his gaze sweeping across the tactical display, "is that not everyone received the broadcast equally. The Lumina's infrastructure is fragmented, but not destroyed. Some regions are still under their direct influence. They'll try to suppress this, Rachel. They'll try to reassert control and discredit anything that deviates from their narrative."

Rachel's eyes narrowed. "That's where we come in. The defectors provided us with the key to their network architecture. While their central nexus is in disarray, their decentralized communication nodes should still be… accessible. We can piggyback on what's left of their network, amplify our own signal, and ensure the truth reaches everyone."

The plan was audacious, bordering on suicidal. The Nautilus, a mere shadow of its former self, did not have a design for extended surface operations. But the alternative was unthinkable. To allow Lumina to regroup, to reassert their control and complete the harvest, was to condemn humanity to a fate worse than death.

"We need to reach the primary broadcasting stations," Rachel declared, her voice gaining strength. "The ones Lumina controlled, but didn't fully integrate into their own network. Their plan was to use them for propaganda, to disseminate their approved version of reality. Now, they'll serve a different purpose."

Jasper's fingers flew across his console, cross-referencing Lumina's preoccupation network schematics with the current, chaotic energy readings. "There are three major hubs that fit the description. One in the Siberian tundra, an ancient Soviet-era facility. Another beneath the Sahara, a hidden pre-invasion complex. And the third… nestled within the ruins of Tokyo, a city that Lumina deemed too chaotic to fully pacify."

"Tokyo," Benjamin echoed, a grim acknowledgment of the city's enduring spirit. "That sounds like a good place to start. If we can broadcast from there, reach the Pacific Rim, and then work our way around the globe…"

The journey to Tokyo was fraught with peril. The Lumina's remaining forces, though disorganized, were still a formidable threat. Automated defense systems, reactivated by residual Lumina directives, patrolled the skies and seas. Rogue harmonizers, their minds still wrestling with the overwhelming psychic influx, lashed out indiscriminately. The Nautilus, a wounded beast, navigated treacherous currents and dodged energy barrages, relying on Benjamin's masterful piloting and Jasper's rapid reprogramming of Lumina's own surveillance systems.

As they approached the shattered skyline of Tokyo, a recent phenomenon became apparent. The Lumina's pervasive influence, the silent hum that had once permeated everything, was gone. In its place was a cacophony of desperate broadcasts, fragmented news reports, and the growing murmur of a populace awakening from a long, controlled slumber. People were emerging from their homes, their faces etched with confusion, fear, and a dawning sense of disbelief. The Lumina's carefully constructed illusion had been shattered, and the raw, unvarnished reality of their subjugation was sinking in.

They located the primary broadcasting tower, a skeletal behemoth rising from the rubble, its once-gleaming metallic skin scarred and blackened. Lumina drones, still patrolling its perimeter, immediately detected their approach.

"They're trying to sever the external connections," Jasper reported, his face illuminated by the frantic scramble of data on his screen. "Cutting off all independent signals, trying to isolate this facility."

"We can't let them," Rachel said, her jaw set. "Ben, get us close enough for a direct interface. Jasper, prepare the counter-frequency.

Elara's work on Lumina's psionic resonance inhibitors will be crucial here. We need to override their silencing protocols."

Benjamin maneuvered the Nautilus with precision, weaving through the ruins of skyscrapers, the submersible's hull groaning under the strain. Energy beams crisscrossed the sky, aimed at the defiant tower. Lumina drones swarmed, their metallic bodies glinting ominously.

"The drones are reconfiguring their targeting," Benjamin warned. "They're prioritizing the tower. They know what it represents."

"That's our advantage," Rachel counters. "They're fighting to suppress; we're fighting to liberate. Jasper, now!"

Jasper activated the counter-frequency, a complex wave of modulated psionic energy designed to bypass Lumina's security architecture. The holographic displays flickered, then stabilized, showing a direct link to the tower's core broadcast system.

"We're in!" Jasper exclaimed, a surge of adrenaline coursing through him. "Uploading our signal. Amplifying it through their own infrastructure."

On the vast screens that now flickered to life across the Nautilus, the world saw it. Not the sanitized, ordered reality of Lumina, but the raw, unfiltered truth. The images revealed Lumina's bio-engineering facilities, the chilling efficiency of their mind-control apparatus, and the horrifying implications of the harvest. But woven alongside the terror was the story of defiance, the courage of those who had fought back, the unwavering spirit of humanity.

The broadcast wasn't just a factual account; it was an emotional testament. It showcased the resilience of the human spirit in the face of overwhelming odds. The broadcast showed the beauty in human imperfection; the strength found in vulnerability, and the profound meaning that could be derived from struggle and self-determination. The raw power of human emotion, the very thing Lumina had sought to eradicate, was now their undoing.

Across Tokyo, people stopped in their tracks, their faces turning towards the broadcasting tower, towards the screens that now displayed an impossible truth. Disbelief warred with dawning comprehension. The narrative they had been fed for so long was replaced by something far more visceral and real.

"They're pushing back," Benjamin reported, his voice tight. "Lumina is attempting to reassert control, to flood the network with counter-propaganda."

"Let them," Rachel said, her gaze unwavering. "We've planted the seed. Now, they have to choose. Do they return to the comfortable illusion, to the sterile order of Lumina and the silent oblivion of the harvest? Or do they embrace the uncertainty, the struggle, the beautiful, messy chaos of true freedom?"

The choice was no longer theoretical. It was a stark, immediate reality broadcast to billions. In the ruins of Tokyo, the first genuine act of global defiance was unfolding. People emerged from their homes, not in fear, but with a newfound purpose. They looked at each other, not as compliant cogs in an alien machine, but as fellow beings capable of independent thought, of collective action.

The Lumina built their dominion on the assumption of human passivity. They had underestimated the enduring power of hope, the indomitable will to be free, and the profound, irrational, yet ultimately powerful, nature of the human heart. Despite the network damage and fractured control, humanity made the final decision. Uncertainty and peril marked the dawn of a new era. The choice was theirs, and for the first time in generations, it was a choice they could genuinely make. The fate of their species, the very definition of what it meant to be human, hung precariously in the balance, waiting for the collective response to the truth that had finally, irrevocably, broken through the alien silence.

If you could call it a victory, it tasted like ashes. The Nautilus, battered but functional, drifted in the scarred waters near what remained of Tokyo. The attack threw their global network into disarray, shattering the Lumina's nexus. Yet, the silence that followed wasn't one of peace, but of a world holding its breath, staring into an abyss it had only just glimpsed. Rachel, Jasper, and Benjamin had indeed unleashed the broadcast, a desperate gamble. It was a wildfire of truth, spreading through the fractured Lumina conduits, igniting dormant minds and shattering generations of carefully curated complacency. But freedom, Rachel was rapidly learning, wasn't a gift freely given; it was a burden, heavy with the weight of responsibility and the specter of unending struggle.

The immediate aftermath of the broadcast was a confusing, chaotic symphony of awakening. Across the globe, pockets of humanity, jolted from their lumina-induced stupor, grappled with the horrifying revelations. The broadcast stripped away the veneer of perfect order and effortless existence, revealing the stark, terrifying reality of their subjugation. In many regions, the Lumina's remaining automated systems, or those whose minds hadn't yet fully broken free from their conditioning, fought back with brutal efficiency. Security drones, designed to maintain Lumina's peace, now hunted those who dared to question, to resist, to *think* independently. Cities that had been models of alien-designed utopias now became battlegrounds, the echoes of desperate skirmishes replacing the once-ubiquitous hum of Lumina's psychic control.

On board the Nautilus, the strain was palpable. Working feverishly, Jasper hunched over his consoles to monitor the global network, or what was left of it. His face was a mask of exhaustion, etched knowing that every signal, every flicker of independent thought, represented a life teetering on the precipice of either true liberation or brutal suppression. "The Lumina are adapting," he reported, his voice raspy. "They're isolating sectors, attempting to re-establish localized control grids. They're also... re-purposing their own infrastructure. The propaganda streams are intensifying. They're painting us as terrorists, as saboteurs of global harmony."

Benjamin, his gaze fixed on the external monitors displaying the desolate landscape of war-torn Tokyo, grunted. "Harmony built on a foundation of mental enslavement isn't harmony, Jasper. It's a prison. And we just kicked down the cell door." He ran a gloved hand over his weary face. "The cost, though... it's already mounting. We've seen reports. Cities are in lockdown. Lumina forces, what remains of them, are rounding up anyone showing signs of 'deviant thought.' It's not just about controlling information anymore; it's about silencing the very idea of dissent."

Rachel watched the fragmented news feeds, her heart sinking with each report. She saw the confusion in the eyes of ordinary people; the fear warring with a nascent spark of defiance. She saw the swift, brutal response of Lumina's automated enforcers. This was the price of freedom they had underestimated. They had believed that simply revealing the truth would be enough, that the inherent human desire for autonomy would sweep away the alien control. But the Lumina had been insidious, their influence woven so deeply into the fabric of society that waking up was not a gentle process, but a violent tearing away.

"We underestimated the inertia of their control," Rachel admitted, her voice barely above a whisper. "They didn't just impose their will; they reshaped our desires, our perceptions. For generations, humanity has known nothing but its curated reality. The broadcast was a shock, a jolt, but the system, our own minds, is fighting to reassert the familiar. The comfort of the known, even when it's a cage, is a powerful force."

Jasper nodded grimly. "And the Lumina know this. They are exploiting it. It's not just us they are fighting. They're reminding people of the chaos before their rule, the struggles, the uncertainties. They're painting the Lumina era as a golden age of peace, and our broadcast as the harbinger of a return to primal anarchy."

"Which is why we need to keep broadcasting," Rachel declared, her resolve hardening. "We need to counter their narrative. We need to show them that the 'chaos' they fear is the fertile ground from which genuine progress, true humanity, can grow. Elara's psionic resonance inhibitors, Jasper, are they ready for wider deployment? We need to break the Lumina's hold on those still susceptible to its subtle psychic influence."

"The prototypes are functional," Jasper confirmed, his fingers flying across the console. "But the Lumina are actively jamming our communication channels, trying to isolate us. Reaching the remaining Lumina broadcasting hubs we identified, the ones with the least direct integration into their core network, will be incredibly difficult. They're heavily fortified, and they're Lumina's last line of defense against uncontrolled information."

Benjamin slammed a fist against a console, the sound echoing in the cramped command center. "Fortified is an understatement. The intelligence from the defectors painted a grim picture. These aren't just broadcast towers anymore; they're Citadel's. Lumina has poured all its remaining resources into these hubs, turning them into virtually impregnable fortresses. They know that if we can seize them, we can effectively dismantle their remaining global influence."

The weight of their mission settled on them, heavier than the crushing pressure of the ocean depths. They had struck a decisive blow, crippling the Lumina's central command. But the empire, though wounded, was far from defeated. Its tentacles still reached into countless corners of the globe, its remaining forces loyal to a doctrine of order that now threatened to consume them all. The fight for freedom had just begun, and it was a fight that would demand more than courage and ingenuity; it would demand sacrifice, resilience, and an unwavering belief in a future that was far from assured.

The first target was the Lumina broadcasting hub located deep within the Siberian tundra. It was a monumental undertaking. The journey itself was a gauntlet. Remnants of Lumina's orbital defenses, though erratic, still posed a significant threat. Automated patrols, programmed to maintain territorial integrity, crisscrossed the desolate, ice-bound landscape. The Nautilus, designed for oceanic depths, struggled against the frozen terrain. Benjamin adapted, using every bit of his skill to navigate the treacherous, snow-blasted wilderness. They encountered pockets of humanity trapped in Lumina-controlled enclaves, their minds still under the alien influence, their eyes blank and uncomprehending. These were the hardest sights for Rachel to bear, a stark reminder of the vastness of the task ahead.

Jasper, working tirelessly in the sub-zero temperatures, established a temporary uplink with a network of independent resistance cells that had sprung up in the broadcast's wake. These cells, fueled by a desperate hope, provided crucial intelligence on Lumina's troop movements and the defenses of the Siberian hub. They learned the hub was not just a broadcasting station, but a heavily militarized complex, bristling with energy weapons and patrolled by Lumina's elite harmonizer units – psionically augmented soldiers whose loyalty was absolute.

"They've deployed a new generation of harmonizers," Jasper reported, his breath misting in the frigid air of the Nautilus's interior. "More potent, more resilient to psychic disruption. And the hub itself… it's shielded. Not just against physical intrusion, but against psionic interference. Elara's inhibitors might not be enough to breach it directly."

Benjamin frowned, studying the schematics. "So, we can't just hack our way in. We'll have to go in hot. That means a frontal assault, which is exactly what Lumina wants. They'll be ready for us."

"Not entirely," Rachel countered, her eyes alight with a dangerous idea. "They expect us to target the hub directly. What if we create a diversion? Something so disruptive, so unexpected, that it draws their attention away from the primary aim? The Lumina's obsession with order is their greatest weakness. Creating enough controlled chaos will force them to react.

Their plan was audacious, bordering on suicidal. Using the Nautilus's limited atmospheric capabilities, they would launch a series of targeted strikes on Lumina supply depots scattered across the tundra, designed to cripple their logistical network and force the harmonizer units to disperse. This would create the diversion. While Lumina's forces were occupied, a small, elite team, including Rachel, Benjamin, Jasper, and a few specialized resistance fighters, would attempt to infiltrate the hub through a poorly defended subterranean access tunnel that Jasper's network contacts had identified.

The assault on the supply depots was a brutal dance of destruction. Benjamin piloted the Nautilus with a ferocity that bordered on recklessness, unleashing its limited offensive capabilities with devastating precision. Explosions ripped through the icy plains, sending shockwaves through the frozen earth. Lumina's automated defenses responded with a fury, unleashing torrents of plasma fire. They were outgunned, outmanned, and the Nautilus operated far beyond its intended operational parameters. The submersible sustained heavy damage, its hull groaning under the relentless assault.

During the chaos, Rachel, along with a handful of hardened resistance fighters, made their perilous descent into the Siberian earth. The subterranean tunnels were a labyrinth of icy darkness, patrolled by Lumina's automated sentinels. They moved with a stealth born of desperation, their breath misting in the frigid air, their senses heightened by the constant threat of discovery. The Lumina's control in these deep tunnels was less pervasive, but the automated defenses were still formidable. They navigated through ice caves and reinforced shafts, their progress slow and agonizing.

They reached the primary conduit leading to the broadcast array, a colossal structure embedded deep within the permafrost, humming with latent energy. Lumina harmonizers patrolled the interior, their psionic presence a tangible weight in the air. Rachel activated Elara's prototype inhibitors, a wave of subtle energy rippling through the chamber. The harmonizers faltered, their movements becoming sluggish, their psionic focus wavering. It was a temporary reprieve, but it was enough.

The ensuing battle was a desperate, brutal affair. Rachel, drawing upon her own burgeoning psionic abilities, fought with a ferocity that surprised even herself. She deflected energy blasts with shields, her mind a razor's edge against the harmonizers' psionic attacks. Jasper, having brought the damaged Nautilus to a precarious position near a secondary access point, provided crucial, albeit limited, fire support. But it was the resistance fighters, the ones who had tasted true freedom for the first time, who fought with the most ferocity. They knew the stakes, the terrible cost of failure, and they fought with the courage of those who had nothing left to lose.

One by one, the harmonizers fell, their psionic energy sputtering out. But the victory was not without its cost. Several resistance fighters fell, their bodies ravaged by energy weapons and psionic feedback. One of them, a young woman named Macy, a former Lumina technician who had defected, gave her life to disable a crucial defense node, creating an opening for Rachel to reach the central broadcast nexus. The young woman's last words, whispered through cracked lips, were a plea for Rachel to remember.

With the last of the direct opposition neutralized, Rachel, her body aching, her mind reeling from the psionic exertion, accessed the main broadcast console. Jasper's voice crackled through her comms, strained but triumphant. "I've rerouted the primary broadcast signal. The Siberian hub is now under our control. We're transmitting the full spectrum of Lumina's atrocities, Rachel. The harvest chambers, the consciousness extraction protocols… it's all going out. And this time, there's no ambiguity, no room for misinterpretation."

The broadcast from Siberia was even more devastating than the initial one from Tokyo. It showed not just the Lumina's intent, but the chilling, systematic reality of their methods. Videos of the harvesting process, previously buried deep within Lumina's encrypted archives, were now laid bare for the world to see. The sterile efficiency with which they dissected and absorbed human minds systematically horrified everyone, and no amount of Lumina propaganda could truly hide it. A surge of amplified psionic resonance, a deliberate counter-frequency designed to shatter any remaining Lumina psychic dampeners, accompanied the broadcast and awakened those whose minds had been most deeply submerged.

As the Siberian broadcast reverberated across the globe, a profound shift began. The initial confusion and fear gave way to a tidal wave of outrage and unified defiance. The sheer volume of irrefutable evidence and the raw, unadulterated horror drowned Lumina's attempts to discredit the broadcast as out it conveyed. In regions where Lumina had maintained tight control, the awakening was more violent. Cities erupted in spontaneous uprisings, the populace, armed with makeshift weapons and fueled by a righteous fury, turned on their former enslavers. The Lumina's carefully constructed order crumbled, not under a strategic military assault, but under the weight of a species finally remembering its own inherent value.

Yet, even as the Lumina's grip weakened, the cost of this dawning freedom became starkly apparent. The world that emerged from Lumina's shadow was not one of immediate paradise, but of profound disruption and immense challenges. The Lumina, though its global network was in tatters, still held significant power in isolated pockets. Their remaining forces, driven by a desperate, dogmatic adherence to their mission, fought with a fanaticism born of defeat. The ensuing conflicts were brutal, often devolving into localized skirmishes and acts of desperate revenge.

The Lumina had not merely controlled humanity; they had altered it. Generations of passive compliance had eroded the very foundations of self-governance. Societies had to relearn how to make tough decisions, how to negotiate, how to rebuild from the ground up, all while grappling with the trauma of their manipulated history and the ever-present threat of Lumina's resurgence. The broadcast had shattered the illusion of comfort and security, but it had replaced it with the daunting reality of responsibility.

On board the Nautilus, the mood was somber, despite the undeniable progress. They had won a monumental battle, but the war for humanity's soul was far from over. Jasper monitored the ever-shifting global landscape. "The Lumina are in full retreat in many sectors," he reported, a hint of weariness in his voice. "But they're not gone. They're consolidating. We're seeing pockets of Lumina resistance forming, highly organized and technologically advanced. They're fighting a guerrilla war now."

Benjamin nodded. "And the world… it's not ready. We've unleashed the truth, but we haven't prepared them for the consequences. There's infighting, power vacuums, old rivalries resurfacing. Lumina's order, as terrible as it was, provided a blanket of stability. Now that blanket is gone, and the cold reality of human nature is setting in."

Rachel looked out at the ravaged skyline of Tokyo, a city that had become a symbol of both Lumina's tyranny and humanity's defiance. The broadcast had been a catalyst, a spark that ignited a global fire. But fire, while cleansing, could also consume. The Lumina had offered a seductive promise of effortless existence, a painless surrender. They had underestimated the enduring human spirit, the innate drive for meaning, for struggle, for genuine connection. But they had also inadvertently revealed the fragility of that spirit when subjected to prolonged subjugation.

"They chose freedom," Rachel said, her voice resonating with a quiet strength. "But freedom is a path, not a destination. It requires constant vigilance, constant effort. The Lumina may be retreating, but the temptation of their ordered reality, the allure of a world without struggle, will remain. Our task is not just to defeat the Lumina, but to help humanity embrace the responsibility of self-governance. To remind them that true strength lies not in the absence of challenge, but in the courage to face it, to learn from it, and to build something better, something truly their own."

The Nautilus had carried them through the heart of the storm. But the real journey had just begun. They were no longer just soldiers fighting an alien invasion; they were architects of a new world, tasked with guiding a fractured humanity through the perilous dawn of its own hard-won liberty. Instead of oblivion, a species clamored to find its voice in the silence. The price of freedom was not a single sacrifice, but a continuous, collective effort, a testament to the enduring, often painful, power of self-determination.

Instead of peace, the silence over Earth was of a world recalibrating. The broadcast from the Siberian hub, a raw, unvarnished exposé of the Lumina's heinous practices, had been a digital wildfire, consuming the carefully constructed illusions of generations. A violent, shattering thrust jolted humanity awake, into the stark reality of its own subjugation. Yet, as the Lumina's centralized network fractured and their direct control waned, a disquieting question rippled through the newly awakened collective consciousness: was this dawn of freedom, or merely a temporary reprieve before an unending watch?

On board the Nautilus, adrift in the quiet aftermath, a gnawing unease had replaced the feverish urgency of battle. Benjamin ran a hand over his stubbled chin. "We broke their grip," he stated, his voice gravelly with fatigue and a touch of apprehension. "We exposed them. But did we truly win?" He gestured to a scrolling feed detailing a violent uprising in what was once Neo-Berlin, where factions now clashed over resources and ideology, reminiscent of the very pre-Lumina chaos the aliens had promised to quell. "Look at this. The Lumina provided order, however brutal. Now… we have a million new warlords, and a planet still reeling from centuries of suppressed thought. This is the price of throwing open the cage door, Rachel. It's not always what people expected."

Jasper nodded from his station. "The Lumina are dispersing, not dissolving. We've intercepted fragmented communications suggesting consolidation into smaller, highly fortified enclaves. It's more of a strategic redeployment than a defeat for them. The broadcast was a devastating blow to their global network, yet they knew humanity's self-destructive nature and remarkable resilience. They've been observing us for centuries; they understand our cycles of conflict and cooperation. They might wait for us to falter, to fall back into our old patterns, before reasserting control in a different guise." He projected a holographic map showing clusters of Lumina activity, scattered like persistent embers in the global conflagration. "Area 291, for instance. Our intelligence suggests it's become a hub for Lumina's remaining logistical operations and, more worryingly, a center for continued psionic research. They're not abandoning their agenda; they're adapting it."

The very nature of the Lumina's intentions remained a profound enigma. They had presented themselves as benevolent overseers, bringing order to a chaotic species. Then, the truth revealed a far more sinister purpose: the systematic harvesting and assimilation of human consciousness. But even this horrifying revelation left unanswered questions. Why Earth? Why humanity? Was it a singular act of predation, or part of a larger, cosmic imperative? Rachel recalled fragments of Lumina psionic transmissions intercepted during the early days of the conflict, whispers of a "Great Alignment" and a "Cosmic Harmony" that seemed to transcend mere resource acquisition. Could their goal have been something far grander, and far more terrifying, than simple enslavement?

"They didn't just want our minds," Rachel mused, her gaze distant. "They wanted something *from* our minds. Our creativity? Our emotional spectrum? The very essence of our consciousness that makes us, us. That encounter in Area 291... it felt like more than just an accidental discovery. It felt like a deliberate test, or perhaps even an initiation. They showed us glimpses of their true capabilities, their understanding of consciousness, almost as if they were... grooming us." The implication hung heavy in the air: had humanity, in its desperate fight for survival, inadvertently proven itself worthy of a more profound, albeit terrifying, integration into the Lumina's grand design?

Benjamin scrubbed a weary hand across his face. "Grooming? Rachel, they were dissecting us. They were feeding on us. To suggest anything else is to romanticize our tormentors."

"But their ultimate goal, Benjamin," Rachel countered, her voice firm. "Was it simply to consume, or to incorporate? If it were the latter, then this 'freedom' we've achieved… it might be a carefully orchestrated phase. We know that maintaining this technological and societal cohesion isn't possible alone after centuries of Lumina dependency. They might wait for us to descend into chaos, to become desperate enough to welcome their 'guidance' back. They've sown the seeds of dependence, and they're patient. Their existence spans millennia; they can afford to wait."

Jasper interjected, his tone grave. "There's also the matter of the Lumina's own internal dynamics. The broadcast exposed their atrocities to the wider galaxy, or at least to those Lumina enclaves capable of receiving it. We intercepted some communications that suggest dissent within their own ranks. Not everyone agreed with the harvesting protocols. Some saw it as a perversion of their species' purpose. This could be a critical weakness, or it could be a trap. They might feign internal conflict to lull us into a false sense of security, or to encourage defections they can then exploit."

The immediate aftermath of the broadcast had seen a surge of unified resistance. Humanity, for the first time in centuries, had a common enemy, a shared understanding of the oppression they had endured. But as the Lumina's immediate threat receded, old divisions surfaced. Nations once united under the Lumina yoke, now fractured along pre-existing political and ideological lines. Rebuilding infrastructure, establishing governance, and re-educating populations conditioned for passive compliance proved difficult for the newly liberated territories. The Lumina, through their subtle manipulation of human history and societal development, had ensured that the path to genuine self-governance would be fraught with peril.

"We've liberated them from the Lumina, but have we liberated them from themselves?" Rachel wondered aloud, her gaze sweeping across the chaotic world map. "The Lumina's presence suppressed our baser instincts – our territoriality, our greed, our tribalism. Now that the censor is gone, those instincts are resurfacing with a vengeance. They're fighting over land, over resources, over ideologies that the Lumina had carefully suppressed or twisted to their own ends. It's a dangerous inheritance."

Benjamin sighs, the sound heavy with the weight of their precarious victory. "We kicked the wolf out of the henhouse, Rachel. Now we've got a pack of feral dogs running rampant. We're dealing with the consequences of our actions. We ignited the fire of truth, but now we have to manage the inferno." He looked at Rachel, his expression softening. "You were right about Elara's inhibitors. They helped to break the Lumina's localized psionic grip. But the wider psionic resonance that broadcasted… it awakened more than just defiance. It awakened the full spectrum of human emotion and thought. And not all of it is pretty."

The world was a tapestry of conflicting narratives. In some regions, liberated populations were already establishing democratic councils, seeking to build a future based on transparency and shared responsibility. These were the pockets of hope, the proof that humanity could indeed chart its own course. Elsewhere, the power vacuum was filled by autocratic regimes, sometimes mirroring the very control they had fought against, or fractured tribalistic societies were locked in perpetual conflict. The Lumina's long game, it seemed, was proving to be a masterclass in manipulation. They had not simply imposed their will; they had reshaped the very foundations of human society, leaving it vulnerable to its own inherent weaknesses.

"The Lumina's greatest threat wasn't their armada or their psionic dominion," Jasper observed, his fingers dancing across the controls as he analyzed incoming data streams. "It was their understanding of human psychology. They knew that true freedom, the kind that requires constant vigilance and ethical responsibility, is a heavy burden. They offered an alternative: a life of ease, of dictated purpose. Many even now crave that simplicity. The broadcasts are intensifying their propaganda again, focusing on the chaos, the violence, the uncertainty that has followed our victory. They're painting themselves as the only viable solution to a humanity incapable of self-governance."

Rachel stood and walked to the viewport, gazing out at the endless expanse of the ocean, a stark contrast to the volatile world unfolding on their monitors. "That's why we can't stop. The Nautilus isn't just a vessel; it's a symbol. We shattered their illusion of invincibility. Now we have to be the constant reminder of the truth, the counter-narrative. We have to continue to expose their machinations, to support those who are striving for genuine liberation, and to understand their ultimate objectives. The encounter in Area 291… it was a turning point, but not an end. They showed us their power, their advanced understanding of consciousness. That knowledge is something we cannot forget. And if the Lumina are truly seeking a 'Cosmic Harmony,' then we need to understand what that means for the rest of the galaxy, and for Earth's place within it."

The Lumina had a sophisticated understanding of consciousness, a concept they had reduced to raw data for their parasitic needs. But Rachel suspected there was more to it. The psionic resonance inhibitors they had deployed, while effective in disrupting Lumina control, had also hinted at the existence of deeper, untapped psionic potential within humanity itself – potential the Lumina had either suppressed or sought to exploit. The lingering question remained: were they now free to explore this potential, or had they merely traded one form of control for another, this time self-inflicted, as old prejudices and power struggles resurfaced?

"Their true intentions… it's still the great unknown," Benjamin admitted, the weariness in his voice now tinged with a reluctant understanding. "They could regroup for a second invasion, or they could watch us, waiting for us to fail so they can swoop in as saviors. Or perhaps, as you suggest, Rachel, they have a more intricate plan, a cosmic agenda that we've only just glimpsed. We don't know how much they truly understand about consciousness, or how much they've deliberately manipulated our understanding of it. Area 291 was a glimpse behind the curtain, but the stage is vast, and the play has many more acts."

Jasper tapped a key, bringing up a new set of readings. "The Lumina is also experimenting with new technologies. We're detecting anomalous energy signatures from several of their known exfiltration points. They're not just retreating; they're preparing. And they're studying us. They're analyzing our responses to the broadcast, our societal fractures. They learn faster than any other species I've ever encountered."

Rachel turned from the viewport, her gaze meeting Benjamin and Jasper. The path ahead was uncertain, shrouded in the shadow of a defeated but not vanquished foe. The broadcast had been a victory, a monumental achievement that had shattered the Lumina's global hegemony. But freedom, she understood now more profoundly than ever, was not a destination, but a journey. It was a continuous process of learning, adapting, and confronting the uncomfortable truths about oneself and the universe. An effortless existence, offered by the Lumina, inadvertently revealed the value of struggle, self-determination, and authentic humanity. The watch had indeed begun, an unending vigilance against complacency, against the allure of false security, and against the lingering, enigmatic threat of the Lumina, who had once again retreated into the shadows, leaving humanity to wrestle with the daunting, exhilarating cost of its own hard-won liberty. The dawn had arrived, but the true light, the light of understanding and enduring self-governance, was yet to break through the horizon.

EPILOGUE

When they all finally got home, it was a whirlwind of telephone calls, emails, and interview requests. Their actions up to this point have been focused on publicizing the Harvest and the aliens. They accepted every single interview request. All three of them were doing interview duty. If it fell on a day when no interviews were scheduled, then they would all go. The big interview was coming up today. Congressional hearing.

The design did not intend the space to feel like a room.

No windows. No clocks. Overhead lights were sunk into acoustic tiles, and the tiles swallowed sound just as snow swallowed footsteps. The carpet was a tight, government-gray weave that looked designed to hide stains and secrets equally well.

Rachel stood behind the witness table and tried not to think about how many people had sweated through this same patch of air.

Benjamin stood to her right, hands folded, jacket buttoned like armor. Jasper stood to her left, shoulders square, eyes forward. He'd shaved. He looked like he'd tried to put himself back into a version of his life that made sense. His curly hair was still unmanageable.

A staffer moved down the table with a plastic bin.

"Phones, watches, anything with a mic," she said. No smile. No small talk.

Rachel placed her phone inside. Then her watch. It felt like handing over a part of herself.

The staffer turned the bin toward Benjamin. He hesitated, then slid a small device off his keychain and dropped it in. The staffer didn't react, but her eyes flicked down as if she'd already known it would be there.

Jasper emptied his pockets like a man who'd done this before.

When the staffer left, the silence expanded.

On the dais, a row of senators and representatives sat behind microphones with their nameplates. A U.S. flag stood in each corner like a reminder of who owned the air.

To Rachel's surprise, not all the faces were hard. Some looked tired. Some looked angry. One or two looked like they'd been awake for a day and were only upright out of spite.

A man in a dark suit leaned toward the central microphone. His nameplate read **Sen. Hartwell.**

"This hearing of the Joint Oversight Subcommittee on National Security Programs will come to order," he said. His voice was steady, practiced. "Let the record reflect this is a closed session conducted under appropriate classification."

He glanced down the line, then back at them.

"You have been advised you are under oath. You understand that?"

Rachel's throat was dry. "Yes, Senator."

Benjamin's answer came at the same time. "Yes."

Jasper was a fraction later, heavier. "Yes."

A clerk stood and lifted a hand. "Please raise your right hands."

Three hands rose.

"Do you swear that the testimony you give before this committee will be the truth, the whole truth, and nothing but the truth, so help you God?"

Rachel almost said something reflexive, something safe. Then she thought of the things buried under the desert, and the things buried under paperwork, and the faces of people who'd never been given a chance to speak at all.

"I do," she said.

Benjamin: "I do."

Jasper: "I do."

The clerk sat.

Senator Hartwell tapped a pen against his folder. "For the record, state your names and affiliations as you understand them to be at present."

Rachel leaned toward the microphone. It picked up the slight tremor in her breath. "Rachel—Rachel Katz. Civilian. Former contractor to the Department of Defense."

Benjamin's voice was smoother. "Benjamin Fine. Research scientist. Formerly affiliated with... multiple federally funded programs."

Jasper's jaw flexed before he spoke. "Jasper Winston. Former U.S. Army. Formerly assigned to operational security under Project oversight."

Hartwell nodded as if checking boxes. "Thank you."

He looked down the line again, then back up.

"Ms. Katz, you and your colleagues are here because multiple agencies have provided the committee with conflicting accounts regarding three subjects: one, the group called the Luminaries; two, an operation referred to as the Harvest; and three, credible evidence of nonhuman presence on United States soil. Do you understand the scope?"

Rachel swallowed. "Yes."

"Good," Hartwell said. "Let's begin with the simplest question that apparently no one in the executive branch can answer without lying."

A few people shifted. Someone's chair creaked.

"What is Area 291?"

Rachel felt Jasper's gaze flick to her, then away. Benjamin's expression didn't change, but she could see tension in the tendons along his neck.

"It's a site," she said carefully, "and it's also a designation. A physical location used for storage and research. And a set of protocols used to keep certain discoveries compartmentalized."

"Discoveries," Hartwell echoed

A woman two seats down leaned forward. Her nameplate read **Rep. Nguyen**. Her voice was sharp and awake. "Let's cut to it. We're not here for vocabulary. What discoveries, Ms. Caldwell?"

Rachel looked from the microphones to the faces behind them.

Then she said the words that had been impossible to say out loud for most of her life.

"Nonhuman technology," she said. "And nonhuman biology."

The room didn't explode. No one shouted. There were no gasps. But the air changed.

Hartwell's pen stopped tapping.

Rep. Nguyen stared at Rachel as if she were deciding whether to believe her or accuse her.

Another man, older, his nameplate reading **Sen. Rivera**, exhaled slowly through his nose as if he'd been holding his breath for years.

"Thank you," Hartwell said softly. "That matches what we've been told in private by people who stopped short of admitting it on record."

He flipped a page.

"Now. The Luminaries. Mr. Katz, our understanding is that the Luminaries are a group of internal actors, a cult, or a cover term for an external influence. Which is it?"

Benjamin didn't answer immediately. Rachel could see him choosing the shape of the truth.

"They began," Benjamin said, "as people."

"People inside government?" Nguyen asked.

"Inside and adjacent," Benjamin replies. "Contractors, researchers, officers. They were drawn together by the same thing everyone in this building is drawn together by: access."

"And then?" Hartwell pressed.

Benjamin's eyes lifted to the flag behind the dais, then back down. "Then they encountered something that—" He paused, and Rachel felt a pulse of fear. Not fear of the committee. Fear of saying it.

"Then they encountered something they believed was… guidance."

Jasper made a sound Rachel couldn't interpret. Almost a scoff. Almost a cough.

Rep. Nguyen snapped her head toward him. "Mr. Winston, do you want to contribute?"

Jasper leaned toward his microphone. "What they called guidance was control," he said. The words came out flat, but there was heat underneath. "They weren't worshipping. They were being handled."

"By whom?" Hartwell asked.

Jasper's gaze stayed steady. "Not a who. A what."

A silence settled, heavy enough to feel.

Senator Rivera finally spoke. "Mr. Winston. Are you asserting that this nonhuman presence can influence human thought?"

Jasper hesitated.

Rachel saw the moment he could lie to keep it simple.

He didn't.

"Yes," Jasper said. "Not like mind reading. More like—pressure. A nudge. A tightening of decisions people already wanted to make. It amplifies obsession. Certainty. It makes people feel chosen."

Benjamin's fingers tightened on the edge of the table, then relaxed.

Rep. Nguyen's voice dropped. "So, you're saying the Luminaries were compromised."

"Yes," Jasper said. "And they compromised others. They got into positions where they could move resources and bury bodies with no one asking why."

The word bodies landed like a stone.

Hartwell's expression hardened. "That brings us to the Harvest."

Rachel's stomach tightened. She'd known this part would come. She'd known the word would be spoken out loud in a room where it couldn't be erased by shredders.

Rachel turned the microphone towards her. "Let me interrupt for a moment, please."

"Of course, Ms. Katz, what information can you provide?" Hartwell asked.

Hartwell slid a folder toward the edge of the dais, not offering it to them, just letting it exist between them like a threat.

Rachel fixed her jacket and collar, cleared her throat and then recalled what she had rehearsed. "Mr. Hartwell, it is our intention to be open and honest with this committee. But what we've uncovered affects every single living person on this planet. Every decision we must make must be considering that. When we first thought of testifying before Congress, I was disappointed to learn it was a closed session. It is therefore our position not to say another word until we reconvene in an open meeting. Every person in the world needs to hear our message. Until that happens, we are and have been granting interviews with every form of international press. Until we meet at an open meeting, we are lawyering up. Thank you." And Rachel put back the microphone.

"Are you, Mr. Winston and Mr. Fine, taking the same position?" Hartwell asked.

Both Jasper and Ben shook their heads.

Rachel forced herself to breathe.

Rep. Nguyen leaned in, voice like a blade. "Define the Harvest, Mr. Fine."

Benjamin's hands folded tighter. "We stated our positions a moment ago, but I will partially answer your question." When you hear what the Harvest is, I promise you will never know what a good night's sleep is again."

Hartwell looked at them one by one.

"You've all committed crimes," he said, and Rachel's stomach dropped again, until he continued. "Not in the way Representative Kelso means. You committed the crime of knowing and not being believed. The crime of holding a truth that was too large for the channels built to hold it."

Kelso shifted, irritated. Nguyen watched Hartwell as if she were reassessing him.

Hartwell's voice stayed steady. "This committee will draft recommendations based on your testimony," he said. "You will remain available for follow-up. And you will not discuss this hearing outside this room."

He paused.

Then, softer: "Do you understand?"

"Yes," Rachel answered.

Benjamin: "Yes."

Jasper: "Yes."

Hartwell nodded once. "We are adjourned."

The red recording light clicked off.

A staffer opened the side door, and for a second a thin wedge of brighter hallway light cut into the room like a blade.

They gathered their papers. Rachel realized she'd been gripping the edge of the table hard enough that her fingers had gone pale.

As they stood, Rep. Nguyen called, "Ms. Katz."

Rachel turned.

Nguyen's expression wasn't warm exactly, but it wasn't hostile either. "You said the public deserves the truth," she said. "You also said disclosure is a process."

Rachel nodded.

Nguyen glanced at Benjamin, then Jasper, then back to Rachel. "If we do this," she muttered, "we'll need people who can speak without turning it into mythology."

Rachel felt Benjamin's attention sharpen. Jasper too, like men who'd learned to detect danger in tone.

Nguyen continued, "We'll need witnesses who can say 'we don't know' without sounding weak."

Rachel's throat tightened. "Are you asking me to do that?"

Nguyen didn't answer the question directly. "They will ask you, I'm telling you," https://booktrovert.zendesk.com/hc/en-us/articles/33081655550231-I-m-an-author-publisher-How-do-I-list-my-books-on-Booktrovertshe said. "Not by this committee. By the country."

Rachel exhaled. "Then I'll answer," she said.

Nguyen nodded once, like that was all she wanted.

They went out through a corridor that looked like every federal building hallway Rachel had ever walked: beige walls, fluorescent lights, doors with keypads. But guards with weapons were stationed at each corner. There were cameras. There were signs that said AUTHORIZED PERSONNEL ONLY in the same cold font that had labeled so many locked rooms.

At the end of the corridor, they stopped at a small anteroom where someone returned their items in the same plastic bin.

Rachel slid her watch back on. The weight felt oddly comforting.

Benjamin clipped his keys to his belt. The small device was gone. Rachel noticed, and Benjamin noticed she noticed.

He said quietly, "Don't."

She didn't asked. She only nodded.

Jasper slipped his phone into his pocket without turning it on.

When they stepped through the last door, it wasn't into daylight, not exactly. It was into a covered loading area attached to the building's lower level. The winter air was sharp, and Rachel's breath came out white.

For a moment, they just stood there, three people who had walked through the center of a secret and come out the other side still carrying their names.

Jasper broke the silence first.

"So that's it," he said. "We tell them the truth, and they put it in a folder."

Rachel looked at him. His face was hard, but his eyes weren't. Not anymore.

"It's not nothing," she said.

Benjamin rubbed his hands together for warmth. "It's a beginning," he said. Then, with a thin smile that didn't quite make it to his eyes: "Congressional beginnings are slow."

Jasper gave a short laugh. "Yeah. Slow enough for the world to end twice."

Rachel surprised herself by smiled back. It felt strange on her face, like a muscle she hadn't used in a long time.

"Or slow enough," she said, "for us to keep it from ending."

Benjamin tilted his head. "You really believe that?"

Rachel looked out toward the street beyond the loading area. There were cars passing. People walking with coffee cups and scarves. A normal city morning continued as if nothing in the universe had changed.

"I believe," she said, "that the worst part was being alone with it."

Jasper stared out too. "We're not alone now?"

Rachel glanced at him. "No," she said. "Now it's on record. Now there are more eyes. More hands. More people who can ask why."

Benjamin's voice was quiet. "More people who can say no."

Rachel nodded.

They stood there for another moment, and Rachel felt something she hadn't expected to feel at the end of all this.

Not victory. Not closure.

Possibility.

A black government sedan idled at the curb. A driver stood by the rear door, waiting. Not rushing them, but not giving them forever either.

Jasper started toward it, then paused and looked back at Rachel and Benjamin.

"Hey," he said.

Rachel met his gaze.

Jasper's voice roughened. "If they decide to bury it again," he said, "we don't let them."

Rachel didn't hesitate. "We won't," she said.

Benjamin nodded. "We'll make it harder," he said. "Every time."

Jasper's mouth twitched, almost a smile. "Good."

They got into the sedan. The door shut with a soft, final thud.

As the car pulled away, Rachel watched the federal building recede behind them. Just stone and glass and flags in the cold.

It didn't look like a place where the future would be decided.

But she knew better now.

Rachel rested her hand against the window, feeling the faint vibration of motion under her palm, and let herself imagine the next room. The next hearing. The first briefing that wouldn't be a lie.

Outside, the city moved on. Inside, for the first time since Area 291, Rachel felt the weight shift.

Not off her shoulders.

Shared.

And that, she realized, was how hope started: not with certainty, but with witnesses.

With names.

With truth spoken into a microphone, recorded in a room designed to swallow it, and still somehow carried out into the world.

The End

I hope you enjoyed reading Area 291. I'll take this time to let you know what is real and what was fictional imagination. First, Area 291 is an actual place and is exactly how I described it. The restricted airspace, and decades of missing boats and people. Even the part about Rob Lowe. If you want to spend an interesting evening, do a Google search. The stories will really bother you.

To look at the maritime maps of Area 291 and its surrounding areas, you'll see a detailed map of the location in question. The area is a ledge. When you go under the ledge, it drops many thousands of feet. My story just weaves these individual facts into what I believe is happening over there. The locals tell tales of watching the lights.

Science is amazing! All the research methods I used are also genuine science. Actually, it is now more advanced than what I used on the Nautilus. This story is my vision of how these tales come together.

The Catholic Church owns and operates one of the most powerful telescopes on earth and it is in Arizona.

History is an amazing thing! When I write my books initially, I don't pay attention to the number of words I use because there will be at least four rounds of editing. My word count was 160,000! Unfortunately, I had to edit out a lot of history that I had integrated into the story. I was sorry to see the scene go! Unlike other genres, science fiction books can take some literary liberties to write up to 120,000 words. This book came in at 90,000 words.

Right now, the movie trailer for Age of Disclosure is coming out, a person is no longer 'crazy' when they talk about UFOs. Is there life out there? That's the $64,000 question. What I will say is that all the chemical principles on Earth is common across the universe.

Humans can be narcissistic enough to believe Earth has the only life out of billions of years. It is that statement that I believe sounds crazy.

If someone wants to learn about things going on out there, many credible sources available. MUFON is a real group. People who make reports of UFO and other paranormal happenings have investigators who will come and assist law enforcement (if they are involved) about how to preserve evidence and interview the witnesses. One of my very favorite sources is the Secret of Skinwalker Ranch. The story of that ranch in Utah is very gripping. It is now owned by Brandon Fugal, and the ranch is now a hotbed of scientific testing.

If you found this book good or you kind of liked it, please leave a review. Authors are like street musicians: we have to sing for our supper. I thank you in advance. If you would like to contact me, my email is jenny@jennyahmed.com. Also, I'm on all the social media sites. I would love to connect!

Warm regards,
Jenny Ahmed